MALEVOLENCE

A HOLLYWOOD MYSTERY

BRITT LIND

Designed and distributed by Bublish, Inc.

eBook ISBN: 978-1-647045-73-9
Paperback ISBN: 978-1-647045-71-5
Hardcover ISBN: 978-1-647045-72-2
Audiobook ISBN: 978-1-647045-74-6

Praise for *Malevolence—A Hollywood Mystery*

Britt Lind has created two excellent lead characters in Rosemaria and Josh, and their loving and supportive dynamic provides a unique backdrop to the grim and dark world of murder and international conspiracy. The mystery at the heart of *Malevolence* is highly engaging with enough twists and turns in the tale to keep audiences on their toes and excited to read what happens next. The dark nature of the subject matter is excellently counterbalanced by Josh's light sub-plot about getting his big break. As with the previous story, Rosemaria proves herself to be a capable investigator and an excellent pair of eyes for the audience to engage with the core mystery. The additional obstacles provided by her professional life contribute to the unpredictable directions that the plot takes as it moves forward.

Readers' Favorite—A Five Star Review

Malevolence—A Hollywood Mystery is the second book in the highly-rated series by Britt Lind. Like the first book, *Malevolence* weaves the themes of commitment and love, along with animal rights, into the narrative. And in the end, those who should get their comeuppance do. For readers who like their police novels with a good heart, strong female leads, and a well-integrated animal rights theme, *Malevolence—A Hollywood Mystery* will excite and satisfy.

Chanticleer

Rosemaria is an endearing and incorruptible protagonist who demonstrates tact and compassion while investigating the teenager's murder and finding witnesses for her court cases... Her tender relationship with Josh and their banter are high points of the novel, and the dialogue ably reveals nuances of characterization... As the murder reveals a political conspiracy with international implications, Rosemaria finds herself pulled in different directions, and she must face the possibility that she may not be able to save everyone she loves...

Kirkus Reviews

Praise for *A Fate Worse Than Death– A Hollywood Mystery Prequel*

Lind's prequel to her A Hollywood Mystery series enlivens the slender police procedural with emotional depth and an appealingly complex heroine . . . the fast-paced plot unfolds smoothly, with a constant sense of dread hanging in in the background. Rosemaria's poignant backstory follows her troubled childhood, and Lind vividly describes the tension the young Rosemaria feels, keeping the reader thoroughly invested. She's also meticulous about describing her characters' particularities as she delves into the fears, insecurities, and individual struggles. In Lind's skillful hands, this story of resilience, strength, and intricacies of familial relationships is both a compassionate character study and a page-turning thriller.

The Prairies Book Review

With a big talent for writing, Britt Lind again captivates the reader with a new mystery.

Jonas Nordstrom—Marketing Head of Adventure Box

Hollywood and mystery are a part of Britt Lind's history—from big screen to little screen and roles ranging from Clint Eastwood's *Play Misty for Me* to the iconic *Columbo*, so it's no mystery why she is a shining star of the written word in her Hollywood Mystery series including this prequel which gives us a glimpse into the childhood of her protagonist Rosemaria Baker.

Bob Linden—Radio talk show host, producer, and vegan activist

A well written book with a great sense of suspense . . . The police sergeant's daughter Rosemaria is as courageous and cunning as her father twice over. Well written in a language that will compel you to read to the end without putting it down.

Amazon Reviews

Praise for *Deception—A Hollywood Mystery*

A thrilling page-turner about a group of flawed, yet compelling characters caught in a cesspool of greed and ruthless ambition behind the scenes in Hollywood. I couldn't wait to find out the ending while simultaneously wishing the book wouldn't end.

Lara Wickman—Writer, producer, actress

. . . the story takes some refreshingly unexpected turns, picking a path through genre clichés and keeping readers guessing. The author has an easy writing style and a cinematic grasp of pace. Fans of silver screen crime should approve, as, in many respects, this reads like the novelization of a movie.

Kirkus Reviews

If you want to read a book that offers romance, suspense, detective work, intrigue, and feels like you're watching a movie, then this is your book. I highly recommend it.

Andreas Michaelides—Writer, reviewer,
blogger, and natural health educator

Deception is a gritty rendering of the classic battle between good and evil played out in the milieu of Hollywood. As an actor herself, Britt is ably qualified to explore and articulate the disappointment and heartache of fame-obsessed performers as they struggle to "make it" in an unforgiving industry where fame is illusive, and disappointment can lead to murder.

Tony Eldridge—Executive Producer of
The Equalizer and *The Equalizer 2*

Praise for *Learning How to Fly*

(Beverly Hills Book Award Winner)

Britt Lind's journey to find her ultimate calling (a voice for the animals) is filled with highs and lows on her road to Hollywood, and you will want to keep turning the page.

> Sylva Kelegian—Actress, writer, and award-winning author
> of *God Spelled Backwards* and *The Dolphin Princess*

Learning How to Fly is the inspiring story of a fellow activist who has hung in there through thick and thin for all of the thirty-two years I've known her. Fighting vivisection is a hard road, and it takes both courage and incredible patience to stay in the battle. But Britt found a way to stay on course and still fulfill her passion for acting. Readers will find this book entertaining and humorous, but it's also her journey that provides guidance on how one can find their own way to a meaningful life.

> With Respect for all Life—Chris DeRose—Founder
> and president of Last Chance for Animals and
> author of the autobiography *In Your Face*

As a young starlet, Britt Lind was a beauty who was cast in a Clint Eastwood movie and found happiness being married to a television producer and acting and raising a baby girl. But in a flash, her marriage ended, riches vanished, the house was foreclosed on, and her career crumbled. Britt's story of disappearing success is poignant and unforgettable, and by the time she is beaten down in Hollywood and heads for New York with visions of Broadway, you cannot help but cheer for her and the animals she has dedicated her life to saving. This is a heartfelt, timeless story of shining on to create a life filled with love, beauty, and triumph.

Janette Turner—Writer, director, and author of the forthcoming memoir *Magazine Crush: My Life as a Cosmo Addict*

These are the adventures of an innocent young girl from Norway, thrust into American culture, driven by a passionate ambition to be an actress in a ruthlessly unpredictable and sexist industry. Britt navigated through a life of obstacles, betrayals, and disappointments with courageous resolve, a resolve deeply rooted in a firm moral foundation and strengthened by a deep compassion and a fiery desire to end the suffering of animals.

Captain Paul Watson—Founder of the Sea Shepherd Conservation Society and author of several books, including *Sea Shepherd: My Fight for Whales and Seals, Seal Wars: Twenty-Five Years on the Front Lines with the Harp Seals,* and *Ocean Warrior: My Battle to End the Illegal Slaughter on the High Seas*

Dedication

This book is dedicated to Billy the elephant, who has been incarcerated at the Los Angeles Zoo for thirty-two years since he was four years old, and the activists who work tirelessly to free him. Thousands of us who love Billy will continue to work toward his release until he finally finds the freedom and happiness he deserves.

"Friendship multiplies the good of life and divides the evil."

Baltasar Gracián

"Man is the cruelest animal."

Friedrich Nietzsche

PROLOGUE

Shivering uncontrollably, the girl crouched in the bushes at the edge of the hotel parking lot. She was wearing a thin minidress, and the leaves were damp from the night watering system, causing goose bumps to pop up on her bare arms and shoulders. Even in Los Angeles, the city of sunny beaches and palm trees, the night breeze carried a sharp chill in late January. The man chasing her had gone back into the hotel but was sure to come back. He had dragged her from the room on the second floor, gripping her firmly so she couldn't escape and holding his hand over her mouth to keep her from screaming. Outside, he had tried to force her into a black town car parked in a space near the side entrance, but she had fought back and screamed "Rape!" as loud as she could, bringing people running from the front of the hotel and other parts of the parking lot. He had released her arms and backed away, head down, avoiding the security camera as best he could. She knew he wouldn't let her escape. She considered running into the lobby of the hotel and asking for help but was afraid no one would believe her.

She glanced around and saw a tall chain-link fence behind her a few feet away. Not an easy climb but going over it was her only way out that didn't involve running back out into the open. Keeping her eye on the side door of the hotel, she slipped off her 6-inch heels, held them in one hand, climbed over the fence, and found a path leading to a private home. Holding her hand on her small purse that hung from her shoulder, she ran through the brush, sharp rocks cutting into the bottoms of her feet. She opened the wooden gate that led into the backyard of a small house with an attached garage and prayed the house wouldn't have an outdoor lighted alarm system. No lights! She tried the side door of the garage and found it open. Should she keep running? Stay here and hide? She was so terrified she couldn't think straight. She looked behind her, and the decision was made for her. Two men were now in the parking lot searching for her. She entered the garage, found her way around two cars in the darkness, and hid underneath a wooden workbench. She couldn't stop shaking but was determined not to let fear overwhelm her and prevent her from finding a way to escape. She had been in plenty of rough situations when she worked the streets in Hollywood. Why had she been stupid enough to come back? Sergeant Baker had gone to so much trouble to help her and had given her money to go back home. But home had been just as boring as before, and she had longed to return to the only city that could give her the life she dreamed of. But beautiful young girls were everywhere in this town, and it took more than looks to get what you wanted. She had discovered that the first time around. Now that she was more than three years older and, she had thought, wiser, she figured she might have a chance. None of that mattered anymore. She just wanted to stay alive.

CHAPTER ONE

Rosemaria Baker, former homicide detective and brand-new deputy district attorney, stood sipping her morning cup of coffee, staring out the sliding glass door of the small one-bedroom apartment she shared with Josh Sibley. Suzi the cockatoo sat on her perch near the window, spitting seeds as she crunched on her breakfast. There wasn't much furniture yet. They had moved in three weeks ago and still hadn't had time to shop for more. They had a bed, a small dining table, two chairs, and a couch from a thrift shop. That was about it, but to Rosemaria, it was heaven. Any place she shared with Josh was fine with her. She had to admit she had turned into a sentimental slob. Her entire personality had changed because of that big lug she was nuts about.

They lived on the third floor of a Mediterranean-style stucco apartment building in West Hollywood that had probably been around since Greta Garbo was buying up Rodeo Drive and Joan Crawford revealed what a truly ungifted dancer she was in *Our Dancing Daughters*. Crawford was almost as terrifyingly bad as Elaine in *Seinfeld*. Rosemaria had actually watched *Our Dancing Daughters* with her mother at a revival theater in the Fairfax district. Her mother, a failed actress and now deceased, loved old movies from the twenties, thirties, and forties and knew all the old stories of Hollywood. She shared them with her young daughter as if they were magical fairy tales of impossibly beautiful heroines and handsome leading men, some flawed, some victims of tragedy, but living in a world her mother wanted with all her heart and soul to become a part of. But it never happened. Success eluded her, and Rosemaria believed her mother died, not of a coronary thrombosis as the doctors had told her and her father, but of rejection and unfulfilled dreams.

Witnessing her mother's deep disappointment had turned Rosemaria off show business forever, or so she thought. Inexplicably, that turned out not to be true. Now, she was madly and hopelessly in love with a musician and singer who was steeped in the business. Go figure. Not only was he in show business, an anathema to her, but he also had briefly been a murder suspect in an investigation she had led two years ago, and he had been drinking a lot then. But somehow, despite the whole deck of cards being stacked against them, including a year apart after she fled to New York to get him out of her system, they found their way back to each other. She couldn't imagine life without him.

This morning, she had an appointment with her new boss, Neelen Summers, the assistant deputy head D.A. at the Los Angeles Superior Court Airport Courthouse near LAX, where county prosecutors had their offices on the sixth floor. After several interviews with LA County high muckety-mucks, she had met with Frank Lattimer, the head deputy D.A. who was Summers's immediate superior, and she had been hired. Even though she had gone to a no-name law school, she had graduated at the top of her class and had passed the bar in both New York and California with flying colors. It helped that she had a sterling record her first year as an ADA in Manhattan and that she was given high recommendations by both Captain Hubbard and Lieutenant Manley of the Beverly Hills Police Department. But now she had to prove she had what it took to be in an LA County courtroom instead of working vice on the streets of Hollywood and investigating murders as well as other high crimes and misdemeanors committed by the famous and not-so-famous denizens of Beverly Hills. She was excited but nervous as well. She looked at the alarm clock on the nightstand. It was only seven. She didn't have to be in the office till nine.

She had crept out of bed while Josh was still asleep, which gave her plenty of time to drink a few cups of coffee, but that only made her even more jittery. Josh had stumbled past her after she had consumed two cups of coffee and given her a quick peck on the cheek before heading for the bathroom.

She listened to him humming in the shower. As it did every morning, listening to the sounds of Josh washing and shaving in the bathroom filled her with a deep sense of contentment. Even today, when her nerves were on edge, his nearby presence was a comfort. She heard him turn off the shower, imagined him toweling off, and then he opened the bathroom door. There he was in all his glory, with a towel around his waist. He was tall—about 6' 2"—and had blond hair that was a little too long and sticking out in every direction. His handsome face showed hints of dark circles underneath his blue eyes, and his body displayed evidence that he had abused alcohol for several years. But now, after more than a year of AA, his physique was coming around nicely, thank you very much. They studied each other for a few seconds.

"Am I interrupting some deep thoughts?" Josh grinned.

"Just thinking about how crazy I am about you."

"Of course you are." He lifted his hands, palms up in front of him, indicating their tiny living quarters. "Look at everything I have to offer."

"You won't use it against me?"

"Never."

She walked over to him and gently smoothed down his hair. "In that case, I'll make you breakfast." Before she could walk away, he grabbed her arm and pulled her close. His soft lips covered hers in a long kiss that took her breath away. As he nuzzled her face and neck, she could barely speak. "I have to leave here at eight on the dot, and if you don't stop, I'll have to redo all this hair and paint."

He pulled back and touched her cheek. "You don't need any paint."

"That's what all you men say." She shook her head. "But you don't mean it."

Rosemaria walked into the tiny kitchen and opened some cupboards, which were almost bare. "How about some instant oatmeal? Or maybe toast with strawberry jam?"

Walking from the bathroom into the bedroom alcove, he shrugged. "Anything, as long as the coffee is strong."

Fifteen minutes later, Josh was dressed in jeans and a T-shirt, and they were seated opposite each other at the small table with their toast and coffee. Josh sipped his coffee and observed the woman he loved. She looked smashing in a blue suit that hugged her figure and a white blouse buttoned up conservatively. Her shoulder-length, curly auburn hair was pulled back behind her ears, and her green eyes were framed by long black lashes.

She took a bite of her toast. "I hope you don't expect me to cook like this for you every day."

"Thank God."

"Hey, I made a nice veggie lasagna last week. You said you liked it."

"What could I say? You still pack a gun in your purse." After a moment, he said, "Just kidding. Yeah, it was good."

"All right then. And the gun is not loaded."

"I know for a fact it is."

"Okay, it is. Anyway, we live in West Hollywood, and there are restaurants we can go to for breakfast, lunch, and dinner."

"Give me some time to find out if I have a hit song on my hands. Then, I'll support you in the style to which you were never accustomed."

"You're screening the entire movie today, right? I hope the composer is everything you and Ken hoped for. You haven't even let me hear Joell sing your opening song yet. I don't know why you want to keep me in suspense."

The movie that their friend Ken had produced and directed had been in postproduction for five months. Josh had written the song for the opening credits and had a bit part as a homeless man. It was while he was in New York for a week filming his small part on the streets of Manhattan that Josh had run into Rosemaria after a year of living on separate coasts. They had first met in LA when Rosemaria had been investigating the murder of Stan Levy, a movie producer Josh was working for, and he had been one of the prime suspects. Rosemaria had eventually arrested the producer's wife, Lila Levy, for the murder. Stunningly beautiful, the evil Lila had captivated Josh's heart from the moment he saw her, while Rosemaria found herself inexplicably attracted to the alcoholic singer/songwriter. When Lila's true character became obvious, Lila lost her hold on Josh and he fell in love with Rosemaria. A tragic misunderstanding between the two of them caused her to leave Los Angeles and begin a new life in New York. A year later, they found each other again when Josh was working on a movie in Manhattan, and they realized that although they were as different as night and day, they nevertheless were a perfect fit. They returned to Los Angeles together and never looked back.

"Yes, we're both happy with the score, but I don't want you to hear bits and pieces. I already told you Joell does an incredible job with my song. You'll see and hear it all at the screening for the cast and crew."

"When you have the premiere, we don't have to do that red-carpet hoopla, do we? Can I sneak in the back door? All that glamour stuff is really not my thing, you know?"

Josh stood up to take his dishes into the kitchen. "It's my big moment. Of course you'll be on the red carpet."

The sound of her cell phone playing generic elevator music interrupted the discussion. It was coming from her purse on the bed. She jumped up, scrambled around till she found the phone, and clicked it on. "Hello, this is Rosemaria." Her face lit up. "Hey, Sergeant, good to hear from you!" She looked up at Josh, who had grabbed his jean jacket off a hook near the door. "Honey, it's Sergeant Osborne, who took my job when I was away."

Josh yelled out, "Show her how it's done, Osborne!" Rosemaria shot him a look and sat on the bed. She listened for a few seconds, and Josh saw a look of concern come over her face. "No, don't send me a photo. I'll come see her in person. I'll be there in about a half hour."

Josh walked over and sat on the bed beside her. "What happened?"

Rosemaria's voice was shaking. "They found a murdered girl in a dumpster at the Island Hotel in Beverly Hills this morning."

"The Island. That's that ritzy place on Santa Monica Boulevard, right? Why are they calling you?"

"She had no ID in her purse, but they found my old BHPD card crumpled up in her makeup bag."

"And they think she might have been one of your girls?"

"It's possible. I helped as many of them as I could, but some just wouldn't listen to me." Rosemaria shook her head and sighed.

Josh put an arm around her and held her close. "Hey, you did your best."

"Damn!" She stood up and looked out the sliding door. "I kept telling them if they didn't get off the streets, this is what could happen. A few listened. A couple of them I talked into going back home if home was really the right place for them to be." She turned and looked at Josh, her eyes glistening. "It was hard sometimes to know what was best for them but working the streets and taking drugs sure the hell didn't make for a rosy future." Rosemaria grabbed her purse off the bed, took out a Kleenex, and dabbed her face underneath her eyes. "This is what you've done to me. Turned me into an emotional dishrag."

"It looks good on you."

"Well, I don't want to embarrass myself at a crime scene and start bawling when I see it's a girl I knew and obviously let down. If it is, I won't even be able to help find out who killed her."

Josh pulled her to her feet and walked her to the door.

She made a wry face. "Looks like I'm going to be late for my first day at work."

"They'll understand."

She made an effort to pull herself together.

"No matter what, we're going to spend next weekend with Noor and Gilbert. Being around them always cheers me up." She pecked his cheek. "Love you." Then, she looked over at Suzi, who was still eating her breakfast. "Bye, Suzi."

She went out the door, and Josh watched her walk down the hall. He wondered for the millionth time how he could be so lucky. Two years ago, he had been well on his way to killing himself with alcohol, working at the zoo part-time as a caretaker, and writing commercials whenever Ken found him work. He could not have imagined his life turning out as it had. Now, his best friends—Noor, a black panther he had taken care of at the zoo, and Gilbert, a mountain lion who had spent a lot of time in his apartment after being injured as a baby—were thriving in a sanctuary up north. To top it all off, the woman he loved more than life itself loved him back. He was afraid she was about to have her heart broken.

CHAPTER TWO

Traffic near the Island Hotel was at a standstill. There was a convention of cop cars for two blocks on Santa Monica Boulevard and several on Wilshire Boulevard as well. Traffic cops had blocked off lanes on both streets. Parking anywhere near the Island Hotel alley, where the actual crime scene was, would be impossible. Rosemaria drove down the open inside lane on Wilshire at a crawl for two blocks, turned right into a side street, and found an available parking spot. She paid the meter with her card and started walking toward the hotel. She was apprehensive of what she would find and dreaded seeing someone she knew lying on the ground being checked by the medical examiner like a piece of meat. A murder that involved a friend was hard to take even for someone as hardened to the sight of violent death as she had been as a homicide investigator. Over a year away from the job didn't make this any easier. The girl had been strangled. That and a few hours in a dumpster would not make for a pretty picture. At least Summers had told her to take her time. Her cases could wait until she came in. There was nothing urgent for her to deal with. So that worry was eased at least.

Rosemaria showed her ID to the cops who were keeping looky-loos at bay, signed in, then started walking down the alley. She saw some familiar faces—Sergeant Darryl Osborne and Jimmy Waite, who had been on her team when she had headed up the homicide unit, were having a discussion with Mal Crews, the medical examiner. She was a plain, middle-aged, no-nonsense kind of lady who did not approve of dark humor around the deceased. As far as Mal was concerned, everyone, even the dead, deserved respect. The victim was lying on the ground next to them as they talked and took in the crime scene. She was wearing a tight black dress that was pulled up to the top of her thighs. At least three people from the forensics unit were collecting evidence near the body and inside a dumpster. A few cops stood at the edge of the crime scene.

There were two dumpsters right outside the delivery entrance that were ready for the trash collectors. There was another walk-in entrance inside an alcove a few feet farther up.

Osborne looked up and smiled, genuinely happy to see her. Tall and skinny, he towered over her as he waved his plastic-gloved hand. "Good to see you, Baker. I wish it could have been under better circumstances."

"Me too." She turned to Waite. The redhead's familiar, friendly grin made her feel like she'd never been away. He held up a plastic bag with a wrinkled card inside. She studied it and said, "It looks like an old one from six years ago, when I was working vice in Hollywood."

Mal gave her a brief wave. "Have a look. We just brought her out of the dumpster. The garbage truck broke down on Wilshire this morning, or she would have been long gone by now. A housekeeper found her when she came out to empty a trash can."

Rosemaria crouched down and studied the girl's swollen face and, as much as she pitied the victim, felt overwhelming relief. "She's not someone I know." Mal handed Rosemaria her flashlight, and she aimed the light into the girl's open, blank eyes, which were beginning to film over. "Petechial hemorrhaging." Rosemaria looked at the bruising around the throat and mouth. "So, she was strangled." She looked up and around her for cameras.

"There are cameras inside the alcove and in the loading area," Osborne said, "but not right here by the dumpsters. Unfortunately."

"Was she raped?" Rosemaria asked Mal.

"No bruising or evidence of semen."

"Any skin under the fingernails?"

"I'll check when I have her on the table."

Rosemaria stood up and handed Mal her flashlight. "I know for sure I don't recognize her. One of the older girls must have given her my card. Maybe there'll be a match for her fingerprints in the computer, if she was ever arrested."

Waite looked down at the girl. "She was probably here to cash in on the big Democratic political fundraiser Saturday and Sunday. Lots of out-of-town politicians looking for a good time away from their wives." One of her high heels had fallen off and lay near her foot. It made the victim seem even more lost and pathetic. It had yet to be bagged. "Pretty girl, not more than sixteen, I'd say."

Mal agreed. "She may have had an appointment or just hoped to meet customers at the bar. With her looks and age, it wouldn't have taken her long." Mal's assistants were waiting next to their van, ready to lift the body and transport it to the morgue. She gave them the go-ahead. To Osborne and Waite, she said, "You want to be there when I do the autopsy, I presume?"

They both nodded yes, and Rosemaria felt oddly excluded. It had been her choice to leave the department. Nine years in Hollywood and then two in Beverly Hills had cemented her decision to become a prosecutor. She wanted to make sure criminals stayed in jail instead of seeing them walk free after doing all the hard work of tracking them down and arresting them. She loved the law and she loved justice—no, she *needed* justice—and she hated when defense lawyers found a way to convince juries that guilty people were innocent. Her connection to victims and their families was a sacred bond, and she mourned when she couldn't give them the verdict they needed to hear. A crime scene and the challenge of tracking a killer used to be what got her up in the morning. She was surprised at how out of place she felt, like she was at a party she was no longer invited to. They all watched the body of the girl disappear into the back of the van.

Osborne was observing her expression. "Thinking of coming back already?" he teased.

"You took my job, remember?"

Waite's blue eyes sparkled. "I could always teach you how to become an internet wizard. We have an opening because a recent hire decided to quit and work for a security firm. You might learn to love it."

Rosemaria shivered involuntarily. "When hell freezes over. I'll just head on over to the courthouse and leave the computers to you youngsters who were born attached to a keyboard."

Osborne walked partway down the alley with her. "We'll call you from time to time and keep you updated. You're still family."

"Thanks. I'd appreciate that. And speaking of family, is Larry still on leave until after Vanessa has the baby? She won't say, but I think he's driving her crazy hovering over her every day like she's a piece of fragile crystal."

Larry was her former partner at BHPD. He gave her a tough time when they first worked together but ended up becoming a good friend. One of the positive things that came out of the Levy investigation was that Larry, a former womanizer and heir to a multimillion-dollar fortune, had found his soulmate in actress Vanessa Sheridan, who had been an acquaintance of Lila Levy and a witness in the investigation.

"With over a month to go until the big event? Rumor has it among our administrative assistants that he'll be back way before then."

She smiled. "Well, if anybody knows what's going on, they do. Thanks for calling me. I'm sad for the victim, but at least she wasn't one of mine. I'd like to think they got out of the life and are alive and well."

He nodded, turned, and walked back to the crime scene. She had a momentary feeling of regret that she was no longer needed there. Then, she shook it off and walked to her car.

CHAPTER THREE

The drive to the Airport Courthouse near LAX took half an hour once she got away from the insanity at Wilshire and Santa Monica. She had managed to save some of her earnings as an ADA in New York to put a generous down payment on a new silver Mazda CX-5 that she was in love with. She'd never owned a new car before, but Josh insisted that reliable transportation in LA was a no-brainer. Ironic coming from a man who hung on to his classic Mustang like it was his best friend.

She called Josh to let him know the victim wasn't one of her girls. She knew he'd be concerned for her. She couldn't stop thinking of the murdered girl, who had been in grade school when Rosemaria had worked vice in Hollywood. How had she ended up as a prostitute? Why had she been in possession of Rosemaria's business card? Conflicting thoughts assailed her brain. She knew why she wanted to be a prosecutor—to put bad guys in jail. She had become a cop partially because her father had been one, and he had been the stabilizing force in their little family. It seemed like a good idea at the time. Then, after she became a detective, she grew to love her work—every crime scene was the beginning of a mystery, and it was up to her and her fellow detectives to unravel it and arrest the perpetrator. That was supremely satisfying. In New York, as an ADA in Manhattan, she had found her new job to be fulfilling as the guilty verdicts were handed down.

But even though every case was a challenge, it was never as exciting as unraveling a mystery. Until this moment, she had been sure she had made the right decision in leaving the force. Now unwelcome doubts were creeping in.

She parked in the courthouse parking lot, made her way to the elevator, and rode up to the sixth floor. There were some smiles as she walked to her office, but most people were engrossed in their work. Her assistant, Karen Weiss, whom she shared with Terrence O'Malley, another prosecutor, had a desk outside Rosemaria's office and was already hard at work. Karen was an attractive African American lady in her thirties. They had met for the first time a few days ago, when Neelen Summers had given her a tour of the prosecutors' offices and had introduced her to her fellow deputy prosecutors. Karen looked up from her computer as Rosemaria stopped at her desk.

"Hey, Karen. Sorry I'm late."

Karen smiled. "It's fine. No one's keeping track here. The file for your first case is in your in-basket and in your computer. You have your password?"

"I do."

"Does Summers still want to meet with me? Show me the ropes and all that?"

"He's in court. He'll catch up to you later."

"Thank you." Rosemaria walked into her office and sat down in front of her almost empty desk. She looked out at Karen, who had resumed typing on her computer. Rosemaria had known she would like Karen as soon as she met her at her orientation. She wore her hair in a short Afro, and her coffee-colored complexion was as smooth and clear as a baby's. Hornrimmed glasses were perched on the end of her nose. Today, she wore a colorful blouse over pleated tan trousers and comfortable Skechers on her feet.

Underneath Karen's officious exterior, Rosemaria sensed a bubbling sense of humor. She liked that. A sense of humor was essential in easing over the speed bumps of life and getting to the other side with your equilibrium intact. Yes, she and Karen would get along fine.

A folder was in her in-basket—an armed robbery at a liquor store. The suspect wouldn't plead out. She breathed in deeply and exhaled. This was it. She was ready to kick some butt.

* * * *

Josh drove through the gate at Universal and waved at the guard. Only a couple of years had passed since he came in through the same gate hoping to get his big break by writing a song for a movie. The movie had never been made, and the whole episode had turned into a disaster. But during those worst four weeks of his life, he had met Rosemaria, and by some miracle, she wanted to be with him. Still, as soon as he woke up every morning, he had to reach over and make sure she was really there.

He drove toward the building where Ken's movie was being screened. Dean Jacobs, the composer, would be there as well as Ken Jordan, who still owned the advertising agency that Josh worked for. Ken was both director and producer of the movie. Ken's nineteen-year-old son, Kevin, who was a trainee on the film, would also be there, soaking up everything anybody was willing to teach him. He was hungry to learn the business. Josh hoped he would never lose his enthusiasm. There was a chance Joell would come if her schedule allowed. She had a gig in LA Saturday night in front of several thousand people and had been rehearsing since she came into town from New York.

He parked near the building and saw that Ken was standing outside the door waiting for him. "Are you nervous?" Josh asked.

Ken was in his forties, with longish blond hair and rimless glasses, and he looked as if he didn't know the hippie generation was but a dim memory. His first movie was about to be released, and his usual cool, calm demeanor had been replaced by anxiety. Worry lines were etched in his forehead.

"Yeah. Are you?"

"Sure. But it's your baby. I just wrote a song."

"I watched every scene about a million times when we were editing, and we know the acting is good, the production values are good, and that our sound editor knows his job but . . ."

"Yeah, when the score is laid in, that makes it official. Your baby is about to be born, and you hope the world will welcome it with open arms."

"Let's go in and face the music, so to speak, shall we?" He opened the door for Josh and followed him into the empty screening room.

As they sat and waited for the others to show up, Ken fell into deep contemplation. Josh decided to leave him to his thoughts and consider what had brought his own life to this moment. Josh's career had had more downs than ups, first singing in a band in nightclubs, then composing songs for commercials. Then, there was the tragedy that brought Rosemaria into his life, and the time he almost got his Broadway musical financed, but then that fell through. If the movie was a hit and Joell decided to put his song on her new album, he had a shot at finally becoming enormously successful. He wanted it for himself and for Rosemaria as well. She had made clear how much she hated show business when they first met, but she had always believed in his talent and backed his efforts without hesitation. Whatever happened, success or failure, she'd be there, and he appreciated that. But his yearning for success and recognition that had burned inside him for all these years had not dimmed. He wanted to know what it felt like. And maybe because of this movie, he would.

They both looked up as Dean and Kevin came in, followed by Ken's assistant, Jennie Seger. Ken greeted them with a nervous wave. "This is it. I hope."

Dean, a veteran movie composer in his sixties, feigned hurt and winked at Josh. "Hey, boss, have more faith in me."

Before Ken could react, Joell came in and gave effusive hugs and kisses all around. Tall, with long blond hair and a perfect figure, Joell was the embodiment of self-confidence and had charisma to spare. But she was such a genuinely good person that it took a really jaded, small-minded person to hate her. Not that there weren't plenty of those types in the music business. After they were all seated, Ken waved at the projectionist, and they waited with nervous excitement for the movie to start.

The lights dimmed, and as the introduction to the theme song began, with full orchestration and movie studio sound, Josh caught his breath and bit his lower lip in anticipation. Joell's voice—part Celine Dion, part Adele, but with its own husky flavor—began softly and then grew in intensity as it played over drone shots of Manhattan, then continued during street scenes while the opening credits rolled. The song ended, the movie began, and Josh counted his blessings that it was Joell who had said yes to recording the song. No one else could have done it justice. He tried to relax and enjoy the movie, but his mind was overwhelmed with the possibilities opening up for him. After years of struggle, this one song could open doors that had been closed for so long.

* * * *

The last credits faded out, and the lights came back on. No one—not Josh, Ken, or any of them—moved. This was Joell's first time seeing the movie, and they waited for her reaction.

"I love it."

Everyone in the room joined together in a collective sigh. There were grins all around and a few high fives. Ken's relief was palpable. He looked at his composer. "Dean, my friend, you're a genius."

Everyone stood and took turns hugging Joell, telling her what a great job she did with the song. Jennie whispered in Josh's ear, saying, "I told you it would happen." Josh watched as she backed away from him with a smile and went over and put her arms around Ken. He took a moment to appreciate the two people who had always believed in him. When Josh first started writing and recording commercials for Ken, it was Jennie who had been his biggest cheerleader. She was young and pretty, with acting ambitions that never came to fruition. But she never let herself get depressed or felt sorry for herself. When Josh was drunk and often late for auditions, Jennie had held him together with spit and coffee and willed him through every drunken session. By some miracle, the jobs kept coming, and he was able to pay his bills.

Ken told everybody that he would screen the movie for the cast and crew very soon, and then there would be meetings with the studio execs and distributors, plus all the other business that had to be done to release a movie. Josh was grateful he could ignore the business stuff.

Josh took Joell aside. She didn't wait for him to ask the question. "Yes, your song will be on my new album, and I'll be shooting a video of it as well in a month or so. Care to be there?"

"Absolutely."

He followed her outside.

"Would you and Rosemaria like to be my guests at the concert Saturday?" she asked.

"Under different circumstances, we would, but we're visiting friends up north this weekend."

"San Francisco?"

She waved to her driver, who was standing by her limousine a few feet up the street.

"No, a wild animal sanctuary. My panther, Noor, and my mountain lion, Gilbert."

She looked surprised. "You have a panther and a mountain lion? How did that happen?"

"I used to work at the zoo, and they both came in as babies. I finally got them out of there and to a sanctuary a few months ago. We visit them as often as we can. We missed last weekend because of work, so we have to go. I'm sorry."

"No, no, I totally understand. I wish I could meet them."

"Maybe someday, but it's not like a zoo. People can't come and stare at them anymore."

"Of course. That's how it should be." She gave him a brief hug. "Enjoy your trip."

Josh watched her walk toward her limousine and saw the driver open the door for her. *That's the life,* he thought, imagining what it would be like to enjoy that kind of luxury, then immediately dismissing it from his mind. His needs were a whole lot simpler than that. He walked back into the screening room a happy man, with the germ of an idea having nothing to do with movies or hit songs forming in his mind.

* * * *

Neelen Summers sat across from Rosemaria in her office. He paged slowly through the folder that contained the file on Rosemaria's armed robbery case, then laid the folder back on her desk. He was handsome, Rosemaria thought, for a conservative, squared-away guy. She figured him to be around thirty-five and too busy to get to the gym very often, considering the bit of a spare tire around his middle. "What are your thoughts about the case?" he asked.

"Well, it looks like a done deal if this Thelonious Rham has any sense." She opened the folder and looked down at the file. "I'm sure his lawyer will tell him to plead."

"How will you press your case?"

"It's pretty cut-and-dried. The store owner has given us a positive ID. The camera in the store, while not showing much of his face because of the camera angle and the hoodie he's wearing, shows that Thelonious was dressed exactly like the robber when he was arrested. He was seen by witnesses walking away from the store in the same clothes and shoes, and he was picked up by the police only blocks away."

"He swears he didn't do it."

"We'll offer him a sweeter deal if he tells us where he stashed the gun and money before the cops nabbed him."

"Except for the ID, it's a circumstantial case."

"A positive ID by a man who stared down the barrel of a gun will be pretty persuasive to a jury. Rham's lawyer will understand that."

Summers stood up and reached out to shake Rosemaria's hand. "Welcome to our office. I wish you luck." And with that, he was gone.

Rosemaria breathed a sigh of relief that her meeting with Summers had been short, sweet, and to the point. It was obvious he was not one to interfere, and while that was a good thing, she was now on her own. It was up to her to do or die without a net.

She was mulling over what time to ask Karen to set up an appointment with Rham and his lawyer when her cell phone sent a message alert. She reached into her purse and read the message. "Meet me outside Manuela's tonight at 12. —Melody"

Rosemaria's heart jumped into her throat, and her hand shook so hard she almost dropped her cell phone. Melody was the street name for one of her girls, Maryanne Compton. She had helped her move back to Albuquerque over three years ago. What the hell was she doing back in LA? And why was she asking to meet at night? She knew that Manuela was one of Maryanne's friends, and former working girl whom Rosemaria had helped get a job in Studio City as a housekeeper for friends of Rosemaria's father. They had believed and trusted in Manuela, and it had paid off for all of them. Manuela became a loving nanny to their six-year-old son. Questions shot through her mind. Why was Maryanne being so cryptic? What kind of trouble was she in? She immediately texted back. "What is going on?!" She waited for several minutes, but another text was not forthcoming. She swore under her breath. This was not good.

She picked up the desk phone and asked Karen to schedule a meeting at the jail for the next day at 10:00 a.m. with Rham and his lawyer. Whatever Maryanne needed; Rosemaria couldn't allow her anxiety to sidetrack her work.

CHAPTER FOUR

J osh and Rosemaria, wearing light jackets to keep them warm against the evening breeze, were out on their tiny balcony sitting on rusted wire chairs. They looked out at the palm trees and rooftops of West Hollywood. Lights in the distance twinkled in the dark. A pizza box and their soft drinks sat on a round wire table. The screen door was shut and firmly in place to make sure Suzi didn't suddenly feel the need to escape into the wilds of West Hollywood. The spoiled little bird wouldn't last long in the real world.

Josh spoke through a mouthful of pizza. "This is the life, my sweet, wouldn't you agree?"

Rosemaria took a bite of her slice, chewed, and said, "God's country for sure. You can hardly smell the exhaust fumes up here."

"True. I'll hate moving away once we make our fortune."

"Me too. And if the movie is as good as you say, that may be soon." She took another bite. "You know, I'm almost getting used to vegan pizza, but it tastes nothing like real cheese no matter what you say."

"You earn a lot of points for leaving the dark side and coming over to mine."

She leaned over, gave him a nuzzle, and took a sip of her drink. "Remember that when I have to work nights and you're all alone and longing for the sight of me."

They concentrated on enjoying their food for several minutes.

He gazed at her thoughtfully. "I know you're thinking about Maryanne. You put a lot of effort into making sure she got away from her life in Hollywood. But you can't let it make you feel like you failed her. Ultimately, it's up to her to decide what she wants to do."

"She's sounds like she's in trouble. I have to help her if I can." She looked at her watch. I'll work on my laptop for a while, then head on over the hill to Studio City around eleven." She picked up the last slice.

Josh grabbed her wrist and took a bite. He waited for her usual objection, but it didn't come. "That was your slice, you know."

She shook her head and smiled, then looked out at the distant lights. Her voice was tinged with sadness. "I tried so hard with those girls."

He put down the slice and took her hand in both of his. "Whatever's wrong, you'll know how to deal with it."

She acknowledged his encouragement with a heavy sigh.

* * * * *

Maryanne didn't dare call Manuela and tell her she was outside the house. Whoever had sent those men after her were obviously important. She didn't want to involve Manuela or the Rollands in anything that would risk their lives. And she knew, deep in her bones, that she had stumbled into something that she shouldn't have and was now in serious trouble. She checked her cell phone, but it was dead. It had to be at least 11:30. Everyone had gone to bed, and Sergeant Baker should be there soon, if she had gotten the message. It had gone through, so she knew Sergeant Baker hadn't changed her cell phone number. Her whole body ached from running and stumbling her way to Manuela's house, and her feet were cut to pieces. Running in her 6-inch heels had been out of the question. She had dropped them somewhere anyway. At least she had managed to hang on to her purse and cell phone. She sat on the ground at the side of the front porch, behind one of the eucalyptus trees that bordered the property. She didn't even know what kind of car Sergeant Baker drove, but who else would stop in front of the house at midnight?

Rosemaria drove up Tujunga and turned right on the Rollands' street. She couldn't remember the exact house number but recalled that it was Mediterranean stucco, like so many of its neighbors, but had a forest-green front door, unlike everybody else's. It was a little difficult to see in the dark. She crawled along the street slowly and came to a stop in front of where she thought the Rollands lived. She turned off her lights and waited. She didn't have to wait long before Maryanne came running out from the side of the house and jumped in the car. "Please, can we drive somewhere out of this area?! I'll tell you everything. Let's go up the freeway away from here!"

"Sure, we can do that. Why are you being so secretive?" She glanced over at Maryanne, whose normally light-brown hair was darkened by perspiration and dirt. Her minidress was torn in several places, and her shoes were gone. She was obviously exhausted and frightened.

"I'll tell you everything once we stop on the other side of the hill. Maryanne continued to look around her as they drove. She didn't relax until they were off the 101 and on the 405. Rosemaria took the Mulholland exit and turned east. She drove to a turnout that overlooked the Valley. "Okay, sweetheart. You're completely safe. Tell me what's going on."

Maryanne was close to tears. "I'm sorry I let you down and came back. I truly am." Her eyes welled up, and tears ran down her face. She put her hands up to her face, her back hunched over, and her shoulders shook as she sobbed. Rosemaria reached past her and grabbed some Kleenex out of the glove compartment. Maryanne took them and tried to stop crying. "I messed up, Sergeant."

Rosemaria patted her gently on the arm, trying to comfort her. "I'm Rosemaria, remember? I'm your friend. And I'm no longer a cop."

Maryanne looked at her, wide-eyed. "You're not? Did you get fired?"

Rosemaria stifled a laugh. "No, I didn't. I became a prosecutor. But we can talk about that later. Tell me what happened."

Maryanne nodded and breathed in and out in gasping breaths as she wiped her eyes and nose. "I thought I could handle this town. Obviously, I can't. The thought of having an audition for an actual movie was so incredible that I didn't think it could be something else. I'm a nobody. Why did I think any producer would cast me in anything legitimate?"

"You auditioned for a porn movie?"

Maryanne looked hurt. "Why would you think that?"

Rosemaria regretted the assumption. "I'm sorry."

"No, it was nothing like that. There was no movie. It was all a lie."

Rosemaria was lost. "Let's start from the beginning."

"All right. Just let me get it all out before you ask questions or try to figure things out, okay?"

"Sure. I'll just listen."

Maryanne cleaned up her face with the tissues and crumpled them in her hands. "I'm sorry, but I hated Albuquerque even more than I had when I grew up there. It's boring, and I don't have any friends except for my aunt and my friend Justine, who helped me get a job in the gift shop at the only nice hotel in town. I used the money you gave me to put down on a studio apartment and really tried for three years to make a go of it, but I just couldn't. Can you understand that?"

Rosemaria nodded. "So, you came back here, and then what?"

"I had saved up my money and got a small apartment in Van Nuys." She turned to Rosemaria in a panic. "But I can't go back there now. I just can't! They could find me!"

"Calm down. You don't have to. Tell me what happened."

"Well, I had been in touch with Tiffany, who you used to know, and she's working mostly as a waitress at El Torito in Canoga Park, but she's with an out-call agency too and gets calls for certain jobs." Maryanne turned to Rosemaria, pleading for understanding, "I'd never do that anymore. You know that, don't you?"

"I believe you."

"Tiffany told me she met this guy at a print shop after she decided to make up a résumé to try and get acting work, mostly extra stuff. Her résumé was all fake, but she said they don't really check anymore. So, this guy told her he had friends in the business who were going to do a movie and they might be interested in someone of her type. They were going to need extras, and some could get silent bits. He asked if she had any friends who might be interested, so she asked me if I wanted to, and I said yes. He told her to be at the Harland Hotel in Studio City Sunday night at 10:00 p.m.”

Rosemaria opened her mouth to voice her disbelief, but Maryanne jumped in before she could say anything. “I know that seems late for an audition, but he said they were working on preproduction or something.” She looked at Rosemaria's face. “Yes, I know it was stupid, but I wanted to believe it, you know? My car is broken down, so I had to Uber, and I got to the Harland just before ten. There was this guy waiting outside for us. He asked who I was, and I told him, and he said Tiffany hadn't come yet. He stayed outside to wait for her and told me I should go up to room 203 and tell them who I was. So, I did that.” Maryanne shook her head. “Stupid, stupid, stupid. I was about to knock on the door when some guy opened it, but he was turned away from me. He was holding a suitcase and was in a conversation with another guy who was on the phone. The guy at the door was blocking him, so I couldn't see him very well. Somebody else was coming out of the bathroom, but all I could see were shadows of the other two. It was so dark in there.”

Maryanne took a deep breath, then continued. “The man on the phone was speaking quietly, saying something like, 'You have to get him out of here tonight. He has to be gone before they find the hooker.'”

Rosemaria interrupted. “Did you see the face of the man on the phone? Could you identify him if you saw him again?”

“Like I said, I couldn't. I only saw him in profile from the other side of the room. He sounded desperate. He said to the guy who opened the door, 'Check us out and pull the car up to the side door. I have to call Julie.' The guy at the door started to come out and saw me, and he seemed shocked. He said, 'What the hell are you doing here?' I told him, 'I'm here for the audition.' He looked at me like I was crazy for a second, then like he remembered something, and said, 'Oh yeah. Wait here.' He didn't close the door all the way, and I heard them whispering. One of them said something like, 'Get rid of her.' When I heard that, I knew I'd better get out of there. I started walking down the hall fast, but he came up behind me and grabbed my arm and dragged me toward the stairs. By this time, I was scared out of my wits. He pulled me down the stairs to the first floor and out the side door. He was dragging me toward a car parked a few feet away, so I started screaming 'Rape!' really loud. Some people who were parking their cars came running toward us, and he ducked back into the hotel. And I ran for it."

"And you got away. Good girl."

"I ran and hid in the bushes and then broke into a garage of a house nearby. But before that, I saw the guy come back out with another man, and both of them started looking around, trying to figure out which way I'd gone. I stayed in the garage behind a workbench all night and all day today to make sure they weren't still out there looking for me. After it got dark, I went from yard to yard, then crossed some streets to get here."

"You did well, sweetheart. Really well. But why didn't you call me when you were in the garage?"

"I was ashamed to face you. I thought I could make it over to the Rollands and ask for their help, but I changed my mind."

"You shouldn't have felt that way about calling me, but I understand. What happened to Tiffany?"

"I don't know. I didn't see her. And I forgot to tell you, the car the guy tried to drag me into was a Lincoln Town Car with government plates."

"How do you know they were government plates?"

"Because they said so."

Rosemaria closed her eyes and tapped her fingers on the steering wheel. "I have to tell you, Maryanne, I think you might have stumbled into something worse than anything you ever encountered on the streets."

"What happened? Why are they after me?"

"I might know more tomorrow, or rather today, after I talk to my friends at the Beverly Hills police station, but I'm going to tell you something because I think you need to understand how serious this is."

"Believe me, I know it's serious!"

"A girl was murdered Sunday night at the Island Hotel. They think she might have been a working girl."

"Oh my God! That's why he said, 'before they find the hooker.' The people who are after me had something to do with it. She looked at Rosemaria, wide-eyed. "What have I done? They'll kill me."

"Please, honey, calm down." Rosemaria grabbed her purse from the back seat and got out her cell phone. "I think I have a place for you to stay where you'll be safe."

"You do?" Maryanne's plaintive gratitude was almost too much to bear.

Rosemaria spoke into the phone. "Vanessa, it's Rosemaria. I'm sorry to wake you up in the middle of the night. No, no, I'm fine, and Josh is fine, but I have an emergency. I have a favor to ask of you."

CHAPTER FIVE

The 405 didn't have much traffic at 1:00 a.m. early Tuesday morning, and that was a blessing. Maryanne was pretty much cried out and was staring straight ahead while Rosemaria was searching for answers. Whoever was in that hotel room was connected to the murder of the girl at the Island Hotel. That was obvious. And they were worried that Maryanne could identify the guy on the phone giving orders and the men who chased her. She would have to call Osborne in the morning and tell him everything. Vanessa and Larry had agreed to allow Maryanne to stay at their condo at the Marina. With Vanessa ready to pop, she and Larry didn't go out sailing on his beloved boat anymore or stay at the Marina. They preferred their house in Beverly Hills.

They arrived at the underground lot of the condo building, and Rosemaria punched in the code that opened the gate. Maryanne was looking around furtively as if any minute someone was going to grab her. "Relax," Rosemaria said as they headed for the elevator.

"I never had anybody actually want to kill me before."

Rosemaria pressed the Up button and smiled. "Lots of people have wanted to kill me, and I'm still here."

"Yeah, but you're a cop, or you were one. You're used to it, and you have a gun."

They arrived at their floor. "Come on, let's get you settled."

She rang the buzzer, and Larry opened the door with a smile. "Welcome, ladies!" He hugged Rosemaria like a long-lost sister and ushered them inside. "Hi, Maryanne. I'm Detective Coleman."

Maryanne stared at him like she couldn't believe what she was seeing. "You're a cop?"

Rosemaria had to admit he was a good-looking guy, in a tall, dark, incredibly handsome kind of way, even in the middle of the night.

Maryanne took in the open concept living room, kitchen, and family room. She realized she was in the presence of megabucks.

"I can't thank you enough for coming here at this ungodly hour," Rosemaria said.

"I better get used to it, don't you think?"

Rosemaria said to Maryanne, "He and Vanessa are having a baby." She looked around at the new furnishings. "I see you've updated the whole place. Lots of new furniture as well."

Larry shrugged. "Got to keep the wife happy."

"Vanessa would be satisfied living anywhere with you, and you know it."

"Okay, so I like to spoil her. She deserves it. But let's show Maryanne to her room. She's probably exhausted."

Rosemaria and Maryanne followed Larry down a long hallway to where Maryanne would be staying. "This is your hideaway for now. You'll be safe here."

The bedroom looked like a decorator's dream. Rosemaria had to admit that Vanessa had a flair for making a home elegant but welcoming. If she ever quit acting, she would have no trouble finding a new vocation decorating houses. Not that she would ever need one, being married to a millionaire.

Maryanne looked at them both, and tears threatened to reappear. "Thank you. I don't deserve this."

Larry looked at her, astonished. "Of course you do. Feel free to take a bath or shower. There's food in the cupboard, and I assume you can cook for yourself. I think you're about the same size as my wife, so feel free to wear whatever you need."

Maryanne was so overcome she could hardly speak.

"Okay then."

Rosemaria assured her, saying, "Take your time. We'll chat for a few minutes before I leave. But remember, no phone calls on the landline. I have your phone, so there's no way to trace you. What happens in the movies when somebody being chased by bad guys is told not to call anybody?"

"They call."

"And then what happens?"

"The bad guys find them."

"We don't want that to happen to you. Go take your bath."

Maryanne made her way into the bathroom and quietly closed the door. Larry was almost jumping out of his skin wanting to know what the hell was going on. Rosemaria shook her head and went back into the living room. "You won't believe this."

A few minutes later, Rosemaria and Larry were seated on stools at the large kitchen island drinking coffee. Larry was flabbergasted. "What a mess she walked into. And who the hell was that guy? If he was at the Island on Sunday and at that fundraiser, he's somebody important and obviously connected to the murder."

Rosemaria said, "Yes, but politicians don't have goons who try to kill people in front of God and everybody. They have executive assistants who know people who know people who take care of problems on the QT."

"Won't be easy to track down."

"This takes dirty politics to a new level. Okay, I'm going to call Osborne in the morning and explain it all. What am I saying? It is morning. I'll call him from my office."

"How's the job so far?"

"I have my first suspect/lawyer meeting in a few hours. I hope this caffeine will keep me from falling asleep."

Larry stood up and gave Rosemaria a squeeze on the shoulder. "I'll be getting back to the wife. If I know her, she'll still be wide awake and ready to grill me."

"Give her a hug from me. Tell her we'll get together soon."

He was almost out the door when she added, "By the way, Larry. Go back to work. You're driving Vanessa crazy."

Larry looked surprised. "Did she say that?"

"Of course not. She wouldn't. But a woman knows. Go back to work."
Looking slightly wounded, he gave her a wave and went out.

Rosemaria sighed, remembering the emotionally unavailable jackasses
they both used to be when they first started working together. She thought
about the unbelievably moonstruck saps they had become. She was everything she had always detested, a woman dependent on a man for her
happiness. She saw herself mirrored in Larry, decided there was not a damn
thing she could or wanted to do about it, poured herself another coffee, and
reached for her phone to call Josh. He would be awake and worried.

* * * *

The twenty-eight-year-old African American man, Thelonious Rham, sitting across from Rosemaria in the interview room at the Santa Monica
jail, didn't look much like a criminal. He was fairly handsome, with short
hair and a medium frame. Not being able to make bail, he was dressed in
jailhouse orange. His lawyer, Ben Stein, apparently was a familiar face in
the Airport Courthouse, but this was Rosemaria's first meeting with him.
Short, pudgy, and balding, he was all business. "We told Summers. We're
not pleading this out."

Rosemaria, still fuzzy from no sleep, struggled to concentrate. "We have
a positive ID from the store owner, the clothes he was wearing when he was
picked up match perfectly with the clothes in the store video, and he was
only five blocks away from the store when he was arrested."

Stein's answer was automatic and slightly bored. "That's all circumstantial, and IDs aren't reliable, especially cross-racial IDs. The store owner is
Korean. We're taking this to trial."

"The store owner got a good look at your client, Korean or no Korean.
He was three feet away, and he's positive. He can't be swayed. That's going
to go a long way with the jury. If your client pleads to attempted robbery
and gives back the money, he'll serve almost no time."

"I can't give back what I never took." Rham's voice was cold. "I'm not going to jail for something I didn't do."

Rosemaria was taken aback by his adamant denial. This was not going to be an easy sell. "I'm sure Mr. Stein has told you that armed robbery is a serious felony, and you could go to jail for fifty years or more if you go to court and are found guilty. We're willing to offer you ten to fifteen if you'll tell us what you did with the money and the weapon."

She could see that Rham was getting angry, and despite Stein trying to stifle him, he said with as much force as he could muster, "I can't give you what I don't have. I didn't rob the store, and the store owner is wrong. How can I make you understand that?" Rham's anger had turned to desperation. "I didn't do it."

"If he can't give you the money and the weapon, what kind of deal can we get?" Stein asked.

Rham exploded, shouting, "No!"

"What kind of deal?" Stein repeated.

"We need the gun and the money."

Stein packed up his briefcase and stood up. "Come on, Mr. Rham, we're done here. See you at trial, Ms. Baker."

Rham stood up and spoke like he was trying to appeal to the deepest part of her. "I didn't do it. Really, I didn't."

They went out, and Rosemaria sat for a few minutes and contemplated what had happened. She had to admit she almost believed Rham. Maybe he didn't do it. Maybe he was arrested while being Black. Or maybe he's very clever and is playing her. But she was just the prosecutor, not the investigator, and the cops seemed to have done a thorough job. Her instinct was to talk to the store owner herself. How would Summers like that? He probably wouldn't, then she would get called on the carpet. Push the envelope on her first case? Not wise. She seriously considered doing it. But first, she had to call Osborne and fill him in on Maryanne's close call.

* * * *

It was a tiny one-bedroom apartment in Van Nuys, but to Tiffany, aka Christina Ross, it was the nicest place she'd ever lived in. Growing up in Texas, she'd been passed around from one relative to the next as her mother wandered the state with various boyfriends, all of them drugged out, hard-drinking losers who had an eye for Eve's pretty daughter. After being raped by an uncle and one of her mother's sleazier boyfriends, Tiffany decided it was time to hit the road.

She hitched her way to LA, ending up in Hollywood, where she met a guy named Gary, who said she could stay with him until she got settled. A part of her knew she was playing out the same worn-out old Hollywood cliché, but when he pimped her out, at least she got paid, and he only took 50 percent. She decided who and where, and he never hit her. That was important. Then, one night, she was jumped in an alley by a slimeball pimp she'd never seen before, and Sergeant Baker appeared out of nowhere. It was like a miracle. The guy talked big, but he shook like a leaf at the sight of her and took off running after yelling out a few empty threats that the sergeant laughed off. That's when Tiffany started getting her life together. The sergeant had helped her get a job at El Torito and her own apartment, but still money was tight, so she took a few side jobs now and then when the opportunity arose.

She was only seventeen but turning tricks had become the easy way out for too long. It made her feel like crap, but money was money. She decided she might as well try to get some extra work in movies, so she typed up a phony acting résumé to be professionally printed. And that's what had landed her in this jam. She felt bad for Maryanne and had heard her screaming bloody murder Sunday night. She felt like a coward for not trying to help her, but she had her own safety to think about. When she saw on the news that a girl was found murdered behind the Island Hotel, she knew she had done the right thing. Maryanne could be dead somewhere too, and she didn't want to be next.

Her broken-down old Camry still got her to work and back, and the rest of the time, she hid in her apartment. That guy at the print shop didn't know where she lived and neither did Maryanne, but she knew she had to figure out another place to stay soon. She still had the sergeant's card. Maybe she'd call in a few days. She remembered the picture and phone number she'd given to the phony talent scout and figured there was no way the bad guys wouldn't track her down.

* * * *

Josh was already seated at a table and waved at Rosemaria when she came through the door to meet him for dinner. Viva Vegan on Wilshire in Santa Monica had become his favorite restaurant, and she agreed their quesadillas were heavenly. Ever since following Josh down the vegan path, she had gained way too much weight. She vowed to exercise more often.

He stood up when she got to the table and kissed her on the cheek. "I'm going to have the nachos. What about you?"

"I'll have the Caesar salad. I need to lose some weight."

"You look just fine the way you are."

"You men always say that, and you don't mean it."

"You keep telling me I don't mean what I say." He leaned forward and said under his breath, "Us men like to have something to grab."

Rosemaria sucked in her breath. "That does it. I have to join a gym and start sweating off this blubber. Something to grab, my ass. And stop trying to talk like a chauvinist. You can't pull it off. Nevertheless, I'm still going to enjoy my salad."

"You can have some of my nachos too."

"Enabler!"

They gave their order to the waitress, and Rosemaria shared her frustrating first day. "You wouldn't believe the cases they're giving me—a woman who poured paint on the car of her husband's mistress, a seventy-two-year-old woman who worked as a receptionist at the Golden Oaks Golf Club and had been embezzling money for eight months. Can you believe it? Am I supposed to put this elderly granny in jail? And now I'm wondering what to do about an armed robbery suspect who swears he's innocent, and I actually believe him."

Josh almost choked on his water. "What?! Baker the hanging judge thinks a perpetrator is innocent?! That, literally, is hard to swallow." "There's just something about him. He really seems sincere. I may have to check things out for myself."

"Uh-oh. I'm feeling some cop vibes right now."

Her phone sounded. She fished it out of her purse and looked at the caller ID. "Speaking of— Hey, Sergeant, what's up?" She listened for a few seconds. "Maria Ramirez. No that doesn't ring a bell. Can you shoot me over her booking photo? I'll run it by Maryanne and see if she knew her. I'd like to avoid showing her the crime scene photo. How old was she?" Rosemaria shook her head. "Fifteen? What a terrible waste. Yeah, I'll let you know what Maryanne says. We're going over there now to bring her some groceries. I'll call you tomorrow." She clicked off the phone and looked at the plate the waitress put in front of her. Her appetite had vanished.

* * * *

Maryanne looked like a different person. She had shampooed and blow-dried her hair and was wearing one of Vanessa's spring dresses. She seemed to have relaxed a little and sat with her legs curled under her on the living room couch.

Rosemaria was seated opposite Maryanne. She gave Maryanne her cell phone. "Do you recognize this girl? Her name was Maria Ramirez."

Maryanne studied the picture and handed back the phone. "No. I've never seen her before." She hesitated. "Is she . . . is she the girl who was killed?"

"I'm sorry, but yes, she's the murder victim. She was very young. You had probably left before she got here. You still doing okay?"

"I'm fine as long as I don't think about the people who want to kill me."

"We'll figure out a more permanent place for you to stay in a few days." She smiled. "But this'll do for now, right?"

Josh was standing near the kitchen island checking messages, and Maryanne kept shooting him curious looks.

"Yeah. I never thought I'd live in a place this nice, even temporarily." Then, she asked Josh shyly, "Are you really in the movies? The sergeant—I mean, Rosemaria—told me you are."

"Kind of. I have a tiny part in a movie coming out soon, but I'm not an actor. I'm a songwriter. I wrote the theme song."

Her face lit up. "Really? That's so exciting! I wish I could be a part of all that."

"Who knows? Maybe you will be," Josh responded.

"You remind me of Nick Nolte in *48 Hours* except thinner. I love that old movie. He was so good in that."

"Yeah, he's one of my favorites."

Rosemaria agreed. "Sexy in a disheveled kind of way." She shot Josh an appreciative glance. Between Josh's rumpled appearance and Larry's perfect looks, for her, it was no contest.

She stood up. "We have to be going, Maryanne." She handed her a burner phone. "You can call me on that. My number is programmed in already. But remember—"

"Don't call anybody else."

"You got it."

They said their goodbyes, and Josh and Rosemaria rode down the elevator, lost in their own thoughts. "I want to help so badly," Rosemaria said.

Josh wrapped his arms around her. "But you are."

"Yeah, but not the way I want to."

* * * *

A noise woke Tiffany up from a restless sleep. She looked at her phone—3:15 a.m. Someone was outside. It had been days since she could sleep all night because of her fear of being discovered. So, she had decided to spend every night in the easy chair next to the front window, in her sweat clothes, with her slip-on sneakers, and with her handbag on the floor next to her. If anyone pulled up in a car outside or approached the walkway, she had a better chance of hearing it. Was she being paranoid? You bet. She hadn't been able to reach Maryanne. Her cell phone number no longer existed. Maybe she was dead too. Maybe they'd gotten to her. But why?! What had Maryanne seen that was so terrible? The only thing Tiffany knew was that she had to stay alert or meet the same fate as the other two girls.

She carefully pulled the front curtain aside barely an inch, just enough so she could see outside her apartment. From the second floor, she had a good view of a dark sedan that had just parked halfway down the block. She knew that because their brake lights were still on. Then, the lights went off. There were two people inside, but they weren't getting out. A chilling fear made her entire body shudder. She kept staring at the car, hoping she was imagining that the two people had any interest in her at all. They could be visiting someone else in the apartment complex next door. *At 3:15 in the morning? Fat chance*, she thought. The two men, who were wearing dark clothes, got out of the car and started walking down the sidewalk toward her apartment. It was time to make her move. She quickly slipped on her shoes, grabbed her purse, tossed in her cell phone, and walked quickly to the back door. She opened it quietly, stepped outside, locked the door, and made her way soundlessly down the stairs to where her old brown Camry was parked behind the building. She almost gasped out loud when she looked behind her and saw a man come around the side of the apartment building and begin to creep up the stairs to her apartment. He didn't see her. Starting the car was going to make noise, but she had no choice. She would drive down the alley in the opposite direction from where their car was parked. She probably knew this area a hell of a lot better than they did, and chances were good they wouldn't catch up to her.

She unlocked the car door with her key. Thank God it was old and didn't have an alarm. *Please let it start, please!* She turned on the ignition and it fired right up. *Yes!* She backed out with a screech, drove like the devil himself was chasing her down the alley, and then turned right. She kept to the side streets, driving fast, hoping she wouldn't hit any stray animals. She knew where she wanted to go, if she could just get there without getting killed.

* * * *

Who the hell were these people?! Tiffany was hunkered down in her car in the front seat. She had parked inside an abandoned car repair shop that Tiffany had passed several times on her way to the laundromat on Van Owen. In panicked desperation, she had managed to pull up the rusty, broken door that led into the car repair bay, and somehow she had avoided driving into the mechanic's hole in the middle of the floor. As soon as she was inside, she pulled the door back down. She figured she was safe here for now. Lots of brush and weeds had grown up around the shop as it waited to be torn down or reincarnated into whatever would rescue it from oblivion. She hoped the men chasing her would figure she had driven far away from here by now and certainly wouldn't be hiding inside this wreck of an old repair shop.

Why, why, why hadn't she called the sergeant days ago? She had thrown her cell phone out the window near her house. She had heard that a cell phone could be tracked, and she wasn't taking any chances. But now she needed another phone to call the sergeant. She would wait another day in case the men were still looking for her. Then, she'd walk a block up to the Super King and buy another phone. Meanwhile, she had a box of crackers and bottles of water in her purse. Using the broken-down toilet was disgusting, but she couldn't risk going outside and doing her business in the bushes. She was safe for now. She had to believe that.

* * * *

The man from room 203 in the Harland Hotel paced the carpeted floor of a luxury hotel room in Washington, DC. He was dressed impeccably, as always, the very picture of the powerful, professional politician that he was. His gray hair was cut short. He had handsome features that were craggy but not old-looking. He was trim and fit, giving the impression that the future was his for the asking. The desperate expression on his face told another story as he spoke in harsh tones to the middle-aged man seated on the couch. The man looked implacable, radiating a dangerous energy.

"How could they lose her?! She's just a young, stupid girl! And the other one might have been outside and could have seen the whole scene in the parking lot!"

"What about the guy who hired the hookers to come up to your room?"

"I've used him before. My people contact him by phone. He's very discreet. But I don't know what he saw."

"We'll find all three and take care of it. Meanwhile, you need to calm down."

"The girl who came to the hotel room might have seen my face. And she sure as hell got a good look at those idiots who lost her!"

"Hiring hookers was a major mistake. You politicians have your brains in your dick."

"I planned to celebrate a little before I went back to DC. What was the harm? The Harland is far away from where the action was at the Island. It wasn't my fault everything turned to shit!" His voice became louder as he spat out his indignation. "I would've agreed to cooperate. Your goons didn't need to threaten me right outside the Island, where somebody could have overheard. And why didn't they get rid of the body after they killed the slut? Why make things worse by throwing her in the dumpster? That was stupid!"

The other man stood up. He could barely conceal his contempt. "Do I have to remind you who's in charge here? You work for our boss, not the other way around. He paid for you and put you where you are. Do as you're told, and keep your mouth shut. If you're questioned by the police, act innocent and tell them nothing. This whole thing will blow over, and we'll all get what we want."

He walked out of the hotel room without a backward glance.

CHAPTER SIX

O sborne, Waite, and veteran homicide detective Sergeant Harvey—in his fifties, with thinning hair, but still as sharp as a tack—were in Lieutenant Manley's office about to go over the case. They looked up to see Larry come through the door.

Osborne grinned and was the first to comment. "So Vanessa finally had enough, huh?"

"She begged me to stay home, but I told her you needed me, so here I am."

Osborne chuckled, but the lieutenant was all concern. "She's about due to have the baby, isn't she?"

"Still a few weeks, but you never know."

"Well, it's good to have you back." The lieutenant gave Larry a brief nod, then focused again on his laptop. "Your reports are always thorough, Osborne, but I like to hear it spoken. Start from the top."

Larry pulled up a chair and took out his pen and notebook. He had a bit of catching up to do, and he liked to keep his own informal notes.

Osborne opened his file folder and glanced down. "Victim: Maria Ramirez, street name: Lorelei Star, fifteen years old, no contact information available regarding her parents, one misdemeanor charge, dismissed with a warning, assigned to live at the Lifeline House, stayed for two weeks, and then disappeared. The Island Hotel cameras show her at the bar."

The lieutenant looked down at his laptop and clicked on the video. Osborne continued, saying, "She walks into the lobby, attempts a couple of times to connect, can't find any takers, sits at the bar for a few minutes, takes out a pack of cigarettes, and glances around the lobby, probably looking for an exit so she can go outside to smoke. She walks down the hallway to the back exit, and that's the last we see of her alive. There were no cameras where she must have been standing."

The lieutenant studied the video. "Several men went down the same hallway shortly after Ms. Ramirez. Is there a restroom there?"

"Yes, the men's room. The women's is down the other alcove a few feet away. No exit on that side."

"I'm counting eight men going in that direction just while I'm watching."

"Most of them, as you can see, do nothing to hide their identity. We can partially see their faces." Osborne moved to stand behind Manley and waited. "If you'll allow me . . ." He reached in to stop the video. "These three keep their heads down and, as best we can determine from what they're wearing, never come back in. Two of them are walking inordinately close to the man in the middle, maybe in an intimidating way. As you can see, a Hispanic busboy briefly bumps into them, but they brush him off and keep going."

"Did he remember what the men looked like?"

"No. Too many people, and everybody pretty much looked alike to him."

"So, they were determined to have a conversation in private outside," Waite said.

Osborne agreed, saying, "And Ms. Ramirez must have been smoking near the exit and overheard something she wasn't meant to hear."

"That must've been one hell of a conversation to have to kill her to keep it quiet," Larry said.

The lieutenant was still looking at the video as Osborne went back to his seat in front of Manley's desk. "There's hundreds of people milling in and out of the lobby. There's no way to tell if those three ever came back and no way to know who they were," Manley said.

"The cameras over the loading dock show one man walking alone down the alley, then two men following him a few feet behind five minutes after Maria Ramirez walked down the hallway. Could be the same men, but we can't be sure," Osborne responded. "They kept their heads down."

"These guys all seem to dress the same," Larry added. "Lots of blue suits, white shirts, red ties, and a flag on the lapel. They want to look patriotic and conservative in case of a photo op. It's difficult to tell these guys apart."

"I'll have to call in extra help for the interviews. We can't do them all. I'll ask Hollywood and Van Nuys for as many people as they can spare," Manley said.

Harvey looked down at his notes. "Most of the attendees have left town already. We'll be doing a lot of phone and Skype interviews."

The lieutenant nodded in agreement. "Tell me about Maryanne."

Osborne read from his file. "Real name: Maryanne Compton, street name: Melody Lane. She came here from Albuquerque, parents long gone, was raised by an aunt who seems like a nice lady but strict. Came to Hollywood at age fifteen, on the streets for two years before Sergeant Baker helped her get back to Albuquerque." He turned to Larry. "You want to take it from there?"

"Well, unfortunately, she made the decision to come back to LA. Somehow, she connected with a girl named Tiffany, who convinced her to come to a fake movie audition at the Harland, where she overheard a man talking about a dead hooker and then barely escaped being dragged into a Lincoln Town Car with government plates. She contacted Rosemaria and now is staying at my condo at the beach. We promised her that no one outside this room can know that. I have a strong feeling they want her dead, and considering those plates, it's somebody who has a long reach."

The lieutenant didn't disagree. "Her whereabouts will stay in this room. But she can't stay there forever. This investigation could end up taking weeks or even months. Hopefully, we'll nail these guys before that, but that's not a sure thing."

"She can stay at our place until we can move her somewhere out of town. Maybe witness protection can help."

"I really don't want the feds getting involved with this case." Manley was adamant. "Find another way. They'll horn in on this as soon as they get wind of the way this investigation is heading. Protecting politicians is second nature with people in DC. We can't have that. Keep everything on the DL. Agreed?"

Everyone in the room assented, but Harvey was skeptical. "If we have all those people from other departments doing the questioning, how are we going to keep this on the down low? Somebody's bound to talk."

Manley breathed out heavily. "You're right. I'll handpick a few men I used to work with. I'm afraid most of the burden will be on us."

"Don't worry, boss, we're up for it," Waite said. "We just won't eat or sleep for a week or two."

Manley ignored the remark. "Any leads on where to find this Tiffany?"

"We're hoping she'll contact Rosemaria," Larry said. "We tracked down her address, but there's no sign of life in her apartment."

"You have my permission to update Baker on the investigation, but make it clear she is not to get involved."

"I'm afraid she's already involved. Maryanne is her friend. She'll do whatever she has to do to protect her."

"Make it clear that that's *our* job, not hers. Understood?"

"Yes, sir."

Manley closed his laptop, and everyone else stood up. The meeting was over. "Organize the interviews, Osborne. Let's hope we get lucky fast."

"Will do, sir."

The group made their way back to their own cubicles. Waite followed Larry into his. "The lieutenant knew I was kidding about not eating or drinking, didn't he?"

"The lieutenant doesn't kid. Haven't you noticed that?"

"I wasn't complaining."

"What are you so worried about?"

"I just want him to know I'm part of the team like everybody else. I don't just sit behind the computer all day."

"He knows."

"Think so?"

"He knows everything, which is why I have to make sure I get Rosemaria to stay out of this."

"Can't be done."

"Tell me about it."

CHAPTER SEVEN

The liquor store Rham purportedly held up was near the corner of Main and Pacific. Rosemaria drove by slowly and saw that there were no cameras at the intersection nor on any of the other buildings nearby. She parked in front and walked inside the small store, noticing a camera over the door that faced the interior of the store. A young man—white, around twenty-five, and wearing a plain blue sweatshirt—stood behind the counter. She gave him a friendly smile. "Hello. I'm wondering if you can help me."

He seemed congenial enough. "Sure. We probably have every kind of beverage you could want."

She took out her prosecutor ID and held it up just long enough for him to read her name and see the official seal. "I'm Rosemaria Baker, and I'm here to ask some questions about the robbery. Is the owner of the store here?"

"No. He's home today. Still a little shook up, you know?"

"Well, he can relax now that the robber is in jail."

"You'd think he would, but he's still scared. I guess it must have been having a gun pointed in his face."

Rosemaria looked around the store, up at the camera, and back at the young man. "So, he's home right now?"

"That's where he said he'd be. I usually just unload stock and put it on the shelves. I'm not at the cash register all that much. Sometimes his wife comes in to help him."

"She works here too?"

"Sometimes."

"Thank you, Mr.—"

"Zimmer. Ben Zimmer."

"Okay, Mr. Zimmer. You've been a big help."

She walked back to her car, cursing under her breath. "Damn." She had hoped to take her lunch hour talking to the owner and make it back to the office before Summers started asking Karen where she was. Now she felt compelled to track down the owner at home and question him there. She didn't even know if Summers approved of this type of thing. In New York, prosecutors talked to witnesses at home or at work if they felt they wanted more information, but who knew how things were done here? Well, she needed some answers, and the only way to get them was to talk to the owner herself.

The owner of the liquor store, Mr. Lin, lived about a mile away in Venice in a small run-down house in a lower-middle class neighborhood. *I guess the liquor business isn't doing too well,* Rosemaria mused. A car was in the driveway, so he must be home. She walked up the cement steps and knocked on the door. She immediately heard loud whispering inside the house that sounded like it could be Korean. She shouted, "Hello, I'm from the Los Angeles prosecutor's office. I'd like to talk to you if you have time." The door opened slightly, and a short, thin Korean man in his fifties peeked out at her.

"We say everything to the police. You ask them what we say."

"I need to ask you some questions myself. Please open the door."

She heard the voice of a woman, who she assumed must be his wife. The woman spoke to him in Korean. He shook his head. "We don't want to talk. We say everything already."

Rosemaria was tired of being jerked around by this guy, victim or no victim. "You can let me in and talk to me now, or you can talk to me in my office. Your choice."

The man turned around, had a whispered conversation with his wife, then came back to Rosemaria. He opened the door wide so she could come in. The wife was also small and thin. Both looked nervous. The wife indicated for Rosemaria to sit, and she chose a chair next to the coffee table. The husband and wife huddled together on the couch. "Mr. and Mrs. Lin, my name is Rosemaria Baker. I'm going to be the prosecutor on your case. You do know that the robbery suspect is in custody and will not be able to make bail? You're not in any danger now."

The wife said something to her husband in Korean, and he turned back to Rosemaria. "We know that. We are not afraid. We don't like talking to government people. We have done nothing wrong."

"I didn't say you had done anything wrong, Mr. Lin. After all, you are the victim. I just have a few questions, and then I'll be on my way. All right?"

He nodded, his face set in a scowl.

"First of all, how long have you owned the store?"

"Why you ask?"

"Just answer my questions, please, and we will get this over with a lot sooner."

"Eight years."

"Have you been robbed before?"

He hesitated.

"Have you?"

"Maybe two times before."

"You don't remember?"

"No."

"Would it surprise you to know that you have been robbed five times in those eight years?"

"Sound correct."

"When you were robbed before, was it the same people or different people?"

"Different."

"Were they arrested and prosecuted?"

"No."

"Had Mr. Rham been in your store before?"

"Don't remember."

"Mr. Lin, you're making this very difficult. Had he been in the store before?"

He squirmed on the couch and hesitated, then said, "Yes."

"How many times?"

"Maybe two or three."

"Had he ever given you any problems before?"

"No."

"Did he always wear the same jacket when he came in?"

"I don't remember."

"Okay, that's fine. I can sit in the car outside your house until you do remember. Maybe turn on my flashers." *Threatening an old Korean couple. Wow. What flashers? She didn't have flashers anymore.* She asked the question again. "Did he always wear the same jacket?"

"Think so. And he have fancy shoes, like Nike, maybe."

"Just like in the video."

"Yes. Just like."

"You had ten thousand dollars in your safe the night you were robbed. That seems like an awful lot to be keeping in the store. Why was so much money in the safe?"

He was looking more and more uncomfortable. "I told other police that I hadn't been to the bank in a week. It had added up."

"Added up? Uh-huh. Mr. Lin, I don't believe a word you're telling me. You're still scared to death even though Mr. Rham is in jail. I think you recognized the real robber, and he's frightened you into lying to us. Is he threatening you, Mr. Lin?"

Mr. and Mrs. Lin engaged in frantic exchanges. Rosemaria couldn't make head or tail of what they were whispering to each other. Finally, Mr. Lin turned back to her. "We have nothing to say. We get lawyer if you try to take us in."

Rosemaria sighed and rolled her eyes. She didn't want to be accused of browbeating a victim. "Take it easy, Mr. Lin. I'm not taking you in. I wouldn't want the real robber to think you're cooperating. But I'm not putting an innocent man in prison because you're scared, do you understand that?"

She got up, walked to the door, and opened it. "This is not over." On her way out, she heard their whispers growing more urgent.

* * * *

After a brief appearance at her office to make sure no one was looking for her, Rosemaria decided to head on over to the Santa Monica police crime lab to look over the evidence from the liquor store robbery. She knew there had to be differences between Rham's clothes and those in the video. Her instincts told her that he was innocent, and as a cop, she had relied on her instincts more than once. Mr. Lin was lying. She had looked at the video repeatedly to try to find something. Some difference. She studied the pictures of Rham after he was arrested wearing the same clothes as in the video. The robber had obviously observed Rham in the neighborhood and decided to make him the patsy for the robbery. He had also observed that the angle of the camera made it difficult to see a customer's face. Maybe the robber himself had managed to adjust the camera to where it was now. But why did Mr. Lin have so much money in his safe, and how did the robber know about it? Did one of the Venice gangs have a protection racket going, and Mr. Lin was paying them off? Maybe her imagination was running away with her. She needed to find something solid to get Rham out of this frame. She wasn't a cop anymore, and she couldn't get involved in investigating gang activity way out of any jurisdiction she had ever worked in.

Frustrated, she picked up one of the shoes Rham had been wearing and noticed how it was laced. A lot of times, gang bangers didn't lace up their shoes at all, but Rham did. Instead of putting the laces into all the holes, Rham had skipped three holes and then resumed lacing to the top. It was that way on both shoes—very odd. She buzzed Gary, the lab assistant, and asked if he could zoom in on the robber's shoes in the video.

Gary, a bespectacled, officious young man in a white lab coat, came through the door, puzzled. "Still looking for something everybody else missed, huh?"

"I think I found it, and with your help, I can get the accused out of jail."

Gary took his place at the computer and ran the video.

"Try to find a spot that shows the robber's shoes that you can zoom in on."

Gary started going through the video frame by frame until he found the best view of the shoes and zoomed in. "Now what?"

"Well, will you look at that?" Rosemaria sounded as smug as she felt. Then, she mentally crossed her fingers and hoped that Summers wouldn't be pissed because she had ruined a perfectly good slam-dunk case.

* * * *

Thelonius Rham looked around the interview room in the Santa Monica jail, nervous and jittery. Neither he nor his lawyer, Ben Stein, had any idea why they had been called to this meeting.

Rosemaria entered the room carrying her briefcase. She greeted them politely and sat down opposite Rham and his lawyer. She took an eight by ten photo out of her briefcase and placed it on the table. "Is this a picture of your shoe?"

Rham studied the picture and said, "Yes. I know because I lace my shoes like that."

"Why do you lace them up like that?"

"Because I have flat feet, so I have to wear inserts and then leave the arch of my foot open. I can't lace up there or my feet hurt. After I started doing what the foot doctor told me to do, my feet don't hurt anymore."

Rosemaria placed another picture of a shoe on the table. "Does this look like your foot?"

"Shit no. I can't lace my shoes like normal people."

"That's the shoe of the robber."

After a few seconds, when the truth had sunk in, he grinned. "Well, what do you know?"

His lawyer nodded, smiling. "Good catch, Ms. Baker."

Rham let his head fall toward his chest. "Hallelujah." He sighed, then looked up at Rosemaria. "Does this mean I'm free?"

"I have to discuss this with Summers, then do the paperwork. If all goes well, I will secure your release before the end of the day. But I must tell you, we don't know who the real robber is yet. I'll have to bring in Mr. Lin and convince him it's in his best interest to give us the name if he knows it. Framing an innocent person is against the law. I'm sure he'll cooperate. So be cautious, Mr. Rham. I don't know if the robber knows where you live, but I'd advise you not to go outside at night. Secure your house both when you're at home and when you go out. This man almost succeeded in getting away with armed robbery by blaming you. He'll be angry that he failed. Mr. Lin is obviously terrified of him, so don't underestimate what the robber is capable of doing to you."

Rham was smiling broadly. "Thank you for believing in me, Ms. Baker. Who'd have thought that my screwed-up feet would get me out of a jam?"

"Thank you, Ms. Baker, for going the extra mile for my client," Mr. Stein added with genuine appreciation.

The meeting was over, so they all stood up. Rham and Stein thanked her again with warm handshakes.

"All in a day's work, Mr. Stein. My pleasure."

After they left, Rosemaria felt a thrill of satisfaction similar to how she'd felt after solving a perplexing case back in the day. Oh well. She was on a different path now, and she was determined to see it through.

CHAPTER EIGHT

Sammy the elephant, standing alone in his small enclosure, was swaying back and forth, his heavy-lidded eyes looking at Josh through the bars of his prison. Sammy's entire body communicated hopelessness. Sammy had been incarcerated in the zoo since he was captured as a baby in the jungles of southeast Asia and brought to LA twenty-five years ago. He had been beaten with bull hooks to make sure he understood that to rebel in any way meant severe punishment. Once his spirit was broken, he was deemed acceptable to be put on display for people to stare at for two minutes and move on. Sammy's life was a living hell for the sake of two minutes' worth of staring.

He had no elephant companions and barely had room to walk around. The large palm trees had been electrified so Sammy couldn't rub against them, as elephants instinctively need to do. The entire time Josh had worked as a caretaker at the zoo, his heart had ached for this elephant. Through the years of Sammy's confinement, various animal groups had tried to free him, protesting outside the zoo entrance, appealing to the LA City Council time after time. Josh was convinced that councilmember Chang, who represented the district the zoo was in, was accepting under-the-table-donations from the zoo to make sure Sammy stayed put. Sammy was an important part of the animal entertainment complex, otherwise known as a zoo, and Ed Hahn, who ran the place, had to compete with Universal Studios, Disneyland, and SeaWorld, among other venues, for tourist dollars. So, Sammy had been forced to endure his prison until, as Josh could clearly see, he was merely a shell of the elephant he was meant to be.

Jerry, the zoo veterinarian and Josh's good friend, was standing beside Josh. "I do the best I can, but his feet and legs are extremely damaged because of the hard surface of his enclosure. He needs natural turf and many miles to roam. I'm afraid he's given up, Josh. I'd like to free them all, but elephants suffer more than any of the other animals because of their size and their need for space. You gave Noor and Gilbert their freedom, my friend. Can you work a miracle for Sammy?"

"I don't know, but if I don't do something soon, he'll die."

Jerry nodded his head slowly and turned away from Sammy's small enclosure. "Come on. You wanted to see our new clinic. I'll give you a personal tour."

"I'll join you there in a few minutes, okay? I'd like to say hello to a few old friends first."

"Sure. I'll see you up there." Jerry hopped into his golf cart and drove up the hill. Then, he glanced back to see Josh, still with Sammy, talking to him softly.

* * * *

Sergeant Kowalski, late 60s, thick arms, big pot belly, was standing behind the desk when Rosemaria burst through the front door of the Beverly Hills Police Department. "Hey, girl! I knew you couldn't stay away!" He came around and pulled her in for a good long hug, dismissive of any political incorrectness that that kind of behavior might entail. She hugged him back, loving the familiarity of his tobacco and aftershave smell.

"Don't get your hopes up. It's just a visit."

He mimed disappointment and let her go. "Too bad. Everybody misses you. Things are way too dull with you gone."

"I hope I don't stir up a hornet's nest coming in. I just wanted to get a firsthand update on the investigation into the murder of the prostitute at the Island. My friend Maryanne is still in danger."

"Got to let the guys do their thing. You don't get to chase down bad guys anymore."

She started up the stairs. "Don't worry. I'll just ask a few questions and then be on my way. I can be very unobtrusive."

"Not in this lifetime," he said, chuckling. "If you need anything, I'm here."

She continued up to the detectives' offices. Shelly, the young blond receptionist who sat behind the reception glass, looked happy to see her. She opened the door and hugged Rosemaria. "Welcome back!"

"It's just a visit. Is anybody in?"

"Osborne is at his desk, the lieutenant is at a meeting downtown, and everybody else is out doing interviews."

"Thanks, Shelly." She walked to Osborne's desk, and he smiled up at her. "I've been expecting you."

"I won't interfere, I promise. But whatever you can tell me, I'd appreciate it."

"Pull up a chair."

Rosemaria did as she was told. "Any more details on the murder victim?"

He turned back to his computer and pulled up a video.

"She wasn't raped, if that's what you're asking. She did have a small amount of skin under her nails. We'll get the DNA, and if we find the killer, we can nail him. Waite tracked down her booking info. She was born in Youngstown, Ohio. Her mother is Meredith Ramirez, whereabouts unknown. Sergeant Harvey and Detective McNamara from the Hollywood precinct are on Hollywood Boulevard as we speak trying to find someone on the street who may have known Maria. We have no leads, just flying blind hoping to find someone there with a connection to her."

"I worked a vice case with McNamara a while back. She's good. She'll find something if there's anything to find."

"Let's hope so." He directed her attention to the video on his computer. "This is Sunday night, after the banquet. That's her in the bar."

Maria—thin, dark, with long black hair, and exquisitely beautiful—walks into the lobby looking ill at ease, with a brave, pasted-on smile. She attempts to speak to a couple of men but is rebuffed. She bites her lip, her confidence obviously shaken, and seats herself at the bar. After ordering her drink and then sipping it slowly, she very subtly eyes possible clients and gets a few looks but no takers. Even politicians are wary of a girl who looks like possible jailbait. She pays for her drink and goes out into the lobby. At least fifty people are milling about, talking and laughing. Politicos are working the millionaires and billionaires for donations. Maria seems lost as both men and women glance at her briefly and continue past. After a few awkward moments, Maria looks around and finds the exit near the men's room sign. She walks toward a short hallway at the back of the hotel. Soon, three men head in the same direction.

A Latino busboy, carrying a tray of dirty dishes and glasses, bumps into two men, who keep their heads down. They are clearly escorting a third man out of the banquet room. The men are annoyed, and the busboy wipes one of the men off with his towel and apologizes.

"Did you interview the busboy?"

"We did, but he couldn't remember even enough to help us with a drawing."

She continued watching. "Too bad."

The three men continue toward the hallway where the alcove and the men's room are located. The camera in the alcove follows them out the exit door, where presumably Maria is taking a smoking break.

"It's unfortunate that there were no cameras covering the door and the dumpsters."

"Management says they're going to fix that. A little late."

"I guess the two goons had already scoped that out. Any video of them checking it out earlier in the weekend?"

"Who knows? They hide from the camera very well. We're looking at videos."

"So that's it?"

"Most of the politicians didn't stay at the hotel. Way too pricey for even them. Maybe it's some sort of violation of the law to use campaign contributions for ultra-luxury hotels. The donors stayed at the Island all weekend. Some politicians had their rooms directly paid for by donors. I guess that's legal. All the others stayed in cheaper hotels or with rich friends. No one so far admits to staying at the Harland. The room Maryanne went to was paid for by an offshore corporation that Waite managed to follow to an account in Qatar."

"Good luck trying to trace that. So, you just have to talk to a few hundred conference attendees and try to find someone who acts guilty."

"You forget that there were plenty of people who gate-crashed the party to network and glad-hand. They wouldn't be registered or have any record of them being there."

"I take it most of the politicians and their aides have left town by now. How are you going to interview hundreds of people by phone and Skype without them leaking it to the feds?"

"We'll have to narrow down the field quite a bit before that's necessary."

"This might take a while, even for brilliant minds such as my former colleagues in the greatest police department in the country."

Osborne's eyes narrowed. "You're going to interfere, aren't you?"

"Absolutely not. I'm shocked that you would even suggest such a thing. I'm up to my eyeballs in work at the courthouse."

"Just keep it to a minimum, okay? I'll share what I can, but if the lieutenant gets wind of you sniffing around, he'll blame me."

Rosemaria showed him her best innocent expression.

"Just so you know," Osborne added, "Maria has an uncle on her mother's side, Malcomb Curtis. She obviously had parents who never gave a damn, and we were not able to track them down. Curtis said he has no idea where they are either. He'll be coming next week to claim the body and bury her."

"I'd love to meet him, if that's okay."

Osborne sighed. "All right. I'll arrange it. And we need to talk to Maryanne. Can you bring her in next week?"

"Your wish is my command."

"If only that were true."

* * * *

"Let's turn on the TV! Let's turn on the TV!" Suzi sat on Josh's shoulder, squawking into his ear as he stopped strumming his guitar to look at her.

"Man, I can't concentrate with you talking so much. What's gotten into you? You have to behave the next couple of days. Gladys, the neighbor lady, will be taking care of you. Be nice to her."

"Let's turn on the TV!"

"We don't have a TV. As soon as I get my next residual check, we'll get one."

He looked up to see Rosemaria coming through the front door, cell phone against her ear. She walked over to where he sat and bent down to buss his cheek but couldn't navigate past Suzi so gave up. "That's wonderful news, Mr. Stein. Tell him he has to keep an eye out. I'm not kidding about that robber being dangerous." She listened. "I'm afraid that's a job for the police. As soon as he's in custody, I'll let you know. Bye." She clicked off the phone.

"I got my armed robber off today." She kicked off her shoes and plopped down on the couch beside him. He was strumming a tune.

"I thought you were supposed to prosecute them, not let 'em go."

"He was innocent. I had to see that justice was done. That's my job."

"What do you think of this?" He lifted Suzi off his shoulder, put her on the back of his chair, strummed a chord, and began to sing.

It was just a dream.
Nothing was real.
I was a fool, all was foreseen.
I wish I had known,
But then, yet again,
I wouldn't have changed
Just being your friend.

His voice gave Rosemaria chills as he soared into the chorus.

I'm living a dream and I'll never let go, of all that you are,
And all that I need,
Never to be, never to have.
In my own world, I let my heart lead.

He stopped and looked at her. "That's as far as I've gotten on that one. It's after Samantha, the rich girl, tells Max, the chauffer who's in love with her, that she's marrying someone else, and he's feeling like life is hopeless. It's still a little too schmaltzy. What do you think?"

Rosemaria could barely contain herself. "You sing like an angel, my love, and like all your songs, it's beautiful!"

"I feel like it's almost ready—maybe."

"Then start putting it out there. You almost did two years ago when Ken thought he had backers for you. You've been working on it for ten years, writing and rewriting. It's time to share it and let other people besides me appreciate how amazing your musical is. It's time! Just do it!"

Josh blew out a big puff of air. "Yeah—"

She took his face between her hands. "What do I have to do to convince you? It's ready. I'll tell Ken, or you can. Okay?"

"Maybe—"

"Tomorrow morning we're driving up to visit Noor and Gilbert. If you don't say yes, I'll nag you all the way."

"That sounds like not too much fun. If I promise to talk to him on Monday, will you not nag me?"

She grinned and put her head on his shoulder. "I promise."

"I don't know what he can do, anyway. One of the backers was a friend of his who decided he'd rather invest in Ken's movie."

"How did his wife work out in the part Ken cast her in?"

"Not too bad, actually."

"There's a part for her in the musical too, right?"

Josh grimaced.

Rosemaria put up her hands. "All right, make it a small part. Schmooze with her husband at the premiere. See what happens."

Josh all but guffawed. "I should hire you as my manager."

"I'm just sayin'. And now that Ken is dealing with a lot of people with money, you never know. Maybe somebody will at least be willing to listen to the demo."

Josh stared at her through narrowed eyes.

Rosemaria smiled and backed away to sit on the bed. "That's all I have to say. Carry on with what you were doing. Just pretend I'm not here."

Josh turned back to his music and, with a great flourish, brought his hand down hard on his guitar strings, filling the apartment with a discordant noise.

"Nice chord," Rosemaria observed sincerely.

Josh threw his head back and laughed. Then, he put down his guitar and jumped her.

CHAPTER NINE

Southern California was showing off her natural beauty as only she could as Josh and Rosemaria drove up the coast past Montecito and Santa Barbara. Josh was behind the wheel of his classic blue-gray Mustang convertible that was barely hanging on to life. The ocean was on the left, the hills of Santa Barbara on the right. Palm trees, beaches, and blue skies with a hint of fluffy white clouds completed the picture postcard.

"We live in paradise, my friend," Rosemaria announced. The top was down, and a warm breeze ruffled their hair.

"And it's for sale at a million dollars per square inch." Josh patted her knee. "We can look but not touch."

"Oh, pshaw, we're a year away from a house on a cliff overlooking the ocean."

"That's a lot of faith you have in this ol' guitar plucker, ma'am."

"Just keep pluckin'. We'll get there."

They drove through Santa Barbara, past Lompoc, and toward San Louis Obispo. Then, they took an exit toward the ocean. A road on their right, unmarked, led them to the Second Chance Sanctuary, where panthers, mountain lions, and other big cats could roam free, surrounded by tall fences that kept them in and people out. These cats had grown up in captivity and were unfit to be released in the wild, so the sanctuary was the next best thing to real freedom. They drove through the entrance and parked next to the office in the main building.

Jason Ruesch—a thin, wiry, thirty-two-year-old man with limitless energy—ran the place with the help of several volunteers and a visiting veterinarian. He had worked at the zoo with Josh, also as a caretaker, and now had a new job more to his liking. He loved animals, but in a short time, he had concluded that the zoo was nothing but a prison. He felt guilty leaving the animals he had grown to love at the zoo but was happy he could now oversee the amazing transformation of cats who had been abused by zoos, circuses, and private owners. He enjoyed observing them as they slowly learned to trust, made friends, and reveled in their freedom. He was at his desk, working on his endless grant proposals, when Josh and Rosemaria came through the door. He leaped to his feet. "Hey, you two! Good to see you!"

They shook hands. "We came to see our kids," Josh said. "They in the closed area?"

"I just coaxed them in there. They know that means you're coming."

Josh was eager to get going. "Let's go then."

Josh and Rosemaria followed Jason out of the office and sat in the back seat of his golf cart while he drove them down a dusty road for half a mile. Jason stopped in front of a gate attached on both sides to a high, smooth fence topped with barbed wire and cameras every 10 feet. The fence kept the animals safe and rendered escape and the invasion of intruders impossible. He unlocked the gate and invited them in.

"Enjoy your time."

"Always," Rosemaria said.

Jason handed Josh a key card. "I had this made for you."

Josh took it and smiled. "I owe you."

They went through the gate, and Jason locked it behind them and headed back to the golf cart. Josh and Rosemaria walked a few feet to another gate, manually unhooked it, then walked quickly to their usual meeting place by a large flat-topped rock surrounded by brush and a few small trees. Josh didn't bother to call out. Noor and Gilbert would know they were there. They sat down, side by side, on a tree stump to wait, smiling wide and barely breathing.

Noor appeared first, settling on top of the rock, her shiny black coat sleeker than ever. She crouched down with a gleam in her eye, ready to pounce. "Hey!" Josh said when he saw her. Noor waggled her rump in excited anticipation, then suddenly leaped on Josh, knocking him to the ground. He tried to push himself back up, but she wouldn't allow it, licking his face and rubbing his shoulder. Rosemaria watched in amazement. Barely giving animals a second thought before she met Josh, she was completely in love with this panther and young Gilbert, the mountain lion, Josh's other best friend.

She saw Gilbert sitting a few feet away, calmly watching the reunion between Noor and Josh. He was full-size now. His gentle yellow eyes, lined in black, studied her carefully. His coat looked healthier and thicker than it had been the last time they had seen him, golden with white on his chest. Like Noor, it was apparent he was thriving. She remembered when she first saw him as a baby in Josh's apartment, healing from an injury. The little cub had grown into a beautiful adult. She held out her hand. "Get over here, Gilbert. We love you too." He stood and walked slowly toward Rosemaria, and she felt honored to have him choose her. She stroked him gently. "Hi, pal. Sorry we didn't come last weekend." He rubbed against her side, and she put her head next to his.

Noor observed what was going on between Rosemaria and Gilbert and decided it was time to say hello to her female human. She moved away from Josh and nudged Gilbert away so Rosemaria could pet her. Josh looked at the three of them with a contented sigh. "Hey, let's go for a walk." He led, and the cats and Rosemaria followed, the cats pushing and shoving, vying for attention.

* * * *

The cabin they had leased was a tiny ramshackle hut with a porch that looked like it was ready to crumble, but it was across the road from the sanctuary, so it suited their purpose. Josh had promised Noor and Gilbert he would have a place nearby so he could visit often. Even though he no longer saw them every day, he knew they both were happier running free. He hoped their years at the zoo would eventually be forgotten. His two cats had an unbreakable connection to him that was essential—like children who had gone off to college but still wanted to know that their parents loved them. And he did.

"Home sweet home," Rosemaria said as they pulled up outside the cabin.

"Be it ever so humble," Josh added.

They grabbed their backpacks and went inside. It was one room and a bathroom. It had running water, a sink, a woodstove, a small refrigerator, a double bed, a rustic wooden table, and two chairs. Their apartment seemed luxurious in comparison. "Let's get some heat going in this place before the sun goes down and it gets cold." Rosemaria dropped her backpack on the bed, grabbed some newspaper and kindling by the pile of wood, and shoved it inside the stove. "I hope I'm doing this right." She added a couple of logs to the pile.

Josh let his own backpack slip to the floor and went to assist. "You're getting good at this." He grabbed the matches off the shelf by the stove, took one out of the box, and lit the paper under the kindling. Soon, the fire was blazing, and the room began to heat up.

She walked over to the bed, shoved her backpack on the floor, and drew back the quilt. She took off her jacket, lay down, and stared up at the rough-hewn wooden ceiling. "You know, I'm not always as strong as I seem to be."

Josh walked slowly to the bed and sat beside her. "Nobody is."

"Do you mind if I borrow your strength every once in a while?"

He lay down next to her and held her face between his hands. "That's what I'm here for."

She smiled, they kissed, and she relaxed with a sigh, letting him explore, touch, heal, and take her where she needed to go. And she did the same for him.

* * * *

They were seated at the table eating their sandwiches and chips hungrily, not talking. Josh had always appreciated that she was not finicky when it came to food but dove right in. "You know how to build up my appetite, girl. You make these sandwiches?"

"I oversaw the making of them at Subway."

"Great job."

She took a long swig from her bottle of Pellegrino and wiped her mouth with her napkin. "I have to call Maryanne and tell her I'm picking her up on Monday to take her to see Osborne." She dug her cell phone out of her backpack. Josh gathered up the remains of their meal and took them over to the sink. While he cleaned up, Rosemaria tapped in Maryanne's number. After a moment, she said, "Hi, hon, how are you?" She smiled and nodded at Josh. "That's good to hear. You keep bingeing. They have every channel known to man on their TV, so I'm sure you'll never run out of shows to watch. Listen, the reason I'm calling is that I have to take you to the station on Monday. I'll pick you up sometime in the morning, but I'll call first. And don't worry, I will bring Larry and a patrolman with me, so you'll be perfectly safe. Okay?" She listened for a minute. "Yes, I'll make sure no one follows us. Don't worry. Bye."

She looked around the cabin. The door was open, and Josh had disappeared. A moment later, he was standing in the doorway, holding his guitar. "Don't mind if I do a little work, do you? I'm recording a commercial for a furniture store in a couple of days, and so far, everything sounds too cliché. It's not fun to listen to."

"Do what you have to do. I'm going to sit outside on the swing for a while." She walked outside and sat down in the rickety, old porch swing, listening to Josh trying out chords on his guitar. She felt just as contented as she had been after tracking down her first murder suspect, testifying at his trial, and hearing him being sentenced to life without parole in the state penitentiary. Being here with Josh was even better than that.

CHAPTER TEN

After Rosemaria left the apartment Monday morning, Josh's thoughts returned to Sammy. He was never far from his mind. The joy that Noor and Gilbert now were able to experience away from their cages at the zoo was in direct contrast to the misery Sammy had been forced to endure every day of his life for twenty-five years. But to do something about it, he knew he had to enlist famous people to help him—like Joell. Judging by conversations he'd had with her, she seemed to genuinely care about animals. But first, he needed to figure out how to get Sammy out of the zoo and to a sanctuary. He needed a solid plan, and he didn't have that yet. He wanted Joell to understand how important ending Sammy's suffering was to him. In return, he had to be her friend as well. No matter how famous someone may be, they still had fears and insecurities that something unforeseen or the wrong move could destroy their careers. He had intended to call and ask how her concert went, even though he had just heard from Ken this morning that it had been a huge success, with standing ovations and numerous encores that lasted half an hour. He had already decided to thank her for inviting him and Rosemaria to be her guests. Maybe she would appreciate his genuine interest and the implied offer of friendship. His conscience told him he was being awfully self-serving, but that couldn't be helped. This was not about convincing Joell to record his songs, but rather about something he cared about a lot more.

* * * *

Karen wasn't at her desk when Rosemaria came in. That was unusual, but she saw Karen's computer was on, so she knew she was there. Maybe she was with O'Malley. She walked into her office feeling refreshed and renewed after her most excellent weekend and looked forward to her meeting with a man arrested for assault and battery on his wife. The wife, after years of abuse, had finally gotten up the nerve to press charges, and Rosemaria would do everything in her power to keep him from getting out on bail and going after the wife and possibly killing her. If he did make bail, she would find a safe house for the wife until she could throw his ass back in jail for good.

She was reading through the file when Karen appeared in the doorway. Her face was ashen.

"What's wrong? You look terrible."

"Summers has been transferred. He's going downtown."

"I like him a lot, and we'll both miss him, but why are you so upset about that?"

"He's being replaced by Walter Atkins."

"Oh, shit." Walter Atkins was the nephew of Ken Folson, the attorney general of California. Atkins had been working out of Van Nuys and had been the nemesis of her friend, assistant DA Celia Mathison, for two years. While Celia had a perfect conviction rate, Atkins's was at a dismal forty-five. He annoyed judges, defense attorneys, victims, and other prosecutors. The only reason he hadn't lost his job was because of his uncle and his uncle's powerful friends. He was nepotism incarnate.

"Oh, God. Karen, please tell me you're kidding."

"Apparently, some of the judges in Van Nuys were so sick of his self-aggrandizement, lack of respect, and all-around bad behavior that they told the attorney general they refused to have him in their courtrooms one more day. So, Summers got promoted to downtown, and somehow Folson got Atkins a job working for his pal Lattimer. If he can't make it here, he's gone."

"Geez, you wouldn't think that coming here would be a punishment. Look at our beautiful views of freeways and airports."

"How can you joke? I've heard horror stories about how he treats assistants. And I believe them. Oh, and he asked to see you as soon as you come in."

Rosemaria smiled mischievously, "As soon as I come in, I'll go see him. And Karen, let's just take this one day at a time, okay? We'll do our work and do our best to ignore him."

Her cell phone rang, and she clicked it on. Karen shot her a miserable glance and went back to her desk. "Baker here." Rosemaria shot out of her chair. "Tiffany?!"

Tiffany was slouched in the front seat of her car in her hiding place at the abandoned garage. Her hair was dirty, her clothes were in disarray, and her makeup was smudged. She looked twelve years old and terrified. "Sergeant?" She tried to keep her voice from shaking. "They found out where I lived. They came to my apartment."

"What?!"

"They came in the middle of the night, but I got away. Is Maryanne okay? Did she call you and tell you everything?"

"She did. Where are you now?"

"I'm in Van Nuys in my car in an old car repair shop. It's abandoned and all grown over. I don't think they can find me here."

Rosemaria's mind raced. *What to do? Where to take her?* "You can't stay there. I'm going to think of somewhere for you to live until this is over. Maybe with Maryanne. These people obviously have powerful connections and tracked you through your phone. Did you get rid of it?"

"I did. I bought a prepaid one at Super King."

"Do you have food to last another day or so?"

"Yeah, I bought some snacks there too."

"All right, then stay where you are. Don't move. They may still be in the area looking for any sign of your car. Will you do that for me?"

"I will. Thank you for helping me." She sounded utterly lost and forlorn.

"That's a given, Tiffany. Of course I'll help you. I'll call you later today." Rosemaria clicked off the phone. Maybe Tiffany could stay with Maryanne at the Colemans' condo for another week or two, but then she had to find them both a more permanent place to live. Rosemaria also needed to go to the Harland, ask a few questions, and then check out the Island Hotel for herself. She was risking annoying her friends at BHPD and taking a chance that Atkins would find out, but what she did on her own time was none of his business.

As she was mulling over her next move, Walter Atkins, the Darth Vader of LA courtroom corridors, appeared in her doorway. "I told your assistant to tell you to come to my office as soon as you came in." Any resemblance to Darth Vader disappeared as soon as he opened his mouth and his whiny, high-pitched voice issued forth.

"She did, but I had to take an important phone call."

"Regarding what case?"

"I hope you're not going to be one of those micromanagers that won't trust us to do our jobs."

Atkins didn't bother concealing his rage. He was younger than her, with a weak chin, thinning hair, and an ample belly hanging over his belt. "You're not a cop anymore. You work for me now. You'll take the cases I give you and do exactly what I say."

Rosemaria stood up and walked toward him. "As I remember, the few cases of mine that you prosecuted, you lost."

"That was because of shoddy police work, not because I didn't do my job."

She stood in front of him and looked him in the eye. "I disagree. But be that as it may, why don't you give me whatever cases you want me to handle, I'll deal with them, and you stay out of my way?"

Atkins was shaking. He could barely control his contempt for her. "You always had a hell of a lot of nerve, Baker, but this is my office. You step out of line, and you're gone.

Rosemaria wasn't through. "I've also heard rumors about how you treat assistants. If you abuse Karen in any way, shape, or form, I will make a formal complaint against you and make it stick. Understand?"

"You can't win this war, Baker. I have the leverage, and all you have is your smart-ass mouth." He gave her a final contemptuous look and left.

Rosemaria contemplated the upcoming battle of wills that was sure to ensue and wondered if her days as a prosecutor were numbered before she'd barely even started. Nepotism was a powerful force. Somehow, she had ended up with another problem to solve.

Karen stepped in her office. "Wow. I can't believe what you said to him."

"Beware of future incoming missiles, Karen, but I think he knows better than to go after you."

* * * *

The man sitting across from Rosemaria in the tiny jail waiting room was huge. If he hadn't been handcuffed to the table with the deputy sheriff, who was twice as big, standing by, she would have been terrified. The man was bald and ugly. For the life of her, she couldn't figure out why any woman in her right mind would have ever married him. But Lisa Hutchinson had done just that, and now the poor woman was going through hell because of it. The report said she had been battered for years, had shown up in the emergency room time after time, but always denied that her husband had beaten her up. Finally, after he had stuck a gun in her mouth, threatened to blow her head off, and then decided to rape her instead, something inside the wife snapped. So, here they were.

Rosemaria looked at the young, court-appointed lawyer, Mal Bergman, who was not concealing very well that he had a scumbag for a client. "Mr. Bergman, right now, I intend to charge your client, Mr. Leonard Hutchinson, with felony sexual battery, which carries a four-year sentence; assault and battery inflicting serious bodily injury, which carries another four-year sentence; and last but not least, attempted murder, which carries a life sentence. I will agree to plead down to no charge on sexual battery and assault and battery, which leaves attempted murder, for which I will agree to fifteen years to life, with the possibility of parole in five years."

Hutchinson looked at her like he wanted to leap across the table and smash her face in. She hoped the manacles on his feet would hold and the table was bolted securely to the floor. He all but growled at her. "I'm not going to jail for one day. That stupid bitch will never testify against me, and you don't have a chance of getting a conviction without her."

"Actually, your wife is now in a safe place, where you will be unable to reach her and intimidate her into changing her mind. I will also make sure you do not get bail and remain incarcerated until the trial is over, at which time you will end up in a federal facility until the end of your natural life."

Bergman was not convinced. "How can you get an attempted murder conviction? He didn't attempt anything. He merely threatened her."

"Wrong. You can still be convicted of attempted murder if you initiated the act and then changed your mind. It's still attempted murder, Counselor. Believe me, I've testified in these kinds of cases before, and I am happy to say, every one of them resulted in a conviction."

"You testified?" Mal asked.

"I was a homicide cop."

Hutchinson looked at her, surprised. She could tell he was starting to see the light.

Rosemaria continued. "I promise you that if you do not take the deal, I will prosecute every charge and make sure you serve your sentences consecutively. You, Mr. Hutchinson, will never get out of prison. I can assure you of that."

Hutchinson looked at his lawyer, his anger diffused. Fear had taken its place. Like all bullies, he was a coward at heart. "If we go to trial, will what she just said happen?"

"There's a chance we might get a lighter sentence, but considering the evidence, your wife's testimony, and the prevailing public opinion of this type of offense, I'd recommend you take the deal."

The fight was gone out of Hutchinson's eyes. He looked like a giant deflated balloon. "I'll take it."

"Once you sign the papers, allocute in court, and receive your sentence, there is no going back. No appeals. Do you understand that?"

Defeated but sullen and resentful, he mumbled, "I understand, bitch." The lawyer looked at her apologetically. "I'll call you this afternoon." "And I'll draw up the papers." She stood. "I'll be on my way then."

She whispered a sigh of relief to the deputy on her way out. "I couldn't have done that without you."

He smiled.

* * * *

On her way back to her office, one of the other prosecutors saluted her as Rosemaria walked past her desk. Another gave her a thumbs-up. She acknowledged their affirmations with a smile. Word of her altercation with the new boss must have spread throughout the office. God only knew what was coming next.

Karen greeted her as soon as she came around the corner to her office. "I just put a folder on your desk. The chinless wonder came by and said you were to be in court immediately, regarding a limo driver who was beaten up by the guy he worked for, who happens to be Dr. Albert Hecht, the chief of staff at Cedars-Sinai. O'Malley went to the hospital with appendicitis. He was just about to begin the prosecution's case after lunch, at which time you are due in court."

"Why on earth wasn't there a continuance?"

"I think Atkins told the judge that you had agreed to cochair with Terrence and were intimately familiar with every aspect of the case. And you need to know, Judge Hopkins only grants continuances if somebody dies or another 9/11 happens. He's known for that."

Rosemaria briefly scanned the files, then stuffed them in her briefcase. "If I fall flat on my face, Atkins will look as much like an idiot as I do."

"From what I've heard about him, he'll figure out how to put all the blame on you."

"Tell him I'm on my way to the courtroom."

Rosemaria hurried down the hall toward the elevators and pulled her cell phone out of her purse. She tapped in a number. "Celia? Thank God you answered." She listened. "I was fine, but now I'm in one heck of a pickle. Atkins is now my new boss." She stepped into the elevator as she listened to a string of curses. "I agree with all of that, but I need your help fast." She quickly explained her situation to Celia, who calmly asked her who the defense counsel was and who the judge was, then told her what to do. "Thank you, sister. I owe you!" Rosemaria clicked off her phone and pressed the elevator button for the floor of the courtroom, where there was a distinct possibility she would face a disastrous outcome.

* * * *

The courtroom was still empty of spectators while the bailiff and other courtroom personnel went about their business. Rosemaria put her briefcase and purse down on the prosecutor's table and waited for the defendant and his lawyer to arrive. She didn't have to wait long. The accused, Dr. Hecht, was brought in. Dr. Hecht was a man of mediocre looks, in his thirties, with a thick head of brown hair and wire-rimmed glasses. He oozed arrogance despite his situation. His attorney, Willeen Sarno, a brittle-looking woman in her fifties, came in and sat down next to him. Rosemaria immediately went over to the defense table. "Hello, I was just assigned to this case by Walter Atkins. Terrence O'Malley is in the hospital with appendicitis."

The other woman looked her over, none too friendly, and they shook hands. "Willeen Sarno. Happy to meet you."

"I told my friend Celia Mathison you would be representing the accused, and she said I should say hello."

Sarno visibly stiffened.

Rosemaria continued. "I'm going to ask the judge for a continuance so I can meet with the people involved with the case. I haven't even had a chance to read Terrence's notes."

Sarno became stone-cold. "If your boss thinks you're ready, then I see no reason for a continuance."

"But I told you—"

"Your problems with Atkins are no concern of mine. I'm here for my client, not to accommodate the prosecution." She looked over at Hecht, who nodded in approval.

Rosemaria backed away and sat down at her desk. She waited patiently as people straggled in after lunch. The judge, in his sixties, looked every bit as harsh and intransigent as his reputation had promised. He took the bench, and the jury came in. Then, he called the court to order and asked if the prosecution was ready to resume.

Rosemaria took a deep breath. "If the court please, Your Honor, could we have a sidebar?" The judge waved them both up to the bench. She stammered slightly. "Judge, I just received this case out of the blue a few minutes ago and have not been given any time to prepare. Terrence O'Malley is in the hospital, and I haven't even looked over the material. I request a week's continuance so I can talk to the victim and the witnesses."

The judge looked down at her sternly. "I was told by Atkins that you were second chair on this case."

"I don't know why he said that. Possibly, he was confused. I am so sorry."

"Confusion in the prosecutor's office is no excuse. I'll give you an hour to review the case."

Rosemaria spoke softly as she pleaded. "That's not enough time, Your Honor. I don't think I'll be ready."

The judge, discomfited by her desperation, looked at Sarno. "What do you say, Counselor?"

By this time, Sarno had built up a full head of steam. "I strongly object to any delay! My client is entitled to a speedy trial. Glitches in the prosecutor's office are not my problem! I see no reason why you should grant a continuance!"

The judge was taken aback by Sarno's vehement outburst. He frowned, then announced his decision. "This trial will be continued until—" He studied his court calendar. "—next Thursday at 10:00 a.m. Step back."

Sarno tried to remain composed in front of the judge, but her disgust at the ruling was evident. Rosemaria calmly walked back to her table and picked up her briefcase. After the judge dismissed the jury, she smiled sweetly at Sarno and went out.

* * * *

Karen looked at Rosemaria warily as she saw her come around the corner and walk toward her cubicle. "What happened?"

"I got the continuance."

"No way! Judge Hopkins hates those."

"I called my friend Celia, a prosecutor who knows both the judge and the defense lawyer, Sarno. She told me Judge Hopkins can't stand overbearing women and expects female lawyers to be sweet and soft-spoken. Celia also told me that Sarno hates her because she's lost so many cases to her. The mere mention of Celia's name makes Sarno's blood boil. My instructions were to mention Celia's name to Sarno, then act meek and mild with the judge. Sarno was certain to object in a loud and overbearing way, which Judge Hopkins finds extremely offensive, so he would grant the continuance just to spite her."

Karen laughed. "Good job, boss! Atkins will spit nails."

"Then, we'll hammer them into his forehead if he gets too mean."

She went into her office, picked up her jacket, came back out, and closed the door. "I'm off to take care of some business for a friend. If Atkins calls, tell him the sad news. This wasn't just about him hating me but also about rich people helping rich people. I'll bet he was hoping I'd blow this case so the good doctor could go free per instructions from his uncle. I'm not giving him the satisfaction."

Karen whispered happily to herself as she watched Rosemaria disappear around the corner. "This used to be a boring job."

CHAPTER ELEVEN

Tiffany couldn't concentrate on the paperback book she'd bought at Super King. She had a horrible thought. What if the people chasing her had access to videos at Super King and other food stores? Maybe take-out restaurants too. They must assume she hadn't gone far and needed the necessities of life and food. She'd used cash but they might have seen her license number and followed her by street cameras straight here. Or maybe she had seen too many movies and her imagination was running on overtime. Or, as they say, you're not paranoid if somebody really is after you.

She got out her cell phone and tapped the speed dial. She drummed her fingers nervously on the dashboard as she waited. There was no answer, so she left a message. "Sergeant Baker, I'm afraid to stay at the garage any longer, so I'm going to sneak out the back door and walk down the street to a laundromat. I'll pretend I'm sitting there waiting for my clothes to dry. Please come pick me up! I'll stay there until you come. It's near Vesper and Van Owen."

She stuffed everything into her handbag and opened the car door. She heard voices outside the sliding door, so she quickly made her way to the back door, pushed it open a few inches, and went outside. She was shaking so hard she could hardly put one foot in front of the other. No one came around the side. She stayed off the sidewalk and walked as close to the buildings as she could, stepping into driveways whenever possible. Finally, she came to the laundromat, walked in, looked at one of the dryers in use, and pretended her clothes were in there. She found a seat in the back and sat down to wait.

* * * *

"Thank God, a human being to talk to!" Maryanne had opened the door to the condo as soon as Rosemaria knocked.

"Hi, sweetheart. I've got a car waiting downstairs. Larry is driving, and a patrolman is in the back seat. So, you'll be perfectly safe. You ready to go?"

Maryanne picked up her bag and coat from the couch and said, "Absolutely."

"Hold on. I need to check if I have any new messages. I've been avoiding my boss, who's called at least ten times. I think I'd better call him back before he has a stroke. She scrolled through her messages. "Darn!"

"What is it?"

"Tiffany called." She tapped in the phone number and waited. "Tiffany, are you all right?"

Tiffany, still sitting in the laundromat, was so relieved she choked up and could hardly talk. "I think they tracked me down somehow. I'm at the laundromat on Van Owen near Vesper. How fast can you get here?"

"It will take at least forty-five minutes in this traffic even with lights and a siren. If you feel you're in danger, go somewhere else, and we'll find each other."

"Where?! There is no place else!" Tiffany spoke in a loud whisper. She noticed the other people in the laundromat, almost all of them Latinos, staring at her.

"I can call the Van Nuys Police Department, and they'll have a patrol car come immediately."

"No! They don't know me. They might hand me over to those people. I have to wait for you."

"Then hide the best you can till we get there. I'm sorry. And get rid of your phone. I hope they haven't traced it already."

Tiffany clicked off the phone, went outside, stomped on it, and threw it in the trash. She returned to where she had been sitting, turned to the woman sitting closest to her, and spoke. "My father beats me. He's trying to find me to take me back home. I'm very afraid of him. Do you understand?" The lady looked at her, comprehending some of her words. "Mi padre es muy malo." Tiffany searched for words she had learned as a child in Texas. "Él me pega. Me está buscando. Me temo que. Si viene, necesito esconderme. Comprende?"

The woman stood up and spoke to a man who had been standing next to her. Tiffany thought he must be her husband. Their conversation was so fast she couldn't understand what they were saying.

The woman came back to her. "No worry. If you see him coming, we hide you. No worry."

"But where? Dónde?"

"You no worry. He no find you."

*　*　*　*

Rosemaria pulled Maryanne down the corridor to the elevator. She punched the button, and the door opened immediately.

"What's wrong! Are they after us?!"

"No, it's Tiffany. They found where she was hiding. We have to go pick her up before they get to her!"

"Oh my God!"

The doors opened to the parking lot, and they ran to the unmarked police car. The back door was open. Maryanne jumped in beside Patrolman Jamison, who was thirty years old and built like a middleweight. He nodded at her reassuringly. Rosemaria slid into the passenger seat and shouted, "Start the car. We have to go to Van Nuys!"

Larry did as he was told. "What the hell is going on now?"

"Whoever is after Tiffany found out where she was hiding. She's in a laundromat on Van Owen near Vesper. She's terrified."

"Well, shoot, what are we waiting for?" He tore out of the garage.

The 405 was jammed. Rosemaria slammed the magnetic red light onto the roof, and Larry turned on the siren. They flew up the side of the freeway. They made it to the 101 in record time and got off on Van Nuys, lights and siren all the way. Rosemaria looked back at Maryanne, who seemed to be in a state of shock. She had probably never ridden in a car going this fast before. "Don't worry, we won't get a ticket." The joke fell flat on everybody.

Finally, they got to Van Owen and started looking for the laundromat. They saw it up ahead.

"Let's make a pass and see if there's any sign of the two men who are following her," Larry said. All seemed quiet around the laundromat. They made a U-turn and pulled into the parking lot. Larry glanced toward the back seat at Maryanne. "Stay in the car with Jamison."

Rosemaria and Larry walked slowly toward the entrance of the laundromat. Rosemaria had her hand on the gun inside her purse, and Larry had his hand on the holster inside his jacket. He waited outside as Rosemaria went into the laundromat. She looked around and saw only a few Latino women and three burly Latino men who looked like they did heavy construction work. She hesitantly approached one of the women. "Has visto a una joven rubia? Ella es mi amiga. Ella me está esperando." Even as she asked the questions, her hopes faded. It was obvious Tiffany wasn't there. A cold fear cramped her chest. She was too late.

One of the women came toward Rosemaria. "Ella es su amiga?"

"Si, mi amiga."

"Para salvarla de su padre?"

This took Rosemaria aback for a split second. *Save her from her father?* "Si, para salvarla!"

The woman indicated for Rosemaria to follow her and led her to a large commercial dryer in the back of the room. She opened up the dryer, and Tiffany peeked through the clothes. She crawled out and threw herself at Rosemaria. "Sergeant, you came!"

"Of course I did." Rosemaria held her close.

The words poured out of Tiffany in a torrent, "They came in here, but Elena, her husband, and the others saved me. There were two of them, and they walked around and looked everywhere. I was terrified they would look in the dryer, but they didn't. I think they must have decided not to confront Elena's husband and his two friends." Tiffany turned back to Elena and hugged her. "Gracias, mi amiga, gracias!"

"De nada, Tiffany." Elena and her husband seemed nonplussed. They had done a good deed. It was the right thing to do.

Rosemaria thanked them all and hustled Tiffany out the door. "We have to get out of here. Let's not have a gun battle in a laundromat in Van Nuys, if we can avoid it."

Larry was already back in the driver's seat when Rosemaria practically shoved Tiffany through the rear door, on the other side of Jamison. Rosemaria hopped in the passenger seat. As Larry backed up and drove out of the parking lot, Rosemaria turned around and looked at the two girls. They reached across Jamison to clutch each other's hands.

"I'm so sorry I got you into this, Maryanne. This is all my fault," Tiffany said.

"We both believed a con man, Tiffany. We should have known better."

"So, do I have two guests at my condo now, or what?" Larry asked.

"Until we find a place more permanent away from LA," Rosemaria answered. "Obviously, these people have the means to track their victims, but there must be some place we can come up with."

She glanced back at the girls, who didn't like the sound of her words.

"Don't worry, I will figure out something. Those bastards will not lay a hand on either one of you."

The girls looked only slightly comforted.

* * * *

The group was gathered around Osborne's desk in his cubicle at the Beverly Hills Police Department. Maryanne, Tiffany, Larry, Waite, Harvey, and Osborne were listening as Rosemaria described what had happened in the last two hours.

Osborne took it all in with his usual calm. "These people have a long reach. We all know Washington, DC is a cesspool of corruption, but obviously we're dealing with politicians who have crossed the line and are willing to commit murder to cover their asses. We don't know what kinds of agencies they have access to and what forces they can bring to bear upon us. So, we must move as swiftly and unobtrusively as we can. We don't want the feds barging in and shutting down our investigation. This murder happened in our city, and we won't let the killers be protected because of political expediency. If a member of Congress is involved in this, he will be prosecuted. I don't care who he is or who he knows."

Osborne continued. "We've talked to some of the attendees, and their whereabouts at the time of the murder has been accounted for. We still have a lot more people to talk to, mostly long distance, unfortunately. They're all back in their states or in DC. Some of the donors live here, so those interviews are progressing. Waite, Harvey, and I have gone through about ten donors. We haven't seen anything yet that raised a red flag. Harvey and McNamara found nothing helpful while talking to the working ladies in Hollywood. Maria seems to have been a bit of a loner." He took a photo of Maria Ramirez and showed it to Tiffany.

"Have either of you seen this girl?"

Tiffany shrank back. "Is that the—?"

"Yes. Do you know her?"

"No."

He looked at Maryanne. "And you already said you didn't recognize her."

"She's too young to have been there when I was."

Osborne laid the picture back on his desk and faced Tiffany. "First of all, do you want to be called Tiffany or your real name, Christina Ross?"

"I prefer Tiffany, if you don't mind. It carries fewer bad memories."

"All right. Since this all first started with you, why don't you tell me how you both ended up at the Harland."

"I told Maryanne. I'm sorry about all this. I was stupid to believe him."

"Tell us from the beginning."

"Well, I thought I would try to earn a little extra money to supplement what I'm earning at El Torito, so I decided to have some résumés made up. You know, fake ones with jobs I really hadn't done since you can't get acting work if don't have anything on your résumé."

"Sounds logical," Osborne said.

"Anyway, I was at Perfect Printz in Santa Monica, telling the printer guy that I wanted it to look professional, you know, and this other guy was there having business cards printed up. He introduced himself, but I'm sorry, I can't remember his name. He looked at me, and after a while, he asked if I was an actress. I said yes, and he told me there were going to be auditions for a movie on Sunday night at ten o'clock at the Harland Hotel in Studio City. He said they had to do them late because they were already working in preproduction. He offered to meet me there so he could introduce me. And he said if I knew another beautiful young girl, she could come too. So, I asked Maryanne, who I had just run into on the boulevard, if she would want to, then all of this horrible stuff started happening."

Rosemaria could see Tiffany was barely holding it together. She wrapped an arm around her shoulder. "You're doing good, honey. You're helping us." Tiffany managed a grateful smile.

"Did you get one of his business cards?" Larry asked.

"No. I should have, but I was so excited I forgot. Like, I had some headshots, but I hadn't even had my resume printed up and already I might get a real acting job. Stupid, I know."

Harvey, who had a daughter only a few years older than Tiffany, spoke to her in a gentle, reassuring voice. "Not at all stupid, Tiffany. You trusted someone who seemed nice."

Osborne turned to Maryanne. "We heard what happened to you at the Harland and how you managed to escape. Well done."

"Thank you."

"Is there anything else you want to add?"

"Well, I know I told Sergeant—I mean, Ms. Baker—that the man on the phone said Julie. It could have been Judy or Junior or something close to that. I'm sorry. I'm just not sure."

"If you remember anything else, let Ms. Baker know, okay? Tiffany, do you two think you could help our police artist draw the man you met at the print shop and the other men who were chasing you? And, Maryanne, can you describe the men who tried to kidnap you at the Harland?"

Both girls nodded. "Sure," Maryanne said.

"All right then. Waite, as soon as they finish the pictures, will you go to Perfect Printz and find out who this man is? I'm sure they'll have his contact info, and we'll talk to him. And see if you can match up the drawings with photos in the database."

"Sounds like a plan," Waite replied. To the girls, he said, "Come with me, and we'll get this done."

After a hesitant backward glance to Rosemaria, who gave them an encouraging smile, the girls followed Waite.

Larry spoke after they had gone. "So now we look for a politician or donor who has an assistant or wife named Julie or Judy or something like that. Oh, man, we are still wandering around in the dark right now."

Rosemaria disagreed. "Now that you have a lead to the man who was in contact with the men in room 203 at the Harland, that will move the case forward. And you know the man in the room who was talking on the telephone had to be someone who attended the fundraiser, didn't go home, and didn't stay in another hotel or with friends, so that narrows it down. Did you find any identifiable fingerprints or DNA in the Harland hotel room?"

Osborne shook his head. "Wiped clean."

"If it's important enough to kill over, that means there's a lot at stake here," Larry said. "Doesn't sound like a personal issue or a minor problem with a donor or bit players in DC. I'd say we're looking at someone high up in government." Larry threw up his hands. "Then again, who knows?"

Osborne was studying his computer. "Waite still has gotten no further than Qatar in tracking down who rented the room."

Harvey was optimistic. "Computer trackers tend to be a little obsessive-compulsive. If it can be found, he'll find it."

Rosemaria checked her cell phone and saw another message from Atkins. "I need to get back to my office before my new and very unpleasant boss fires me. Larry, I know I'm pushing my friendship to the limit right now, but I don't know what else to do. Could you take both girls back to your condo and let them stay there for now? I promise I'll figure something out in the next few days."

"As long as they need to."

"Thank you."

She got up to leave, but Osborne stopped her. "Maria's uncle will be coming in tomorrow at four. Do you still want to talk to him?"

"Absolutely. I'll be here."

Walking down the stairs, Rosemaria was wondering how she was going to pull off doing two jobs at once, which is what this was turning into. With Summers, she might have gotten away with it. Atkins would use it to bludgeon her to death. Couldn't be helped. She dialed his number.

CHAPTER TWELVE

Rosemaria stood in Atkins's office in front of his desk. Expected to act like a recalcitrant child, she just couldn't make herself hang her head in front of this schmuck.

Atkins, smug and sure of himself, leaned back in his chair and addressed her. "You have wasted an entire day on your own personal issues. That is not acceptable in this office."

Rosemaria tried to sound pleasant. "Actually, I was able to get a plea deal from a murderous brute who assaulted his wife and a continuance on the Albert Hecht case. I consider that a good day's work."

"And the rest of the day was spent doing what exactly? What was this life-or-death situation that needed hours of your time?"

"I'm afraid that's personal, Mr. Atkins. But it's been handled, and I'll be able to devote myself to my cases from now on."

"Have I told you how much I hate your condescending tone?"

"No."

"Well, I do. But maybe your arrogance will be the thing that ends up being your downfall, and I won't have to listen to it anymore."

"I don't know why you hate me so much. Everybody else around here likes me."

"You can't win this, Baker. And that continuance you got, there's still a trial coming up, and you are in untested waters. I wouldn't count on winning if I were you."

Rosemaria was stunned that he would admit that he wanted her to lose the case. "Am I hearing you correctly, sir? Is the prosecutor's office rooting for the accused?"

Realizing that his hatred for Baker had made him slip up, he changed his tune. "Of course not. That's ridiculous. I'm merely stating that you, as a neophyte, will have an uphill battle against a seasoned defense attorney."

"Thank you for your support, sir. Is that all?"

Atkins leaned forward and glared at her. "Don't get too comfortable in that little office of yours. I look forward to forgetting you were ever here."

* * * *

Karen opened the door to Rosemaria's office and saw that she had fallen fast asleep, with her head resting on her arms on top of her desk. She hated to wake her, considering the last twenty-four hours, but she had no choice. "Rosemaria, you need to wake up. I need to know when you want to schedule the Carreras' interview tomorrow."

Rosemaria sat up groggily. "Huh?"

"Mr. and Mrs. Carrera. They're coming in tomorrow. What time do you want them here?"

"Ten o'clock should be fine. Is there anything else I need to do before I leave?"

"No. I think you should go home before you're too tired to drive."

"You're right. I can't die in a traffic accident. That would make Atkins too happy."

Rosemaria stood up, leaning on her desk. "Whoo, I haven't had much sleep the last couple of nights. I'm so tired I'm dizzy."

"Do you want to Uber?"

"No, I'll make it. Thank you for taking such good care of me."

"Part of my job. I want you to be well rested and alert so you're fit and feisty to fight another day with that, that—"

"Running out of names for him?"

"No, but I can't say any of them in polite company."

Rosemaria picked up her things and made her way to the door. "Don't ever worry about that. Being polite is highly overrated." She almost sounded drunk and needed to pull herself together. "I'm good to go, Karen. I'll see you tomorrow at eight, and we'll work on winning the Carrera case if it kills me."

"It'll kill Atkins if you do."

"Hold on to that thought." She continued out the door and wove her way down the hallway, vaguely remembering something about a dinner date with Larry and Vanessa that evening.

* * * *

Josh was standing in the kitchen, munching on a sandwich, when Rosemaria came wobbling through the door. She didn't look left or right, but just headed straight for the bed and collapsed without taking off the coverlet. Josh put down his sandwich and was by her side in two seconds. "I will have your clothes off before you know it." He pulled off her jacket and started unbuttoning her blouse.

"I don't think I'm in the mood for that kind of thing right now," she mumbled.

"Relax and let me take care of you." He pulled off her blouse, skirt, and shoes and then moved her over so he could cover her with the sheets and comforter. "Go to sleep, and don't worry about going out with Vanessa and Larry tonight. I canceled. Larry is almost as tired as you are."

"Thank—" And she was sound asleep.

* * * *

Ricardo and Sofia Carrera were seated in the conference room, nervously waiting for the prosecutor of their case to appear. Ricardo was in a wheelchair, and his arm was in a cast. They were a matching pair. Both were in their sixties, had gray hair, were a little overweight, and came dressed in their Sunday best. They didn't know what to expect from this meeting. The man they had been working with and trusted was now in the hospital, and someone new had been appointed. They hoped that this new prosecutor would be as dedicated to finding the doctor guilty as he had been. Karen came through the door carrying their coffees.

"One black for Mrs. Carrera, and cream and sugar for Mr. Carrera."

"Thank you," Mr. Carrera said in a heavy Spanish accent. He lifted his cup and took a sip.

"Will the new prosecutor be here soon?" Sofia was anxious and impatient. She spoke in an accent heavier than her husband's.

Karen sat opposite them and organized the folders in front of her. "She's been going over your case this morning in her office and should be here any minute."

"Good coffee," said Mr. Carrera, indicating to his wife to try it.

Everyone was relieved to see Rosemaria come through the door carrying her purse and briefcase. She reached out to shake hands with the Carreras. "Thank you for coming." She sat next to Karen. "I want you to know I fully support Terrence O'Malley, the other prosecutor, in not accepting a plea deal. We'll be moving forward with the trial next Thursday, and I will be calling you as witnesses. But first, I need to hear—" She stopped short when she saw Atkins walk through the door.

"You don't mind if I sit in, do you?"

Rosemaria forced herself to sound civil for the sake of the Carreras. "Certainly not."

Atkins pulled up a chair next to Karen. He introduced himself to the Carreras, who were a bit confused.

"Are you our prosecutor too?" Mr. Carrera asked.

"No, I'm not on this case. She," indicating Rosemaria, "works for me."

Rosemaria bit her tongue and began again. "I've read Mr. O'Malley's report, but I'd like to hear from you what happened. You can take your time. Try to remember everything that happened. The smallest thing can be important, okay?" Rosemaria was so furious with Atkins she was trembling.

Mr. Carrera took another sip of his coffee. "First, you must know that this Dr. Hecht is a very abusive man. One of the neighbors told me he has had many drivers, and none of them stay more than a couple of weeks. He pays a lot of money to try to get drivers to stay longer, but after a while, the money is not worth it. I stayed because I lost my position as an apartment manager, and we got way behind on our bills." He looked at his wife, and she nodded at Rosemaria. "I was desperate for a job when he hired me, and I thought we would finally be able to get out of debt."

"How long had you worked for him before the attack?"

"About four months. Four months of abuse every day, but I took it because I had to. The day this happened—"

Atkins interrupted him. "You were badly hurt, were you not, by Dr. Hecht?"

"Yes, I was."

"Are you planning on bringing a personal injury lawsuit against him? Is that why you are against a plea deal?"

"Rosemaria could barely contain her anger. "Mr. Atkins, you are speaking out of turn. We are not here to talk about civil litigation."

"I will talk about whatever I wish, Ms. Baker."

She stood up and walked to the door. "I need to speak with you in private. Now."

Atkins didn't move. "You are the one out of order."

Rosemaria gave the Carreras a reassuring smile. "Karen, would you take the Carreras into my office, please?"

Before Atkins could stop them, Karen had wheeled Ricardo out of the room, with Sofia trotting in quick little steps to keep up.

When Atkins tried to follow, Rosemaria blocked his path.

"Stop trying to subvert this case, or I'll have to write up an official complaint and take it to Lattimer myself."

Atkins snorted contemptuously. "You think I'm worried about Lattimer?"

"You should be, since he's our boss and has the power to fire you."

"And my uncle is his boss."

"Not quite."

"Close enough."

"You're not the only one with connections."

"You got nothin'."

"Try me."

Atkins couldn't keep up his false bravado against Rosemaria's well-honed hard-ass attitude. He didn't really know who her connections might be, but he knew he was going out on a limb for the sake of his uncle's biggest contributor to his campaign chest.

Rosemaria's voice was soft and threatening. "The next witness conference I have will be behind locked doors in my office. You will not be invited in. And if you try to interfere with any of my witnesses again, I will have you in front of the disciplinary board, uncle or no uncle."

"You have no idea the can of worms you just opened."

He left before she could respond with a remark that was on the tip of her tongue, which was probably a good thing.

* * * *

The Carreras seemed more comfortable in Rosemaria's office even if it was a bit cramped. Karen sat on a folding chair, squeezed between two file cabinets. Mr. Carrera was in his wheelchair, facing Rosemaria, who sat behind her desk. Sofia sat in a chair beside him. Mr. Carrera was speaking freely. He felt safe now that the unpleasant man was no longer near them. He spoke calmly through the entire recitation, having repeated the same things several times already to the police and O'Malley.

"I had waited for Dr. Hecht in his house like I always do. He likes me to carry his briefcase, so I come promptly at 7:45 a.m. and sit and wait on a bench in the hallway. When he comes downstairs, I take his briefcase from him, but that morning, he didn't have one. I was going to ask where it was, but he was already in a bad mood. He was shouting at his wife, who was in another room. I just followed him outside, opened the door, and then he said, 'Where's my briefcase?' I said he didn't give me one. He started calling me insulting names and told me to go back in the house and get it. I told him it wasn't in the hallway, and I couldn't go upstairs to look for it. He became even more angry and yelled at me. He said I had no right to disobey an order." Mr. Carrera trembled slightly and put his hand on his thigh when it began to shake.

Sofia reached over to steady her husband's hand, and he continued. "At that point, I couldn't take any more. I told him to stop blaming me for something I didn't do and to stop swearing at me. Dr. Hecht looked like he was going to hit me, and for once, I wasn't going to back down. That surprised him. He came so close he was almost touching me. Then, he shoved me hard, and I fell. I tried to get up, but he kicked me in the head, and I fell back. He kept kicking me all over until I passed out. Then, I woke up in the hospital, and they told me I had three broken ribs, a broken arm, and a concussion. My neighbors had called the police and told them what had happened. Dr. Hecht had already left, but they went to the hospital and arrested him there."

Rosemaria was looking at her computer screen. "I see there are several witnesses to the attack. Two witnesses, Mr. Lydon and Mr. Mangini, saw Dr. Hecht shove you to the ground. The others came in somewhere in the middle. Dr. Hecht is accusing you of starting the fight. Mr. Lydon and Mr. Mangini are very important to our case. Do you know Mr. Lydon?"

"He is the owner of a very fine restaurant on Melrose. I think he's had enough of Dr. Hecht."

"So, he probably has seen him abuse other drivers."

"And employees who work inside the house too. He told Mr. O'Malley he could hear the yelling from outside on the sidewalk."

Rosemaria glanced over at Karen and then back at the Carreras. "I can see why Dr. Hecht's lawyer asked for a plea deal. Dr. Hecht has no chance whatsoever of getting off if he goes to trial. The one thing that worries me is that someone in this office may make a plea deal and get him off with a slap on the wrist."

Mr. Carrera was alarmed. "There must be a way to stop him! Dr. Hecht is a violent man. He should be in jail, not working in a hospital!"

"I need to think about this. We'll finish the interview later."

Karen opened the door to usher the couple out, and Rosemaria and the Carreras shook hands. They had barely left the room before Rosemaria picked up her cell phone and dialed. "Celia, will you call me back as soon as possible? I need your advice again. Thanks." She tapped in another number. "Hello, yes, is Mr. O'Malley there? This is Rosemaria Baker. I'd like to speak to him, if possible— Oh, I'm sorry. No, that's okay." She clicked off the phone and glanced up at Karen. "O'Malley is not coming back anytime soon. They found an intestinal blockage when they opened him up for his appendectomy, and he had major surgery two days ago. Darn!"

"What are you going to do?"

"I don't have a clue. Do you have any ideas?"

"I'll bet anything that Atkins is talking to Sarno right now and offering a deal."

"Then, whatever I come up with, it'll be too late anyway."

"Pretty much."

"Do you think he'd take a case away from me without getting the okay from Lattimer?"

"He might."

"But he'd want his approval. When will Lattimer be back from Sacramento?"

"Tomorrow."

"They could have talked on the phone already."

"Poor Mr. Carrera. He so badly wanted his day in court." She jumped as her cell phone rang. "Oh, Celia, I'm sorry I called. I don't think there's any way out this time." Karen gave a wave as she left the room.

Celia, a beautiful African American woman in her late twenties, was in her Mercedes driving on the 101, talking into the speakerphone on her dash. "One of these days we'll have to get together and have an enjoyable conversation."

"We will, someday, after I know what I'm doing." Once again, she explained her predicament to Celia.

"Okay, first of all, there's no easy way around this. My suggestion is to call Lattimer on his cell phone in Sacramento, and hopefully, you'll get through to him before Atkins does."

"You think that's kosher? In all my years as a cop, I never went directly to a superior to complain about another cop. It just wasn't done. You'd lose all respect from both sides."

"I get that, but this is political, and whether or not you like it, this is where you are now. Yes, Lattimer is cozy with the attorney general of California, but they look out for number one first and foremost, and that's what you count on."

"Like how?"

"Briefly explain the case because he won't give you a lot of time. Emphasize how dangerous and brutal Hecht is. Make it clear how he could have killed Mr. Carrera and could very well end up killing someone if he pleads out. Use hyperbole, give Lattimer something to worry about if the press gets wind of the fact that his prosecutors let this guy walk when they had him dead to rights. And, finally, accentuate the Carreras' race and vulnerability and how this will play out in the media if it seems that his office puts wealth and status above the well-being of the average citizen. And say all that in under two minutes. Can you do that?"

"How do I get his cell number?"

"Your assistant should be able to get it, but hold on, I think I have it here." She took a few seconds to locate it. "Okay, I'll send it to you."

"You know I can never repay you for all your help."

"No worries. And who knows? I may need something from you one of these days."

"I'm calling now." They both hung up, and Rosemaria waited until she got Celia's text message and dialed. No answer. She left a short message and crossed her fingers.

Ten minutes later, Lattimer called her back, and she followed Celia's instructions to the letter. She couldn't read his intentions from the curt responses he gave, but at least he didn't brush her off. She thanked him for his time and clicked off her phone. She'd move forward with the case and see what happened.

Rosemaria called Osborne to tell him there was no way she could get away to meet Curtis at the station and to ask if he'd meet her near his hotel at the Starbucks or coffee shop of his choice later in the afternoon. She was looking forward to having dinner that evening with Josh, Vanessa, and Larry at Pura Vita, Josh's other favorite vegan restaurant. They'd been putting it off for weeks. Something always came up for one of them. Finally, they were going to have a relaxing evening eating delicious food and listening to Vanessa and Larry make plans for the new baby. If her own plan went according to Hoyle, in a few days, Maryanne and Tiffany would be safely out of town until the bad guys were behind bars. With those pleasant thoughts in her head, she pulled up the Carrera file on her computer to prepare for her meetings with the witnesses.

CHAPTER THIRTEEN

Malcomb Curtis had chosen to meet Rosemaria at the Starbucks on Beverly Boulevard in Beverly Hills. She found a parking space nearby and walked up the street toward the coffee shop. She recognized Curtis from the photo Waite had sent her. He was seated at a table outside, sipping his coffee. Osborne must have described her to him because he gave her a short wave when he saw her.

"I was given your description, and you match it perfectly," he said, confirming her thoughts.

She smiled and shook his hand as he stood up.

Curtis was single, in his late thirties, and around 5' 11". He had piercing blue eyes and hair cut like a Marine. Indeed, he had been in the Marines for two decades. Rosemaria knew all this because she had asked Waite to check him out thoroughly, down to what boxer shorts he liked to wear. Considering what she was about to ask him, she figured she'd better know everything about the man.

"What can I get you?" he asked.

"You don't have to do that."

"Sure I do."

"All right then. How about a soy decaf mocha, small?"

After he went inside, she wondered how best to approach him. He was a loner. Never been married. Maybe he liked it that way. He must be a considerate type of person to come all the way from Ohio to bury a niece he barely knew existed. That was a good sign.

He came back out, handed her the mocha, and sat down. "Sergeant Osborne told me the same people who murdered Maria might be after two friends of yours. I'm not sure why you want to talk to me."

Rosemaria set her coffee on the table. "First of all, I have to tell you, I'm so sorry that your niece died at such a young age and in such a terrible way."

"Thank you."

"How were you related to her?"

"Maria is—was—my sister Meredith's daughter. Her father was married to Meredith for about two minutes before he took off for parts unknown. I joined the Marines when I was nineteen to get out of Youngstown. When you're dirt poor like we were, you either end up in jail or dead. Maybe it's not so bad now. I don't get back there much."

"Where's Meredith now?"

"I have no idea. Meredith left Maria with my mother's sister when she was ten. My aunt died five years later, and Maria took off. If I had known Maria had come out here and was doing what she was doing, I would have flown out and dragged her back to Ohio whether she wanted to or not."

"You can't blame yourself for what happened."

"I can, and I do. She's my one and only niece. I retired last year after a back injury would have made me deskbound. I should have looked her up then. My fault." His composure slipped only slightly but enough for Rosemaria to see he was carrying plenty of guilt, with layers of protection covering it up.

"There is a reason I asked to meet with you."

"I figured there was."

"There are two other girls who used to be in Maria's occupation. Their lives are in mortal danger from the same people who murdered Maria. The people who want to kill them have powerful connections, and they seem able to track down the girls, wherever they are. We need to move them somewhere they'll be safe until we can find the people responsible for Maria's murder and lock them up."

Curtis mulled this over. "Why not put them in witness protection?"

"We want to keep the feds out of this as much as possible. We're afraid if the FBI takes over, and if these people have the connections in DC we think they have, the whole thing will be covered up. We can't trust them, and we don't trust them with the girls."

Curtis whistled softly through his lips. "They don't have family?"

"Maryanne has an aunt in Albuquerque. Tiffany has no one."

"That's their names?"

"Yeah. Right now, they're safe in an unoccupied condo that belongs to a cop, but I want them far away from here."

"I'm a single man, living alone."

"Well, to tell you the truth, I did check you out, so I know that. Everything I found out about you assures me there is no one else I know who would do a better job protecting the girls."

Curtis looked off into the distance, taking it all in. "I guess you need me to tell you right away."

"Before you leave, yes."

He waited another minute. "Okay, I'll do it."

Relief washed over Rosemaria. "Thank you."

He gazed at her intently. "Life sure does take a lot of strange twists and turns, doesn't it?"

He had the kind of gaze that made her feel like he could read her mind. "I'm a walking example of that," Rosemaria said.

They both sipped their coffee in silence for a few moments.

"I'm very grateful to you for doing this."

"They'll be safe with me."

"We can discuss all the particulars before you fly out on Friday. And I'll see you at Maria's funeral tomorrow."

"It's nice of you to come."

"She didn't get what she deserved when she was alive. The least I can do is give her my respects in death." She looked at her watch. "I need to go visit someone in the hospital. I'll see you tomorrow."

They both stood. His blue eyes met hers. His face softened for the first time. "Thank you for giving me a second chance."

Rosemaria's breath caught in her throat. She didn't know how to respond. She managed to say, "You're welcome," then turned to leave but changed her mind. "This isn't something that was made public, but Maria had my business card in her purse. It was crumpled up as if it had been there a long time. It was from four years ago, when I was working in Hollywood. I used to pass them out all the time. Someone gave it to her, but she chose not to call. I wish she had."

He looked at her kindly. "We're making up for it now."

* * * *

The corridor at Cedars-Sinai was empty except for Rosemaria, who was walking quickly, glancing at room numbers as she passed. Her phone was to her ear. "Honey, I know you're in the studio right now. Why don't you go straight to the restaurant, and I'll meet you there? See you." She hung up and dialed another number. "Karen, hi, did Lattimer call? — No? That could be a good sign. I'll be in tomorrow morning to meet with the witnesses. I have to go to a funeral first, but I'll be back afterward to go over O'Malley's notes. I haven't heard from Atkins. Have you? — That's either scary or good. Guess we'll find out tomorrow. — You too." She put her phone away and entered O'Malley's room.

He was hooked up to an IV bag hanging on a post, and even though he was at least five years younger than her and had the innocent face of a choirboy, he now looked like death warmed over. His voice was weak and scratchy. "Good to see you, Baker. You must be in some kind of trouble to show up here."

She pulled up a chair by his bed and replied, "I was going to come by anyway. Honest. I appreciated how kind you were to me when I first came.

You know that. If it had been just appendicitis, I would have come here and begged you to come back. I ended up with all your cases." She sat down and studied him. "Why do you sound like a ninety-year-old smoker?"

"They had a tube down my throat until this morning. That's why I sound like this. I'm okay."

"Well, I did have a bit of a problem, but I think it's been dealt with. Walter Atkins, who replaced Summers, assigned me to the Hecht case. He wants me to plead down as a favor to his uncle."

"What!" O'Malley looked like he was about to have another medical incident. "Summers said nothing about that to me!"

"Well, now Atkins thinks he has Lattimer in his pocket because the attorney general is his uncle."

"Lattimer is in no one's pocket. I take it you accomplished the impossible and got a continuance."

"I did."

"Good job. If you can do that, you can handle Atkins."

"I'm not so sure about that. He hates my guts."

"Use it against him."

"How? It's him, Lattimer, and the attorney general of the state of California on one side and me on the other."

"Lattimer and Folson will always do what is politically expedient. I wouldn't worry."

"Why is Hecht so important to them?"

"He's a big donor to Folson's campaign and every other Democrat in the state. They overlook his shortcomings for the sake of dollar signs." He closed his eyes for a moment, and his voice was becoming softer. "They made their play to use Atkins to get him off. It failed, am I right?"

"So far."

"Did you talk to Lattimer?"

"I did."

It was becoming an effort for him to speak. "Good girl." He paused, then added, "No offense."

"None taken."

"Lattimer will want no part of this. It's assault and battery and attempted murder. If Hecht is convicted, he's persona non grata. Atkins is irrelevant."

"What do I do if Atkins keeps trying to sabotage my cases?"

"I'll make a prediction. If he's as thoroughly loathed wherever he goes as I've heard he is, and everybody knows he's gunning for you, spies will come forth. You'll know what he's going to do before he does it."

O'Malley's voice was getting softer, and his eyes were almost closed again. "He can't do his job in secret. There are rules and procedures to follow. If he's stupid enough to meet with defense attorneys to make secret deals and is found out, he's gone. I don't think he'll be that stupid."

"Whew! You've given me hope. I'm going to let you rest now. I don't know how I was lucky enough to end up with two awesome mentors like you and Celia." She stood up and looked at her watch. "I better get going. I have to meet some people for dinner."

He whispered, "You'll do fine. People like Atkins are their own worst enemy. You'll see."

Rosemaria turned at the door to say goodbye, but O'Malley was already sound asleep.

On her way to the parking lot elevators at Cedars, Rosemaria thought about what O'Malley had said regarding Atkins and his hatred of her: use it against him. But how? That was the question. She hoped that he would become as obnoxious and difficult as he had been in Van Nuys, and then she wouldn't have to deal with him at all. But his uncle had his back, and this was his last chance. He had won a few of his cases in court, so she knew he wasn't a complete idiot. That is what was so scary.

As she walked to her car, she felt happy that she and Josh were finally getting together with Vanessa and Larry just to relax for a couple of hours and enjoy each other's company. They would eat the best Italian food in town at Pura Vita, and she would let go of her worries for one delicious evening.

* * * *

Detectives Waite and Harvey had no problem getting the name of Tiffany's would-be talent agent/sex procurer from the manager at Perfect Printz, but the address they had for him proved to be a post office box in Van Nuys. Waite used his laptop in the car to try and find records for a Tyrone Lawton, but as far as the state of California or any other state went, he didn't exist. They drove over the hill and talked to a woman who was the owner of Mailboxes R Us, a run-down mailing and print shop in a sleazy area near the police station on Van Nuys Boulevard. They asked about the man who rented Lawton's mailbox and showed her the police drawing. She said she had never seen Tyrone Lawton, but the man in the drawing looked just like Seymour Dobransky, who rented the box and was a very nice man, middle-aged, not bad-looking, small, and thin. Sometimes mail came for Tyrone in care of Seymour, who didn't talk much, just bought his stamps, sent out a few packages, and that was about it. At their insistence, she looked up his credit card information and, in the car, Waite quickly tracked down Dobransky on his laptop.

"He has an apartment in Tarzana, north of Ventura. No arrests, not even a traffic ticket. How about we pay Mr. Lawton a visit?" Waite asked.

"This poor guy is a wannabe of the most pathetic kind. I almost feel sorry for him," Harvey said.

"I can't figure out how that loser had any connection to the kind of powerful people he was finding hookers for. I'm wondering if he had provided other girls for this guy before."

"Waite smiled. "I'm sure we can convince him to tell us."

"You want to talk to him in his apartment or bring him in?"

"I think we should bring him in. He sounds like the type of guy who will open up more easily in an official setting if we make it clear he could be implicated in a murder."

They drove to the address they had for Dobransky. It was an old but well-kept apartment building on a street of similar apartment buildings. There was no security gate, and they were able to walk right up to the apartment door. Waite knocked and they waited. There was no answer. Waite peered in the front window and saw no one. Inside, the apartment appeared to be in perfect order. Harvey went around to the side window and saw nothing suspicious. "Let's park up the street and wait for him. I don't want to call and tip him off that we want to talk to him."

Two hours later, they were still waiting. Waite wasn't used to stakeouts and was getting antsy. "This is agony. I don't know how you guys do this."

"I don't know how you can sit at a computer all day."

"I'm going to need to take a leak soon."

"That's what bushes are for."

"I wonder why Dobransky didn't just hire prostitutes from an agency?"

"He saw an easy opportunity to hire two beautiful young girls and took it."

"It's getting dark. Where the heck is he?"

"I have a bad feeling about this."

"Let's wait another hour and call Osborne. Maybe he can get us a warrant to go in."

"I'll make that half an hour just for you."

* * * *

Rosemaria drove slowly up a side street that was near Pura Vita, but she was getting farther away from the restaurant on Santa Monica Boulevard. Parking was always tough in this area. The parking signs were so confusing. It was hard to tell if and when nonresidents were allowed to park on the streets at all. Finally, several blocks up, she spotted an empty space, read and reread the parking sign several times, and concluded it was okay to park there. She grabbed her purse, got out of the car, and walked quickly down the sidewalk. She saw a couple of cars driving slowly up the street and muttered to herself, "Good luck finding a space."

The attack happened so fast she didn't have time to react. A dark sedan screeched to a halt in the street beside her, and a tall Black man in a leather jacket jumped out from the passenger side and wrenched her arms behind her back. He dragged her toward the car, where another man was waiting in the driver's seat.

The man had an iron grip on her arms, but Rosemaria's cop training kicked in, and she drove her heel into the man's instep. He howled in pain. She managed to free her arms and took a massive roundhouse swing with her heavy purse. It slammed into the side of the man's head, making him stumble. She was about to finish him off with a kick to the kidneys when the driver jumped out of the car, launched himself at her, and knocked her to the ground. Leather Jacket and Driver each grabbed one arm and tried to pick her up, but she managed to land a solid kick to Leather Jacket's knee, and he went down howling. Driver landed a punch to the side of her face, and she retaliated with a kick to his groin. He grabbed his privates and yelled, "I told you we should've just shot her!" Leather Jacket was still trying to get back on his feet. Driver fumbled in his jacket pocket for his gun, but before he could grab it, a loud voice from behind their car echoed up and down the street. "Police! Down on the ground!" A Glock 22 was aimed in their direction, and Larry looked like he meant business.

Rosemaria had no mercy. "Shoot them both! They tried to kidnap me!"

Her piercing scream scared the crap out of the two men, and they froze. Leather Jacket had told Driver this would be easy. Grab the prosecutor off the street, take her somewhere, torture her, and when we're done, we'll shoot her. Driver had been willing to help because the bitch had wrecked his friend's liquor store plan to blame the holdup on somebody else and get away free and clear. Instead, the cops were hot on his partner's tail. As soon as they offed the bitch, they would grab the money and head to Mexico. They had followed her from place to place all day until finally they decided this dark street was the perfect place to grab her.

Yeah, a brilliant plan, but Driver was not ready to die to help his friend get revenge on this crazy broad. Larry approached, aiming his Glock at the two men while Rosemaria yanked Driver's gun out of his coat pocket.

"Down on the ground before I blow your brains all over the sidewalk!" Larry yelled. Driver threw himself flat, spread eagled. He'd played this gig more than once and knew what to do.

Larry came around to the side of the car and stared at Leather Jacket, who was barely able to stand. "On the ground, pal!"

Leather Jacket looked at Driver, at Larry's Glock, and at Rosemaria pointing Driver's gun at him. He grimaced, his knee in agonizing pain, then slowly bent down and laid flat on the ground.

Larry took two flex cuffs out of his pocket and tossed one to Rosemaria. "Wow, you really wanted me to shoot both of them?"

"Nah, I just wanted to give these two saps something to think about." She pulled the cuff tight on Leather Jacket's wrists, and he winced from the pressure. She picked up her purse off the ground.

They heard the sirens and saw the flashing lights of half a dozen cop cars coming down the street. Leather Jacket looked up at her. "Who the hell are you, bitch? You're no prosecutor."

Rosemaria glared at him.

"I dare you to tell me that in court, dimwit."

* * * *

The deputies at the scene had wasted no time getting Leather Jacket and Driver into squad cars and on their way to the West Hollywood jail. The real name of Leather Jacket was Grover Vick, a suspect in the Korean liquor store robbery who had been identified by the liquor store owner. Driver's name was Castro Hernandez. Both had a string of misdemeanor and felony convictions and had started their criminal careers while minors. Now, both faced spending the rest of their lives in prison for a measly $10,000.

The Airport office had jurisdiction over the assault and attempted kidnapping, as well as the robbery. Rosemaria regretted the fact that because she was the victim, it would be impossible for her to be assigned the cases.

Rosemaria and Larry walked down to Pura Vita, where there were still a couple of squad cars parked outside. Josh and Vanessa, her long blond hair in disarray and her face wide-eyed with apprehension, were waiting by the entrance. Vanessa walked toward Larry as fast as her swollen belly would allow as soon as she saw him. "Are you all right?! What happened! Who were they?!" Larry and Vanessa had spotted Rosemaria fighting with the two men when they drove up the same street to look for parking. He had jumped out of the car, telling Vanessa to call 911, park in front of the restaurant, place his cop card on the dash, and wait for him.

Larry put his arms around Vanessa to try and calm her down. "I'm fine. No problem. The perpetrators practically volunteered to get arrested."

Vanessa looked at him skeptically. "Yeah, right. I'm sure."

"I'm sorry you were upset. You need to take it easy. Do you want to forget dinner and go home and rest?"

"No way! I have every intention of enjoying dinner with our friends." She looked over at Josh and Rosemaria. "Was it really as easy as he said?"

Rosemaria waved her hand in the air. "Absolutely."

"Then why do you have blood on your cheek?"

"Oh, that. I accidentally tripped and fell against the door getting one of them into the squad car."

"That is the lamest excuse I ever heard, but I'll accept it because I don't want my dear husband to insist that this is all too much for me and make me go home."

She headed into the restaurant, and Larry followed her. Rosemaria turned to thank the two deputies, who were ready to drive away. "I appreciate you keeping our family safe here while we took care of that business up the street."

"No problem. Happy to help," they said in turn, tipping the brims of their hats. Then, they took off.

Josh took Rosemaria's arms and turned her to face him. "Family?"

"Yeah, that's what you are, aren't you?"

"I like the sound of that."

"Keep liking it, and maybe we'll get somewhere."

"I can do that, but how am I going to keep you out of trouble? You're not supposed to be involved in shoot-'em-ups anymore. And I'm not fooled by your explanation to Vanessa of how you got that blood on your face."

"The situation may have been a little dicier than I described, but this was an aberration, I promise. From now on, our lives will be as dull as dirt."

"I'll hold you to that."

Larry appeared in the open doorway of the restaurant. "My wife is starving. Get in here so we can order." He popped back inside.

"I'll explain it all later. I promise."

He held her tight. "If anything happened to you, my life would be over."

She pointed at herself and then him. "Me same you. Double."

She took his hand and led him inside.

* * * *

Vanessa was in heaven. "This lasagna is sooo good. I can't believe everything here is vegan. Who knew?"

Larry took a sip of his wine. "It's all Josh's fault. He'll have us all become vegan and turn us into animal activists. We'll have to arrest ourselves at protests."

Josh was digging into his pesto and spoke with his mouth half full. "I'll look forward to it."

Rosemaria was busy with her carbonara, having given up temporarily on her diet, and was letting other people keep the conversation going. She hadn't eaten all day and didn't realize how hungry she was.

Josh took time off from chewing to take a swig of his grape juice. "What's going to happen to those mutts now anyway?"

Vanessa was still in the throes of ecstasy over her lasagna. "No unpleasant talk tonight. I have to decide what I want for dessert."

"The chocolate fudge cake is fabulous," Rosemaria managed to say between bites. "You'll love it. I can't have any, but you should. As long as—" She stopped.

Vanessa's eyes narrowed. "You mean, as long as I'm big as a house, I might as well indulge?"

"Well, I wasn't—"

"Yes, you were, and you're right! I'm going to eat whatever I want, and after I have the baby, I'll starve myself."

Larry protested, saying, "Let's not get ahead of ourselves. You're not going to starve yourself on my account."

"If only I had the willpower to do that," Rosemaria mumbled as she took another bite of her carbonara.

Larry's cell phone rang. He looked at it and immediately clicked the call button. "It's Osborne."

Rosemaria put down her fork and felt a lump in her stomach. "Now?"

Larry spoke into his phone. "Coleman here. — Yeah, I knew they were going over there. What happened? — Oh shit.— How?— Sounds like they're cleaning house.— Listen, I'm going to drop Vanessa off at our house, and then I'm going over to the condo to check on Maryanne and Tiffany. I want a double guard on them until we can find a safer place for them to stay. — Yeah, I'll see you tomorrow." He clicked off the phone. To Vanessa he said. "I'm sorry, honey, we can get dessert to go."

"Forget dessert. You take care of those girls."

"What happened?" Rosemaria asked.

"Harvey and Waite tracked down the talent scout. Turns out his name is Seymour Dobransky. They found him in his bathroom dead. Strangled."

Vanessa gasped. Josh inadvertently grabbed Rosemaria's arm.

"I have to tell you all something," Rosemaria said. "Malcomb Curtis has agreed to take both girls home to Ohio with him."

They all looked at her, surprised. "How did you manage that?" Josh asked.

"I met him today at Starbucks. He feels guilty about Maria and promises he will keep the girls safe, and I believe him. He's a former Marine, he has guns, and he knows how to use them. Besides which, only we at this table and Osborne, Waite, and Curtis will know where they are. I had Waite check him out thoroughly. I wouldn't want to be the guy who goes up against him."

Larry nodded slowly and thoughtfully. "I like it. When do they leave?"

"Tomorrow is Maria's funeral, and he's making arrangements with Osborne for the three of them to fly out Friday."

Larry waved at the waiter for the check. He looked at Vanessa. "Are you all right with me leaving you at home alone for a while?"

"I knew what I was getting into when I married a cop. Do what you have to do."

"Do you want me to go with you to the condo?" Rosemaria asked.

"No. You'll see them before they leave. I won't tell them about Dobransky. I'll let Curtis tell them after they're safely back in Ohio."

"Sounds good."

The waiter boxed up what was left of their dinners, and they parted company, all of them feeling more than a little unnerved by how their pleasant evening had turned into a nightmare.

* * * *

The next day, the mood was glum in Osborne's cubicle. Larry was leaning back in his chair staring at the ceiling, and Waite was typing on his laptop, which rested on Osborne's desk, in his continued futile efforts to track down the ultimate owners of the offshore corporation that had paid for the room at the Harland.

"We still have a lot of people to interview and alibis to track down," Osborne said. "We have a few extra detectives, close friends of the lieutenant, from other units working on it—with strict instructions not to be too threatening, only cajoling. It's not easy to extract the truth from any of them. The politicians and their aides are being less than forthcoming."

Larry sat up and chuckled. "Away from their wives and families, a lot of drinking and eating in the near vicinity of hotel rooms. It's a chance for politicians to have some fun on the side, and no one need be the wiser."

"You'd think that with a murder rap hanging in the balance, they'd be willing to be honest," Osborne said.

Waite looked up from his typing. "They're more afraid of their wives than they are of us."

Larry injected a note of optimism. "Forensics got a nice fresh fingerprint off the back door at that broken-down car repair shop where Tiffany was hiding. We got a positive hit on a real piece of work."

Waite read from his laptop. "Ralph Coulter. Spent two years in the army, dishonorable discharge for attacking another soldier, was convicted of petty larceny in Camden, New Jersey, and spent five months in jail, arrested and convicted for beating up a bartender in Camden, spent three months in jail, worked as a security guard at a chemical plant, then at their corporate headquarters. Disappeared, no further job history. Obviously, somebody found good use for him. He's 6' 3" and weighs 230 pounds. That's a guy who stands out in a crowd."

Osborne looked up from his note-taking. "Now all we have to do is find him."

"He'll show up again. He has too much fun trying to kill people," Larry said.

Waite stopped typing. "You think there'll be another attempt on the girls' lives?"

"If they can find them."

CHAPTER FOURTEEN

Rosemaria walked from her car to the courthouse holding her morning Starbucks coffee. Inside were hundreds of hardworking, dedicated professionals doing their best to dispense justice to the denizens of their part of LA County. It had to be Rosemaria's luck to end up in a war with the only bad apple in the barrel.

Atkins hated her more than some vicious murderers she'd locked up. His hatred was like nothing she'd ever experienced. He sent ripples of loathing in her direction anytime she was within a few feet of him. And why? Because he had been prevented from delivering to his uncle the most important favor he had ever been asked to do—get Hecht a sweet deal and make him even more amenable to donating money to his uncle's campaign. Her phone call to Lattimer, per Celia's instructions, had put a nail in that coffin. Lattimer had called Rosemaria that morning and told her to proceed with the trial. That was it, full speed ahead. Rosemaria had turned Atkins into an abject failure, or at least that's what she assumed he thought. But with his hubris, he probably concluded it wasn't failure, but rather the fault of one ex-cop who had no business being in this building at all.

Josh had suggested she take a little time this morning to meditate and feel thankful for her blessings. (He shared a lot of things he learned at AA with her, and his going to AA and being sober was the number one thing she was most grateful for.) He thought it might help prepare her for the turmoil she faced inside her office. So, she had done just that while sipping her decaf soy mocha. (Multitasking was her forte.) Josh was right. After five minutes of meditating, she was ready for anything Atkins threw her way. She opened the door and went inside.

Karen was at her desk early, as usual. (One more thing to be grateful for was her smart, efficient secretary.) "Good morning, boss. No meetings this morning."

"Good. I'm going to go over the Hecht case for about the millionth time. Conviction seems like a no-brainer, but I don't want Hecht to walk on my account. Do you know when the arraignment of my attempted kidnappers is?"

"The clerk said 9:30, but you know that's just approximate."

"Okay. I'll go down to the courtroom in about an hour and then to Maria Ramirez's funeral. I'll be back in time to meet with the witnesses. Fredrik Palmer is up first, right?"

"Fredrik Palmer at two, then Henry Lydon at three thirty, Mary Jacobs at four, and Sylvio Mangini at five."

Rosemaria went into her office and put her briefcase on her desk. She turned on her desktop computer and clicked on the Hecht case. She had been working on her opening statement and lining up all the facts so she could describe them in order to the jury right up front. Since O'Malley had been in the middle of his statement when he became ill from appendicitis, she had the opportunity to start from scratch. Voir dire had already taken place, so she would be plunging right in without knowing much about the jury except for their histories, which were in the computer.

It was a straightforward case. Hecht had committed the act. In cases like this, he would admit to the fight, but the defense would claim, as they always do in these kinds of cases, that it was the fault of the victim. Then, the victim bashing would begin. It was her job to make sure every single minute of the attack and exactly how it started were accounted for. There could be no wiggle room. On her side, she had several witnesses who knew the truth, and on the defense side, Hecht had his lies. Convincing lies told by people of professional distinction who, in this case, would be portrayed as a savior of lives, had been known to sway a jury.

* * * *

Reid Smith, who had been assigned to prosecute the case of Grover Vick and Castro Hernandez, was seated in the back of the courtroom, going over his notes and waiting for his turn. Cases had been called in a steady stream since he got here at nine o'clock. Amanda Logan, their defense attorney, was seated up front. Smith had talked to Logan briefly and was told that Vick and Hernandez would plead not guilty. How they planned to get away with that was baffling. They had rejected a plea deal. He would be more than happy to give them a full-blown trial and watch them get convicted of attempted kidnapping and assault. With their records, they'd never get out of prison.

He looked at his watch. Almost 9:30. Hopefully, he would be up soon. He smiled when he saw Rosemaria come through the door and sit next to him.

"I was afraid you were going to miss all the excitement."

"Not a chance."

"They're both pleading not guilty. What do you think the defense will be?"

"Insanity, drugs, or their father beat them as children. How'd you get the case?"

"I only had to beg a little."

"Thank you for that."

"I guess Atkins doesn't know we're friends. We'll keep that our shameful little secret for now."

"Safer for you. Which one will you try first, the robbery or the kidnapping?"

"This one. Then, we'll go after Vick for the robbery."

"Who'd you draw?"

"Judge Lawford."

"I heard he's fair, leaning toward the prosecution."

"Nice."

Judge Lawford was a short, pudgy man in his fifties, with beady eyes that looked as if he missed nothing. The bailiff barked out the names of the defendants, and Smith walked to the front of the bench to stand beside Logan. Vick and Hernandez, both manacled, were brought through the side door to wait behind the glass near the front. The judge asked for the pleas.

"Not guilty," Vick said.

"Not guilty," Hernandez repeated.

"I'll schedule the voir dire to begin four weeks from now. Does that suit the defendants and the prosecution?"

"Fine with me," Smith said.

Logan agreed. "That is acceptable to us, Judge."

Rosemaria stared at Vick. He had been glancing around the courtroom since being brought in. When he spotted her, his face contorted into an ugly scowl. If looks could kill, she'd have a knife in her throat. Fortunately, she had become immune to the murderous stares of perpetrators. Hundreds of them had been aimed in her direction. On a scale from 1 to 10, his stare registered at about 1.5.

The judge continued. "Are you asking for bail, Counselor?"

"We are asking for release on recognizance or bail at $50,000 max."

"We request remand, Your Honor," Smith said. "These defendants brutally attacked an officer of the court and attempted to kidnap her. Her life would be in imminent danger if the defendants were released."

The judge wasted no time agreeing. "The defendants are remanded until trial. Next case."

Vick aimed daggers at Rosemaria one last time, complete with flaring nostrils. She returned his implied threat with a dismissive shrug that caused his anger to explode. He wrenched his arm away from the sheriff's deputy and made a move in her direction, at which point two more deputies grasped Vick firmly and held him back. They shoved Vick out the door, causing him to bump into Hernandez, who whirled around and pushed Vick hard into the wall. Rosemaria thought there was going to be a full-fledged scuffle between the two defendants, but sadly the deputies quickly regained control.

Smith came back to where she was standing, ready to leave. "I didn't tell you this, but Atkins suggested I agree to bail, not that there was a chance in hell I would do that."

"Wow, he actually wants me dead."

"It would seem so."

"Thanks for having my back."

"Always."

She waved at him as she left the courtroom and walked down the hall to the elevators. She leaned against the wall by the elevator buttons, feeling a little shaky. As a cop, she had witnessed petty feuds, differences of opinion, and political backstabbing by the higher-ups, but never had any of her coworkers tried to sabotage her. It just wasn't done. You never knew when you might need each other in life-or-death situations. This kind of vendetta hadn't happened in the New York prosecutor's office either. She went down the elevator to the first floor and walked outside. She really liked the people she worked with, and there was so much opportunity to do good. Why did Atkins have to spoil it all?

* * * *

Curtis had bought a plot for Maria in Forest Lawn cemetery, overlooking Glendale and the mountains beyond. He had given her nothing in life, so he wanted to, at the very least, give her a beautiful resting place. His niece had never had a chance. She had been a girl just struggling to survive and a product of her misbegotten childhood. He had lived his life only concerned with his own survival and finding escape from a dead-end environment. His entire focus had been his military career, staying alive in combat zones, and making sure his fellow Marines were safe. He looked down at Maria's coffin. Before now, this girl, his niece, and what she had been going through had never entered his mind. He considered the dangerous predicament Maryanne and Tiffany were in, safely watched over by guards hired by

Coleman, whom he found to be generous to a fault. Tomorrow morning, he would pick them up, they would be driven to the airport under armed guard, and by this time tomorrow, they would be in Dayton, Ohio. He had a home there. With any luck, the killers would not find them. But he would be prepared. He would make up for what he hadn't done for Maria. No one would touch them.

Rosemaria had told him that a few cops might show up at the burial, and he hoped they would. A tall man with blond hair stood several yards away, intently looking out over the valley, and he figured that must be one of them. He seemed to be lost in thought and decided to wait before approaching him.

Josh, unaware that Curtis was studying him, was remembering the last time he had been in this same cemetery. Stan Levy, a producer who had hired Josh to teach his wife to sing, was buried not too far from where he was standing. He remembered falling under the spell of Stan's breathtakingly beautiful wife, an image of perfection that didn't exist in real life. He thought what he had felt for her was love. But it wasn't. It was a deep longing to fill a void in his life that neither his music nor alcohol could fill. It had been the worst mistake of his life. But if he hadn't been suspected of murdering Stan, he never would have met Rosemaria. Every miserable, sordid minute of the investigation and trial was worth it, because now his life was on a new track. Whatever happened, good or bad, nothing could break the bond between him and Rosemaria, and that's all that mattered.

"You sure have a satisfied grin on your face." Curtis had walked up and was standing next to him.

"Oh, I'm sorry. I was thinking of something else."

"That's okay."

Josh held out his hand. "Josh Sibley. I'm Rosemaria's friend."

Curtis took his hand. "I'm Malcomb Curtis. Pleased to meet you."

"Maria didn't deserve what happened to her."

"I like to think she's in a better place now."

"I believe that from the bottom of my heart," Josh said sincerely.

Josh was surprised to see a small crack in the stoic expression on Curtis's face. Then, the mask was back in place, and only his steel-blue eyes gave any hint of the pain inside.

"I believe the subject of your thoughts is coming up the hill toward us," Curtis said. They both turned to see Rosemaria approaching. The minister he had hired was walking toward the grave site from the other direction, and Curtis left Josh to greet him.

As soon as Rosemaria reached Josh, he folded her into his arms. "I know," she said, noticing the look on his face. "This place is a reminder of some very bad things."

"Yeah, but we don't have to think about them anymore."

"We do not. Let me go over and give my best to Curtis."

He watched her give Curtis a hug and her condolences. He wondered if anyone else would show up to honor Maria's life. When he saw Osborne and Waite pull up in an unmarked police car, he breathed a sigh of relief. For whatever reason, it was important to him for Maria to have more people at her memorial service than just Curtis, Rosemaria, and him. He saw a familiar Lexus pull to a stop in the parking area. The car doors opened, and Larry helped Vanessa out of their car. He held her arm as they slowly made their way up the hill. Josh relaxed. Maria had not been forgotten.

The small group gathered solemnly around Maria's casket. It was clear that Curtis had told the minister about the realities of her life. In his eulogy, the minister, wearing a black suit and crisp white shirt and looking like everyone's idea of a kindly grandfather, talked about her beauty, her suffering, and the life she had never been given a chance to live. He talked of redemption, love, and release from all earthly concerns. Rosemaria could see that Curtis was having a hard time controlling his emotions. Watching him, she was suddenly overwhelmed with regret that she hadn't been there to help this girl and all the others like her who were lost, alone, and preyed upon.

The minister finished the eulogy with the Lord's Prayer, closed his Bible, and opened his mouth to say the benediction. Then, unexpectedly, Curtis cleared his throat and hesitantly began to sing the first words of "Amazing Grace," his voice wavering and off key. Vanessa, seeing him struggling, quickly joined him in her soft soprano voice. Rosemaria, who couldn't carry a tune, tried to follow along anyway. Larry, Waite, and Osborne sang hesitantly, stumbling over the unfamiliar lyrics until Josh's mellow baritone took the lead. Everyone relaxed, and their voices floated imperfectly but sincerely over the hillsides.

Amazing grace! How sweet the sound
That saved a wretch like me.
I once was lost, but now am found,
Was blind, but now I see.
Through many dangers, toils, and snares,
I have already come.
'Tis grace hath brought me safe thus far,
And grace will lead me home.

As the last note faded into silence, one by one they picked up a rose from a folding chair near the minister and placed it on the casket. They stood in silence for a few minutes. The only sounds were birds chirping and the muted roar of cars on the freeway a few miles away.

Looking at Curtis, with his lined face set in granite, Rosemaria thought about how hard he was being on himself. But the tragedy of Maria's cruel life and death wasn't just his to bear. If Rosemaria hadn't left Hollywood, she might have reached out to Maria as she had done with other girls. If pedophiles didn't exist, if her mother had cared for her, if pimps didn't infest the streets, if more help was available, Maria might still be alive. *We're all to blame*, Rosemaria thought, *but guilt accomplishes nothing*. There are two girls still in need of saving and two young lives to be lived.

Josh was speaking in hushed tones to Curtis. She joined them and said that she would see Josh at home after work once she had stopped by the condo to check on the girls. She thanked Curtis for sheltering them, shared hugs all around with the others, and headed for her car. Maria was now safely home, but Rosemaria would do whatever it took to make sure Maryanne and Tiffany didn't join her there anytime soon.

CHAPTER FIFTEEN

Karen led Fredrik Palmer into Rosemaria's office, introduced him, and went back to her desk. Rosemaria knew Palmer was fifty-two years old and a widower with no children. He was nice-looking, dressed casually, and exuded confidence. As heir to a department store fortune, he not only was set for life but also had access to a terrific wardrobe. A man in his position didn't have to pander to anyone.

Palmer looked her straight in the eye and said, "I want to help you nail this bastard."

Rosemaria indicated for him to have a seat.

"I already told all this to the other prosecutor."

"I know, but I like to hear firsthand what you have to say."

"Fine. I've watched him abuse and eviscerate more than one poor desperate soul ever since he moved in next door two years ago."

"I'd like to hear about the times you've watched him mistreat other people who worked for him, and if you remember names, that would be helpful." If the defense opened the door and claimed that Hecht was a saint, she would be allowed to introduce prior bad acts, and she wanted to include as many as she could.

"I never knew the names of all the people he abused, but I do know the name of his last driver."

"And what was the name?"

"His name was Perry. That's what I heard Dr. Hecht call him as he screamed at him every time he did something Dr. Hecht didn't approve of."

Rosemaria was typing into her computer. "Thank you. We can find out his last name. What exactly happened with Perry?"

Palmer shook his head in disgust. "Once Dr. Hecht happened to see a small scratch on the bumper of his car and went ballistic. He accused Perry of driving his car without his permission, threatened to turn him in to the police, and repeatedly shoved him into the side of the car."

Rosemaria was typing furiously. "What did Perry do?"

"He did nothing. What could he do? He was an elderly Black man who looked to be in his late sixties. He was defenseless. I never saw him again. Then, Mr. Carrera became Dr. Hecht's driver, and the abuse started all over again—shoving, yelling, name-calling, and then finally, almost killing him."

"Did you ever call the police and report the abuse?"

"Of course. I'm sure you have that in your records. But Dr. Hecht always talked his way out of it. He's a doctor and the chief of staff at Cedars-Sinai. Who was going to take our word against his? And his victims would never say anything to the police. I assure you, we did try to put a stop to it."

"Did anyone ever confront Dr. Hecht directly?"

"Yes. Mr. Mangini did. He's a very large young man. He lives on the other side of Dr. Hecht, three houses down. Once, when Dr. Hecht was berating a middle-aged Hispanic fellow who was bringing Dr. Hecht's garbage containers to the curb, Mangini came out and told him if he didn't stop yelling at the man, he was going to kick the crap out of him. And he looked like he meant it. It stopped Dr. Hecht for a while, but of course, with men like that, nothing ever stops them for long."

"You didn't see the actual beginning of the attack, did you, Mr. Palmer?"

"No, but Mr. Lydon did. He happened to be going to work just as Dr. Hecht started his rampage."

"Okay, thank you. I'll be talking to him later. Did Dr. Hecht ever have people over, any parties, get-togethers of any kind?"

"Oh yeah. Huge parties. Famous people, politicians, all arriving in their limos dressed to kill. Sometimes photographers would show up outside. Even his mousy little wife would get dressed up and look halfway decent."

"Did Mrs. Hecht ever try to stop him from abusing the help?"

"Are you kidding? Have you ever seen her?"

Rosemaria shook her head.

"She's skinny, nervous, frail, and never says a word. She looks like an empty shell where a person used to live. I think she fled years ago and only the outside is still there, going through the motions of being his wife. I have no doubt he prefers it that way."

"Thank you for sharing all of this with me, Mr. Palmer."

"Whatever I can do to help."

"It's particularly important that when we're in court, you only answer the questions that I ask. Don't add or embellish or let your anger show. Just be matter of fact in your responses. That goes double for when the defense lawyer cross-examines you. She's a very experienced lawyer. She will try to make it seem like you are lying because you hate Dr. Hecht. She will do everything in her power to try and evoke rage and disgust from you. You absolutely cannot allow her to manipulate you."

"Manipulate me?" Palmer was insulted. "I invite her to try."

Rosemaria was confident Palmer would make an excellent witness. One down, three more to go.

Henry Lydon was tall, thin, and in his late twenties. He was as laidback as Palmer was straightforward and slouched in his chair as he studied Rosemaria. "You know we've been to the cops more than once about this creep?"

"I do know that, Mr. Lydon, but this time I intend to get justice for his victims. I need your full cooperation to do that."

"The man is rich and has influence. Are you sure there won't be any deals made before this even gets to trial?"

"That's one thing I can assure you of, Mr. Lydon. There will be no deal made on behalf of Dr. Hecht."

"Then why did somebody call me and try to get me to not testify about what I saw?"

"What?!" Rosemaria almost bolted out of her chair.

"They said something about my bank accounts and hinted that my identity would be stolen if I didn't say that Carrera started the fight."

Rosemaria had to take a few deep breaths. "It had to be a friend of Dr. Hecht's or a political or business associate."

"I had one of my tech guys try to trace the call, but no luck."

"This is beyond depraved. It's downright stupid. Did it frighten you? I know that kind of thing, stolen identities, has happened to other people. It can destroy lives."

"I have internet protection up the ying-yang and the best computer people money can buy. I guarantee you that no one will steal my identity or my money."

"I'm relieved to hear you say that. Then let's move forward and put this guy behind bars."

"In that case, I'm all in. I want to get that SOB. I saw exactly what happened from start to finish."

Rosemaria would have felt satisfaction at having two impeccable witnesses if not for Atkins's clumsy attempt to influence Lydon. Well, she assumed it was him. It was clear Atkins was no longer functioning with a full deck. He was off the rails, and his wheels had fallen off. She gave Lydon the same speech she had given Palmer, but she doubted that even Sarno, with all her tricks, could get Lydon to express even a hint of anger toward Hecht. She could jab away at him all she wanted, but all it would do is aggravate herself. Rosemaria had seen that happen already and looked forward to a repeat performance.

Mary Jacobs was third on her list. She lived two houses down from Hecht and had experienced his abuse firsthand. She had been walking her dog when the dog peed off the curb outside Hecht's house. She sniffed as she recalled the incident. "You'd think the poor little thing had defecated like a horse right outside Dr. Hecht's door, the way he laid into me." She had picked up her dog and hurried home so she wouldn't have to hear the foul language spewing out of Hecht's mouth. She'd also seen his attack on Ricardo Carrera and was not afraid to come forward. She was small, around

5' 1", seventy-five years old, and as nice as could be. But Rosemaria sensed a core of steel inside this lady. After all, she had successfully run a design firm for forty years and had made a small fortune doing it. Let Sarno try to intimidate this sweet old lady.

They said their goodbyes, and Karen stuck her head in the doorway to say that Sylvio Mangini was going to be late. He was coming from Redondo Beach, and there was an accident on the 405.

"Darn, I wanted to leave a little early this afternoon so I could spend time with Maryanne and Tiffany before going home."

"He said he'll be here in half—" She abruptly stopped as something caught her eye out in the hallway. Then, she stepped out of the doorway and made room for Henry Constanza, the mayor of Santa Monica. Rosemaria's eyes widened in shock and disbelief as he entered her office and stopped near the door.

"Mr. Mayor, this is a surprise." She came around the desk and held out her hand.

He shook it warmly and smiled. "I don't want to disturb your busy schedule, but I had a meeting down here today and decided to come by myself and congratulate you on your work on behalf of the county and the citizens of Santa Monica. Not only do you investigate and find the real perpetrators, but you also survive an attack on your life and arrest them as well. I do commend you for your courage, but I hope you won't have to go to those extraordinary lengths again to put criminals in jail."

Rosemaria laughed. "I sure hope not, as well."

"I understand you used to be a police detective."

"Yes, I was, for several years."

"I'm sure that came in handy when you dealt with your would-be kidnappers."

"It did. But I had help from my former partner. He's the real hero in this."

"I appreciate your modesty, Ms. Baker. I'll leave you to your work, and I hope to see you again under less stressful circumstances."

Rosemaria was all but genuflecting. "Thank you, Mr. Mayor. I'm honored you came to my office."

He nodded and was gone. Karen came in, and they stared at each other. Together, they mouthed, "Oh, my God!"

Rosemaria pulled herself together and addressed Karen as if nothing had happened. "Call Mr. Mangini and find out where the heck he is." She looked to the ceiling in awe. "I can't believe the mayor of Santa Monica came to see me!" She looked sternly at Karen. "Get a grip on yourself, girl. All in a day's work." Rosemaria had a thought and said, "Maybe now Atkins will back off a little." They looked at each other for a moment and said in unison, "Naw," laughing uproariously.

They waited a half hour before Mangini finally showed up. He was nineteen years old, lived with his parents, and was a weightlifter. He looked like a young, better-looking Arnold Schwarzenegger. Rosemaria took one look at him and thought, *No wonder Hecht had fled after Mangini came after him.* He explained he had been heading for a competition the day of the attack. He was just pulling out of the driveway when he saw Hecht confront his driver. Carrera said something to Hecht and Hecht punched him in the face. The old man was on the ground and Hecht was kicking him in the head by the time Mangini got within a few yards of the confrontation. As soon as Hecht saw Mangini, he jumped in his car and drove off. Mangini could already hear police sirens.

When Rosemaria asked if he felt confident in his ability to stand up against an experienced defense lawyer, Mangini said he couldn't wait to get on the stand to describe what he saw. He assured Rosemaria that no lawyer was going to aggravate him to the point of him losing his temper. His father was a lawyer, and he'd been watching him work since he was a kid. He knew every trick in the book that defense attorneys used to destroy prosecution witnesses.

After Mangini left, she felt like she had truly hit the jackpot with all four witnesses. She was debating if she should put them on the stand first or if she should call the EMTs, doctors, and nurses to describe the massive injuries before bringing in the witnesses. She'd think about it later. She told Karen she was going to check on Maryanne and Tiffany, but that was not really where she was going first. Why worry Karen needlessly? She walked down the hallway to Atkins's office. She was disappointed to find he wasn't there, and neither was his secretary. Talking to Atkins to try to convince him to declare a truce would have to wait for another day. She wondered if Lattimer had called him personally and told him to back off the case. That would have stoked his hatred toward her into a massive bonfire. This couldn't go on much longer. Atkins was on a self-destructive path, and she didn't intend to get dragged down with him.

* * * *

A patrolman was seated by the door outside Larry's condominium. He stood up as soon as he saw Rosemaria. They had met before, but she showed him her ID, not wanting to break the protocol that Curtis had demanded. He knocked on the door, announced Rosemaria, then waited for the female cop, Officer Boa, to look through the eyehole and open the door. The girls ran to greet her.

Maryanne hugged her hard. "I'm so happy to see you," she whispered.

Tiffany hung back. Rosemaria could see the fear and doubt in her eyes.

"I was afraid we wouldn't see you again before we left," Maryanne said.

"I told you I'd come by."

"I know, but you're probably very busy."

Rosemaria sat on the couch, and Maryanne sat down in a chair facing her. Tiffany leaned against a stool next to the kitchen island.

"You're right. I do have a lot on my mind, but I'm telling you the absolute truth when I say that nothing is more important to me than your safety. And, of course, finding the thugs who are responsible for Maria's death and are trying to silence you."

Tiffany hesitated, then asked, "Do you think that Mr. Curtis will be able to protect us? I mean, do you trust him?"

"You couldn't be in better hands, okay? Whatever happens, do whatever he tells you to do."

Maryanne was alarmed. "Do you think something will happen? Do you think they'll find us?"

"There are no guarantees about that. But I do know that Mr. Curtis faced enemies a whole lot tougher than these creeps when he was in the Marines, and he beat them every time. If things go sideways, you just follow his orders, and he'll keep you safe."

Rosemaria looked over at Officer Boa, who was now seated at the dining room table. She was probably only a couple of years older than the girls. "So, have your charges been behaving themselves?"

"Maryanne's been killing us both in poker. Thank God we're not playing for real money, or I'd be broke. Other than that, we watch movies, read, and eat. I wish their lives didn't have to be so boring right now."

Rosemaria laughed. "After what these two girls have been through, boring is good!"

Tiffany clasped her hands in her lap. She seemed to be searching for the right words to say.

Maryanne spoke first. "It's kind of hard to say this, but we feel bad that because of what we did, other people have to put their own lives in danger. You know?"

Tiffany jumped in. "It's not her fault. It's mine. I was stupid. I got us into this."

They both looked at Rosemaria as if seeking absolution. She slowly shook her head and relaxed back against the couch.

"What is going on now is happening because of something very evil and ugly that has to do with politics and greed. We don't know exactly who murdered Maria or who is trying to protect the murderer by coming after you. We know it apparently started at the Island Hotel, but maybe not even there. This whole ungodly mess probably began when ruthless men decided to force their will on someone else. They have decided to let nothing stand in the way of achieving their goals. That is something that the detectives are trying to figure out."

"And you too?" Tiffany asked.

"And me too. But the point is, whatever these men are up to, anyone could have been a witness to their crimes, anyone could have inadvertently seen or heard something they shouldn't have and become a target.

It happened to be you two. They believe you've seen and heard things that can do them harm, and they can't allow that to happen."

"So, if— I mean, after you catch them, we can testify, right?"

"Absolutely. You can be part of the reason they are convicted and put in jail."

The girls looked at each other. "I'd like to think that my life can be of some use," Tiffany said.

Rosemaria started to say something, but Tiffany stopped her. "No, no. Let me say this." She was again searching for words. "I'm not saying I've had some sort of religious experience or anything, but all my life, people made me feel worthless. Everybody around me used drugs, so I did too. I talked the way they talked, using language that makes normal people cringe, so I talked that way on purpose. You know? I didn't care what people thought of me because what did it matter anyway? I was going nowhere, and I knew it."

She looked at Maryanne, who was nodding in agreement. "When I came out of that dryer and saw you standing there, I really felt like somebody cared about me. And now I actually have people risking their lives to protect me. It's almost too much to take, you know?" Her eyes appealed to Rosemaria to understand.

"Yeah, I know. But get this into your head: you *are* worth saving. Both of you are."

They sat in silence for a while, and Rosemaria knew it was time to say goodbye. She stood up, hugged both of them, and walked to the door. The girls followed her and put on brave faces. Rosemaria waved to Officer Boa and left before her emotions ran away with her, which seemed to be becoming a pattern for her these days.

* * * *

"They're so scared and vulnerable, Josh. A part of me wishes I could go with them." They were walking along the beach in Santa Monica near the pier. The sun had set, and the lights were blinking on the Ferris wheel and the carousel.

"Wow."

"Wow what?" Rosemaria asked.

"How times have changed. I remember how you used to accuse me of wanting to rescue broken wings. You told me it was my fatal flaw, or words to that effect."

"Hoisted on my own petard."

"What's a petard, anyway?" Josh asked.

"Who knows, but this is different."

"Mm-hmm."

"Okay, forget I just said that. You've turned me into an emotional dishrag. I now am the mother of two cats and a bird, and I find myself caring deeply for Maryanne and Tiffany. I always did my best to help the girls working the streets in Hollywood, but now it's become personal. Get it?"

Josh pulled her close. "I do."

"Now that I got that out, the mayor of Santa Monica came to my office today."

"What for?" Josh said, only mildly surprised.

"To thank me for catching two dangerous criminals."

"As well he should have."

"You're not impressed that the mayor of Santa Monica personally came to my office to thank me?"

"He's just acknowledging what I already know, that he's lucky he's got a prosecutor like you taking care of business."

"Maybe I'll agree with you once I get Hecht convicted and behind bars for twenty years."

"I think you brought me here to tell me something."

Rosemaria stomped a foot in the sand. "Darn! You can always sense things! Okay, you're right."

"So, what is it?"

"Well, now, don't get all excited, but instead of going with you to visit our kids this weekend, I want to snoop around the Island Hotel."

Josh took a step away from her and threw up his hands, speaking in a Cuban accent. "Aye, yay, aye, yay, yay. Lucy! Not a good idea!"

She protested, saying, "Just this once, okay? I'm not being clued in on the investigation—not even Larry will tell me much. I don't know who they've interviewed, what they've found out, nothing. I need to see what I can find out on my own and if they've missed something. It's the weekend. My time off from being a prosecutor. What can it hurt?"

Josh shook his head and looked up at the sky. "I thought you became a prosecutor to spend your life in a cramped office and stuffy courtrooms. Now you're ready to go back to chasing dangerous criminals and putting your life in danger. Why?"

"I'm not doing any chasing. Just a bit of snooping."

He put his arm around her waist and pulled her close. "I won't try to talk you out of it. You may have your law degree, missy, but you still bleed blue. If you catch the scent of this bastard, I have no doubt you'll follow it till you nail him."

"You better believe it, buddy. I got *you*, didn't I? Race you back to the pier!"

She took off running, and he followed at a leisurely pace, admiring the sight of her backside in shorts and a T-shirt.

* * * *

The unmarked car pulled up outside LAX. Two girls were hustled inside and surrounded by four men in suits and one wearing jeans and a camouflage jacket. They moved quickly through security without delay and boarded the plane, without waiting. Lieutenant Manley had called in his connections, and the operation went like clockwork. Once inside the plane, Curtis and the girls settled in their seats, and the men in suits disappeared. To Maryanne and Tiffany, the entire operation suddenly seemed like an exciting adventure. As for Curtis, he was fulfilling a pact he had made with Maria at her grave site, and it was one promise he didn't intend to break.

CHAPTER SIXTEEN

Noor lay on her soft bed of leaves and grass, stretched luxuriously, and looked around. Gilbert was already asleep a few feet away. She felt rather than knew that Josh would be coming in the morning. Days and nights came and went, and when it was time, she sensed it. Her life now almost made her forget the terrible years when she had lived in a cage. She loved having the freedom to roam and climb for many miles. She also had a little pond that she dipped her feet into on hot days. Her love for Josh and their special bond would never diminish, but freedom was everything. Now she didn't have to run and climb rocks only in her dreams. Her freedom was real. And with the rising sun, she would also have Josh. After a contented sigh, she closed her eyes and fell into a dreamless sleep.

* * * *

Josh was in his Mustang, driving through Santa Barbara with the top down, when his phone rang. He picked it up. "Yes, my darling."

"I'm on my way to the Island Hotel now. Where are you?"

"You're outta control, that's where I am."

Rosemaria turned right on Wilshire Boulevard and headed west. "I'll do a bit of unobtrusive looking around, and that's it."

"You know what will happen if you get fired."

"What, besides I'll have more time to cook for you?"

"God forbid. No, it would mean I'd have to write more inane commercial jingles to support us. That could make me a little grouchy."

"Won't happen, and I'm deeply hurt you said that about my cooking. Love you." She clicked off her phone and pulled into the parking structure at the Island.

Rosemaria stood near the entrance of the hotel and surveyed the lobby. The hotel emitted waves of affluence that washed over her like warm tropical breezes. This was the life. The furnishings were luxurious: plush couches and chairs around stunning coffee tables with a deep, rich wood finish—probably cut from trees that grew in some endangered rain forest. But what did rich people care about such things? Money and air conditioning shielded them from the realities of global warming. She saw the bar where Maria had sat for a few minutes, waiting for an invitation that never came. She looked toward the back of the room and saw the hallway where she had gone to smoke a cigarette and never returned.

Rosemaria had to ask herself what she was doing there. What could she hope to discover that Osborne and Larry hadn't? She had figured out her cover story and hoped no one would call her bluff. The young man at the front desk seemed friendly enough. She would give it a try. He saw her walking toward him and offered a friendly smile.

"Hello. May I help you?"

Rosemaria tried to be officious yet personable, but it was not easy to pull off. "I'm hoping you can. I was supposed to be at the fundraiser last weekend with my boss. I live here, but I had been in New York for a couple of days. My return flight to LA was canceled, so I missed the event."

The man behind the desk was wondering what this had to do with him.

"I'm wondering if you can help me, Sy," she said, reading his name tag. "Would you happen to know if you have any leftover material from the fundraiser—any leaflets, programs, list of attendees, that sort of thing? I'd like to go over the names to see if there might be any possible donors for our own work in South Central and Watts." Using the plight of the disadvantaged for her own benefit seemed wrong, but she needed to appeal to this guy's conscience. He came through.

"I totally understand. Yes, I believe the banquet manager still has the unused material. She usually throws it out to be recycled, but maybe she still has it in her office." He pointed. "It's right down the hallway behind me and to the left. Her name is Magda." He laughed. "She likes to talk, so if you want to get out of here by dinnertime, just take what you need and go."

A talkative witness? That was music to Rosemaria's ears. She followed his directions and introduced herself to Magda, whom she found seated behind a desk, typing into a laptop. "Sy told me you might have some material left over from the fundraiser that I could have. Would that be possible?"

"And you are?"

"I work for a community organizer in Watts. My boss neglected to save any of the pamphlets and other information that might help us find donors. Would it be okay if I take some of the information with me?"

Magda, a shapely redhead with what sounded like a Russian accent, was surprised anybody would want that junk but was amenable. "Sure. I haven't gotten around to taking it to the recycling bin yet. You're welcome to it." She showed Rosemaria the boxes of papers and booklets that sat on a small table in a corner. "Take what you want."

Rosemaria started sifting through the material, taking out papers that looked interesting and making a pile on another tabletop. "It must have been quite an event, all those hundreds of politicians and rich people." Oops, what a dumb thing to say. Everybody who comes to this hotel had to be rich. But Magda didn't notice.

"Yeah, never saw so many billionaires and politicians together in one place. You hear every kind of con and pathetic story when you oversee the banquets. I don't think they eat as much as they beg. That's a politician's life, I guess. They beg for money, and other people beg them for favors. Makes me glad I don't have to deal with them on a daily basis. Our normal guests are usually very quiet and private."

"I guess some people must get pretty aggravated when they don't get what they want from the politicians. I mean, favors and such."

"You mean like, I contributed to your campaign, so you better keep my coal plant open?"

"Yeah, like that."

"Usually, what I hear is about bills. You vote for this or that, and I'll ask my friend so-and-so to contribute to your election fund. But nobody gets really angry and makes threats or anything. I've never seen that."

"Except somebody must have gotten angry at the poor girl who was killed."

Magda's face fell, and she shook her head sadly. "That was so awful. Nothing like that has ever happened here before. Who would do something so terrible to a young girl?"

"Must have been someone lurking in the alley. I can't imagine a politician doing something like that."

"Are you kidding? From what I've seen, those people have zero morals. They'd sell their souls to hang on to their power." She suddenly realized that she'd said too much. "Don't mind me. I tend to have strong opinions." She smiled. "And right now, I need to get back to work."

Rosemaria picked up her stack of material, put it all in her oversize bag, and thanked Magda profusely for her help. She waved goodbye and noticed Magda looking at her with a curious expression as she left.

She couldn't exactly start interviewing maids and busboys as if she were still a cop, so that was out. Besides, she was sure the detectives would have interviewed them all by now. There was always the bartender. Maybe he had been here last weekend and seen something. She sat at the bar and ordered a wine spritzer knowing if this came back to Osborne, there would be hell to pay. The bartender, whose name tag said "Mel," set her drink in front of her. She sipped it slowly as he watched her to see if she liked it.

"Very good. Thank you."

"Are you staying here?" Not a come on. He was just being polite.

"No. I came by to pick up some material for my boss. He was at the fundraiser last weekend."

The bartender acknowledged this without responding. He walked to the other end of the bar to wait on another customer, then moved back to her.

She continued. "My boss was horrified to hear a girl had been killed right outside the hotel. You can't help but think that someone who was here acting like a normal person could have done it."

"I felt worse. I had talked to her."

Bingo. Hit the jackpot. Rosemaria was unfazed. "She looked so young, considering her—you know, what she did." She sipped her wine and continued to look unconcerned.

The bartender added, "Yeah, she showed me some fake ID, but I only gave her a soda. She was way too young to be here looking for action."

"I thought maybe she was here to meet someone. You know, maybe some rich guy had called an agency."

"No. She was alone. Alone and totally lost. She didn't say a word, just looked around like she was waiting for someone to rescue her. She was obviously in the wrong profession. I wish I could have done something for her."

Rosemaria took out some bills and laid them on the bar.

"You're a good guy, Mel. A really good guy."

He gave her a two fingered salute and moved down the bar.

Rosemaria figured she had done as much as she could without getting into trouble and walked back to her car.

* * * *

The Sun Café was on Ventura Boulevard in Studio City, near Lankershim and Universal Studios. It was a restaurant Josh liked that was also close by the studio where he had almost had his first big break. Now, two years later, he was going to see that dream realized. It was also halfway between Rosemaria's apartment in West Hollywood and her father's house in Simi Valley, with a whole lot of cheat in her direction. But they both loved the restaurant, so her father didn't mind driving farther to meet her for dinner whenever Josh was working late at the studio and she needed to talk.

They settled at a table on the patio, which was surrounded by trees sparkling with lights. A slight breeze cooled off the warm winter day. She opted for the Caesar salad, and her father ordered the baked lasagna. It would take a bit of willpower not to ask for a bite or two of that. After the usual inquiries about home and health, Steven Baker, a man who didn't beat around the bush, got to the point. "I'm sensing that, right now, you're going off in several directions at the same time, and you need to find a bit of focus. Am I right?"

Rosemaria looked at her father, who'd been a cop on the beat for five years, then a homicide detective for thirty years. Even though he was now retired, he was still strong and vital. Anyone looking at him would think he was ten years younger than his sixty-five years. He was also the smartest man she knew.

"Dad, I've got a big trial coming up, more cases in my in-basket, a boss who hates me, two girls to worry about, and what I really want to do, in the worst way, is spend all my time tracking down the SOBs who murdered Maria and are trying to kill Maryanne and Tiffany. The fact that I can't is driving me crazy."

Her father poured them water from the carafe and took a sip. "I get it."

"You do?"

"When you were a detective, there were times when you had several cases begging for your time, and you didn't think there were enough hours in the day to do what you needed to do."

"Yeah?"

"And you managed just fine. This is no different, except for one thing. You have been hired to work as a prosecutor, not as a detective. You could handle all of this if your friends at the BHPD included you in the investigation, and if you didn't have to hide what you're doing from them or your boss at the courthouse. That's what's stressing you out. You're not allowed to be a real part of the process of putting the pieces together. They've made you feel like you're interfering. And the fact is, you are. Unless you are there with your friends every day, interviewing and following leads, you can't know what direction the investigation is heading."

"So, what do I do?"

The waiter brought their plates, and Rosemaria eyed the lasagna longingly.

"Do you want a bite?" her father asked. "It's too much for one person."

She looked at her salad and quickly made up her mind. "Just a little, okay? You can put just a smidgen on my plate."

He gave her a couple of generous forkfuls and answered her question. "What do you do? Exactly what you are doing. Using your days off to find out what you can, and if you think you discover something helpful, pass it on to Osborne or Larry. These girls are important to you. So, don't feel bad about trying to help."

"You have no idea how good it feels to have someone who understands me!"

"Why wouldn't I? I'm your father."

"Tomorrow I'm going through the material I collected at the Island. I'm not sure what I'm looking for."

"Look for connections between politicians and lobbyists. Lobbyists for big corporations wield a lot of power in DC. There are always bills coming up for a vote, and lobbyists are willing to do just about anything to make sure bills get through committee and out on the floor."

"Somebody else said almost the same thing today," she mused.

"Pharmaceutical companies, agribusiness, gun manufacturers, military contractors, oil companies, and the like all stand to lose or gain billions of dollars depending on what bills are passed in Congress and signed by the president."

"I'll go through it all tomorrow and see what I can find. I just wish I didn't have a boss who wants to destroy me. He is liable to stab me in the back any minute, and I mean that literally."

"From what you've told me about him, he sounds like he's been emotionally disturbed for some time. You happened to run across him when he's ready to self-destruct. The people you work with are aware of the problem. Ask for their help, if need be. I think you'll do fine."

They tucked into their meals, appreciating every bite. Rosemaria spoke with her mouth full of lasagna. "Now that you've solved my problems, I want to know what's going on with you and the house. Are you going to sell or what?"

"Since you and Josh are dead set against living in Simi—"

"We love the house, Dad, but Simi is just not for us. Too far away from everything."

"I know, I know. I just would have liked to see you living in the house you grew up in."

Rosemaria took another heavenly bite of the lasagna and chewed thoughtfully. She should have just forgotten about her diet and ordered her own. "I do wish you wouldn't move back to Tahoe for a while though, Dad. I may have an idea about the house."

"You care to share it with me?"

"No. I don't want to jinx it, okay?"

"As you wish. I'm in no hurry to move. I kind of like being close to you and being asked to solve your problems."

"You always did, Dad."

They enjoyed the rest of their meal in silence.

* * * *

Suzi couldn't seem to stay in one spot for more than a minute. She was always restless when Josh was away for more than a day. "Turn on the TV! Turn on the TV!" she yelled from atop her perch.

Rosemaria, at the dining table, hunched over papers and her laptop, tried to be patient. "We don't have a TV, okay? And if you keep that up, we'll never get one!"

Suzi, feeling chastised, stopped complaining and perched on a chair next to Rosemaria. "You can watch my computer screen, okay? There are pictures on there sometimes and even videos. That'll have to do for now." Suzi, responding to the gentler tone, hopped on Rosemaria's shoulder and peered down at Rosemaria's hand as she shuffled through papers. Then,

Suzi saw the hand stop moving as Rosemaria brought it up to chew on her thumbnail and stare straight ahead.

Rosemaria had found some connections between certain senators and lobbyists just by seeing what meetings and seminars they had signed up to attend. There was a wealth of information here. But she had to assume Osborne had all of that himself and someone had already gone through it. She needed to find out what important bills were in committee and which ones were up for a vote. Maybe there was one huge one coming up. That might give a hint as to who was desperate enough to maybe blackmail a senator and kill a girl who overheard them plotting. She would have to keep narrowing down the list of suspects. There were around a hundred or so.

Suzi started squawking and flew to the door. She landed on Josh's shoulder as he came in and pecked at his ear. "Whoa! That's quite a welcome." She jumped on his outheld arm.

"Don't mind me. I'm just the hired help," Rosemaria said.

He walked over to Rosemaria as Suzi flew off his arm and landed on her perch. Josh looked down at the piles of documents that covered the tabletop and gave her a kiss on the top of her head. "Looks like you found something."

"I think I did, actually. I just have to sort through it while also preparing for my first trial."

"You got this."

"Everybody has so much faith in me. How come I don't?"

"Oh yeah, how was dinner with your dad?"

"Great. I went off my diet. Now I have a huge case of the guilts."

He pulled her up from her chair. "I'm going to take a shower, and then I will help you with that."

"Have you noticed that you're a lot like a doctor, always fixing one thing or another on me?"

"Any complaints?"

"Can't think of any at the moment. How are the kids?"

"Happy and healthy. A new cat came in from a roadside zoo. She's in very poor shape and had to be in quarantine for a week. She's in the main area now. She walked up to the fence and hissed at me. Noor told her to back off in no uncertain terms."

"Ooh, I wouldn't want to be on Noor's bad side."

"It'll get sorted out."

He mussed her hair and headed for the shower. She sank back down in her chair and kept staring at her list, hoping something would jump out at her.

CHAPTER SEVENTEEN

Holmby Hills is arguably even more exclusive than Beverly Hills or Bel Air. It's the home of the Playboy Mansion and where Aaron Spelling built the biggest house in the neighborhood. This is where the really big money resides, and this is where Larry Coleman's mother and stepfather lived in their $200 million mansion. Larry's own modest house on Tower Road in Beverly Hills was worth a mere $10 million. When he was a bachelor, he had held off on buying a house with the money he inherited from his father because he felt no need for it. He loved his condo at the Marina, where he could look out the window and see his sailboat that he used to sail at every opportunity. But after Vanessa came into his life, he wanted to shower her with everything she had never had. She would have been happy living in a cottage in Sherman Oaks, but he could see how much she enjoyed what he offered her. When he thought of the lonely, inept boor he had been when he first met Rosemaria, he shuddered. Vanessa had saved him from that, and nothing he could give her would ever be enough to pay her back for agreeing to be a part of his life.

He pulled up to the massive wrought iron gates that protected the entryway onto his parents' property and spoke into the mic attached to a post next to the gate. "I'm here."

After a moment, he heard a buzzer sound, the gates opened, and he drove in. The estate was massive. Every time he saw it, he thought, *Two people need all this?* The style was Mediterranean, tan with white trim, surrounded by extensive landscaping. Every kind of tropical tree and plant was represented here, all arranged in a seemingly natural flow that kept the groundskeepers busy every day of the week.

After his father died when Larry was in grade school, his mother, Loretta, married Andrew Collins. At the time, Collins was still a detective working in downtown LA. Because Hill Street was near the station, Larry always connected it with the TV show, and that made his stepdad being a cop all the more exciting. Larry swore he'd be just like him when he grew up. He was horribly disappointed to find out that the Hill Street station building on TV was actually in Chicago and that his stepdad's office was somewhere else entirely.

Collins was an excellent politician and moved quickly up the ranks. He had now been police commissioner for two years. As a young man, Larry strove to emulate him because, like Larry, his stepfather had inherited money (in his case a huge publishing fortune) but chose to work at a difficult job and work his way up the ranks to become a success in his own right. But the main reason he admired his stepfather was because he loved Larry's mother and treated her like the intelligent, gracious woman she was. His stepfather recognized that she was at least half responsible for his political success.

His mother opened the door to greet him. He always marveled at how she kept her beauty fresh without the facelifts or lip injections that were so popular among Beverly Hills matrons. She had been too busy running her deceased husband's business and turning it into a bigger success than it had been when Larry's father was alive to obsess over her looks. She accepted the face that God had given her. Now she was retired, spending her time raising money for various charities.

Larry was grateful that his father had left him enough money in a trust so that all Larry had to do was invest the money well and live off the interest. But a life of indolence was not for him. He needed challenges that made life worthwhile.

Larry hopped out of his car and strode quickly up the stairs. His mother threw her arms around him and held him so tight it was as if she hadn't seen him in months when it really was only two weeks. "We don't see nearly enough of you and Vanessa. Why is that?"

"It's my fault. She's getting close to her due date, and I'm afraid I'm a little overprotective. I've turned her into a homebody."

She led him into the massive black and white tiled entrance and steered him toward a sunlit conservatory, which was decorated with white wicker furniture, massive palms, and an array of flowers throughout the room. "I've been pregnant too, you know. Women are perfectly capable of functioning normally until the last minute."

Larry looked at her, contrite. "You got me there, Mom. We'll come by soon. She'd like that very much."

They made themselves comfortable in chairs by the glass coffee table.

"At least you went back to work and stopped hovering around her."

Larry was taken aback. "She said that to you?"

"No, my dear. She never would, but I can read between the lines."

"It's my first. I'm a little nervous."

A maid in a gray and white uniform who looked to be in her fifties came in and smiled at Larry.

"Hello, Mr. Coleman. Nice to see you."

"You too, Martha."

Larry's mother looked at her son. "Can Martha bring you something, dear? Soda, coffee, tea, anything?"

"Water would be nice, Martha. Thank you."

"And Martha, please tell Mr. Collins that Larry is here," his mother added.

Martha left, and Loretta was all business. "You sounded very serious when you called. I know it's Andy you want to talk to, but I just want to say that I'm so proud of you."

"Have I done something special I don't know about?"

"For a while, I was very worried about you. You were doing fine with your career, but you seemed so emotionally rudderless, always searching for something. I don't know what. Then, two years ago, when you began working with Detective Baker to investigate that horrid woman who was married to the producer, you seemed to suddenly find focus. And because of that case, you found your lovely Vanessa and had the good sense to marry her."

"I feel very lucky."

His mother looked over at the entrance of the conservatory. Her husband had come into the room. She stood up, and they embraced. She glanced over at Larry. "I'll leave you men to talk over whatever it is that you have to talk about. Say goodbye before you leave, dear." And with that, she was gone.

His stepfather was not conventionally handsome like his father had been. He was medium height and carried a little extra weight all over, but he had something else that was intangible, a charisma and charm that commanded a room. Larry automatically stood out of respect. Andy's voice was a booming baritone, and he greeted Larry with an affectionate half hug. "Sit, sit. Is Martha bringing you anything?"

Just then, Martha walked in with a tray. On it sat a large bottle of Perrier, two glasses, and a crystal bowl filled with ice chips. "Right here, sir." She set down the tray, and the two men helped themselves to ice and glasses of Perrier. Martha excused herself and left.

The commissioner wasted no time. "In answer to your questions, yes, I was there at the fundraiser last weekend, and yes, I was there when the prostitute was killed."

"Maria Ramirez," Larry interjected.

"Poor, unfortunate Maria. I stand corrected. Of course, we didn't know what had happened until Monday morning, when she was found in the alley. I immediately called Manley, and he filled me in on the details."

"I guess he must have asked you some questions about what you saw."

"And I told him I didn't see anything. At the time she was probably killed, I was in a meeting with a Sacramento legislator who always votes in our favor regarding police issues, which was the reason I was there."

"Were you there on Saturday as well?"

"For a few hours, to do a bit of schmoozing, and then I stayed to have dinner with a couple of friends in the department."

"Can you give me an idea of the general atmosphere there? Who was talking to whom? Was there a lot of wheeling and dealing going on that you might have witnessed?"

"Good questions. I'm not one for making friends with politicians, even though you might say I am one on a much smaller level. I don't trust them. They will say whatever they have to say to win your support and get election contributions. That's how they spend the majority of their time, not legislating. Their staff does most of that. But because of my position, and because the police department is on the defensive much of the time, I like to get a feel for who is on our side and who will have our backs when push comes to shove."

"So, about the wheeling and dealing. Was there much of that?"

"That's the whole reason for the weekend. Speeches are just for show and for politicians to self-aggrandize. These fundraisers are like being at a carnival, with the barkers speaking in dulcet tones with good grammar instead of yelling and acting like two-bit con men. But, make no mistake, they are con men. Lobbyists have taken over our political system. They have bought and paid for most politicians and write the bills they want passed so our legislators won't have to bother with anything other than fundraising."

Larry laughed. "Doesn't sound like what they taught us in school about democracy."

"I moved up in the system because I believed I could help my fellow police officers, but more often than not, it's been a matter of compromising and soothing the hurt feelings on both sides. No one ever gets everything they want. But I think I've done some good. On a federal level, it's worse because you have multinational corporations jockeying for position. I don't have to list them. You know who they are. They have the money to get what they want. I heard blatant offers of payoffs if the politicians would support a certain policy or bill. I would have found it shocking if I hadn't been already aware of exactly what goes on."

"Are there any politicians whom you find especially repugnant, if I can use that word?"

"It's actually the perfect word. California state senator Jerry Hector is a major panderer and will say anything to anybody to get what he wants.

His assistants are nothing more than pimps, offering Hector's services to anyone who will pay the price. Senator Haynes from Kentucky is a real smooth operator. He has no morals and is a snake who will take a bite out of you before you know what's happening. Another senator, I think his name is McConnell or McDonnell, I can't remember, has a reputation for being fond of prostitutes. His wife is one of those downtrodden types that puts on a brave face whenever the rumors of other women surface. He was always lurking in corners looking like he was having secret meetings with big donors. He came up to talk to me Saturday night, and I had to excuse myself because I found him to be so off-putting. I'd put him high on my suspect list."

"You never heard anyone say they were staying at the Harland?"

"No, I didn't. Manley told me what happened to—"

"Maryanne."

"To Maryanne and—"

"Tiffany."

"I hope you have them locked up somewhere really safe because lobbyists have the resources to find anybody anywhere."

"I do believe they're safe right now. So, you think it's lobbyists who are responsible?"

"I'm sure I'm not the first person to suggest that. They don't hesitate to do whatever it takes to get what they want, and that includes blackmail and murder."

"It's depressing to think that that's how our country is run now."

"Like I always tell my officers, get involved. You want to change things? Get involved."

"I'd like to go find Mother, if you don't mind. She'll kill me if I just say a quick goodbye and don't spend more time with her."

They both stood up. "Let's do that," his stepfather said. "I believe she was going out to the vegetable garden to see if any of her plants have started to come up yet. Maybe we can pry her away and convince her to have some lunch with us on the patio."

"I'd like that very much."

Commissioner Collins led the way.

* * * *

Curtis's house in Dayton was in a middle-class neighborhood, with trimmed green lawns and large old maples that shaded the streets and sidewalks. Most of them, like his, were mid-century craftsman, bought for a song in the fifties and worth ten times that now. Inside, the décor was simple and the furniture comfortable but spare. Curtis's house looked like it was owned by a Marine who didn't put much time and effort into decorating. A woman's touch was lacking.

Curtis, Maryanne, and Martin Smith, one of the guards hired by Curtis (salary courtesy of Larry), sat at the simple pine dining table. Martin was not only a fellow ex-Marine but also Curtis's best friend. A 6-foot-tall, big bear of a man, the girls had fallen in love with Martin five minutes after meeting him. He was forty years old, and his brown hair had grown out from his Marine cut so that it was long enough to partly cover his ears. The girls thought he was handsome for an old guy. He had a muscular build but was still just as spry and agile as the smaller Curtis, who seemed to have overcome the back injury that had forced him into retirement.

The group was waiting in suspense for what was coming. They heard Tiffany's voice from the kitchen. "You know I haven't spent much time learning how to cook for people, so I hope you like this. If you don't, eat it anyway, or I'll feel bad." The three people at the table looked at one another. *Uh-oh, will we have to come up with polite compliments we don't mean?* They all took turns cooking, and this was Tiffany's first time.

Tiffany came through the kitchen door, "Ta-da!" She was holding a large bowl of pesto pasta. She lifted it high and then set it down on the table. "Totally homemade from a recipe I found online and with ingredients Martin bought." She brought out a plate of garlic bread, then used a large fork and spoon to dish out the pasta to everyone. "I wish I could serve you wine, but of course, considering our circumstances, we all have to stay sober." She sat down in the empty chair. "So, eat. And be kind."

They each looked at their plates and tentatively took bites. "Maryanne's face lit up. "This is good!"

Tiffany was wary. "You're not just saying that?"

"No, it's really good." She brought another big forkful to her mouth.

"Not bad," Curtis said, chewing slowly. "Not bad at all."

Martin agreed. "You've done it, Tiff. You're now our official cook."

"Really?" Tiffany didn't seem put off by the idea.

"No." Curtis was emphatic. "We all take turns."

Tiffany dug into her own pasta. "I'm a success at something, finally." She emitted a huge sigh of satisfaction.

They enjoyed their food and engaged in idle chitchat about nothing important.

* * * *

Rosemaria was staring at the screen in rapt attention. She and Josh were with the cast and crew watching Ken's movie, *New York Nights,* in a screening room at the studio. It was a romantic thriller/mystery, and it captivated Rosemaria from the start. When Joell sang the opening song, she squeezed Josh's hand so hard he flinched. God, she was proud of him! She hoped and prayed that finally his incredible talent would be appreciated. His tiny role as a homeless man wasn't bad either. She had to laugh when she remembered how she had run into him accidentally in New York, when he was about to do his scene. For a few minutes, she had thought he really was homeless.

The two young leads were breakout stars, according to Ken, and never again would work for the salary he had paid them. This movie would make their careers. Positive thinking was Ken's mantra, and she was on board with that. She loved the climax when the murder mystery was solved and cheered when Josh's credit came on the screen. She leaned into Josh's shoulder and marveled that she was there, in the center of show business, the only place her mother had ever wanted to be. It never happened for her mother, and Rosemaria finally had a hint of the magic that had drawn her mother in.

It was like she finally understood her, and she admired her for never giving up. Only death had ended the dream.

* * * *

In Dayton, in Curtis's living room, Tiffany was watching a Netflix romance movie on the TV, while Maryanne and Martin were playing cards at the dining table. Curtis was sitting in a chair near the front door, lost in thought. He suddenly stood up, told Martin to stay inside, and slipped out the back door.

Curtis knew he was being hypervigilant and maybe overly cautious and paranoid, but the enemy he was facing now was as silent and unseen as the Taliban had been in Afghanistan. He couldn't track them, trap them, surround them, take them prisoner, or kill them as he had there. The four of them in this house were like bait, and the enemy could strike at any minute.

It would have been difficult for anyone to track down the girls to this house. Only a handful of cops and his personally selected ex-Marine buddies whom he had hired to be guards even knew that he had taken the girls home with him. He had bought this house only a month ago, and its address wasn't in any of his service records, on his driver's license, or passport. The only people who knew about the house was his realtor, the mortgage company, and the bank. Those records would be difficult for anyone to access. Yet he knew if these people were as powerful as he believed them to be, he and the girls wouldn't be impossible to find. He had seen the same SUV drive by twice last night, once at 12:30 a.m. and again at 3:00 a.m., while he was sitting watch on the ground behind the rhododendron bush at the side of the house. Both times, his danger radar had gone off. His instincts were rarely wrong.

He crept over the side fence and into the neighbor's yard without a sound. He moved along the back of the other houses on the block, sat behind a car parked in a driveway, and waited. He saw a car parked a half a block away in front of a vacant house. Inside the house, one of his friends was watching for anything that moved in the neighborhood, while two of his other friends sat unseen in the car. He stealthily made his way back to the house and went in the back door.

Martin gave him a knowing look as soon as he walked into the living room. Maryanne and Tiffany were wide-eyed. "Is something up?" Maryanne asked him.

"Just being overly cautious. It's my nature."

"Whew!" Tiffany said. "We thought you saw something."

"No, but I'd like you girls to go to bed. I want all lights out in half an hour."

"Will do, Mr. Curtis. You're the boss," Maryanne agreed.

After they left, Martin asked. "What's up?"

"As I said, I may be a little paranoid."

"You want to take first watch?"

"Yeah. All lights out, okay?"

"You got it."

In half an hour, the house was pitch-dark. Curtis had seen to it that the nearest streetlight was out as well. He worked best in darkness. He called his friend in the house down the block. "Time for you guys to go." He clicked off his phone, and a few minutes later, the door to the house opened. A man wearing jeans, a casual shirt, and a jean jacket walked out, got in the car, and drove off. Curtis made another phone call.

He walked to the living room closet, pulled down the ladder, and climbed up to the attic. He walked hunchback under the eaves over to the tiny, crescent-shaped front window and peered out. He looked at his watch. It was ten o'clock. Too early, if anything was going to happen. He would sit and wait. He had done it a hundred times.

At 1:00 a.m., his acute hearing told him an SUV had driven into the neighborhood and parked a few blocks away. He trusted his gut. He spoke into his phone. "They're here." He slid down the ladder and woke up Martin, who followed him to the girls' bedroom. He gave the girls explicit directions. "Maryanne, Tiffany, do exactly as I say. Follow me, lie down in the tub, and don't move. Martin and I will be outside the bathroom door.

No one will get in." The girls looked terrified but stayed calm. "Let's go." He led them out of the bedroom.

Four men dressed in black suits and shirts climbed out of the SUV. SIG Sauers bulged inside their jackets. They separated and disappeared between the houses. Two of them took the same route as Curtis behind houses on his block. The other two waited out of sight across from Curtis's house for fifteen minutes to see if there was any movement inside or outside the house. One of the men across the street took out his phone and texted. "Now!"

The two men across the street walked quickly up to Curtis's house. One of them used an automatic lockpick to unlock the front door, and the two entered, guns drawn. In the back, the two others did the same. They moved quietly through the house, room by room, puzzled at finding no one. One of the men pointed upward, and they opened one closet door after another until they found the ladder to the attic. One of the men nodded and started up the ladder.

Noise, bright lights, and yelling hit the four men like a grenade launcher. "DPD SWAT! The house is surrounded! You cannot escape! Come out the front door, throw your weapons down on the porch, and put your hands up! Do it now, or we will smoke you out! We will not ask you again!"

The four men were stunned. They knew they had no choice but to surrender. Then, it would be up to their lawyer to get them out. They knew that would happen. It was only a matter of time.

Maryanne and Tiffany were lying flat in a bathtub as the commotion outside broke the silence of the night. They were in a vacant house behind Curtis's that was on the street parallel to his. Curtis had led them through his backyard, with Martin following, Glock out, aware of every sound. Curtis had helped them climb over a short wooden fence and into the other yard and house. He had ushered them into the bathroom and repeated the order for them to lie down in the tub. "We'll be right outside. Not a peep." They had nodded and done as he ordered.

After the noise had died down and the sound of sirens had disappeared, the girls still waited, afraid to speak, clutching each other's hands. They stared at the bathroom door, their hearts in their throats. They almost cried with relief when they saw Curtis stick his head in. "You can come out now. They got 'em."

An hour later, Maryanne and Tiffany were still shaking. They, Curtis, and Martin were seated at the dining room table with cups of tea in front of them. It was still dark outside, and only one lamp lit the room. The girls were happy to be alive, but the mood was somber.

"Do you know where we'll be moving to now?" Tiffany almost whispered.

"I have a couple of ideas about that," Martin said, his voice gentle. "Someplace not associated with us or any of our friends and family."

Curtis chuckled. "How do we accomplish that?"

"After I served my country in Afghanistan with my compadre here," he indicated Curtis, "and before working for the security firm I work for now, I had occasion to use fake IDs and passports while working for another company. That security firm no longer exists since the CEO was convicted on ten counts of fraud, but I still have the ID. I can rent a house over the phone, using a burner, give them my ID, which I checked is still verifiable, and have our generous benefactor, Larry, wire the broker the cash using an anonymous bank account." He raised his eyebrows and looked at Curtis for approval.

"I like it. But we can't move too far. I don't want us traveling and exposing the girls to possible sightings. With all the cameras everywhere these days, the farther we travel, the more likely it is the eyes of this organization will find them."

"How about Akron? Any of us ever live there or have any relatives there?" Everybody shook their heads.

"I've been there once," Curtis said, "but I've been to a lot of places once."

"Okay, I'll pick a broker off the internet, ask to see a few properties online, call Larry, and we'll be out of here by tomorrow afternoon."

* * * *

Rosemaria, groggy with sleep, reached across Josh's sleeping form to pick up her cell phone. "Baker here," she managed to get out. She listened for a few moments. "Oh no!"

Josh sat up, instantly awake. "What's wrong?!"

"It's Curtis. They were attacked last night!"

"How the hell did that happen?!" Josh was on his feet.

Rosemaria threw back the covers and all but leaped out of bed. Into the phone, she shouted, "How the hell did that happen?!"

Curtis was pacing back and forth in the living room. "We have a leak."

Rosemaria was adamant. "Not in this department. I'd stake my life on that."

"I trust every single man I hired to guard the girls. So, who told them they were with me? We had three decoy caravans going in different directions in LA. How'd they know which one to follow?"

She sat down at the table and put her head in one hand and held the phone with the other. "Let me think." She stood up and walked to the window. "Oh, hell, I don't know!" She looked at Josh and shrugged.

"Cameras," Josh said.

Curtis heard and agreed. "They could have gotten access to airport videos or checked passenger manifests."

Josh walked into the kitchen and began making coffee.

"That's an awful lot of work on a maybe," Rosemaria said. "You three could have driven anywhere or even stayed in the area. It would take a lot of man hours to check the videos when they didn't even know what airport you'd fly out of or even if you would be flying."

"If they saw videos of the girls boarding the plane, they would have seen that I was with them and, since they seem to have access to some kind of enforcement agency, used facial recognition to ID me."

"These people have access to everything—hired killers, computer experts, and God only knows what else. We're just guessing here, Curtis. But I'm telling you, it's not a leak. It's criminality in the highest circles."

"Whatever it is, we're moving in a few hours. We're telling no one where we'll be. If their hired goons find us this time, it will be the last thing they ever do."

Rosemaria was taken aback by the menace she heard in his voice. Josh put a cup of coffee on the table, noting her stricken expression with a questioning look. "You won't take any chances with my girls, will you?" she asked. "You won't put them in a dangerous position just to get these guys?"

His voice was flat. "I'll do what I have to do. Would you like to talk to them?"

"Yes, yes, absolutely."

She held up her hand for Josh to hold and hoped she could make herself sound like everything was going to be perfectly all right.

* * * *

Osborne had tracked down Senator Hector's chief of staff, Jeff Mulder, and found out he was still in Los Angeles wrapping up the details of a large donation, according to his assistant. The senator was back in his office in San Francisco but not available. Mulder was staying at the Santa Monica Palm Hotel, which was quite a bit less expensive than the Island.

Osborne and Larry found Mulder in the hotel restaurant and introduced themselves.

"I guess this must be about the murdered girl?" Mulder asked. "Have a seat. I don't know anything, but I'll be happy to answer your questions."

Larry's first impression was that he didn't seem like the odious slime his father had described.

Osborne started. "You and your boss were at the fundraiser at the Island last weekend?"

"Yes."

"Were any other staff members at the fundraiser?"

"Yes. His assistant, Patty Enker, and my secretary, Paul Hudson."

"And you're all staying at the Santa Monica Palm?"

"We don't want to spend taxpayer money on luxuries, except for the senator, of course. It was more important for him to stay at the Island."

"That's very considerate of you," Larry interjected. "Were all of you at the Island at the time of the murder on Sunday?"

"Since we don't know when the murder occurred, that would be hard to say. We all left to go out to eat or run errands at various times on Sunday."

"What about Senator Hector? Was he at the Island the entire day and evening on Sunday?"

"We were all extremely busy with meetings, seminars, and unofficial gatherings. I didn't keep track of where the senator was every second."

"You do know that the murdered girl was at the Island working as a prostitute?" Larry asked.

"That's what I heard."

"The senator is known for his predilection for prostitutes. Do you know if he had hired a girl for Sunday night?" Larry asked.

Mulder did a slow burn. "The senator is a happily married man. He does not cheat on his wife."

"Like Donald Trump?"

"Absolutely not. More like Jimmy Carter, I'd say."

At this, Larry couldn't help but laugh out loud. "Miles away from home, staying at a luxurious hotel, no one to check up on him, you're telling me the senator wouldn't take advantage of that?"

Mulder stood up.

"Is there anything relevant you would like to ask me? If not, I have nothing more to say."

"We'll be talking to other witnesses. If we find out you're lying, and if you personally contacted a call girl service on his behalf, you could be implicated in a crime." Osborne smiled. "These days, everything leaves a trail. It's unavoidable. For your sake, I hope you're telling the truth."

"Leave the senator alone," Mulder said, his voice cold with rage. "I'll tell you something about Hector. He may like a little action on the side, but he doesn't have the juice to hire hit men or the balls to kill anybody himself. He's a two-bit hustler who gets elected in his district because he pretends to care about every liberal cause that comes down the pike. And if you ever tell anybody I said that, I'll deny it."

He slammed a few bills down on the table and walked out of the restaurant.

"Well, I guess he told us," Larry said.

"And I think, for once in his life, he wasn't lying."

* * * *

The employee parking lot of the Beverly Hills Police Department had lots of empty spaces as Osborne pulled into his parking spot at 7:00 a.m. He sat in his car and pondered the last twenty-four hours. He had been devastated to hear that Maryanne and Tiffany had come close to getting killed, by four assailants no less. He was helpless to do anything to protect them. All he could do was continue to interview the attendees at the fundraiser and hope for a break. At least they had eliminated Hector. After talking to his secretary, and despite her efforts to cover up for him, it was clear that Hector had had a succession of women in his room on Sunday afternoon and evening. He had left the fundraising to his employees. The fundraiser was a perfect cover for indulging in his vices.

Osborne suddenly had an overwhelming feeling that he wasn't up to the job. When Rosemaria was his boss, Osborne was the competent plodder, doggedly pursuing leads that she provided, doing most of his work on the computer. She never failed to give him credit, and he became more confident in his skills beyond those on the computer, leaving most of the internet searches to Waite. He became more adept at interviewing suspects, and even some of Rosemaria's intimidation tactics rubbed off on him. Now he was up against a more powerful enemy than he had ever faced. The murder occurred in his town, but any minute the FBI could try to interfere and snatch it away, giving cover to any entity that might have connections above and beyond any Osborne could dream of. Maybe he shouldn't have gotten this promotion after all. Maybe Larry would have been a better choice.

A sharp tapping on his window brought him out of his morbid thoughts. He looked up and saw Rosemaria staring at him, none too happy. He rolled down the window.

"I'm sorry, Rosemaria. I am so sorry. I don't know what else to do." He stepped out of the car and faced her.

"I'm not blaming you, Darryl. I'm not. And I don't know of any other solution except for the Witness Protection Program, and if these people are tied into the government like we think they are, the girls would be even less safe with them."

Osborne took his briefcase out of the back seat. "I agree. So, what brings you here this early in the morning?"

"I have a request, Darryl."

He was wary. "And what would that be?"

"I'm not asking you to share leads with me if the lieutenant doesn't want you to, but I want your permission to poke around, and if I find something, I'll report back to you. I don't want to feel like I'm interfering. Maryanne and Tiffany mean a lot to me, and if I don't try to find the people who are after them, I won't be able to live with myself."

Osborne thought this over for less than a minute. "Okay. I don't see how it can hurt. The lieutenant doesn't need to know."

Rosemaria breathed a sigh of relief. "Thank you."

"And if we find something we think would help with what you've got going, we'll share it with you."

"I don't just want to catch the people responsible for this. I want the person who murdered Maria to pay. I want the person who choked the life out of her, and I want him in the worst way. Can you understand that? This is personal."

"I get that."

"By the way, they've moved again. And Curtis is not telling anyone where they are. I think that's best. Okay, I'm off. I have a trial tomorrow to try and put a bad guy in jail."

"Good luck." He waved and headed for the elevator.

* * * *

The courtroom was packed. The Carreras' supporters sat on the prosecution side and filled every bench. Hecht had, at most, ten supporters on his side of the courtroom, or they could have been court followers and media who happened to sit on the defense side. Hecht's wife was seated directly behind the defense table and was as previously described, thin and pale, her face devoid of expression. Rosemaria guessed that secretly she hoped Hecht would be convicted so she could finally be free of her abusive husband and find some happiness in life. Two television cameras were set up so they could monitor the front of the courtroom except the jury box. A phalanx of reporters had greeted Rosemaria and Karen when they came off the elevator. Rosemaria responded to all questions with a polite, "We're here to make sure justice is done for Ricardo Carrera."

Rosemaria and Karen sat down at the prosecutor's table. Sofia Carrera was seated directly behind them, while Ricardo waited in the witness room. Rosemaria gave her a reassuring smile. She offered a brief nod to Willeen Sarno, who barely acknowledged her existence. Hecht avoided looking in their direction. His demeanor was that of a doctor displaying his most pleasant bedside manner. He was dressed in a dark blue suit, light blue shirt, and blue tie. None of it looked expensive. He was just a man of the people who lived to serve.

"Is Lydon ready to go?" Rosemaria whispered to Karen.

"I saw him sitting in the hall on a bench, listening to his iPod, cool as a cucumber."

"All of a sudden, I'm worried about calling only four eyewitnesses. Do you think it's enough?"

"It's enough."

They brought out their laptops and arranged their papers on the desk in front of them. Rosemaria was nervous but anxious to get started. She whispered to Karen. "You'll be glad to know that after much indecision, I finally decided on the order of witnesses. Lydon will be first, to establish straight off who was the instigator of the attack and to tell how he had been warned against testifying. Next, we'll win the jury's sympathy when sweet Mary testifies about what she saw, then Palmer will add more credibility with his sterling reputation. Finally, Mangini will solidify the facts when he testifies as to whom started the attack. We'll have one of the EMTs next, then Carrera's doctor, and finally Carrera himself."

"Sounds good. No sign of Atkins," Karen said.

"He'll show up. You can bet on it."

"Will Josh be here?"

"I told him he'd make me nervous."

"You did this for a whole year in New York. You've got this."

Everyone stood as Judge Hopkins came in and then the jury. The murmuring died down, and the bailiff called the court to order. Rosemaria heard the judge ask if the defense and prosecution were ready, and she stood and said, "Yes, Your Honor." Sarno did the same.

Rosemaria knew that she couldn't mention Hecht's reputation as a bully in her opening statement. Prior bad acts couldn't be introduced unless it was as rebuttal. She knew Sarno was too smart to maintain that Hecht had a reputation as a kind and wonderful man who wouldn't dream of attacking anyone except in self-defense. But if Hecht testified and was provoked, she felt sure he would lie about never having struck anyone and describe himself as the saint of Cedars-Sinai who didn't have a violent bone in his body. (This would be her dream come true.) Then, every prior act could be described in detail by a long list of witnesses. So, in her opening statement, she merely outlined the events, described Carrera's injuries, and summarized what her witnesses had observed. She called for the jury to convict the accused of attempted murder in the brutal attack of a defenseless elderly man.

Sarno's opening was brief and devoid of passion. She asserted Hecht's innocence and claimed that evidence would show that he was the victim in this case. She mentioned his many years as a doctor, his admirable accomplishments, and his position as chief of staff at the renowned Cedars-Sinai hospital. She described him as a true healer and comforter of the sick. She didn't dare suggest he had a history as a kind human being and employer. That would open the door for Rosemaria and all her rebuttal witnesses who would testify to the contrary.

The bailiff called Henry Lydon to the stand and swore him in.

"Mr. Lydon," Rosemaria began, "what do you do for a living?"

"I own and manage The Studio restaurants on Melrose and on Ventura in Sherman Oaks."

"And are these restaurants you own successful?"

Willeen Sarno stood up. "We stipulate that this witness is a successful restaurateur."

Rosemaria appealed to the judge. "We are establishing his credibility, Your Honor."

"The witness may answer questions regarding his business acumen. Continue."

"Thank you, Your Honor." She turned back to the witness. "Is your company successful?"

"So far, so good, knock on wood. We're opening another restaurant in San Diego next year."

"And you run all of your restaurants with a hands-on approach?"

"Absolutely."

"Are you married, Mr. Lydon?"

"No, I've never been married."

"Have you ever done business with Dr. Hecht, had any personal contact with him, owed him any money, borne any kind of grudge or personal resentment, or sought revenge in any way?"

"No to all of those."

"And the only reason you are here is to testify truthfully about the brutal assault of Mr. Carrera?"

"Sarno stood. "Objection. That it was an assault has not been established."

"Sustained," the judge said.

"Has anyone tried to prevent you from testifying in this case?"

"Yes. I received a threatening phone call from a man who said that if I testified, my identity would be stolen and my personal bank accounts would be emptied."

There was a gasp from the spectators. Sarno looked startled and inadvertently looked over at her client. She quickly regained her composure and made an objection, saying there was no corroboration of this phone call.

The judge overruled her. "The jury decides if a witness's testimony is credible."

Rosemaria continued. "Do you have any idea who made this phone call?"

"No, I do not."

"Did you attempt to find out who made the call?"

"Yes, but I was not successful in tracking it down."

"You were not intimidated or frightened by the call—because here you are."

"I have the best computer people on my payroll and extensive internet protection for my business and my personal bank accounts. I'm not worried about my identity being stolen."

"Tell us what you saw the morning of the incident, Mr. Lydon."

"I live right next door to Dr. Hecht. I was pulling out of my driveway when I saw Dr. Hecht yelling at Mr. Carrera, telling him to go back inside and get his briefcase. Mr. Carrera looked like he was offering an explanation, but it only made Dr. Hecht angrier. A few more words were exchanged, then Dr. Hecht shoved Mr. Carrera to the ground. By this time, I had gotten out of my car, and I heard Mr. Carrera yelling in Spanish. The neighbor on the other side of me had come out and was watching the confrontation. We both started walking toward the two men when we saw Dr. Hecht start kicking Mr. Carrera in the head and in his stomach. Then, Mr. Mangini, who lives on the other side of Dr. Hecht, ran toward them. As soon as Dr. Hecht saw Mr. Mangini, he jumped in his car and drove off. By that time, we could hear police and ambulance sirens. After they showed up, I and some other neighbors stood and watched as they put an oxygen mask on Mr. Carrera, loaded him into the ambulance, and drove away. The police took our statements, and I got back in my car and drove to work."

"Is there any doubt in your mind that Dr. Hecht instigated the attack?"

"None whatsoever."

"Thank you, Mr. Lydon." She turned to Sarno. "Your witness."

Willeen Sarno stood up and addressed Lydon. "When you were witnessing the altercation in your car, could you hear what Mr. Carrera said to Dr. Hecht?"

"He has a heavy Spanish accent, which makes him difficult to understand, so, no, I don't know what he was saying to Dr. Hecht."

"So, you can't be sure that Mr. Carrera wasn't insulting or threatening Dr. Hecht?"

"No."

"Did Mr. Carrera seem angry at Dr. Hecht?"

"I would say annoyed and defensive."

"Your police statement said you thought Mr. Carrera became angry at some point."

"Yes, he did look angry after Dr. Hecht shoved him in the chest."

"So, as far as you know, Mr. Carrera could have said something threatening to Dr. Hecht that made him feel like he needed to defend himself."

"It's possible but not likely."

"And that is your opinion."

"Yes."

"I'm done with this witness."

Rosemaria stood up. "Redirect, Your Honor?"

"Go ahead."

"Mr. Lydon, do you know how old Mr. Carrera is?"

Sarno stood up. "Objection."

"Overruled. She asked if he knew."

"Do you know, Mr. Lydon?" Rosemaria asked again.

"I was told by you that he is sixty-eight."

"Do you know how old Dr. Hecht is?"

"When I looked up his résumé online, it said he is thirty-six."

"Thank you, Mr. Lydon."

Rosemaria addressed the judge. "I have nothing further for this witness."

The judge looked at Sarno. "Do you have any more questions?"

"No, Your Honor."

Rosemaria said, "I would like to call Mary Jacobs to the stand."

The bailiff called out, "Mary Jacobs!"

A cheerful Mary walked into the courtroom on the arm of a deputy sheriff who looked as protective of her as if she were his own dear grandmother. She approached the bench, patted the sheriff's deputy on the arm, and smiled at the judge. The bailiff helped her up on the stand and swore her in.

Rosemaria addressed Mary warmly. "Thank you for being here, Mrs. Jacobs. I know it must be difficult for you."

"Not at all, young lady. I'm happy to do my civic duty."

"Do you mind if I ask you a few personal questions first, before getting to the incident in question?"

"Ask away. I have nothing to hide."

"You're how old, Mrs. Jacobs?"

"I'm seventy-eight years old next month."

"How is your hearing and your eyesight."

"My eyesight is 20/20 after my cataract surgery last year, and as you can see, I have the best hearing aids money can buy." She pulled back her hair to show her hearing aids. She was beaming as she added, "You can test me if you wish."

"That won't be necessary, Mrs. Jacobs. We believe you," Rosemaria assured her.

Sarno looked like she wanted to say something but decided it was futile and kept silent.

"And you live alone, Mrs. Jacobs?"

"Yes. I've been a widow for twenty years now. My Albert passed away from a heart attack."

"Did you work after your husband died?"

"Oh, yes!" Her enthusiasm was evident. "We ran a design firm together that we started in our twenties. It was a passion for both of us. Ten years ago, my son suggested I retire and go on cruises and some such boring things. But I do think I might go on a photographic safari to Africa one of these days. That sounds much more interesting."

Sarno stood up. "Your Honor—"

The judge looked kindly at Mrs. Jacobs and said to Rosemaria, "I think we can get to what she saw, Counselor."

"Yes, Your Honor." Then, to Mrs. Jacobs, she said, "So, tell us what happened the morning you witnessed the attack on Mr. Carrera."

Sarno again looked like she wanted to object but refrained. Hecht was starting to lose his bedside manner.

"Well, I had opened the door and was about to take my little Pierre, my baby poodle, for a walk when I heard some terrible shouting. So, I left Pierre inside with Tanya, my housekeeper, and went outside. I saw Dr. Hecht first shove Mr. Carrera, then hit him, and Mr. Carrera fell to his knees and down to the ground. Dr. Hecht started kicking him something terrible. I didn't dare get too close, but some of the other neighbors came out of their houses and started walking toward them and looked like they were going to intervene. Before they could, that nice young man who lives with his parents ran toward Dr. Hecht and yelled something. Then, Dr. Hecht got in his car and raced off. We all stood and watched while the paramedics worked on poor Mr. Carrera and drove away with him. That's when the police started asking me what I saw, and I told them."

Rosemaria gave Mary a grateful smile. "Thank you, Mrs. Jacobs." She turned to Sarno. "Your witness."

Sarno did not treat Mary with the same consideration and kindness as Rosemaria had, which Rosemaria thought was a huge mistake. The jury was going to hate her for it, and the judge already disliked her.

"So, you say you had to have surgery on your eyes recently, and your hearing is so bad you need hearing aids."

"Yes, that's what happens when you get old."

"Is there any chance that you didn't see or hear everything that was going on between Mr. Carrera and Dr. Hecht?"

"It's possible, I suppose."

"Is it possible that you might not have heard everything that Mr. Carrera was saying to Dr. Hecht, or any kind of verbal attacks on Dr. Hecht?"

"It's true that I couldn't hear everything."

"And you didn't see the beginning of the confrontation, did you?"

"No. As I said, I was in the house when the shouting started."

"You don't know who attacked whom first, do you?"

"No, I don't."

"Thank you, Mrs. Jacobs. That will be all."

The deputy came back and helped Mary down from the stand. She leaned down and whispered to Rosemaria. "You didn't ask me about how mean he was to me and Pierre."

Rosemaria whispered back. "Maybe we can do that later."

Mary perked up at hearing that and let the deputy help her out of the courtroom.

Fredrik Palmer was the next witness, looking splendid in his expensive tailored suit, fitting for the owner of an exclusive department store chain. She established his impeccable credentials, and his testimony was the same as Mary's and Lydon's. He witnessed Hecht attacking Carrera but didn't see or hear how it started. Rosemaria was counting on Mangini to join Lydon in eliminating any doubts about that. Sarno repeated her unspoken assertion that Carrera somehow must have threated Hecht to the point where Hecht felt he needed to defend himself against this dangerous sixty-eight-year-old limo driver. Rosemaria thanked Palmer, and he stepped down. Rosemaria was about to announce her next witness when Karen whispered her name. "I just had a message from the office. Mangini is refusing to testify."

Rosemaria was startled. "Why? What happened?!"

"I don't know. He didn't give a reason. The call was made from the landline at his parents' house."

Rosemaria stepped up to the bench. "Sidebar, Your Honor?"

The judge beckoned Sarno and leaned over to hear what Rosemaria had to say.

"Could we adjourn for lunch early and extend it possibly forty-five minutes or an hour? My witness has been delayed, and it will take that long for him to get here."

"Do you have other witnesses you can call?"

"They're not here either. I told them they would be testifying after lunch."

Sarno was looking none too happy. The judge addressed her.

"What can I do, Counselor? Her witnesses are not here. I'm adjourning for one hour and forty-five minutes."

Karen was standing by the prosecution table. Rosemaria snatched up her purse and said to Karen, "Take my stuff with you, okay? I'm headed over to Mangini's. I hope he's still there!"

CHAPTER EIGHTEEN

Rosemaria raced up the 405, weaving in and out of traffic. She exited on Wilshire, headed west on San Vicente, and turned right on Carmelina. She had an idea of what this was about and could have kicked herself for not heading it off at the pass. She pulled up outside the Mangini house, ran up to the door, and knocked. The door opened, and Rosemaria brushed by a startled middle-aged maid. "I'm from the prosecutor's office. Is Sylvio here?"

Sylvio and his father appeared at the entrance of the living room. Rosemaria was in no mood for amenities. She pointed at Sylvio. "I know exactly what this is about, and you are going to testify whether you like it or not."

Mr. Mangini picked up the phone on the hall table. "I'm calling my lawyer and telling him to call the police and have you thrown out of here. How dare you invade our home like this!" He was outraged but no match for Rosemaria's wrath.

She addressed Sylvio. "If you don't come with me, I promise you that the reason your father talked you out of testifying will become public!" Mr. Mangini froze and set down the receiver.

"You were threatened, weren't you?" Rosemaria asked Mr. Mangini. "And I don't have a lot of time to get Sylvio back to the courthouse, so talk fast!"

Mr. Mangini was shocked. "How did you know about the threat?"

Rosemaria ignored the question. "You embezzled money from your law firm five years ago when you had personal financial problems. An unscheduled audit revealed your crime, and the auditors notified the prosecutor's office. But because you were able to borrow money to pay it back, no charges were made. Your partners hushed up your crime, and life went on as if nothing had happened. Now someone is threatening to expose what you did if Sylvio goes ahead and testifies."

Sylvio was mortified. "You're right. I'm sorry. I want to testify, but my dad said that if this came out and all the reporters hash over what he did, it could impact the firm. Clients would lose trust and go elsewhere."

"So, for that, you would let this monster get away with his crime?"

"You have other witnesses."

"Only one other who was there at the beginning of the attack and heard what was said."

Mr. Mangini was adamant. "He can't testify. This could ruin me."

"I'm going to tell you something, Mr. Mangini. Your son is going to testify. The only people who could have found out what you did five years ago are people who work in the prosecutor's office. If Hecht's lawyer uses this information, she will become involved in a criminal conspiracy, and the person in the prosecutor's office who threatened you will go to jail."

"You know who it is?" Mr. Mangini asked, shocked.

"I'm not at liberty to answer that. But, Sylvio, I will tell you what will happen if you don't come with me right now. I will have the judge issue a subpoena, a deputy will escort you to the courthouse, I will put you on the stand and ask you why you refused to testify, and everything that happened with your father will come out. The only chance the two of you have is to cooperate with me, and I will do everything in my power to make sure that what you did will not become public."

Sylvio looked at his father.

"Okay, you better go with her," Mangini said quietly.

"Good choice." Rosemaria headed out the door, with Sylvio right behind her. Then, she looked at her watch. She had time to spare.

* * * *

Rosemaria raced back into the courtroom, where Karen was already seated at their table. "He's here, out in the hallway. I'll explain later."

She walked over to Sarno and confronted her, saying in a hushed whisper, "This witness received another threat, probably from the same person who threatened Lydon. The threat contained confidential information that is not public. If you have been contacted by this person and reveal that confidential information here in court, I will see that you are both disbarred."

Sarno whispered back, "How dare you accuse me of conspiring with this person! We both know who it is, and I loathe him. I would not risk my career making any kind of deal with him over this client or any other." She glared at Rosemaria with as much venom as she could conjure up. She saw her client being led into the courtroom. "That's all I have to say about this, so back off!"

Sure, you weren't going to use it, Rosemaria thought as she walked back to the prosecution table. *Never crossed your mind.* Atkins probably called her or had someone else call to offer leniency for one of her other unappetizing clients and happened to mention what Sylvio's father had done five years ago. If Sylvio and his father were not sufficiently frightened into stopping Sylvio from testifying, Sarno could have used his father's crime to infer that Sylvio knew what his father did, that Sylvio is a liar who can't be trusted, and that his testimony should be discredited. It was a stretch. The judge might have stopped her in her tracks, but Sarno's defense was so weak who knew how far she'd go to raise doubt about Hecht's guilt? And if doing Atkins's dirty work could get another client off, then there was no telling what Sarno was capable of. They both hated Rosemaria to the point that they'd do it just for the heck of it. They didn't count on her having done her homework.

Sylvio took the stand, and Rosemaria asked him nothing about the threat regarding his father. She had him describe his bodybuilding awards and work as a personal trainer. When she asked him about what he had seen the morning of the attack, he was laser focused. His anger at being the target of an unfair attack and, worse, giving into it simmered beneath the surface. Rosemaria hoped he would stay calm and not allow himself to be baited by Sarno.

"So, you saw what happened from the beginning."

"Yes, I was getting in my car when I saw and heard Dr. Hecht start berating Mr. Carrera."

"Did Mr. Carrera say anything back?"

"Yes. He said that the briefcase had not been in the hall when Dr. Hecht came down, and that's why he didn't bring it out to the car."

"You could understand what Mr. Carrera was saying?"

"Every word."

"What happened next?"

"Dr. Hecht called Mr. Carrera some ugly names, and Mr. Carrera told him to stop."

What kind of names?"

"Do I have to say?"

"Yes."

"He said that Mr. Carrera was a shithead wetback, a worthless piece of crap beaner, and that he should have stayed in Mexico where he belonged."

"Did Mr. Carrera become angry at hearing these insults?"

"He looked like he was about to cry and said to himself, in Spanish, 'Stay calm, you have to keep this job, no matter what, for the sake of Sofia.' That's his wife."

"And you understand Spanish?"

"I grew up in Santa Monica. Half the guys I know at the gym are Latino."

"Then what happened?"

"Dr. Hecht shoved Mr. Carrera hard in the chest, and Mr. Carrera stumbled."

"What happened next?"

"Dr. Hecht punched him. Mr. Carrera fell on the ground, and then Dr. Hecht started kicking him hard. That's when I got out of my car, yelled at him, and ran down the sidewalk. Dr. Hecht saw me and took off."

"I don't understand. Why didn't you intervene earlier when you saw an old man being threatened?"

"The yelling only lasted a few seconds. The same with the shove and punch. When Dr. Hecht started kicking him, I ran."

"At any time during this attack, did Mr. Carrera say or do anything threatening to Dr. Hecht?"

"Nothing."

"Thank you. Your witness."

Sarno stood up. Rosemaria knew she didn't have much to work with.

"Mr. Mangini, you waited a long time to intervene. Is it possible that you thought this was not a serious argument and that Mr. Carrera might have whispered a threat that set Dr. Hecht off?"

"That's the most ludicrous question I have ever heard."

"Your Honor," Sarno almost whined.

The judge looked like he agreed with Sylvio. "Answer the question."

"No, he didn't whisper any threats to Dr. Hecht. While he was down on the ground, he was moaning and groaning, saying, 'Please stop, please stop,' in Spanish until he passed out. By that time, Dr. Hecht was gone."

Sarno looked like she wished she had never asked Sylvio the time of day. "I'm through with this witness."

As Sylvio left the stand, he cast Hecht and his lawyer a contemptuous glance, nodded at Rosemaria, and left the courtroom.

Rosemaria called one of the EMTs who had treated Carrera as her next witness. He spent several minutes describing Carrera's condition when he arrived at the scene of the assault. Then, Carrera's doctor, who had overseen the medical team in the emergency room and continued on as Carrera's chief physician, described the medical procedures they performed to save Carrera's life. Sarno's objection that showing the jury the graphic photos of Carrera's injuries was prejudicial was overruled by the judge.

Carrera was up next. He described his attack just as the other witnesses had. He explained how important this job was to him and his wife and how he was willing to put up with just about anything to keep it, but he wasn't willing to die to keep any job.

"How much longer do you have to stay in a wheelchair, Mr. Carrera?"

"Maybe two or three weeks more. I had three broken ribs and a broken arm, but the cast will have to stay on for another month."

"And that is besides a concussion and a ruptured spleen?"

"Yes. The doctors told me I was a tough old bird. They didn't think I would make it." He smiled.

"How long before you will be able to work again?"

"Six months, maybe longer, but I have disability, and Sofia works part-time for a neighbor up the street. We'll get by."

"Thank you, Mr. Carrera. Your witness."

Sarno stood up. "Are you planning on suing Dr. Hecht to get a big settlement? Is that why you provoked this attack by not bringing out his briefcase as you were supposed to do?"

The courtroom became dead silent. The most hardened courtroom watcher was stunned. Sarno realized she had finally gone too far. Later, alone in her office, drinking several shots of bourbon, she would blame it on temporary insanity caused by having the most revolting and stubborn client she had ever been forced into defending. Her astronomical retainer had blinded her to reality.

The judge was striving to hide his contempt. "Don't bother to object, Ms. Baker. You are out of order, Ms. Sarno. Next question?"

"That's all I have for this witness," she said. "If Your Honor please, I would like to confer with the prosecution before we hear any more witnesses."

The judge looked at Rosemaria. "Is that amenable to you, Ms. Baker?"

"That's fine, Judge."

* * * *

Sarno and Hecht were seated across the table from Rosemaria and Karen in the conference room down the hallway from the courtroom. Sarno had made a fool of herself from start to finish, and she knew it. Her fee for doing so must have been in the six figures, not nearly enough to willingly make herself look like a colossal idiot in front of a courtroom of spectators and the press.

"I'm asking you again," Sarno said, "will you plead this down to at-tempted voluntary manslaughter, five months to a year max?"

"Doesn't fit, because he wasn't provoked. He tried to kill Mr. Carrera, and he would have if Mr. Mangini hadn't been there. It's attempted murder."

Hecht sat and listened, stone-faced. Finally, the bully was getting his comeuppance, and there wasn't a damn thing he could do about it. Folson and Lattimer had washed their hands of him.

"How about second-degree attempted murder, five to ten?"

"I'm not making a deal, and the victim doesn't want me to. My sugges-tion to you is have your client plead guilty and throw himself on the mercy of the court. If this goes to the jury and he's found guilty, I have a long line of witnesses who will testify at sentencing as to your client's past behavior. After they get through, I guarantee he'll get life, and I will be at every parole hearing. If you plead guilty, the judge may be lenient. Who knows? But it probably won't be as bad as it will be if this goes to the jury."

Hecht finally spoke. "I'll plead guilty."

"We can still fight this," Sarno said half-heartedly.

Hecht said, "Let's get it over with."

* * * *

Hecht pleaded guilty and threw himself on the mercy of the court. Judge Hopkins asked Hecht if he had anything to say before he pronounced sentencing, but he declined. The judge then asked Mr. Carrera if he had anything to say.

But this time, it was Sofia's turn to speak. She stood up and walked to the lectern. She spoke in halting English, with her heavy Spanish accent. She looked at Hecht as she spoke.

"You are a very cruel and terrible man. My husband work hard for you, but he never good enough. You treat him like dirt. And this he put up with so we could pay our bills and I would not have to work so hard. And for that, you almost kill him. Doctors are supposed to be nice people who make people feel better. You make everybody feel bad. You think money and knowing famous people will protect you so you can do whatever you want. Now you have to pay. I do not forgive you. Maybe God will, but I look at my husband suffering, and I will never forgive. It is not possible to forgive un pedazo de scoria." She said it with such contempt there was no disguising it's meaning.

The judge waited until she was seated, then proceeded with the sentencing.

"You, Dr. Hecht, have betrayed your oath as a physician in an unconscionable manner. You pander to the rich and famous in public, but in reality, you are a monster who seeks out victims to belittle, threaten, and physically abuse. You target those who are the most vulnerable in our society. Because you have pled guilty and have accepted my sentence with no means for recourse, I use my own discretion to sentence you to second-degree attempted murder and nine years in prison without the possibility of parole. Deputies take this man away." The judge pounded his gavel. "Court's adjourned."

Rosemaria turned around to face Ricardo and Sofia Carrera. "Are you fine with the verdict?"

They nodded. "We did not want revenge, only justice and to be able to tell the truth," Ricardo said.

"My advice to you, if you're going to sue for damages, is that you wait until the publicity dies down. You have a perfect right to sue him, but after that last question by Sarno, don't give the media any reason to come at you. You deserve whatever you can get. He's very rich. The money will be there, so you have time to wait."

"Thank you. Yes, we do not want to talk to any more reporters. We want to live a quiet life and be happy."

"I can't give you any legal advice or tell you what lawyer to hire, but I'll bet Mr. Mangini would love to take your case. And there's nothing Dr. Hecht or his lawyer can do about it."

She could tell they liked the suggestion. Sofia wheeled her husband out of the courtroom as Rosemaria and Karen gathered up their things. Sarno had already left, and Hecht was going to prison where he belonged.

If Atkins had been there, she hadn't seen him, and if he witnessed the fireworks, he would have been long gone by now.

She walked out into the hallway and saw Josh standing there with a grin on his face. He walked up to her and kissed her. "Hail the dragon slayer," he whispered in her ear.

"You weren't supposed to be here," she protested.

"I've been known not to follow orders."

"Were you proud?"

"Are bears Catholic?"

My God, she loved this man! She dropped her purse and briefcase on the floor and threw her arms around him. "Yeah, they sure are. They sure are."

CHAPTER NINETEEN

The house Martin had rented in Akron that Larry had paid for was a modern two-story building. The small garden in the back was entirely fenced in, with trees shielding it from neighbors' prying eyes. Curtis had checked out the gate in the back, put a padlock on it, kept one key, and given the other one to Martin. His other four guards were encamped down the street inside another house. They were the most highly trained group he had ever been in combat with. Curtis had bought ten burner phones and distributed them. Maryanne and Tiffany could only use them to receive calls from him, Martin, or Rosemaria. They were not allowed to make calls, and every week they would destroy the old phones and receive new ones. Martin had inquired about the neighbors, and the realtor told him this was a quiet neighborhood with mostly elderly homeowners. That suited them perfectly. And yet, Curtis knew he had to have an escape plan in case they were discovered. He always had an escape plan. Escape plans were embedded in his DNA.

Curtis was contemplating his options when the girls walked into the room that had become his office. He burst out laughing when he saw them and the expressions on their faces. They had chopped each other's hair short and used the hair color he had bought them. Maryanne's hair was bright red, and Tiffany's was raven black.

"I'm not keeping this look once this is over," Tiffany said.

"I am so not a redhead," Maryanne complained. "I can't stand looking at myself in the mirror."

"The important thing is that you look different. Now, if I could just fatten you up, you'd be able to fool anybody."

"All we do is sit around and eat, so that'll happen." Maryanne thought for a second. "I'm sorry. I'm not complaining."

"It's okay. I'm used to being in war zones, sitting and waiting. Being bored was the norm. But we can't grow too complacent."

"Should we be nervous? Are you expecting something again?" Tiffany asked.

"If you mean has my radar picked up anything, no, nothing like that. You can relax. I'm looking forward to making dinner tonight. A casserole, I think."

The girls looked at each other.

At that moment, Martin came through the door with two pizza boxes.

"Yes!" Maryanne exclaimed. "Saved."

Curtis's feigned look of hurt was interrupted by his cell phone. He listened while the others set up the dining table with plates and utensils.

The look on his face told them that the news was bad. "All four of the assassins made bail. All four have disappeared."

The looks on the girls' faces caused him to quickly reassure them. "But they don't know where we are. And they are probably long gone by now."

Martin's good mood could not be dampened. He opened the pizza box and said, "Let's eat this thing and worry later."

Curtis sat down, and they all dug in. "Just one more thing. Maryanne, the prosecutor sent me booking photos of the four men. You want to have a look and tell me if you recognize anyone?" He handed her the phone, and she thumbed through the pictures. She didn't recognize any of them.

Tiffany looked at the pictures too. She pointed to one. "This guy was at the laundromat." She gave the phone back to Curtis. "Why'd they let these guys out when they know they tried to kill us?"

Curtis looked at the photo of the man she had picked out—Ralph Coulter, like the other thugs, was a hired assassin. Neither Ralph nor the others would give up until the girls were dead or their boss called them off.

"Who knows? The lawyers must've been convincing, or maybe the judge was bought off or threatened." We won't worry about that. We'll take care of ourselves. The cops in Beverly Hills will investigate all four and find out who hired them."

Martin took another piece of pizza and stuffed half of it in his mouth. "All this talk of payoffs and corruption is making me hungry. It's just more incentive to get these dirtbags."

Tiffany looked at him steadily for a few seconds. "Maybe they should get a hint where we are so you can set a trap for them."

"You mean use you girls as bait?!" Curtis said. "No way. I'm counting on the cops to find them first. I'm not risking your lives. Forget it."

"It was just a thought," Tiffany said quietly.

"If this keeps up much longer, can we consider the option?" Maryanne asked.

"Wow. You two girls have a lot of guts for two scrawny kids with crazy hair," Martin said.

"It's not that we're so brave. It's just that waiting for something horrible to happen is worse than just facing it."

"If you girls eat up one whole pizza, I'll give it some consideration," Curtis said. He regretted saying it as soon as he'd said it. The girls snatched up two pieces each and filled their mouths with pizza. He didn't tell them using them as bait would happen when hell froze over.

* * * *

Curtis was outside, at the side of the house, doing his usual rounds. It was one o'clock in the morning, and he had an hour to go before Martin relieved him. He was walking toward the back of the house when he heard the back door open. He froze and peered around the corner. He saw Tiffany standing at the edge of the porch, staring up at the sky. He was about to go to her when Maryanne came out. He quickly stepped back and pressed himself against the wall.

Tiffany heard the door close and turned to see Maryanne standing behind her. "You shouldn't be out here," Maryanne whispered. "It's not safe."

Tiffany turned away. "Sometimes I think I just want to run away and let them kill me."

Maryanne, alarmed, stepped forward and stood next to Tiffany. "Why would you say such a thing? You want to die?"

"I'm a phony, Maryanne. I act like I'm a normal person like everyone else, but I'm not. Inside I'm ugly and disgusting."

"Where is all this coming from? Why are you talking like this?"

"You know when we met up again at Lifeline House a few weeks ago?"

"Yeah."

"I had been working at El Torito for almost two years." She hesitated. "And yet, I thought I might as well earn extra money turning tricks for some slimeball agency that a friend turned me on to. I hated it, but I did it."

"Why did you?"

"Because I needed money, and that's who I am. That's who I've been since I was ten years old. Something to be used like trash and thrown away."

Maryanne sighed deeply. "And you came to Lifeline because . . . ?"

"I went to the boulevard to remind myself of where I used to be and convince myself I'm better than some crack whore with a mouth full of missing teeth standing on the corner, waiting for a car to pull up."

Maryanne said nothing. Just waited.

"I walked by Lifeline, where Rosemaria had taken me to when she first found me, and I just wanted to sit there by myself and try not to feel like those crack whores. But you know what? I am like them. How am I any better?"

The sadness Maryanne felt for Tiffany was like a heavy rock in her chest. "You know why I was there?"

"No."

"I came because, after a month of being back in LA trying to figure out how I was going to become rich and famous, and failing, I needed to remember how much worse it could be. I looked around at all the familiar places and knew a life on the streets was not for me. Yeah, my dreams may be beyond my reach, but at least I have to try."

"You have an aunt who cares for you. You have someone to go back to."

"You have people who care for you now."

"They see the outside. Inside, I'm garbage." Muffled sobs shook her body. "That's all I am or ever will be. It's too late for me."

"It's not too late, Tiff. You never had a chance. No one let you be who you really are. You can't think about yourself like that."

"I'm just like my mother. Even worse."

Maryanne shook her head and whispered harshly. "I don't know what brought this on all of a sudden, and I don't know how to convince you you're wrong, but you have to stop thinking about yourself like that. You have to stop feeling sorry for yourself." She grabbed Tiffany's arm and whispered sharply, "I mean it!"

Tiffany looked at her, surprised. Maryanne continued. "Do you know what it would do to Curtis if you took off and got killed? He'd never forgive himself. Do you want to do that to him? And Martin, and Rosemaria, what about them? You told Rosemaria you've changed, that you felt like a new person. If she heard you talk like this, she'd kick your butt around the block."

Tiffany wiped the tears from her face and drew her lips into a sharp line.

"And what about me?" Maryanne asked. "How do you think I'd feel if something happened to you? Did you ever think about that?"

Tiffany shook her head.

"Like it or not, we're in this together. We have to be strong now. Stronger than we've ever been in our whole lives. And when we get through this, we can stand up to anything and anybody, because what we're going through now is so god-awful scary and horrible that nothing will ever be as bad."

Tiffany's voice was barely audible as she said, "I don't want to let Curtis and Martin down."

"And not Rosemaria either."

"No, not Rosemaria either."

"Let's go inside, okay?"

"Okay."

Curtis, still pressed against the side of the house, heard the back door open and close. A sense of sadness enveloped him. He continued his rounds with a heavy heart. All he could do was protect them. He could never change what they'd been through.

* * * *

Josh and Rosemaria were having Starbucks coffee and rolls at their tiny dining table. Suzi was perched on Josh's shoulder.

"I'm seeing Joell today before I drive up to visit Noor and Gilbert," Josh said.

"Should I be jealous?"

"Absolutely not."

She gave him a skeptical look. "You say that with a lot of certainty."

"When I'm right, I'm right."

She leaned over and gave him a peck on the cheek, then took a bite out of her cinnamon roll.

They chewed in silence for a minute before Josh added, "I'm taking Joell to the zoo to see Sammy."

"Have you figured out a plan yet?"

"It's percolating. Nothing definitive yet."

"And Joell can help?"

"I think so."

"Then make it happen, my love."

Suzi hopped down and picked at some crumbs on the table.

Rosemaria observed her helplessly. "We have no control over our kids, you know that?"

"I'll tell them you said so."

"Tell them I'll see them soon."

He crumpled up the Starbucks bag, stood up, and threw it in the garbage pail under the sink.

"You know I'd go if I didn't have to—"

"Love means never having to give excuses." He grabbed his jacket and pulled her to her feet.

She made a face. "Don't quote that revolting, mushy movie to me. You know I hate it."

He bent her over backward so that her head almost touched the floor. He yanked her back up. "If you like it rough, lady, I can accommodate." He gave her a short but passionate kiss and was gone.

Rosemaria was trying to catch her breath when her cell phone rang. She answered, still gasping for air. "Yeah? Curtis— No, I'm fine. What's up? Are the girls all right?"

Curtis was standing in the backyard of the townhouse, his eyes searching the perimeter nonstop. "The four men who tried to kill the girls made bail. They're probably long gone by now."

"Damn! Unless they come back for another try."

"Them, or somebody else."

"Yeah, probably soon."

"If anybody comes, I'll be ready."

"Thank you, Curtis." She hung up, hating the helpless feeling that constantly nagged her.

* * * *

Joell drove her silver Mercedes CLS down the freeway. Traffic was bumper to bumper, and the air was thick with smog. Not a fun day to be driving. She glanced over at Josh in the passenger seat. "Does your wife know we're meeting like this?" she joked.

"She's a cop. She's knows everything."

"I thought she was a prosecutor now."

"She was born a cop. It's in her blood. No matter what else she does, that's who she really is."

"She sounds passionate about her work."

"You have no idea."

"But you accept that."

"We accept each other, warts and all."

"I wish I could find somebody who would accept my warts."

Josh laughed. "You're already ahead of the game. The first step is to recognize that you have them."

"Oh, yeah. That I do know. Now tell me, why are we going to the zoo today?"

"I have an idea that I want to run by you."

She took the zoo exit and headed down the two-lane road to the parking lot. "You're being very mysterious, but okay, I can wait."

Since it was Saturday, the parking lot was almost full. She pulled into a spot, placed a Ram's cap on her head, and put on a pair of large sunglasses that almost covered her entire face. They managed to walk to the ticket booth and buy their tickets with only a few surreptitious glances. *Was that Joell? Couldn't tell. Better not bother the lady.* They entered the zoo, and immediately Josh was hit with a feeling of frustration and sadness for the animals imprisoned in their cages. When he had worked there, he had shoved that feeling deep inside because he needed a job and because he had Noor's company every day. Now, the frustration that had always been there was given free reign.

Joell echoed his thoughts. "You know, I really don't like zoos. I'm only here because of you."

"We won't stay long, I promise. There's someone I want you to meet."

They walked past a few exhibits, where children were peering at the animals, excited at seeing lions and tigers close up. Neither the children nor their parents gave a thought as to why the animals were restlessly pacing back and forth or lying inert on the ground, nothing left of the wild animals they were born to be. Josh and Joell approached Sammy's enclosure, and he could see that the elephant was bobbing and moving his head nonstop. His eyes were almost closed, barely acknowledging the world around him as people stopped to stare, yell out his name, and move on, quickly bored.

For Joell, looking at him was unbearable. "I've heard about Sammy and the people who have tried to have him moved to a sanctuary, but coming to see him in person and not being able to do anything is not something I've wanted to do." She turned away from Sammy to look at Josh, visibly upset. "A lot of celebrities have been working on this for years. What more can I possibly do that they haven't done?"

Josh did not apologize for bringing her here. His opinion was that cruelty should not be hidden. It should be aired out and faced by everybody. Looking away was cowardice. He didn't say that to Joell but stood his ground against her growing irritation. He led her to a bench sheltered from the sun by trees and invited her to sit.

"I have the beginnings of a plan, Joell. It's not completely thought out yet, but I'm hoping to come up with a solution."

"Why me, Josh?"

"You have to understand something. Last weekend when I went up to see Noor—"

"And why aren't you up there now? I thought you went up every weekend."

"I am going after you drop me off at my apartment. But the point is, when Noor saw me last Saturday, she smiled!"

"Cats don't smile, Josh."

"That's what Rosemaria said, but Noor did. She wanted me to know she is happy. Even if we can't be together, she's happy being out of her prison."

"I think you're crazy as a loon, but good for Noor."

"I want the same for Sammy. Elephants, more than any other animal, need hundreds of miles to roam to be healthy and happy."

Joell sighed heavily. "So, what is this great plan of yours?"

"It's not fully formed yet, but here is the jist of it." He hesitated, not wanting her to reject it out of hand.

"Don't stop now. You got me here where I really do not want to be."

"All right, but let me finish before you say anything. I was thinking that somehow, maybe with a concert, maybe with a fundraiser, your famous friends could raise a million dollars for Sammy. Since the zoo is owned by the city, we can't buy his freedom outright, but we could go to the City Council and offer to give the million dollars to the homeless in exchange for moving Sammy to a sanctuary. Then, we could have a huge press conference and back the City Council into a corner so they'd be forced to do it."

Joell mulled this over for a minute. "That sounds like it might be doable."

"But it's not. We'd be criticized for not just handing over the money to the homeless whether or not they let Sammy go. I don't know how to get around that. Homeless advocates already criticize celebrities for coming to the City Council to testify for Sammy instead of for the homeless. And celebrities care a lot about what people think. I sure don't want to make a million-dollar donation to the zoo in return for Sammy's freedom either. I won't support a place we want to put out of business. Whenever the zoo gets grants and donations, they don't use it for the animals. They use it to turn the zoo into even more of an amusement park." Josh rubbed his forehead and grimaced. "This plan should be a win-win for both sides, but right now, it comes across as the homeless versus Sammy."

Joell took her time answering. "You're right. That's a sticking point. Maybe my PR people can come up with a solution. And I'll be thinking about it too."

"No one can know about this yet. Tell your people to keep it quiet for now."

She smiled. "I'm leaving for a tour of Europe next week. But I promise I won't forget." She looked at Sammy swaying back and forth and gazing at them through eyes that reflected his suffering and hopelessness. "Let's get him the hell out of here."

CHAPTER TWENTY

The Harland was a nicely landscaped, upper-middle-class hotel conveniently situated near Universal Studios, which made it a perfect place for families to stay who wanted to see a real Hollywood studio up close and enjoy the rides and restaurants on Universal City Walk. When Rosemaria came in the front entrance of the hotel, a tour guide was gathering a group of people and herding them out to the tour bus parked outside. Rosemaria walked up to the desk, relieved that she no longer had to hide what she was doing from Osborne. She told the clerk, a young lady who looked like she could still be in college, that she was there on behalf of the Beverly Hills Police Department. The clerk seemed slightly alarmed.

"Is everything all right?"

"I'd like to talk to the maid who cleaned up rooms on the second floor two weekends ago. Would that be possible?"

The clerk searched her computer and came up with a name. "That would be Consuelo Vargas. She should be up there now."

Rosemaria thanked the clerk and walked upstairs, noting this was the stairwell closest to the side door that led to the parking lot. So, Maryanne had probably been dragged down this stairwell. She opened the door to the second floor and walked leisurely past several rooms, then stopped in front of an open doorway to a room in the process of being cleaned. She peeked inside and called out, "Hello? Consuelo?"

A young Latina lady came out of the bathroom, somewhat concerned and nervous. "I am Lupe Saldana. Consuelo is down the hall."

"Thank you."

Rosemaria continued down to the next open door and saw a pleasantly plump Latina woman in her thirties vacuuming the room. Her back was turned. Rosemaria walked in and tapped her lightly on the shoulder. The woman, startled, turned toward Rosemaria, and turned off the vacuum cleaner. "Oh, excuse me, room not ready until one."

"I'm sorry I scared you. I'm not staying here. I just want to ask you a few questions about what happened here two weeks ago."

"Por qué?"

"I'm working with the Beverly Hills Police Department." When she saw the worried look on Consuelo's face, she hurried to say. "I'm not with ICE. I don't work for them or have anything to do with immigration." Consuelo looked somewhat relieved. "Really, I just want to ask you about someone who was staying in room 203 that weekend, someone who seemed important and had people working for him. Comprende?"

"Si, enchilada grande."

"Exactamente. You remember him?"

"No one ever saw him too good. He was very secret. His people were here all weekend, but he only come one time Saturday and late Sunday. And then that poor girl ran away from them in the parking lot. Lots of people saw that. But they moved out fast, before police come."

"After they left, did you find anything they might have left behind? Any papers that you threw away before the police came to search the room?"

"No, no papers. I tell police that. But two days later, I found calzoncillos under the bed. So sorry I not do good job cleaning."

Rosemaria was excited. "You found some boxer shorts? You think he had left them?"

"Pretty sure."

"What did you do with them? Do you still have them?"

"I wash them and give to manager to send to his address, but he had no address, so I don't know where they are."

There goes the DNA, Rosemaria thought. Well, she almost had a clue. "If you can find them, call the Beverly Hills Police Department, okay? Someone will pick them up." Maybe forensics could still find some DNA.

"Did anybody who works here see or hear anything that you think might help me figure out who this guy is?"

"Lupe heard man talk on phone for a few minutes. She was outside the door when he was talking. She had finished her floor and was helping me, like today."

They both walked back to the room where Lupe was cleaning. As soon as she saw them, she started backing away in fear.

Consuelo tried to reassure her. "Está bien. Ella no está con inmegracion."

Consuelo turned back to Rosemaria. "She frightened. Immigration came to her neighborhood in San Fernando to arrest undocumented people. She hid with some nice people till ICE gone. She came back to work today."

"Tell her she doesn't have to worry about me. I just want to ask what she might have heard two weeks ago from the people in room 203."

"Ella preguntar sobre un hombre malo," Consuelo explained to Lupe.

"He seemed like a mean man, but you didn't meet him?" Rosemaria asked Consuelo.

"His people not nice to us. She hear hombre malo yell at them sometimes."

Rosemaria addressed Lupe. "Qué le oiste decir?"

"No entendí."

"Even if you didn't understand what he was saying, was there anything about the way he talked? Cómo habló él?"

The two women exchanged words, speaking too fast for Rosemaria to understand. Consuelo turned back to Rosemaria. "She say he talk like her favorite TV show. She watch it to learn English."

"What show is that?"

They chattered fast to each other again.

"She say on channel with old shows. Very stupid people on show but funny."

Rosemaria mulled this over. *Stupid people? A lot of those on TV.* "Is it a comedy?"

Lupe told Consuelo something else in Spanish. "She say is funny. She say name is Greefis."

Greefis? Comedy named Greefis. The light went on. "You mean Griffith? Andy Griffith?"

Lupe came to life and smiled. "Si, Andy Greefis! Man in room talk like him."

"Thank you, Lupe! You have helped very much! If anybody else was working here and saw or heard anything, will you ask them to call me?" She handed Consuelo her card. "Muchas gracias, señoras."

Consuelo took the card, and they promised to call if anyone else knew anything. "No quiero ser despidida," Consuelo said.

"Don't worry, I won't let them fire you," Rosemaria said and walked toward the stairs.

As she walked down to the ground floor, she felt elated. Well, well, well, now they had confirmation that the big shot was a Southerner. That narrowed it down to O'Donnell, Maxwell, Haynes, Lorenzo, and Sackheim—unless he was a lobbyist or government official, which was entirely possible. The guy in room 203 obviously had something to hide if he didn't even allow the help to get a glimpse of him. And where did he stay when he wasn't at the Harland? Maybe at the Island under a different name? Before the murder, he obviously thought he was going to spend time with hookers at the Harland without being recognized, hence all the secrecy.

She decided she'd better call Osborne right away and tell him what she'd found out. She dialed his number as she walked out the entrance. If Lupe could listen to recordings of these guys talking, they might nail the SOB.

"Darryl, I've got good news." She told him what she had found out from Lupe. "Tell Waite to get voices off the internet of the five Southern politicians and possibly others on your radar, and send them to me so I can play them for Lupe. Oh, and Consuelo has his boxers, or will have, after she tracks them down. Somebody should come pick them up. Unfortunately, she washed them, but you never know."

"And get photos of all the male assistants who work for Haynes, O'Donnell, Maxwell, Lorenzo, and Sackheim. See if any of them match up to the police drawing we have of Maryanne's attacker."

Osborne was elated. "Will do. Good work, Rosemaria. If Lupe recognizes the voice, then all we have to do is find evidence he was at the Island when Maria was murdered and connect him to all these other crimes. Hopefully, we can match the drawing of Maryanne's attacker with one of the pictures. By the way, we all but eliminated O'Donnell, but we'll let Lupe listen to his voice as well."

"I'll leave the easy stuff to you." Rosemaria laughed. "But I'm here if you need me."

She was just about to pull out of the driveway entrance to the hotel when she saw a black van drive in. She noticed the government license plates. "No, no, no!" She did a fast U-turn in the driveway and pulled into a parking spot. Two men from the van, with the acronym ICE on the back of their shirts, were already on their way inside. She jumped out of her car and followed them. Maybe they weren't here for Lupe, but they were about to turn somebody's life into hell.

The two men got into the elevator. Rosemaria raced up the stairs to the second floor, two at a time. She arrived a few seconds after the two men. They had already seen Lupe and were about to take her into custody.

Rosemaria was horrified. "No! She hasn't done anything wrong! You can't do this."

The men from immigration ignored her and proceeded to handcuff Lupe, who was shaking and crying. Consuelo came down the hall and was shocked to see Lupe being led away.

Rosemaria followed Lupe and the men from immigration into the elevator. She pulled out her ID. "I'm from the prosecutors' office. We need this woman to testify in a case. If you want to take her later, okay, but not now. I'm talking about a murder case. We absolutely must have her stay in the country."

The men from ICE looked at her like she was a bug they wanted to stomp on. One of them said, "Not our problem."

They reached the ground floor, and Rosemaria followed them out to the van, still trying to convince them to release Lupe, who was looking at Rosemaria, her eyes imploring her to help.

"Lupe, don't give up, honey. I'll get you back. Stay positive, okay? I'll find you."

The door of the van slammed shut. The men from ICE didn't give her another look.

Rosemaria watched, helpless, as the van pulled out into the street. She pulled out her cell phone, hit the speed dial, and waited for someone to pick up. "Larry, I need a huge favor."

* * * *

Larry didn't disappoint. After he talked to Rosemaria, he immediately went into action and called his lawyer. Larry detested ICE and was infuriated that the girl had been arrested. Not only would she have been able to point them to the politician responsible for Maria's murder and the assassination attempts on Maryanne and Tiffany, but Lupe also did not deserve to be taken away and locked in a cage like a criminal. The thought of it made his blood boil. His nanny when he was growing up had come from Guatemala. She didn't have her papers, but his parents had made it possible for her to stay and become a citizen. She was like a second mother to him. He saw more of her than his mother, who spent all day at her office. The lawyer told Larry that tracking Lupe down and getting her back would be difficult, but Larry's only response was "Just do it." He didn't want to hear any excuses.

* * * *

Karen was already hard at work typing up briefs when Rosemaria arrived at her office Monday morning. She stopped typing and was about to take a bite of a scone lying on a Starbucks bag when she looked up and saw the concerned look on Rosemaria's face.

"Sorry. No time for breakfast at home."

"What?" Rosemaria noticed the pastry. "Oh. It's not that. A maid at the Harland was taken away by ICE a few minutes after I talked to her. She was terrified of this happening. I hope to God she doesn't think I had anything to do with it."

"I hate those ICE bastards."

"Larry has people who are going to try and track her down. He thinks they could intercept her while she's still at the holding center. He told his lawyer that he and Vanessa will be her sponsors so she can stay here legally."

Karen shook her head slowly. "You already told me he's really handsome, and now it turns out he's a good guy to boot. Why can't I hit the jackpot like that?"

"You're still young. He's out there somewhere. If he doesn't find you, he's an idiot. Meanwhile, keep your fingers crossed that Larry's people got to the ICE holding center while she was still there."

She held up her crossed fingers. "I'll have to type a little slower, but I will."

"I'm not sure how well I'll be able to concentrate, but tell me what I have to look forward to today. Oh, by the way, is there any word on the DL how Atkins is handling the Hecht plea and sentencing?"

"He's been ominously quiet according to all my sources."

"That doesn't bode well for me. Or maybe he's changed his ways, and I won't have to have that talk with him about how satisfying it could be to turn enemies into friends."

"That would go over like a lead balloon."

"I know. But I was going to try. Tell me what's facing me on my desk."

"There's that granny who embezzled fifty thousand dollars from the country club, where she was a receptionist. And there's another case where a cop was working undercover with a ring of teenage burglars and got caught in a sting. Claims he hadn't gone over to the dark side, but no one believes that but him."

"All right, let's deal with the granny first. See if they can meet with me here at eleven. I take it she's out on bail?"

"She is, and I'll call right now."

Rosemaria went into her office and turned on her computer. She looked at the file of the crooked granny and made a face. She didn't want to prosecute a seventy-two-year-old grandmother with four grandchildren. But apparently, she didn't want to plead guilty. She was claiming temporary insanity. How do you have temporary insanity for eight months while you're steadily stealing money from the club? Sounded like the definition of chutzpah.

* * * *

Constance Berkstadt, like Mary Jacobs, turned out to be the epitome of the sweet, lovable grandmother everyone loves and adores. Her lawyer not so much. Tovah Feinstein was a tough-looking woman in her fifties who had a gravelly voice and a face to match. "You don't have much of a case against my client. She obviously just made some mistakes with the books and can't remember doing any of it. She's almost eighty years old and can't be expected to keep track of what she did months ago."

"Excuse me," Rosemaria said, confused. "How is that temporary insanity, which is what I have in my file?"

"Don't be ridiculous," Feinstein said, her voice sharp with rebuke. "Mrs. Berkstadt said that out of confusion when she was being interrogated by police after her arrest. There was no attorney present, and she had not been Mirandized. She had no idea what she was saying."

"So that's where the insanity comes in?"

"Don't be smart, Ms. Baker. We're pleading diminished capacity and welcome the opinion of a court-appointed psychiatrist as to the validity of that diagnosis."

Rosemaria looked at Mrs. Berkstadt, who seemed to be a little confused as she listened to the conversation. "Are you okay with this defense, Mrs. Berkstadt? You could end up losing control over your assets and having your children decide what happens to you." She looked down at her file. "I see you have a son and a daughter."

"Address your comments to me, Ms. Baker," Feinstein admonished.

Rosemaria ignored her. "Mrs. Berkstadt, you have been charged with felony embezzlement because of the large amount of money you stole from the club. You are facing two to three years in jail and a substantial fine, if you are convicted. You obviously were able to fulfill your duties as reception-ist, so the diminished capacity defense has little chance of getting you off. If anyone is pressuring you to claim diminished capacity, you need to tell me."

Mrs. Berkstadt opened her mouth to say something, but Feinstein jumped in. "She has nothing to say. We'll wait for you to arrange a ses-sion with a psychiatrist." Feinstein stood up and helped Mrs. Berkstadt to her feet.

Rosemaria watched them go out the door. She knew that something was not kosher about this whole thing. She wondered if Berkstadt had assets her kids wanted to get their hands on and if they were looking to commit her to a mental hospital to get her out of the way. She walked out to Karen's desk. "Karen, I want you to ask the detective on this case to reopen the investigation. I want to know if Berkstadt's son or daughter could have had anything to do with the embezzlement and what their financial situations are. I'm also wondering what their relationship with Feinstein is, specifically if she represents them as well as their mother."

"Will do." She brushed scone crumbs off her skirt and took a sip of her coffee. "You want to set up a meeting with the undercover cop and his lawyer?"

"Yes, let's bring them in tomorrow at two. Right now, I need to go over what happened. He could be telling the truth." She walked back into her office and sat in front of the computer. She tried to familiarize herself with the undercover cop's case, but she found it difficult to concentrate when her mind was really across town wondering what was going on with Lupe and the investigation into Maria's murder. Nevertheless, this was a cop who had been accused of a crime. She knew from working undercover herself that things could get dicey. But in this case, he was working with teenage burglars. This should have been an easy assignment. She suspected greed had gotten the better of him. She concentrated on reading the report.

A twenty-five-year-old undercover cop, Bernard Kazinsky, who looked at least five years younger, was suspected of having crossed the line and voluntarily engaging in criminal activity. He was assigned to go undercover because at least two burglars had been breaking into homes in the Santa Monica, Brentwood, and Pacific Palisades areas. From the crime scene evidence, it was determined that as many as three burglars could be involved. Apparently, the burglars had a way of finding out when owners would be on vacation and knew how to get past security. One thumbprint had been found at the scene of one of the robberies that belonged to a sixteen-year-old male who was a resident of Pacific Palisades and lived with his parents, who were owners of a real estate company. His prints were available from his driver's license application. It was decided to bring in an undercover cop instead of arresting the boy to find out where the stolen goods were being fenced and who his accomplices were. They knew if the boy were arrested, his parents' lawyers would see to it that he was never charged, and at some point, the burglaries would resume.

Bernard befriended the boy on a basketball court, and in a few weeks, he had earned his trust and that of his fellow delinquents. Instead of coming forward with information in a timely manner, Bernard was suspected of taking part in the burglaries and sharing in the profits. Bernard evaded police surveillance twice when homes were burglarized, but two officers followed him to a parking lot one night, where an exchange of money and stolen goods took place with only one of the burglars present. Later, the police arrested the fence, a former security system salesman, and convinced him to cooperate for a lighter sentence. He was told to find out the burglars' next target and let the police know. The sixteen-year-old and two other boys, aged seventeen and eighteen, broke into the house, along with Bernard. They were in the process of stealing valuables and placing them in large garbage bags when the police entered the house and arrested them.

All the boys were residents of Pacific Palisades and had rich parents. The sixteen-year-old broke down and confessed to taking part in several burglaries and implicated the other two boys as well as Bernard. All the defendants pleaded guilty. The judge ordered the two juveniles to two months in a juvenile detention center and court-supervised counseling sessions. The eighteen-year-old, an adult, was sentenced to two years in state prison with possible time off for good behavior. The fence was given probation and ordered to recover all the stolen goods. Bernard insisted he was innocent and demanded a trial.

Whoa, Rosemaria thought, *that judge was not fooling around.* The juveniles could have gotten off with probation, but the judge must have taken into consideration the number of homes they had burglarized and their lack of need to steal from other people. Two years for the eighteen-year-old might also be considered severe. As for Bernard, he was clearly guilty. She usually gave cops a break when their stories didn't quite add up and chose to believe them until facts proved otherwise. But this guy didn't have a leg to stand on. He had ruined his career, and maybe his life, for a few thousand dollars.

She pondered her options. If he insisted on going to trial, she would charge him with the max. Burglary of a residence is a first-degree felony, and he could get six years if he had the misfortune to get the same judge as the other four numbskulls. If he decided to plead guilty, she would offer him one to two years with time off for good behavior. That was apt punishment for terminal stupidity, lack of morals, and betrayal of his badge.

She reached for the landline to ask Karen to remind her when Bernard and his lawyer were coming in. Her cell phone rang, and she clicked it on. "Baker." It was Consuelo. "Consuelo, have you heard from Lupe?"

Consuelo was standing outside the Harland in the parking lot. "No, no, hear nothing. So sad. Can you do anything to help?"

Rosemaria felt devastated. "I have friends working on it, Consuelo. They'll get her back." She bit her lip. "You know I had nothing to do with ICE coming, don't you?"

"We know that, señora. Don't worry. And thank you. I know you would help. I pray a lot meantime."

"You do that, Consuelo. Prayers are sometimes answered."

Rosemaria hoped this was one of those times.

CHAPTER TWENTY-ONE

O sborne was updating Larry, who was at his desk in the next cubicle. "Waite and the other computer whiz kids have been busy focusing on politicians and conference attendees who have Southern accents. They're tracking down where they were Sunday night and getting confirmations on their alibis."

Larry's desk was near Osborne's, and he followed along on his own computer. "So, we have four suspects right now who are holding public office, who come from the South, and who would have a lot to lose if some terrible secret were to be revealed."

"Yeah. We eliminated O'Donnell for sure. He's a total creep, but his alibi for Sunday night is credible. After he agreed to be questioned on Skype, I went after him pretty good until he gave me names of women he'd been with. He's a scumbag but not a murderer."

"We have Senator Maxwell from Oklahoma, Senator Haynes from Kentucky, Representative Lorenzo from Louisiana, and Representative Sackheim from Alabama." Larry was getting irritated. "Why can't we get alibis for these guys?"

"All of them and their assistants have gone back to DC. None of them want to talk about where they were Sunday night. We have no way of compelling them to talk to us, and they haven't cooperated in sending us pictures of the people who work for them. Tell Waite he'll have to dig those up."

Larry joked half-heartedly. "Let's fly to DC and put on some pressure."

"Dream on, pal." Osborne said.

"I wonder why they're trying so hard to hide their whereabouts."

"Could be meetings with people that they don't want the press or their constituents to find out about—arranging to get bribes from lobbyists, meeting with foreign governments to sell their services, deviant sexual practices, and the usual pastime for politicians with hubris, a rendezvous with a mistress. In other words, our democracy at work."

"We don't have the juice to pry those kinds of secrets out of the useless bastards. If they were here, we might have a chance."

"We need to know who wanted a favor bad enough to kill for it. Who do these politicians get money from so they'll do their dirty work? Maxwell is in bed with big oil. They always want something. Haynes gets huge amounts of money from agribusiness and coal companies. Lorenzo gets money from everybody, and Sackheim is married to drug companies. They all have the means to hire hit men and lawyers to help them get away with it."

Larry's temper was flaring. "One of these guys might very well be the one who hired thugs to kill Maryanne and Tiffany. Yet, he's going about his business, acting important, sucking up our tax dollars, and not giving a damn about anything but money and power. And he's willing to have two innocent girls killed to protect what he has. Now all four would-be hired assassins are out on bail and in the wind."

Osborne tried to calm him down. "Just because it's hard doesn't mean our tech guys won't come up with something. They'll keep trying to trace the whereabouts of the guys arrested in Ohio, and I intend to keep calling every politician on our list at their offices and at home. Maybe one of them will admit where he was Sunday night so we can narrow the field."

"Good idea. I'll do the same. I need some catharsis right now."

They both looked up phone numbers on their computer and dialed.

Osborne hesitated. "But let's not be too scary. We don't want them to run crying to the FBI."

*   *   *   *

Osborne felt like he'd been up for two days straight. His stomach was in knots, so he couldn't eat because he'd just get indigestion. Senator Maxwell's assistant had really pissed him off. She acted like Maxwell was God and had no intention of speaking with a small-town cop about a murder he knew nothing about. She refused to look at Maxwell's calendar and tell Osborne what had been on his schedule the Sunday night of the murder. After a curt goodbye, she hung up. Maxwell was the recipient of huge amounts of money from oil companies. They probably wanted permission to drill in a wildlife area where endangered species had their homes. What does it matter if a tiny little bird or gopher goes extinct if it means more money in their pockets? He never realized before how much he hated politicians. He looked at his watch—eleven o'clock. He had to go home and get some sleep. At least he lived alone and didn't have to answer to anybody.

The phone on his desk rang, so he picked it up. "Osborne here. Yeah, Waite, you working late too?"

Waite was sitting at a desk in the deserted computer room. "I'm here. Our new tech guy Elliott just went home."

"Anything?"

"Yeah, you could say that. Elliott just discovered that the lawyer who represented the would-be assassins who invaded Curtis's house used to work for the NRA."

Osborne's face lit up. "I get the feeling there's more."

"Lots more. Elliott is a veritable Sherlock Holmes of the internet. The lawyer, Sanford Keller, tried to hide his association with the NRA. He took it off his résumé online and buried that piece of choice information but not good enough to fool Elliott. Our boy then traced the bail money to another offshore account in the Philippines. The lawyer wants no one to know he works for a company in the Ukraine, which is a subsidiary of a gun manufacturing company called Dillon and Gold, owned by Harvey Dillon and Ken Gold in Austin, Texas."

Osborne sucked in his breath. "Dillon and Gold paid for the hit men's lawyer, which meant that there's a good chance they hired the hit men." *Wow! Finally!* He felt like his brain was moving in ten different directions. He knew from the conference research material that a bill to ban assault weapons was being considered in Congress. If it passed, that would hit Dillon and Gold hard. They needed to stop that bill from passing, no matter how many people they had to kill. "Keep overseeing the whiz kids. They need to look into the past and present of our suspects and see who has the most to lose by being blackmailed. Tomorrow, I'm calling Larry to tell him we're going to Austin, Texas. I'm going to call the police in Austin and fill them in. They're the ones who have to apply for an arrest warrant. I'll have to initiate extradition proceedings, should things go our way."

"What if Dillon and Gold aren't in Texas right now? They could be anywhere."

"The Austin police can check on that. If they're somewhere else, we'll go pick them up there. I don't give a damn where we have to go!"

"I think this is the first time I've ever heard you get excited, Darryl," Waite observed with a grin.

"I'll get more excited when we have those two murderers in jail. They think they're above the law."

"Maybe they are in Texas. You don't know how the police will react."

"Cops want to catch criminals. I don't care what state they work in. Have some faith, Jimmy," Osborne said, trying to convince himself.

"Just covering all the bases."

"Go home. Good work, Detective. Get some sleep."

"See you bright and early tomorrow."

"You got it." Osborne was only somewhat relieved. They had to get these guys out of Texas to Beverly Hills. It was worrisome. Waite wasn't the only one wondering if Dillon and Gold would be protected by Austin police.

* * * *

Rosemaria was at her desk finding it difficult to keep her mind on granny and junior undercover. She ran her fingers through her hair, and for one split second, she wished she lived a life of leisure like Vanessa, with nothing to do but figure out ways to spend her husband's money. She immediately shook off the thought, realizing she would be bored stiff within two hours of having nothing to do but issue orders to servants. She stared at her computer screen and jumped when her cell phone rang.

"Larry, do you have good news for me?"

"We found Lupe, and my lawyer is working on getting her released."

"Thank you!" Rosemaria leaned back in her chair and felt several pounds of stress leave her body.

"Because you witnessed the arrest and we got on it so fast, the investigators got to the ICE holding center at the same time Lupe did. My lawyer went to work, and I'm now the sponsor of a very nice lady who, hopefully, will become a citizen in a few years. As soon as she's released, I'll let you know. We'll have her listen to the recordings of the politicians ASAP."

"You are my hero."

"By the way, I wanted to ask you, will you stay with Vanessa for a couple of nights? We got a huge lead. We traced the killers' lawyer to a gun manufacturer in Austin. The owners probably paid the assassins. We need to extradite them and bring them back here. These guys will fight it like crazy, but we have probable cause, so we hope the judge in Austin will see it our way."

"That's wonderful! Good work, guys. Even if you can't get them back here now, we have a connection that you can trace to the killers."

"I hate to leave Vanessa, but I know she'll be in good hands with you. I'd rather have you there when I'm gone than somebody else. Hannah's great, but you're family, you know what I mean? She only has a couple of weeks before she's due."

Rosemaria wanted to say that babies didn't always arrive when scheduled, but she restrained herself. She didn't want him to worry when he was obviously so excited about the possibility of cracking the case wide open. "I'll take good care of her. I'll go there after work, stay all night, and in the morning, Hannah can take over. She won't be alone for a second." Hannah was Vanessa's housekeeper, who would be living in once the baby was born.

"That's a load off my mind."

"Go to Texas and bring back—who did you say?" She was so happy with the news about the case that she was having a difficult time concentrating.

"I didn't. Harvey Dillon and Ken Gold. They own Dillon and Gold Gun Manufacturers. Whatever they want from the politician must be mighty important for them to go to all this trouble."

"I'll tell Josh he has to do without me for a couple of nights, and then I'll drive to your house. Have a good trip."

"I owe you."

"You owe me nothing. You saved my life, and you saved Lupe."

She finished talking to Larry, then called Josh to tell him the news. Josh said that he was happy for Lupe and would miss Rosemaria. He would be going to an AA meeting that evening after he visited with Martha, a homeless lady who now lived in Josh's old apartment, to make sure she was all right.

Rosemaria told him to give Martha a hug from her, hung up, and got back to the business at hand. She knew what she wanted to say to the undercover cop burglar but needed to think more about the larcenous granny. She'd see them both tomorrow. Her cell phone rang, and she clicked it on.

"Baker here." It was Consuelo.

"Consuelo! You heard about Lupe?!"

"Yes, I just hear. Everyone is very happy."

"I'm so relieved we didn't let her down."

"I also have something for you. I have person for you to talk to."

"You mean about the man in room 203?"

"Yes. You come now? Jose be here soon."

Rosemaria was afraid to hope for too much. "I'll be right over, Consuelo. Thank you."

She clicked off her phone, her heart beating a little faster. Suddenly, she felt like she was chasing and not just snooping. Like old times, but without the badge.

* * * *

The Harland Hotel was jam-packed with tourists again when Rosemaria arrived. She wondered if the murderer-politician had known how crowded it was when he decided to stay here and invited prostitutes to his room. Or maybe that's what he wanted—to blend in with the crowd and be completely unnoticed. The man at the front desk told her Jose would be working in the kitchen, cleaning the floor, at this time of day, so she headed back there. She soon found him. He was a Latino man in his fifties. His dark hair had a few slivers of gray, and he was very thin. She saw him dipping a mop in a bucket of water. When he noticed her come in, he stopped what he was doing.

"Buenos días, senorita."

"Buenos días."

I'm Rosemaria. Are you Jose?"

"Yes, and I speak English. I'm a citizen now," he added proudly.

"Congratulations. I'm happy for you. I don't want to take up too much of your time, but if you could tell me what you saw?"

"Consuelo said you are interested in the men in room 203."

"That's correct."

"I saw two of them around noon that Sunday, before everything happened."

"Where were they?"

"I was called to clean up coffee that had been spilled on the floor at the souvenir stand. That's where I saw them."

"Did they buy anything?"

"They said they had to buy a present for a boy. He didn't care what it was, just something that said Hollywood or something like that. They said charge it to room 203. That's how I knew who they were."

"Can you take a minute so we can go to the souvenir stand and see if you remember what they bought?"

"We can ask the salesman to look it up."

"Thank you, Jose. I should have thought of that."

Rosemaria followed Jose to the souvenir stand by the front entrance, and Jose explained to Alfredo, the clerk, what they needed. He was happy to help and looked up the sales receipt by room number in his computer. He pointed to a revolving rack with lots of cheap souvenirs hanging from it. "That small bear that has a collar that says Hollywood on it. That's what they bought."

"Do they sell these all over town or just at this hotel?"

"Everywhere, I think, not just here."

Rosemaria's disappointment only lasted a moment.

"But we have the barcode underneath that says it comes from us."

That was better news. "And the bear would have that too?"

"Sure."

She held up her phone. "Would you print out the receipt so I can take a picture of it?"

He nodded and did as she asked. "Thank you, Alfredo. I'm going to show you both some drawings of two men. Tell me if you recognize either of them."

She brought the police drawings up on her phone, and Alfredo studied them carefully. He pointed to Maryanne's attacker. "He bought the present while the other man waited, but I don't see that one here."

"How about you, Jose?"

"Yes, I recognize this one. The one who waited isn't there."

"You've been a huge help, both of you."

She turned to go when Alfredo yelled after her. "Wouldn't you like to see the video?"

Rosemaria stopped dead in her tracks. She almost slapped her forehead with the heel of her hand like the idiot she was. "Alfredo, I think you should have my job."

A few minutes later, they were in the security office looking at videos. Emil, the aging security guard, who was more than happy to help, pulled up footage that captured images in the time frame they were looking for. They all waited patiently as they watched customers moving in and out of the shop. "That's him!" Alfredo pointed to a man at the counter. They continued to watch the video.

The man quickly peruses the merchandise and picks something off the rack that faces away from the camera. The man's back hides whatever he is buying, and there is no glimpse of it as Alfredo puts it and the receipt in a bag. The other man hangs back out of camera range.

To Rosemaria's great relief, for one moment, the man's face was visible. Now there was a chance they could make a positive ID. She dialed Osborne to tell him to have someone come to the Harland to pick up the video and the receipt. She also sent him a picture of the receipt and of the bear, including the barcode. They both agreed the bear, if they could get their hands on it, could connect them to the man in room 203 and lead them straight to whoever hired Maria's killers.

* * * *

Rosemaria and Vanessa sat in chairs opposite each other across a coffee table. They were in the living room, both enjoying a creamy chocolate dessert Hannah had whipped up for them. The living room and the whole house was decorated in the modern Scandinavian style that Vanessa loved. There were some pastel prints on the walls and lots of bookshelves with books and mementos Vanessa had collected through the years. It was homey yet elegant and not the least bit pretentious.

Vanessa apologized, saying, "I'm sorry it's not vegan. Next time, I'll tell Hannah to make sure."

Rosemaria shook her head. "Don't worry about it. I haven't acquired the willpower to resist something this good yet." Then, she thought about it and realized she already was starting to feel guilty. She had an image of Josh standing behind her shoulder, tsk, tsking. But she took another huge forkful of whatever the heck it was anyway, enjoying it immensely. "Listen, I may have an acting job for you," she said around a mouthful.

"Uh-oh, I don't like the sound of that." Vanessa was wary.

"It'll be fun. You'll be good at it."

"You want to involve me in some underhanded scheme."

"You'll be great at this. You're the only person I can ask."

Vanessa put down her plate and her fork. "Okay, lay it on me. But I'll probably say no."

Rosemaria put her plate down as well. "Okay, it's like this. There are four DC big shots that Larry and the others have homed in on. None of them will talk. They all have something to hide. But maybe, if you pretend to be working for the White House press office and call the wives to invite them to some kind of event or other, the wives will talk to you. I need to find out if one of the suspects brought back a toy bear as a present for a son or grandson."

Vanessa looked at her, astounded. "Are you out of your freaking mind?! I can't do that!"

"Why not?"

"That would be breaking some sort of law, wouldn't it? Lying about working for the White House?! They could trace it back to me, and I'd get into trouble. Larry would kill me."

"You have to say you're calling from the White House. That way they can't ignore you. I have a burner phone for you to use. I'll ask Waite to get me their home numbers, and we can do it tomorrow." She gave Vanessa the most pleading expression she could muster. "You're an actress. You'll be practicing your craft." That was a reach.

Vanessa laughed. "You are too much. But all right. I know catching these guys and protecting Maryanne and Tiffany is important to you. That's the only reason I'll do it."

Rosemaria breathed a sigh of relief. "Okay then. Tomorrow around ten. That's one o'clock back east. The suspects probably won't be home."

Vanessa picked up her plate. "I should have my head examined."

"It'll be fun. But let's keep this between you, me, and Waite. No need to get anyone's hopes up that we'll find anything."

"I don't care if you call yourself a prosecutor or not. You'll never stop being a cop."

"Just this one case, then I'm done. Really. I'm done."

CHAPTER TWENTY-TWO

J osh parked behind the liquor store as he always did when he had lived in his Hollywood apartment. He took a bag full of groceries out of the back seat and walked down the alley to Hollywood Boulevard. Unexpectedly, waves of dark memories washed over him. He shook them off and kept walking. Those bad old days were long gone. Thanks to AA and Rosemaria, life was no longer filled with the demons that had once threatened to devour him. He had faced them all. Regularly sharing in AA what had happened when he was a young man in Wisconsin had dissipated his guilt and his regrets. He had discovered that life needn't be a painful journey soaked in booze to make his daily existence bearable.

His next step would be initiating a relationship with his mother, who was still in Wisconsin. It was something he had resisted. His resentment of her was too strong. Her part in her younger son's murder by her abusive husband made it difficult for Josh to forgive her. Her weakness and cowardice gave her husband the opportunity to shoot Scott, forcing Josh to kill his father. He blamed his mother for not taking her sons away from the nightmare they had lived in. She forced her mentally handicapped son to endure years of emotional and physical abuse even after Josh thought he was safely away, living in a home with other kids like him. But Josh hadn't counted on his father bringing Scott home for a final deadly confrontation while his mother huddled on the ground in fear. He had reviled her for that his entire life.

Maybe that's what made him admire Rosemaria so much. Her feisty nature caused her to stand up to anybody anywhere and protect the ones she loved, even at the risk of her own life.

That's how a mother should be toward her children. But that was not who his mother was, and her youngest son had died because of it. Everyone had agreed that the shooting was justified, but Josh got an honorable discharge from the army and was scarred for the rest of his life. Through AA, he was dealing with his part in the horror, and the heavy load of Scott's death had almost lifted. He just needed to find a way to forgive his mother and accept her for who and what she was.

He saw Martha walking ahead of him on Hollywood Boulevard. She headed up Cherokee. Josh had turned his apartment over to the homeless woman when he moved in with Rosemaria. He still paid the rent but had obtained permission from the absentee landlord to "sublet" to Martha. The landlord didn't care who lived there as long as he got his money. When Josh first met Martha, he had no idea where she found shelter during the night. She was very secretive. Martha did not like being around most people. Jack Daniels was her best friend. Back then, she had bathed when she could sneak into a Starbucks restroom, and her clothes hung on her body in dirty tatters. For some reason, Martha had allowed Josh to befriend her. Begging on the street was a necessary evil to her. She had to do it to survive and to keep up her supply of Jack Daniels. Josh discerned her feelings about charity in a short time and had talked her into coming up to his apartment to take care of his plants. She was happy to accept a "salary" for doing that and was proud that his plants thrived under her care.

As Josh watched Martha walk ahead of him in her determined strides, it was gratifying to see how her appearance had changed since the first time he noticed her five years ago. Her hair was still gray and thinning but was clean and nicely combed. She was wearing the flowered dress and short brown jacket that Rosemaria had bought for her at the thrift store, where Martha loved to browse until a salesperson would hustle her out. The sneakers that

Josh had given her two months ago were scuffed and dirty, but she wore them every day because they were her favorite. She was willing to accept money and gifts from Josh and Rosemaria because Josh had made it clear to her that they needed her to stay in the apartment in case he ever wanted to move back in. The music business was undependable, he told her. You never knew what might happen. Until that time came, Martha was doing him a huge favor by staying there. On some level, Martha probably understood what he was really doing, but it assuaged her pride to be useful, so she tucked the truth somewhere in the back of her brain.

He caught up with her inside the entrance of the building. She was holding something level inside a shopping bag. She saw him and happily exclaimed, "Look what I found in the dumpster behind Dexter's Pizza! It's not even burned! I have to hold it like this, or all the cheese will slide to the bottom!"

Josh joined in her celebration. "That's wonderful, Martha. Not even burned. The customers must not have been happy with what they ordered."

"Yeah, and now I can heat it up and have a whole pizza for myself."

They stood waiting at the elevator that had been on the blink the entire time Josh lived there but mysteriously was now working. That was a good thing, since Martha always had a hard time walking up even one flight of stairs. The elevator door slid open, and Josh ushered Martha inside.

"I bought some groceries for you too. Everything you like."

"But nothing's as good as hot pizza!"

They arrived at the second floor and got out.

They walked down the hall to the apartment, and she opened the door without unlocking it.

He gently scolded her as he followed her inside. "I've told you to be sure and lock the door, Martha. You don't want anyone to come in here and steal from you."

She looked chastised. "I'm sorry. I'll do better."

"I'm not mad, Martha. I'm just reminding you for your own good." Josh carried the grocery bag into the kitchen and started putting the groceries away.

She carefully took the pizza out of the bag and turned on the oven. "Look, Josh, I'm using the cookie sheet you bought me." She took it out of a bottom cupboard and showed it to him proudly. "Still looks like new, huh? I'm taking good care of it." She opened the pizza box and slid the pizza onto the cookie sheet and into the oven. "It'll be ready soon. Want some?"

"No, thanks. I ate before I got here. I didn't know you were going to offer me dinner."

"Next time then?"

"For sure. Next time."

He sat on the lumpy couch, where he had sat many times writing his songs and working on his musical. He would buy her a new one as soon as she would allow it. He looked around and saw his plants were still as healthy as ever.

"You're doing a great job with the plants, Martha."

"Yes, I do have a green thumb, don't I?" She took off her jacket and hung it in the living room closet. "Want to share a little Jack with me then?"

"I don't drink anymore, Martha. I'm in AA."

She looked downcast. "Oh, that's too bad. I'm sorry."

"AA is a good thing. I've told you I'll take you with me some time."

The very thought horrified her. "Oh, no, I couldn't do that. I don't want all those people looking at me."

"That's fine. No worries. But if you ever change your mind—"

"Pizza should be hot soon." She went into the kitchen and opened the oven door. "Almost ready." She came out with a glass and a bottle of Jack Daniels. She held up the bottle, which was half full. "See, I'm taking it easy. Not too much gone."

"That's excellent, Martha. You keep on taking it easy. It'll last a long time then."

She poured herself an inch and took a sip, enjoying it immensely. "Nothing like it. Sure you don't want some?"

"I'm sure."

The pizza did smell good, even to Josh, who hadn't eaten real cheese in years. She put her glass down, went into the kitchen, brought out the pizza on a large plate, and placed it on the dining table. He watched her pick up a piece and take a bite. Her contentment as she chewed was more fulfilling to him than a roomful of people applauding his music. He wished he could convince her to come to AA, but it had to happen in her own good time, which at her age might be never. Meanwhile, she was happy and safe.

"So, Martha, have you made any friends since I saw you last?"

"No. I don't like people."

"I know that. I just thought maybe someone new had come into the neighborhood."

"They come, they go. None of my business what they do."

"Is Lenny still around?"

"I see him sometimes."

"Is his dog still with him?"

"Bob would never leave Lenny."

"I hope he has enough money to keep Bob fed."

"People like to give money to people with dogs. Sometimes cats too, but they run away."

"I admit I worry when I see people on the street with animals. I wonder if they're going to be okay."

Martha carefully lifted up another piece of pizza. "Just because they live on the street doesn't mean they don't take care of their animals," she said, a bit put off.

"I'm sorry. I'm sure that's true."

"How are Suzi and little Gilbert doing?"

"Suzi is as sassy as ever, and Gilbert is not so little anymore. He's at a sanctuary up north. I go see him and Noor every weekend."

"Is it a nice place? I wouldn't want them to be unhappy."

"It's very nice. It's run by a friend of mine. There's lots of room for them to run free."

Martha got up to put what was left of her pizza in the kitchen. Josh was tempted to help her, but he knew she liked and needed to be self-sufficient. He wandered around the room while she puttered around in the kitchen.

Her Jack Daniels stayed on the table. He heard clattering as something dropped on the floor, but he resisted going in. "Everything all right?"

"Fine, just fine. Just dropped a pot."

She came back in and slumped down on the couch. "I'm feeling a little tired, Josh. Always do after I eat. I think I'll take a bit of a rest."

"Sounds like a good idea, Martha." He picked up the bottle of Jack Daniels, took it and the glass into the kitchen, put the bottle back in the cupboard, washed the glass, and placed it on the drainboard. He saw that she had put the rest of the pizza back in the box and in the refrigerator. He leaned on the kitchen counter, remembering when he had lived there and reflecting on what had brought Martha into his life. He had reached out to her because she was fiercely independent, and he respected that. But maybe his concern for her was partly explained by his relationship with his mother. Did Josh feel like he needed to make up for the fact that he had rejected his mother after his brother's death?

He wondered what had caused Martha to be homeless. Had she fled from an abusive relationship? Had her life been destroyed by alcoholism, or had a terrible event driven her to drink? She never talked about it, and he never asked. But he knew in a crazy way he admired her.

He came out of the kitchen and saw that Martha had fallen asleep on the couch and was snoring softly. He nudged her awake. "Come on, Martha. I'll help you into the bedroom. You'll be more comfortable."

He gently helped her to her feet, and she sleepily let him guide her into the bedroom and onto the bed. He covered her with the bedspread. She closed her eyes and fell sound asleep.

He let himself out of the apartment and locked the door with his own key. He decided to take the stairs the way he had hundreds of times before. He remembered how Rosemaria had come to visit him at the apartment, and how he'd been a little ashamed of how he lived. She had never cared or noticed. That's not who she was. The police had considered him a prime murder suspect, but as soon as she had seen him with Noor, when Noor was sick and had almost died, she dismissed that possibility. She saw his heart like no one else.

He went out the front door to go back to his car but decided he wanted to walk around his old neighborhood for a few minutes. Something was percolating in his brain and needed time to bubble up to the surface. He walked along Hollywood Boulevard and saw that new stores and cafés had sprung up since he had walked here before. There were still some shabby buildings, where the homeless found refuge in their doorways. But they needed homes, not doorways. He saw the mission, where Pastor Diehl fed and clothed a lot of the homeless in the area. Even Martha trusted this man. He never turned down anyone who needed help, and he didn't talk down to them.

Josh stopped at a kiosk and bought a cup of coffee. He stood and sipped, looking up and down the street, lost in thought. He had the germ of an idea. He needed to talk to Joell. He wondered if he could get through to her in Berlin now. He had no idea what the time was there. If she answered, she answered. He dialed her cell phone. After he talked to her, he would head to his AA meeting at the Presbyterian church nearby.

CHAPTER TWENTY-THREE

Atkins sat at his desk, unable to concentrate on the case he was taking to court that day. He had picked the easy ones for himself. Cases he was sure to win. The first one was this morning—a stubborn defendant who didn't have a chance in hell of getting off. An eyewitness with a smartphone camera had caught him in the act of stealing his neighbor's dog out of his doghouse and driving off with him. A neighbor was just getting home from a late shift at work and saw him put the dog in the car. The defendant said he took him to the shelter, but there was no record of it. The dog had disappeared, probably thrown out of the car somewhere. When the dog owner confronted the defendant, the defendant took a swing at him and knocked him to the ground. Two witnesses saw it happen. The idiot should have pleaded out, but he wanted to go to trial and complain about how the dog's barking was keeping him up and destroying his health, blah, blah, blah. A rinky-dink case to be sure, but a sure win, and the animal rights people would love him for it. Atkins needed easy cases for his win percentage. He would use these sure wins to build up his percentage rate to the point where they might let him transfer downtown.

Almost as important was his determination to destroy that Baker woman. She not only treated him with overt disrespect, but she also had humiliated him in front of Lattimer and his uncle. Now Lattimer avoided him, and his uncle wouldn't take his calls. He needed to explain and tell them Hecht's conviction was not his fault. But, of course, they wanted to pretend they had never heard Hecht's name, as if the man had never given his uncle hundreds of thousands of dollars for his election campaigns. He would get his revenge, although he never thought of it that way. It would be pure justice to ruin Baker's career. With someone as shifty as her, who went her own way whenever she felt like it, he would find something to use against her. He was certain of that. Just visualizing her disgrace brightened his day. He collected his files and headed to the courtroom and another sure win.

As Rosemaria stepped off the elevator on the way to her office, she saw Atkins walking toward her to the elevators. She forced a smile, but he ignored her as if she weren't there. Good. She wouldn't have to make polite conversation.

Karen wasn't at her desk, but her computer was on, and Rosemaria's office was unlocked, so she knew Karen was here. Rosemaria put her briefcase on her desk and stood at the window, looking out at the view of the parking lot, the 405, and beyond. She had called Waite first thing, and he had quickly given her the phone numbers she asked for. It only took a minute for him to track them down on the computer. He asked no questions, so she never had to avoid telling him anything she didn't want him to know. He was good that way. Who knows? Maybe Vanessa could dig up something that would narrow down the list of suspects. But first, she had to deal with the undercover cop case. How could Kazinksy possibly explain away what he had done? Well, she'd find out soon enough.

She looked up and saw Karen standing in the doorway of her office. Rosemaria had barely said hi when Karen beckoned her to come out of her office. Surprised, she stepped out. Karen shut the door behind her. She looked at Karen questioningly. "What's wrong?"

Karen was not happy. "You know Tariq, the intern who used to work for Summers, then briefly for O'Malley, and now works for Reid Smith?"

That reminded Rosemaria she hadn't called O'Malley in a week. "Shit! How is O'Malley? Is he home yet? I need to call him."

"He's home and doing fine. Never mind that. Tariq, like everybody else, hates Atkins. Another intern told him that he overheard Atkins hiring someone to put a tail on you."

Rosemaria shook her head slowly. "Wait a minute. Why would he do that? That's a little extreme even for someone as demented as he is."

"He hates your guts. He's obviously hoping to find something to use against you. He's probably heard that you're involved in the investigation of Maria's murder and have been to BHPD more than once. He wants to find dirt on you. He wants to get you fired for not focusing on your job, or worse. He might even make up something."

"I'm doing good work. It'll never happen."

"You need to take this seriously, boss. Stay away from BHPD and just do your job here. Whatever you do with those detectives, be discreet. And I'm going to have your office searched for bugs. I'm not taking any chances on losing the best boss I ever had."

"Okay, if you think it's necessary. Really? I'm your best boss?"

"Are you kidding? Coming into work used to be nothing but drudgery. I could hardly wait to get the day over with. Now, I never know what to expect."

"I guess that's a good thing. I didn't mean for it to be that way."

Rosemaria opened the door to her office, and Karen spoke as if nothing untoward had happened. "Is there anything you want me to work on before the cop and his lawyer come in at one?"

Rosemaria knew she better not say too much. "I have to go out for a while. I'll be back before one."

Karen rolled her eyes and shook her head, wanting to ask, "Now what?" Instead, she complied sweetly for the sake of anyone who might be listening. "Yes, ma'am."

* * * *

"Okay, so let me get this straight." Vanessa sat at a small desk in her office, located next to her bedroom. She was looking at a piece of paper Rosemaria had handed her. "Maxwell is from Oklahoma and has two sons, one in grade school and one in high school. Haynes's first wife died after insurgents in Cambodia murdered her and their two children." Vanessa shuddered. "How horrible for him."

"Keep going. I want to get started."

"Okay, okay. Don't act like a pushy director. Haynes remarried and has a six-year-old boy. Lorenzo is married, has one son who is a doctor, and a grandson who is three. Maxwell is a widower with no children, and Sackheim is older than dirt." Vanessa looked up. "I take it you made these notes?"

"He's almost eighty," Rosemaria explained. "He has children that are long gone. Even his grandkids are old. I think we can forget him."

"Okay, so I take it you are looking for whoever may have bought that bear for a small child and who may or may not have someone working for him named Junior or Julia or something close to that. I can't out and out ask, you know."

"Try anyway."

"Why not just look up kids and grandkids on the internet?"

"Because it could be a friend's kid or a neighbor's that doesn't show any connection to the senator on the internet."

"Okay." Vanessa sighed. She picked up the phone and started dialing while Rosemaria roamed around the room. She noticed a few scripts next to the books on the bookshelves. She fully expected Vanessa to go back to acting once her child was in school. But acting was definitely third on her list of passions now.

Vanessa spoke authoritatively into the phone. Rosemaria was impressed by her tone. "Hello, this is Meg O'Brien calling from the White House. Is Mrs. Maxwell there? Yes, I can hold." She nodded excitedly at Rosemaria and remembered to put the phone on speaker. "Mrs. Maxwell? This is Meg O'Brien calling on behalf of the banquet manager here at the White House. We are planning on arranging a luncheon for congressional wives toward the end of next month. Will you be available at that time? We're trying to figure out the best time so as many wives as possible can attend."

Mrs. Maxwell was standing in her large white kitchen, speaking on the landline and holding a coffee cup while the maid cleared away some dishes. "Well, I'm not sure. I usually don't plan that far ahead."

"Yes, I imagine you like to travel with your husband when he goes on trips."

"Actually, I prefer staying home with the children, but yes, at times I have to go with him."

Vanessa chuckled. "Well, at least he must bring you and the children presents from his trips, since he has to be away from home so much."

Mrs. Maxwell sounded uneasy. "He only travels when he has too. He doesn't have to buy us presents for just doing his job."

Vanessa made a face, then recovered. "And I know he does do a wonderful job for his constituents."

"What did you say your name was again?"

"Meg O'Brien. I can call back in a week and see if you've finalized any plans for the end of next month."

Mrs. Maxwell was interrupted by the maid telling her someone was at the door. "Yes, yes, you can call me back then." She hung up.

Vanessa clicked off the cell phone. She laughed. "Ah! That did not go well! Too obvious!"

Rosemaria disagreed. "Mrs. Maxwell sounds like a straight shooter. She puts her kids ahead of everything else. She doesn't guilt-trip her husband, and she doesn't expect presents for her or her children. I think we can cross her off our list."

"This doesn't seem very scientific."

"We have to let Waite and the others find out who's the most blackmailable. We'll concentrate on the next one."

Vanessa dialed the phone and pressed the speaker button. She heard a young voice say, "Lorenzo residence. Mark speaking."

"Hello, Mrs. Lorenzo, please. I'm calling from the White House."

Mark said, "Please hold."

"Of course."

Mrs. Lorenzo was in her bedroom putting a touch of makeup on her face in front of a dressing table mirror when a little boy came into the bedroom. "Grandma, phone for you." She smiled at her grandson, who gave her a hug before running out. She looked after him fondly. Mrs. Lorenzo was in her sixties, physically fit, and gray-haired. She was dressed in comfortable pants and a loose top. Nothing about her appearance indicated that she was the wife of a man who had been a distinguished member of Congress for several decades. She was as unpretentious as they come.

She picked up the receiver of the phone on the bedstand. "Hello. This is Miriam Lorenzo."

Vanessa heard the warmth in Miriam's voice and mirrored hers. "Hello, Mrs. Lorenzo. This is Meg O'Brien calling on behalf of the banquet manager in the White House. We're planning a little luncheon here for some of the congressional wives, and I'm wondering if you'll be available toward the end of next month. We haven't nailed down the date yet because we want to see who can come."

"Oh dear. I'm not sure I can. I'm not much for social activities anymore. I'm a retired schoolteacher. Sometimes I'll get it into my head to go someplace and I go. But for not too long because I don't want to be away from my grandson for more than a few days. He visits me whenever I can talk his mother into letting him come. We both enjoy that. Me and my grandson, that is. I tend to be a little more lenient than his mother."

Vanessa lowered her voice confidentially. "My grandmother did the same thing with me. I got away with murder at her house. It drove my mom crazy!"

"That's the benefit of being grandparents. We can spoil them rotten but don't have to discipline. I always hated that with my son. I never allowed him to be spanked, of course. That's just plain wrong."

"Is your son in politics too?"

"Oh, no. I think my husband wanted him named after him so he could continue the legacy, but my son never enjoyed that life. He's a doctor. They live close by though."

Rosemaria passed a note to Vanessa, who read it and nodded.

"Your grandson said his name is Mark. So, is he Mark Lorenzo Jr.?"

"Oh, no, that's my son. My grandson is the third, but we don't call him that, of course. Too pretentious."

"I imagine your husband spoils Mark too. My grandfather bought me anything I wanted, which aggravated my parents to no end."

"He brings Mark gifts from his trips, all kinds of toys and games. I can't even keep track of it all. We keep them here so we won't get in trouble with his parents."

Rosemaria signaled with her hands for Vanessa to keep going on this track.

"I always loved when my grandpa gave me bears. I used to collect them. I must have had dozens of them."

"Yes, Mark loves those too. But I have to hang up now, young lady. It's been lovely talking to you. Maybe I can call you back later when I can tell you for sure about the luncheon."

"Oh, that's okay, Mrs. Lorenzo. I can call you back. Don't worry about it."

"It sounds like it might be fun to see old friends. I'll make an effort to be available."

"Very good. Goodbye, Mrs. Lorenzo."

"Goodbye."

Vanessa breathed a sigh of relief. "I hated lying to that nice old lady. Did you get anything out of that?"

"Well, she has a son called Junior, which Maryanne might have interpreted as Julie. But he's a doctor, and I can't see him involved in covering up his father's peccadillos. They sound like wonderful grandparents, but both he and Maxwell don't want anybody to know what they were up to that Sunday night. And I still don't know why. I hope Lorenzo isn't cheating on that wonderful woman."

Rosemaria pointed to the list. "One more." While Vanessa dialed, Rosemaria asked, "Did your grandparents really give you bears?"

"My grandparents made it clear they had no intention of becoming babysitters when they retired. They traveled the world and never brought me back a thing." She smiled. "But I got over it."

"Hello, this is Meg O'Brien. May I please speak with Mrs. Haynes?" Vanessa hit the speaker button.

A gruff voice said, "This is she. Who's calling?"

Vanessa went into her spiel. Mrs. Haynes was less than impressed.

"I don't know why you're calling me. I never go to those things."

Rosemaria thought she sounded like she was half in the bag at eleven o'clock in the morning. This one could prove productive. She indicated to Vanessa to go for it.

"I'm so sorry you feel that way. Have you had bad experiences at the White House?"

Mrs. Haynes was outside in a lounge chair by the pool, a bloody Mary in her hand. She was reasonably attractive and looked to be about thirty-five. She wore shorts and a halter top and had her blond hair tied up in a messy ponytail. "It has nothing to do with the White House. I'm just not into politics or hanging out with other politicians' wives. They bore the hell out of me." She took another sip of her bloody Mary.

"I can totally understand that, Mrs. Haynes. All the social functions you have to attend must get tedious."

"What are you saying that for? You're the one arranging them."

"I'm just saying I get where you're coming from. Every day I deal with politicians and see how they're totally involved with their work and have little time for their families."

"You can say that again. Make that no time. He has no time for me or my son. Couldn't care less about either one of us."

"I hear ya. Some of the other wives I talk to say the same thing. The husbands ignore them and try to make up for it with presents."

"Oh, yeah. But not for me, for the kid. Half the time he forgets to give them to him."

"That's a shame. You'd think with what happened to his first wife and kids that he'd value you all the more."

Mrs. Haynes snorted. "Are you kidding? He didn't have much time for his other family either. But he sure plays up what happened to them whenever he wants the sympathy vote. You'd think he practically lived at their grave sites. Believe me, he couldn't care less."

"Yes, I heard they were brutally killed in Cambodia. Terrible tragedy."

Mrs. Haynes wrinkled up her brow. "Why are you so interested in me? You sound like a reporter. You're not, are you?"

"Absolutely not. I'm just a scheduler here in the banquet room. I don't know how much longer I can stand it though. Too much intrigue and people who think they're better than everybody else. Don't tell anybody I said that though."

Mrs. Haynes took a big gulp of her bloody Mary. "You forgot cheating." Her words were now becoming slurred. "Cheating makes the world go round in this stinking town. And my husband does it better than anybody. Very sneaky. But I know. I know only too well."

"Well, I don't want to intrude on your privacy much longer. Should I call you back in a week or two to see if you've changed your mind?"

"With any luck, I won't be here." And she hung up.

Rosemaria and Vanessa couldn't believe what they'd just heard. Haynes just moved to the top of their suspect list.

Vanessa handed the burner phone back to Rosemaria. "Well, that was fun. I think she hates him."

"Understatement of the century. He's mean, he cheats, he couldn't care less about his son, and if the man who bought the bear turns out to be his assistant, we've nailed him. The only downside is that the whiz kids haven't found anything blackmailable. He must be hiding his mistresses pretty well, and these days, that's not much of a reason to kill somebody."

"Did I do good?"

"You were Emmy-award good. I might hire you again."

"Oh, please don't. I think I'll be busy that day."

"Be that way. I'm going to call Curtis later and fill him in. He wants me to keep him updated. He says he has time to be on the computer looking up stuff."

"I hope I helped."

"You were magnificent."

She picked up her purse, bent down to give Vanessa a peck on the cheek, and headed out the door. "See you tonight." And she was gone.

Vanessa buzzed the kitchen. "Hannah, could you bring me some chocolate chip cookies and a jar of martini olives? I'm in need of sustenance."

Rosemaria breezed out the front door of Vanessa's house, started down the stairs, and stopped for a moment to appreciate the lush green hillsides of Beverly Hills. She walked to her car parked in the driveway, clicked open her car door, then looked back at the sleek modern structure of Vanessa's house, admiring the straight lines and the minimalist landscaping. Very Vanessa. As Rosemaria opened her car door, she thought about how she'd like her own dream house to look—maybe a Cape Cod with white shingles, surrounded by flowering bushes everywhere in riotous colors. And maybe a view of the ocean. She got in her car, visualizing how she'd decorate the interior. All in good time. Right now, she had more important things on her mind.

CHAPTER TWENTY-FOUR

Because it was lunchtime, Subway was jam-packed. It took forever for Rosemaria to work her way to the head of the line and order a sandwich for Karen and herself. As soon as she paid, she grabbed her order and ran. She had called Curtis after she left Vanessa's house and filled him in. She told him the names of the three politicians who might be prime suspects, with Haynes at the top of the list. She suggested he dig into what happened in Cambodia to his family. Mrs. Haynes seemed to think something was a little off there. But she might be prejudiced because she obviously loathes the man. Curtis already knew about Dillon and Gold and their connection to the lawyer who had gotten the four assassins out of jail. She asked about the girls and briefly talked to each of them. They seemed subdued but not frightened. God willing, Curtis would keep them safe.

When Karen saw the sandwich bag, she almost snatched it out of Rosemaria's hands. "I'm starving! I didn't have a chance to eat yet."

"Take it easy, girl. You need to start getting up earlier and make time for breakfast." She handed Karen her sandwich. "You'll have to get coffee out of the lunchroom. Will you get me some too?"

Karen opened the sandwich wrapping and took a bite. She spoke with a mouthful. "Just to help me make it to the lunchroom."

Rosemaria walked into her office and put her purse in a drawer in the filing cabinet. She had volunteered to pick up lunch for herself and Karen and didn't mind treating her to a meal as often as she would accept it. For one thing, Karen worked her tail off and deserved to be waited on, and for another, this morning Karen had told her she had a friend from a security firm come over and check Rosemaria's office for bugs. He found nothing but said he would sweep the room regularly for her. He also replaced the lock and gave Karen the only two keys. Rosemaria now felt reasonably secure from Atkins's prying eyes and ears.

After her meeting with Kazinsky, she intended to make plans to turn Atkins's schemes right back on him. Meanwhile, she would check what was happening with her other cases as she ate lunch. Yes, she did have a flair for doing several things at the same time. Too bad Atkins wouldn't be around long enough to fully appreciate her talents.

* * * *

Maryanne and Tiffany had separate bedrooms in the house, but they invariably found themselves mostly hanging out together in Maryanne's room. It had a bigger TV and the Netflix/DVD box, and they liked having their pick of movies. Most of the Netflix lineup consisted of war, violence, murder, and revenge, which had now become a part of their own lives. Hiding from killers had become normal.

Maryanne was browsing on Netflix, flicking from one movie to the next. She stopped and looked at Tiffany, who was slumped in an easy chair looking listless and bored. "Do you think if I asked Curtis, he would let us go out somewhere for an hour or two?"

"I'd love to get out of here," Tiffany said, "but where would we go?"

"Let's go ask Curtis. Maybe he can think of a place. Somewhere enclosed but not inside. Somewhere safe but not confined."

"You're talking like him."

"I hope so."

The girls walked downstairs and knocked on Curtis's door. They heard him say, "Come in," and went inside.

He looked up from his computer. "What can I do for you girls?"

Maryanne ran her idea past him.

Curtis looked thoughtful. "Believe it or not, I've been thinking it was time to let you two get some breathing space. Safe but not confined, huh? I may know just the place. Let me set some things up, and we'll see if we can't make it happen."

Tiffany breathed a sigh of relief. "Thanks, Curtis. We're pretty much going out of our minds."

"Will we have the whole contingent with us?"

"Of course. But you won't see them."

The girls were on their way out the door when Curtis asked, "Whose turn is it to make dinner tonight?"

In unison, they both said, "Yours!"

"Already? Okay, I'm sure I can whip up something."

Maryanne and Tiffany looked at each other. "Maybe not beans again?"

"But I'm so good at opening a can. It's my specialty."

"We'll go see what there is in the kitchen. Maybe we can put something together and relieve you of KP duty."

"Sucking up to your superior officer and getting me to ease up on the rules. But it's working. You definitely get to go out today."

The girls pumped their arms. "Yes!" And they left him to his laptop.

Curtis's computer search on the politicians had yielded little helpful information. Maxwell was pretty much bought and paid for by oil companies and had been for decades. That was nothing new. They were looking to drill in the Arctic wildlife area and had been pushing for that for years, but lawsuits by environmental organizations had stopped them cold. He couldn't see any bills coming up in Congress to make it any easier for them. If there were, Maxwell wouldn't be risking much voting for it. Drilling in pristine areas wasn't much of a concern in Oklahoma. Any kind of hard-nosed tactics weren't necessary for him to do the bidding of oil companies. But why wouldn't he agree to be interviewed by the cops and tell them where he was the Sunday night of the murder? He had heard of upstanding citizens being into all kinds of kinky situations, but digging that up would be difficult. There were so many avenues of possibilities Curtis didn't have time to try and find it.

Lorenzo got his main money from gun manufacturers. They always had bills in Congress—more, more, and more guns, that was their motto. There was a bill in committee to ban assault rifles and tighten up regulations on handguns that the NRA was having apoplexy over. Over their dead bodies would that pass. But Lorenzo was a Republican from Louisiana. They didn't need to strong-arm him to vote against it. Lorenzo was a genteel old family man. Weird sex? A mistress? He didn't think so. But why avoid the cops? You never knew about these people.

And that led him to Senator Haynes. As a Democrat, he was in favor of the assault rifle ban. It would destroy his career if he voted against it. Only some hard-core blackmail could make him go against his party. He had a wife who hated him, a kid he hardly ever saw, and he fooled around—but was it with prostitutes, or was he simply having affairs? Rosemaria said she couldn't tell which from what his wife said. But what really interested Curtis was finding out what actually happened in Cambodia. He had read the newspaper reports about the tragedy, and every one of them made him out to be a hero.

Apparently, Haynes was filming a TV interview when Cambodian rebels attacked tourist spots in Phnom Penh. They had been breaking into restaurants and stores, killing and looting, and coming close to the hotel where Haynes was staying. When the killing began, the army assumed that they could stop the rebels easily, so they didn't raise the alarm in time for people to run for safety. Haynes's wife and small son and daughter were having lunch in a restaurant several blocks from the hotel. As soon as Haynes was told about the violence, he ended the interview, ran down to the lobby, and tried to force his way out the front entrance. Security guards stopped him. They told him a helicopter had landed on the roof to fly him and other American officials to safety. Haynes had only minutes to get up to the roof, but he refused to go. He had to be carried by security guards and shoved onto the helicopter. He was devastated at leaving his family behind. The army managed to quell the violence before the insurgents could attack the hotel, but Haynes's family and everyone who had been in that restaurant were slaughtered.

From the way his wife had described Haynes to Vanessa, he didn't seem like the heroic type to Curtis. He wondered what had really happened. He searched for an hour but came up with nothing. He contacted a friend at Veterans for Peace. Those guys had the connections in the military to find out anything.

After speaking to his friend and to the other bodyguards, Curtis told the girls they were going on a little field trip. He led them out the side door and to the SUV that was pulled into the backyard. Thick flowering bushes hid the SUV from the street. The girls were so eager to end their confinement, they were practically quivering with anticipation. Curtis hadn't told them where they were going. Martin was in the driver's seat of the SUV, and Curtis had both girls get in the back. He told them to buckle up and keep their heads down. Not a word was exchanged as Martin drove for approximately half an hour and then stopped.

"You can sit up now," Curtis said.

Maryanne and Tiffany did as they were told and peered out at what looked like a small, abandoned school surrounded by woods.

Maryanne was apprehensive. "What are we doing here?"

"Follow me," Curtis said.

Martin stayed with the car.

Maryanne and Tiffany exchanged nervous glances but followed Curtis into the abandoned building. Huge chunks of plaster and paint were hanging off the walls. Broken chairs, desks, and tables were strewn about the hallways. It felt as spooky as a horror movie.

Curtis didn't look around at the chaos. He led them forward to an exit door and out into a small field.

The girls followed Curtis's gaze, and broad smiles lit up their faces. Facing them at the far end of the field were several shooting range targets.

Curtis turned to the girls and gestured at a couple of large metal cases on the ground in front of them. "Ready to learn how to shoot?" "Yes!" they said in unison. "We're ready!"

* * * *

Rosemaria studied the two people who sat across from her in her office. Bernard Kazinsky was nervous, not a good trait to have when you work undercover. His lawyer, Alvin Mailer, was all business. Bernard looked like he was no more than nineteen. He was wearing a T-shirt with a logo of a rock group she had never heard of, was tall and lanky, and probably had played basketball in high school. Rosemaria made a mental note of the fact that he also had well-defined muscles, which meant he probably worked out at a gym. Mailer was a minuscule man with a high-pitched voice and pasty complexion. He looked at Rosemaria and asserted, as forcefully as he could manage, "You have no case against my client. The only witnesses you have are the three boys who were involved in burglarizing several homes. They are the boys whom Officer Kazinsky was assigned to find. His job was to infiltrate their gang and bring them to justice. This is exactly what Officer Kazinsky did. You need to drop the charges against my client, or we will file charges against you for prosecutorial misconduct."

The last statement made Rosemaria's eyes narrow. "Prosecutorial misconduct? How dare you threaten me. You don't have a leg to stand on, and you know it. Kazinsky refused to pass on information regarding the gang members to the police, he took part in a burglary and was caught red-handed in a sting. The police brought this case to our office, Mr. Mailer. I do not pick and choose whom I get to prosecute. Kazinsky is a dirty cop and a discredit to the Santa Monica Police Department. They want his head on a platter, and after what you just accused me of, I will do everything in my power to give them exactly what they want. I'll see you in court." She stared them down, making it clear she wanted the two of them out of her office.

Bernard panicked. "Wait a minute." He cast anxious looks at his lawyer. "Don't I get to say anything?"

Mailer tried to shut him up. "No. Anything you tell her she can use against you."

"But I'm innocent. I want to talk to her."

"I'm advising you not to talk, Mr. Kazinsky."

"I don't care. Ms. Baker, will you just listen to me for a minute?"

Rosemaria stood up. "Excuse me for a moment. I haven't had a break in a while. I have to go powder my nose. I'll be right back."

Kazinsky was taken aback, threatening to pout and whine. Mailer looked annoyed but shrugged, saying, "What the hell."

Rosemaria walked up to Karen's desk, bent down, and whispered, "Call Tariq. When these two guys come out, I want Tariq on their tail all the way to their car. I don't want to know what they say. That would be privileged. I just want to know Kazinsky's attitude. Make sure Tariq knows that."

"Got it. Kazinsky's attitude."

"I'm actually in the ladies room right now."

"Would you like to make small talk while you're in there?"

"Seen any good movies lately?" Rosemaria asked.

"I'm waiting for a good thriller with Leonardo DiCaprio."

"He was fabulous in *Once Upon a Time in Hollywood*."

"Invite him to Josh's premiere, and I'll come."

"I'll ask Ken. Maybe he can arrange for you to sit next to Leonardo. Back to the brutal interrogation."

Rosemaria went back into her office and looked at her watch as she sat down. "You're on the clock, Bernard."

Bernard ran his fingers through his thick dark hair. In Rosemaria's opinion, this guy had no business going undercover. He was a child with a badge.

"Okay, so this was my first undercover job, okay? Maybe I didn't know exactly what I was doing or what the procedure was, but I knew I would be able to gain their trust." He looked at Rosemaria for some sort of affirmation, but she was hard to read. "So, I said I'd do it. The kid whose fingerprints they had, Conner, played pickup games on a court in Santa Monica, and since I played in high school and was pretty good, they let me play. It took a while, but when I kept helping Conner and his team win, he started to trust me. We hung out for a while. I let him know that my family was hard up, that I was always looking for extra work apart from my regular job as a welder, and that I'd been laid off a week ago. After talking to the other guys, he decided to let me in on what they've been doing. I went with them on two jobs, and they knew there was no doubt they could trust me."

Rosemaria was implacable. "Why didn't you let your contact at the Santa Monica PD know what was going on? Why didn't you give him the names of the other boys?"

Kazinsky agonized over the question and squirmed in his seat. "I know I should have done that, but I really wanted to wait until I could give them the whole case, you know. I wanted to wrap the whole thing up. I wanted the names of all the fences because they always used different ones, and I wanted the name of the security guy too. They hadn't told me that yet."

"So, you wanted to play the hero, is that it?"

"Well, yeah, you could say that. I was so close. They didn't have to arrest me like I was some sort of criminal. When they handcuffed me, I thought it was just some kind of show not to blow my cover, but then they accused me of taking part in the crimes. Unbelievable."

"So, this is all just a mistake, is that it?"

"Absolutely. You believe me, don't you? You used to be a cop. You used to work undercover."

"You found that out about me, huh?"

"Well, yeah."

Mailer had heard enough. "So, what do you say, Ms. Baker? Are you going to drop the charges?"

Rosemaria pretended to mull it over. "Let me think about it, okay? I'll check into a few things and get back to you."

They all stood up and shook hands. Kazinsky looked relieved. "Thank you for listening to me, Ms. Baker."

She smiled. "No problem. We'll be talking in a couple of days."

The two left, and after saying goodbye and thank you to Karen, they headed for the elevators.

"Is Tariq on their tail?"

"He's on it."

She went back into her office to call Waite. She had plans to make.

CHAPTER TWENTY-FIVE

The headquarters of Dillon and Gold were impressive—a five-story, glass-and-brick building set in a beautifully landscaped industrial park. Rolling green lawns, blooming bushes, flowerbeds, and young evergreen trees gave the appearance of a city park just waiting for kids and their families to throw Frisbees in the air for their dogs to catch. You almost forgot that this building and this business was built on violence and death and that greed ruled supreme in this blissful setting. Larry and Osborne, as cops, were only too aware of that truth. The parking lot was dotted with trees, and they pulled into a nicely shaded visitors' spot.

Larry was in the driver's seat. He looked at his friend. "Let's see what Dillon has to say for himself."

"How fortunate for us he just got back from vacation in Bermuda."

"Visiting his money, no doubt. I hope Gold is in his office too."

"I love surprise visits. You never know how criminals are going to react."

They got out and started walking toward the entrance.

"So, do you remember exactly where Dillon's office is?" Osborne asked.

"Fifth floor, southeast corner office," Larry said. "No locks or key cards for the elevators. Love those whiz kids."

"In a few years, they won't need us regular cops. Computers will do everything."

Larry shook his head. "Naw, they'll need us. We'll just be working for them."

"I was happily surprised by the attitude of the Austin police."

"They'd be insulted if you said that. They're just doing their jobs, like us."

They reached the entrance and went in. The lobby was massive—a huge atrium with marble everywhere and many tall palms reaching toward the glass ceiling. The security guard sat behind a black marble, 12-foot-long reception counter. He was huge and wore a no-nonsense expression. His name tag said Chester.

"What can I do for you gentlemen?"

Osborne showed him his badge. "Yes, Chester, we're here to talk to Mr. Dillon and Mr. Gold, if they're in." He was desperately trying to suppress a snicker.

"Mr. Gold is out of the country. Do you have an appointment with Mr. Dillon?"

"Yes, we should be in your computer. Detectives Coleman and Osborne of the Beverly Hills Police Department." Osborne used his most officious tone.

Chester was not intimidated. "You're a little out of your jurisdiction, are you not?"

"Investigations take us wherever they may lead." Larry sounded cold. "And they led us right here."

The guard was searching on his computer. "I don't see your names here."

Osborne acted shocked. "We were told Mr. Dillon would be here and possibly Mr. Gold as well. We came all the way from Los Angeles to talk to them, and now you're saying we're not in the system?" Osborne took out his cell phone. "I'm calling my boss to find out what the hell is going on."

The guard seemed uneasy. "Hold on. I'll call upstairs and see—"

He was interrupted by the squealing of brakes as a gray sedan screeched to a halt in the parking lot by the front door and an Austin police car with lights flashing pulled up behind it. The cops got out, as did the driver of the gray sedan, and the sound of loud yelling and arguing carried into the lobby.

Chester seemed torn. "You two stay right here." He got up from behind the counter and went outside.

Larry and Osborne didn't wait around to see what happened next. They ran toward the elevators, and Larry pushed the Up button. They jumped in the elevator as soon as the doors opened. Larry pressed the button for the fifth floor, and they were on their way.

"And everybody said Dillon would refuse to see us."

"What do they know?" Osborne replied.

They got off on the fifth floor and didn't stop at reception, where a young blond stared at them with her mouth open. They opened the glass doors behind her and walked down the hall to the southeast corner office.

They found Dillon's office and didn't bother to knock.

Dillon was standing behind a shapely brunette who was seated in a chair typing on a tablet as he massaged her shoulders.

"Sorry, you forgot to lock the door," Larry said.

The brunette was so shocked she fumbled her tablet and dropped it on the floor. Dillon turned around and looked at the two men who had the unmitigated gall to invade his office. "Who the hell are you, and how did you get up here?!" he roared.

The brunette picked up her tablet and raced out of the office.

Larry and Osborne walked forward together until they were up close and personal in Dillon's space. "We're Beverly Hills cops, Mr. Dillon, and we want to know why you had one girl murdered in our fair city and are trying to murder two more?"

Dillon reached for his landline but whipped his head around as he heard Osborne locking the office door. Larry quickly placed a bug under Dillon's desk. Two locks on the door? Osborne mused. Guess Dillon found the need for privacy now and then. Dillon looked scared.

"You may be able to get away with these kinds of tactics in Beverly Hills, but you can't get away with this in Texas." Dillon all but spat out the words.

Osborne was in his face again. "You want to tell us about the lawyer you hired to get your assassins out of jail?"

"And where they all disappeared to?" Larry asked. "You planning another hit on the girls? You still think you can shut them up?"

Dillon was trembling with rage. He'd been protected from the ugly reality of his business for decades. Every necessary evil had been relegated to others, and he paid plenty to make that happen. Protests, petitions, crying parents, and Black Lives Matter never touched him. He tuned it all out. Everybody blamed the NRA, who were mere lobbyists, while nobody even knew his name. He made money for stockholders. That was his job, and he did it well. How dare these people come in here and try to intimidate him.

"Get out!" he screamed. "I want you out of here now! You two bastards won't have a job to go back to after this. I have connections everywhere, and that includes the state of California. Not everybody there is a lily-livered, piece-of-shit, gun-hating liberal." He was on a rampage now. "You are dead meat, you hear me? Dead!"

Larry's voice was like ice. "Like Maria Ramirez?"

He stopped cold and stared at them. They heard a fist pounding on the office door and Chester's voice yelling. "Open up! Open up the door."

Dillon was rooted to the spot. Osborne walked to the door and put his hand on one of the locks. "You ready to blow this joint, pal?"

Larry joined him. "Yeah, I believe I need a bit of fresh air."

Osborne unlocked both locks and opened the door to find the astounded guard standing there. "You okay, Mr. Dillon?"

"He's fine, Chester. We didn't hurt him at all," Larry said.

They walked down the hall, through the glass doors, unscathed.

Outside, they walked quickly to the car. "Think it'll take him long?" Larry asked as he used the remote to unlock the doors.

"Our job was to make him mad enough to call. I think we did our part."

They sat in the car, and Larry started it up. "That was fun and not bad acting on the part of the Austin police either. We don't get to do that nearly enough." He looked at the GPS screen. "We'll be there in five."

"Hopefully he'll call, give up somebody's name, and we can get them both extradited. Then, we'll go after the politician if we can track the phone number. Too bad we didn't have a chance to check on Gold."

"He's semi-retired. Spends a lot of his time flying to his various homes on his private jet."

"Ah, the life of the purveyors of violence. Do they ever feel even a smidgen of guilt?"

Larry's eyes were glued to the road and the GPS, but disgust registered on his face. "Remember how excited the NRA guys were when kindergarten children were murdered? Remember that? Right away, they wanted teachers to be locked and loaded. They envisioned gun battles in grade schools between teachers and shooters. Their wet dreams come true."

"You do realize that getting CEOs indicted and in jail is next to impossible. They have the best lawyers in the country on retainer and the money to fight this until they die of old age, not to mention the connections to make everything we find out disappear."

Larry was looking around. "We're getting close. Look for a plumbing van with a discreet satellite dish."

Osborne pointed. "There it is, on the left."

The van was parked on a street with run-down industrial buildings and vacant lots. Larry drove a block past the van. They both got out of the car and walked nonchalantly toward the vehicle. Not seeing anyone looking at them with any interest, they jumped in when the door slid open.

"Anything?" Larry asked as he and Osborne settled on seats facing a monitor. They had already met the Austin cops Mitch and Tony.

The two cops had headphones on. Mitch—curly-haired, with freckles, and in his mid-twenties—had a mischievous expression on his face. He put a finger to his mouth. Tony was more intense and slightly older. He solemnly handed Larry and Osborne each a headset.

"He just dialed his cell phone," Tony whispered. "We got the warrant to listen in just an hour ago. Our attorney general is all in on this, and he knows the few judges in Texas who are anti-NRA."

They stopped talking as they listened to Dillon scream into the phone. "I want to talk to your boss right now!"

A man on the other end said, "Dillon? Why are you calling? You're not on your own phone, are you? I don't recognize the number."

"Don't question me. I'm the one who pays the bills around here."

At this, all the cops gave a thumbs-up.

"And no, I'm not on my own cell phone or my landline. I've got lots of disposable cell phones, so don't worry about it."

"Are you in your office?"

"I have it swept three times a week. It's safe."

"Well, he can't talk directly to you, and you know it. Things are too hot."

"They're going to get a lot hotter if he doesn't."

"He's not here. He's in committee right now, working on the bill you want him to kill. He's still several votes short of making that happen. We might have to take our chances in the full Senate."

"He'd better make it happen, or I will ruin him. That assault weapons ban could cost me billions of dollars. If it passes, I will wash my hands of all of this."

The other man sounded desperate. "You can't do that! You were the one who blackmailed him into committing political suicide! He's going to have to change parties after this. Democrats will have his hide!"

"Calm down. All we have to do is get rid of the girl who saw and heard him at the Harland. I don't know what the other girl knows, but probably as much as the pimp who hired them. I've got some Beverly Hills cops here right now sniffing around and asking questions about the hooker at the Island."

"Maybe they're just fishing."

"They connected Keller to me. They're getting too damn close for comfort."

"What do you want me to tell him?" The man sounded desperate.

"Tell him to keep his head down, don't talk to any cops, and see if he can get his friends in high places to tell the Beverly Hills cops to back off. They're the ones driving this investigation, and if we can stop them, we're good to go. Meanwhile, I'm heading someplace they can't find me. I'll make sure the whores from LA are eliminated."

"But if they know that Keller works for a company you own . . ."

Dillon cut him off. "Keller could work for a lot of people. There's no record of me paying him to do anything. The only person who'd want the prostitutes dead is that dickhead you work for. The yahoos from Beverly Hills can't prove I hired the hit men. Those so-called hit men have been banished to Kazakhstan, and they better stay there."

"You can't throw Haynes under the bus. You two are connected like Siamese twins."

At the mention of Haynes's name, the faces of all four cops lit up. "Yes!" Larry whispered.

"Nobody's throwing anybody under the bus. But tell Haynes to do as I said. Nobody can stand up to the feds, especially not those numb nuts in Beverly Hills."

"I hope you're right."

"Get rid of the phone you're on. Get another one and give me the number."

"I'm not an idiot."

"If you're anything like your boss, you are." And the line went dead.

Mitch dialed a number on his cell phone, put it on speaker, and spoke into it. "Did you trace the call?"

A voice came over the phone. "Sorry, we traced the phone to a location near the Washington Monument. If we'd had people close, we might have caught him. We couldn't trust the Capitol Police."

"No problem. We know who he's working with," Osborne said. "I think we've got enough on Dillon to extradite him to California." He looked at Mitch and Tony. "You agree?"

"Let's find out what the judge says. We'll have to see what Dillon's lawyers come up with."

Osborne started dialing. "I have to warn Curtis about what's going on. He waited impatiently while it rang. "Curtis, Osborne here. I'm fairly sure there's going to be another attack. Tell me where you are, and I'll send some people." He put the phone on speaker.

Curtis was in his room on the computer. He stared straight ahead, closed his eyes, and breathed deeply. "No, that won't be necessary. I got it covered."

"You're sure?"

"Any idea of when it's supposed to happen?"

"No. Probably soon." He told Curtis he was on speaker and filled him in on what had gone down.

"These guys act like they're untouchable." Curtis sounded disgusted.

"They have been for decades," Larry said.

"I wonder how many other people they've killed to get what they want?" Osborne asked rhetorically.

Larry gave a crooked smile. "They made a mistake when they brought their sordid little game to us."

Tony nodded. "I hope it's their last mistake."

Curtis was somber. "I'll make certain of that. Thank you, gentlemen." And he hung up.

Osborne addressed the Austin cops. "Dillon has the means to escape your jurisdiction within the hour. He has homes all over the world. We need him locked up until we can get him extradited."

"I'm on it," Mitch said, making another call on his cell phone. He listened for a few seconds. "What?! How could that happen?! They were supposed to be watching him! He looked at the others. "Dillon has disappeared. He's not in his office. For all we know, he has an underground tunnel that leads to another building where he can escape. He thinks because he hires mercenaries, he is one. Having a tunnel is probably how he thinks."

"We'll cover all the airports, public and private. We'll have roadblocks on all the roads out of town. Texas Rangers will join in the hunt." Mitch looked at the other cops and waggled his eyebrows. "Are we having fun yet?"

"Speaking for us numb nuts from Beverly Hills," Larry said, "I'd have to say catching Dillon will be more fun."

* * * * *

Tariq, good-natured and gregarious, who welcomed novel challenges, was about to enter the courthouse when he saw Rosemaria walking up to him from the parking lot carrying two Starbucks coffees and a pastry bag. She handed him a cup and sipped from her own. "Did you see anything inter-esting in the way our undercover cop behaved after he met with me?"

He sipped his coffee, enjoying the taste for a second. "I thought he had an unusual reaction for someone accused of burglary who is at risk of destroying his career."

"How so?"

"He looked pretty smug. Then, his lawyer said something, and Kazinsky laughed and slapped him on the back, like he was saying don't worry about it. Not that I heard anything, you understand."

"Of course you didn't. It's confidential. And repeating it to me would be illegal."

"I'd say the guy looked like he had no worries."

Rosemaria handed him the pastry bag. "Your reward. A few yummy rolls fresh out of the microwave. You can share with the others. But keep this little adventure between you, me, and Karen."

"As you know, I can be bribed by cinnamon rolls."

"Why don't you go on ahead? I have to make a call."

She punched a key on her cell phone as he walked away. "Vanessa? Rosemaria— No, wait. This isn't another acting job. But do you know somebody who kind of looks like me?"

* * * *

As soon as Rosemaria got to her desk, she called Curtis on her newest pre-paid cell phone. He was working on Haynes's background, and she wanted to see if he'd found anything. She knew something was wrong as soon as she heard his voice. "What is it? Are the girls okay?"

"I took them on a little outing and hoped to do another. Looks like that's canceled."

"Why? What happened?"

Your cops found out that Dillon's goons are going to make another attempt to kill the girls, and Dillon has disappeared. He and Haynes are working together."

"Shit!"

"Yeah, up to our eyeballs. But we'll be ready for them."

"I wish I felt as confident as you. And the girls know what's coming?"

"No, I haven't told them yet. I have some things to arrange, and when I have everything set up, I'll share the news with them." He chuckled. "But I gotta tell ya, these two are something else. I think when they find out what I have planned, they'll dive right in. They are fearless. Maybe they've been watching too much violence on Netflix and think that bullets aren't real. Or maybe they're just sick and tired of being victims and want this to be over. Either way, you can be sure, they won't let me down."

"You're scaring me."

"Didn't mean to. They're terrific kids. We'll talk later." He hung up.

She took the battery out of the cell. She wasn't taking any chances.

She used the landline to make another call. "Yeah, Howard. Do you have any news for me on the granny case?"

Howard Meeks, the veteran detective who had arrested Constance Berkstadt for embezzlement, was at his desk in the SMPD. "You were right. I think her kids want her locked away. Constance owns an old house on the beach near the Marina that is about ready to fall down. But the property could be worth a few million if they can sell it, which their mother won't do. I don't know if they forced her to steal from the club or how they would do that. And yes, her lawyer represents the kids too. You need to get her another lawyer and talk to Constance, away from the circling vultures."

"Thank you, Howard. I'll see what I can do. I'll have to go in front of a judge, but the conflict should be obvious. Maybe Feinstein will make it easy for me so I don't have to go through all that hassle."

"If you ask me, it's elder abuse, clear and simple. I just wish I knew how they convinced her to steal the money."

"Don't worry, I'll find out."

* * * *

Rosemaria picked up her tail as soon as she left the parking lot. It was a newer model silver Ford Focus. It followed her up the freeway and off the Wilshire exit, where she knew of a way to get behind him so she could read his license plate. She wanted proof of what he was doing just in case she might need it. He stayed two or three cars back to avoid detection. She turned right and then left, behind a Starbucks, and sped through the parking lot. Then, she went past the alley and turned left toward Wilshire. With any luck, the driver of the Ford would assume she turned left at the alley and then pulled out onto Wilshire when he didn't see her. She waited at the intersection in front of an impatient driver in a red Honda who honked his horn for her to drive forward. She waited patiently until she saw the Ford pull out onto Wilshire. She sped up and pulled up behind him. She had her cell phone ready and punched the button to call Waite. "Waite, are you near a computer?"

Waite was in the computer room with about ten other people who were staring at their monitors and typing on their keyboards. "I should be out in the field right now, but yes, I'm shackled to a computer again."

"Will you please do me a favor and run down this California license plate?" She gave him the number. "Any time today will be fine."

"You have your own people who can do that. Why ask me?"

"It's better this way."

"Uh-oh. You're up to no good. But then again, I'd be disappointed if you weren't."

"I strive not to disappoint."

"I'll get back to you in a few."

"Thank you. I owe you big time. Anything new on Haynes?"

"We're pretty sure he's the one, but we need more proof."

"If it was his assistant that bought the bear at the Harland, you've got him."

"His name is Bernie Braverman, but he's not listed on Haynes's staff. He's worked for several people in DC. Never stays in one place for long."

"But he had to be working for Haynes that weekend."

"Yeah, but we'd like to get our hands on the bear. We found out Haynes has a pied-à-terre in DC for his private use that the wife might not know about. It could be there. If he forgot he bought it, it may still be somewhere in a drawer. Getting a subpoena to go in there would be tricky. We'd tip off his lawyers, and they'd fight it tooth and nail, giving someone time to get rid of it."

"I may be able to do something about that."

"You've got to be kidding. What are you plotting now?"

"Never mind. Curtis is working on something too. You heard they may come after Maryanne and Tiffany again."

"If they can find them."

"Let's hope they don't. Got another call. Thanks again."

She clicked her phone, keeping her eye on the Ford. "You have good news for me?"

Larry was in a Starbucks in Austin waiting for his latte. He had a smile on his face. "Lupe should be getting out today sometime."

Rosemaria was ecstatic. "Yes!"

"My lawyer played the voice tracks for Lupe, and she identified Haynes as the man in room 203."

"And Waite says he identified the man who bought the bear at the Harland!"

"We have even more than that now. We'll fill you in when we get home." The barista called his name, and he reached for his latte. "I gotta get back to work." He hung up.

She clicked off her phone, wondering what Larry meant by the last remark, and moved alongside the Ford. She drove past him without acknowledging his presence. Might as well pretend she didn't know he was following her. From now on, she would make it really easy for him.

Another call was coming in, and she answered it. "Jimmy, what have you got?"

"The car is owned by a leasing company, and it was rented today by a Mitch McGuire, who works for Saunders and Bergman Detective Agency. I hope that helps."

"It does. Just one more thing."

"Uh-oh."

"If I give you a name, could you check out gyms in Santa Monica and find out if he belongs to one in that area?"

* * * *

Maryanne and Tiffany looked uneasy as they came out of the kitchen and saw Curtis and Martin sitting in the living room. Curtis had a pensive expression on his face, and Martin was looking down at the floor.

Maryanne tried to joke. "You're interrupting the making of our latest culinary creation, sure to delight your palates."

"What's up?" Tiffany asked. They stood by the dining table, waiting for an answer.

"Sit down, girls," Curtis said. His tone added to the tension in the room, and they complied.

Maryanne sat on the couch next to Curtis and Tiffany perched on the coffee table.

Curtis breathed in and out heavily, then said, "We have credible information that the assassins will try again."

The girls took a few seconds to process what he said.

"How could they possibly find us?" Maryanne asked. "No one knows where we are except your friends."

Martin answered her. "Somehow, they have access to every kind of technology the government has—satellite, street and store cameras, cell phone tracking, and they're possibly tracking Curtis's computer. He's been extra careful, but if they have the means, they can circumvent every safeguard."

"If I'm responsible for them finding you," Curtis said, "I can't tell you how sorry I am. I thought I could help with the investigation. Instead, I might have led them right to you."

"You don't know that," Martin said. "And finding proof that Haynes and Dillon are responsible for this is of vital importance in bringing them all to justice. Let's concentrate on how we're going to throw a wrench into their plans. They may be able to hire trained assassins, but we're better." He looked first at Maryanne and then at Tiffany. "You can believe that. And keep in mind, we don't know that they have found us. We only know they're planning another attempt."

"So, what do we do?" Maryanne's voice was calm.

"I, for one, am happy that they're coming," Tiffany said. "I'm sick of being a victim."

Maryanne put her arm around Tiffany's shoulders and pulled her close. "I don't want to be a victim either. We'll do whatever you say."

Curtis stood up and started pacing back and forth. Something else was weighing on his mind. This was going to be more difficult than he thought. Sharing his feelings was not something that had ever come easily to him, and he had never wanted to until now. But he felt compelled to say what was on his mind, no matter how difficult it might be. He might never get another chance.

Maryanne, Tiffany, and Martin watched him, waiting expectantly.

"Okay, this is a little hard for me to explain, but you need to understand where I'm coming from. I never wanted to have anyone in my life that I had to give any consideration to except my fellow Marines. I was so intent on getting out of Youngstown and far away from the people who called them-selves family that I didn't give them any thought as I moved forward with my life. My father was a car mechanic who drank himself out of a job. My mother had to support us by working as a cleaning woman in a hospital. He was abusive, and she took it. I was the only child and could hardly wait to leave home. After my mother died of a heart attack and my father killed himself in a car crash, I was relieved. I would never again have to feel any guilt about not going back to Youngstown and seeing them."

"Maria had a worse upbringing than me, but her aunt, my mother's sister, took her in. I never knew about the hell Maria ended up in after she left her aunt—not until she was murdered. Then, the guilt came pouring in, and it was just too damn late to do anything about it. When I had a chance to make up for what I hadn't done for Maria by protecting you girls, I grabbed it. I was looking for absolution for my entire self-centered life.

But I got a whole lot more than that." His face softened as he looked at the girls. "I got a family. Because that is what you are to me. My family. You two, Martin, and my friends who are willing to put their lives on the line for two girls they don't know. Right now, when our lives may be in danger, is probably the happiest moment of my life. If that makes any sense, I don't know, but it's true."

Maryanne and Tiffany sat for a moment, at a loss for words. Martin, clearly moved, said, "That's the most I've ever heard you say at one time in all the years I've known you."

Maryanne cleared her throat. Her voice sounded raspy, filled with emotion. "We have something to say to you two as well."

"Yeah," Tiffany said. "But I'll make mine short and sweet. We went from having no one who cared about us to having so many people care that we can hardly believe it. We want to do better with our lives. And we will. I promise you what you are doing for us will be worth it."

"It already is, Tiffany," Curtis said. "You owe us nothing."

"I think we do," Maryanne said. "All we ever wanted was to show people who we really are, and now we can." She broke out into a smile. "Just keep us alive, guys. It's all we ask."

Curtis stood up, all business again. "Everybody sit at the table, and we'll talk about what we're going to do in case the assassins come. We may never have to do anything. Maybe the cops will arrest them and lock them up. But just in case, let's be ready."

The four of them sat at the table, and Curtis and Martin laid out their plan.

CHAPTER TWENTY-SIX

It was after closing at the zoo, and Sammy was standing still as Jerry examined him and took pictures of Sammy's legs and feet. Jerry had examined Sammy many times before, but now he wanted pictures of his wounds and videos of his endless swaying and bobbing, indicating that Sammy was in danger of complete mental collapse. He spoke soothingly to Sammy, who was familiar with his voice and knew he was a friend. Jerry was almost finished with his examination when a harsh voice startled them both. Sammy backed away slowly to seek protection behind a tree, and Jerry looked around for whoever was yelling.

He didn't have long to wait as Logan Peterson, 6 feet tall and 20 pounds overweight, came in through the gate carrying a bull hook. He waved it at Sammy. "Get inside! Get inside now!" He walked toward Sammy and held up the bull hook. Sammy, terrified, walked in agonizing slowness into the small barn that was his home at night.

Peterson turned to face Jerry. "What the hell are you doing here?"

Jerry was not intimidated. "I work here, remember?"

"You have no business in the elephant compound. Nobody asked you to examine Sammy."

"I'll examine him whenever I feel it's necessary. And I felt it was necessary."

Peterson stood a foot away from Jerry. "I'm reporting this to Hahn. Taking pictures? You'll be lucky if you hang on to your job."

Jerry moved closer to Peterson. "I don't work for Hahn. I work for the city. And you need to stop threatening me. You are the one who is in danger of losing his job. The way you threatened Sammy with that bull hook is illegal, and you know it. I took a picture of you waving that thing. You're the one who will be lucky to hang on to your job."

Peterson's face turned red, and he looked like he was about to have apoplexy. "You little twerp. Don't you try to threaten me. Hahn hates your guts." He poked a finger into Jerry's chest. "You think you have any leverage here? Think again." He shoved Jerry, forcing him to take a step back. "You're a wuss. You're a pathetic—"

He didn't have a chance to finish as Jerry gave him a powerful shove, slamming him into the trunk of the palm tree behind him. Peterson shook like he was being electrocuted, which he was. All the trees in the compound were wired to cause electric shock. The trees were there for decorative purposes, not for Sammy. Peterson stepped away from the tree and shook himself like a dog shaking off water. His hair stuck out in every direction.

"How do you like it?" Jerry asked. "That's what Sammy gets whenever he follows his natural instinct to rub against a tree."

Peterson was subdued, but his rage was palpable. "Who gives a damn about his instincts? Soon, you and all those mealymouthed protestors won't have anything to complain about anymore. Sammy will be gone. He'll be somebody else's problem." Peterson made his way shakily to the gate, unlocked it, and walked away.

Jerry knew better than to try to find out from Peterson what he meant. He thought he already knew, but he had one friend on the zoo board who would tell him if his suspicions were correct.

* * * *

Josh was home eating dinner. He had recorded two commercials in one day, which was unusual, but work at Ken's agency had not slowed down.

Ken intended to keep the agency up and running despite the fact that his movie was coming out later that year. The sales agents had done their job and distributors, foreign and domestic, had been found. All that was left to make everybody happy was to have a great big hit. Meanwhile, the agency paid everybody's bills and, considering the fragility of show business success, Ken would make sure producing commercials would always be a viable alternative if moviemaking turned out to be a bust.

Josh had called Rosemaria, who was spending another night with Vanessa. Except for a couple of times when he went up to spend the night at the cat sanctuary without her, he and Rosemaria hadn't spent a night apart since he had convinced her to come back to Los Angeles. Until now, he had taken her being with him night after night for granted, as if that's where she belonged and always would. He had been alone most of his adult life until Rosemaria came along, and that had been normal and preferable to him. There had been no one to prod, nag, and inspire him to do better or to tell him to stop drinking. He thought that's what his life would be. He was contemplating all this as he dug into his lettuce, tomato, and avocado salad, with Suzi perched on his shoulder. Then, his cell phone rang.

He answered. "Jerry, what's up?"

Jerry was at his desk in his office at the zoo. "Whatever it is you and Joell are planning for Sammy, you better hurry up."

Josh dropped his fork and stood up. Suzi fluttered upward and landed on the chair. "What are you talking about?"

"I found out that Hahn has been talking to the Milwaukee Zoo about selling Sammy to them."

"That bastard! He can't do that unless the City Council approves it."

"He's working with Councilman Chang to convince the others to vote to sell him."

"Thanks for letting me know, Jerry. I'm calling Joell now."

Josh hung up and dialed. He waited impatiently as the phone rang, but there was no answer. He left a message. "Joell, it's Josh. We have to put our plan into action now. Hahn is trying to send Sammy to Milwaukee, which is one of the worst zoos in the country. He won't last six months there. We've got to get him to a sanctuary now. Call me as soon as you get this. I forget when you're due back. Call me."

Josh told Suzi to hop onto her perch, grabbed his jacket, and ran out. He hoped Pastor Diehl would be at the mission.

* * * *

The mission was quiet at night, and the door was locked. No overnight guests were allowed here, as was the case with most daytime feeding missions. Josh peered in the storefront window and saw Pastor Diehl straightening chairs and putting away hymnals. Pastor Diehl was in his forties, with thinning hair, glasses, and a face that revealed his gentle nature. Josh knocked on the window, and Pastor Diehl looked up. He immediately came to the door when he saw Josh. "Can I help you with something?"

"Yes. I need your help, and so does my friend Sammy."

Pastor Diehl opened the door wider. "Well, come on in and tell me about your friend."

Josh followed Pastor Diehl inside. They sat in chairs facing the small wooden pulpit in the front. Diehl pulled a chair around to face Josh.

"I hope you have time to talk to me," Josh said. "This could take a while."

"Of course I have time. I'm here to listen."

"It's a long story. It started when I was working at the zoo. While there, I was able to help my friends Noor and Gilbert, a couple of animals who were being kept there. I had them moved from the zoo to a sanctuary. I want to do the same for Sammy, an elephant, but I'm afraid Sammy is going to be much more difficult to help." Josh proceeded to tell Pastor Diehl everything about his work at the zoo, his career as a songwriter, and getting Noor and Gilbert to a sanctuary. He talked about Joell and her love for animals and how she wanted to help get Sammy the elephant out of the zoo and to a sanctuary as well. He described Sammy's suffering and how the zoo was negotiating with a horrendous zoo in another city to sell Sammy in order to get the protestors off their back once and for all.

Pastor Diehl listened intently, and his face showed a great deal of compassion, but he looked perplexed. "You say you would like my help, but I don't think I would be able to do anything to influence any decision made by the zoo or the City Council."

"Joell and I have come up with a plan, and this is where you come in. Joell will raise at least one million dollars putting on a concert featuring herself and all the singers and musicians she can persuade to take part. All of the proceeds will be donated to the homeless in return for the City Council sending Sammy to a sanctuary."

Pastor Diehl's face lit up. "But that's a wonderful idea. A wonderful outcome for both the homeless and Sammy!"

"The problem is, it's likely homeless activists will want us to give the proceeds to the homeless whether or not the City Council allows Sammy to go to a sanctuary. To them, the homeless are more important than any animal, and it would be wrong to withhold the money for the freedom of an elephant."

"I see what you're saying." Pastor Diehl was thoughtful. "And what is the solution to that dilemma?"

"The solution is to get the homeless on our side. Right now, my friend Martha is living in the apartment I used to live in on Cherokee."

"You're the one who gave Martha a home! Good for you!"

"Well, it was my pleasure. She's my friend. But she reminded me the other day that the homeless are not faceless derelicts who want handouts and think only of themselves. Sure, some of them are addicts and alcoholics, but a lot of them are good people who love their animals and take good care of them. They are willing to reach out to helpless creatures just like anybody else."

"And you think that if we can get them to support the project, the homeless activists will have to go along."

"Exactly."

"I know what you're saying about the activists. They mean well, but they can have tunnel vision when it comes to the people they presume to represent. The people who come here don't want to live in tents on the streets. They want and need housing, and they help each other as best they can. Many of them have lost their jobs and then their homes and families because they couldn't pay their rent. And some are families living out of their cars because serious illness and medical bills wiped out their bank accounts. They're all different. They're all individuals."

"Will you help us organize it, Pastor Diehl?"

"First, tell me this. If you give that money to the City Council, it may very well disappear down a deep dark pit, as it often does. We have to guarantee the money will actually go to the homeless."

"Yes, we thought about that. Councilman Moretz has formed a committee made up of community leaders, former homeless people, and social workers. He also has voted time after time to release Sammy to a sanctuary. We will give the money to him and suggest that you be the one to help the committee disperse it. We don't trust politicians for the main part, but we trust you."

"So, what do you want me to do?"

"We have to arrange a press conference as soon as Joell comes back from Europe. She may cut her tour short as soon as she hears what the zoo has planned for Sammy. We have to move fast. We don't want any activists to raise hell and end this before we get started. So, once she's back, it's important that we have as many homeless people on our side as quickly as we can for the press conference. We emphasize their humanity and compassion, not their victimhood, explain how we will make good use of the money, and make sure it goes where it's supposed to go. The City Council won't be able to say no to both Sammy and the homeless."

Pastor Diehl needed no time to think. "This is the most exciting thing that's happened to me and this mission since I set up shop. I will do it. I will only confide in my friend Bertha, who works here too. She's great at organizing. You just wait and see."

Josh stood up. "I can't tell you how much this means to me. People have been trying to get Sammy out of that hell hole for a long time. Sorry for my language."

"Perfectly all right." Do you mind if we say a prayer before you leave?"

"No. Not at all."

Pastor Diehl stood, and they both bowed their heads. He prayed, saying, "Dear God, thank you for bringing Josh into my life. Guide us as we prepare to do all in our power to help those who have so little and to rescue poor Sammy from his prison. We place it all in your hands as we go forward, knowing that where many are gathered together in love, there you are as well. Thank you, Lord. Amen."

"Amen."

They said their goodbyes, and Josh walked out the door feeling certain that everything was going to come together. He walked toward his car and took out his phone. He pushed a button and waited for Rosemaria to pick up. "Hello, is this the most beautiful woman in the world?"

Rosemaria was sitting across from Vanessa at a card table, playing gin. "No, but she's sitting right here. Do you want to talk to her?" Vanessa looked at her, puzzled.

Josh laughed. "One of these days, you have to look in the mirror for more than two minutes, and you'll see what I see."

"I don't have time for that stuff. What's up?"

"I just talked to Pastor Diehl, and he's on board with the plan."

Rosemaria pumped her free hand. "Wahoo! Now all you have to do is get Joell back from Europe and get this done." Vanessa finally realized what they were talking about and did an arm pump of her own.

Josh got to his car, opened the door, and looked up and down Hollywood Boulevard. *What a beautiful town, and what beautiful people live here*, he thought. He slid in, started the car, and headed home. They were going to make it happen. God willing.

Rosemaria looked at Vanessa. "Pastor Diehl is all in. We're going to help the homeless and get Sammy out."

"Yes! Larry will want to contribute to the freedom fund. And you can contribute all that money you're winning from me."

They went back to playing cards and chatting.

"Melinda is all set to be you," Vanessa said. "I've bought matching outfits for the two of you. You can take yours with you when you leave."

"I'll pay you back with my earnings." Rosemaria slapped down her cards. "Gin."

CHAPTER TWENTY-SEVEN

Curtis was sound asleep in his room when the phone rang. He sat up, instantly awake, and grabbed the cell phone. "Yes?!" He relaxed slightly when he heard who was on the other end of the line. "Enright. I thought it was someone else. Have you got anything for me?"

Jack Enright was another Marine Curtis had served with in Iraq and Afghanistan. Now, he headed up Veterans for Peace that was headquartered in Minneapolis and was living somewhere in Southeast Asia.

"It's like you thought. Haynes is no hero."

"What'd you find out?"

"My friend, Janice Ku, who was stationed in Cambodia at the time of the massacre, knew another soldier who was in the hotel at the time. He was one of the people who was standing guard outside the door when Senator Haynes was being interviewed by a Cambodian TV station. He saw for himself Haynes run out the door and up the stairs to the roof. He never went down to the lobby and never tried to rescue his family. It was all a lie."

"Why didn't the soldier ever say anything? Why didn't anybody?"

"What was the point? It was their word against Haynes and his handlers."

"And it still is."

"Not quite."

"What do you mean?"

"Word is the Cambodian cameraman who was filming the interview didn't stop filming when he was told to. He filmed Haynes getting hysterical. He followed him as he went out of the room, ran down the hall, and took the stairs up to the roof, with his handlers close behind."

"So, who has the video now?"

"The cameraman died a few years ago. He tried to sell the video to the highest bidder but wanted too much and didn't have any takers. My friend's friend thinks the cameraman's wife has it. I'm trying to track her down through some people I know who work in a casino there."

"Your tentacles spread far and wide."

"I should have the video in a couple of days."

"That fast?"

"I hate politicians worse than you do, especially a phony hero. We know people who died in war and were buried and forgotten. They were the real heroes, not this useless piece of garbage."

"Then let's expose the bastard and make sure he pays the price."

"Will do. Over and out."

They disconnected. Curtis was feeling hopeful. Maybe they could get this guy before he had a chance to come after his girls. That would be ideal. But he was prepared for any eventuality. He placed a call to Osborne in Austin to fill him in.

* * * *

Rosemaria appeared in the courtroom early Monday morning to ask the judge in the Berkstadt case to get Feinstein removed and a new lawyer appointed for Constance. He didn't need much convincing. The conflict of interest was obvious. Feinstein didn't put up much of a fight, just enough to impress her real clients, Berkstadt's son and daughter, and make it look as if she was doing her best for them.

A few hours later, Constance walked into Rosemaria's office looking confused and agitated. Her lawyer, Ezra Silverstein, was almost as old as she was and seemed like a sweet old guy. *Probably a real killer,* Rosemaria thought. You never knew with lawyers. And seeing as she now was one, she could say that with certainty. She just hoped that Ezra had Constance's best interest at heart.

Constance sat down. "I don't understand why I have a new lawyer. My kids said it wasn't necessary. Why is this happening?"

Rosemaria spoke to her softly. "Mrs. Berkstadt, you need to have a lawyer who is working for your interest, not your children's. I'm sure Mr. Silverstein explained that to you."

"But that's the same thing, isn't it?"

Mr. Silverstein was trying his best to be patient but ended up being perfectly blunt. "As I was saying on the way here, Mrs. Berkstadt, it definitely is not. You could end up locked up in a mental hospital if they have their way."

She looked at Rosemaria. "Surely that can't be true."

"I'm afraid he's right, Mrs. Berkstadt. Your children are getting very impatient with you because you don't want to sell your house. You're spending money on repairs, and in their minds, that's a waste of your money. They want you declared mentally unfit and moved to a home. They want to take control of your property and sell it for millions of dollars. I'm afraid that's why they convinced you to steal from the country club."

Mrs. Berkstadt looked deeply hurt. "My children would never want me locked up somewhere. They know what that house means to me. It's where my husband and I lived all our lives and raised our children. It's my home."

"They've been pressuring you to sell it for over two years, isn't that right?"

"They're just worried that I can't keep it up, that's all."

"Is that why they told you to steal?"

Mrs. Berkstadt sat and stared at the two of them and seemed at a loss for words.

Silverstein tried to coax his client into telling the truth. "You can tell this lady everything, Mrs. Berkstadt. Be honest."

"But the other lawyer said I shouldn't tell her anything. She'd use it against me."

"The other lawyer didn't care about you," Silverstein said. "She was the one working against you."

Rosemaria, again, was as gentle as she could be. "I have the evidence I need to convict you, Mrs. Berkstadt. But I know there were extenuating circumstances that will reduce your sentence quite a bit. You need to tell me what they are so I can help you."

Mrs. Berkstadt was still unsure what she should do but decided to trust her lawyer and this nice young lady who seemed to really want the best for her. "You see, I went back to work because I just didn't have enough money to pay bills. My kids were right about that. And I did love my job. There were so many nice people there. Some of them used to be my friends a long time ago when my husband and I had money and were members. But I never could make enough to cover all the costs of keeping up the house. I worked and worked, but I was getting deeper into debt. I told my son what was going on, and he said the only answer was to sell the house. I said I couldn't do that. He told me that if I didn't, both he and my daughter would shut me out of their lives. I couldn't stand the thought of that happening." Her eyes started to tear up. Rosemaria handed her a tissue.

"One day, I called my daughter and begged her to bring my grandchildren to see me, and she said she couldn't as long as I insisted on falling deeper into debt. She jokingly said that I could always borrow from the club's membership fund. They wouldn't miss it. It was in the millions, and I had access to it. At first, I thought, I can't do that. But I missed my kids, and I couldn't lose my home. So, I thought I'd just take out a little. Then, the next month, I took out a little more, and before you know it, I had my bills paid off. It was wonderful. And I swore to myself I would pay it all off somehow before anyone would know. I enter all kinds of contests and lotteries I'm sure to win eventually, and then everything will be fine. But then one day, the police came and arrested me." She blew into the tissue, and Rosemaria handed her another.

"I'm afraid it was your children who turned you in, Mrs. Berkstadt. It was an anonymous phone call from a landline in a store near where your son works. They wanted you arrested so they could have your lawyer make a deal with me to have you committed. Then, they would have power of attorney, sell the house, and divide the proceeds."

"You have to face it, Mrs. Berkstadt," Silverstein told her. "They concocted this entire scheme to get their hands on your money. You can't go on closing your eyes to their true character any longer. You've been doing it for years, and they were on the verge of having you locked up. Are you willing to close your eyes to the point of losing everything you have, including your freedom?"

Mrs. Berkstadt sat quietly, with tears running down her face. Her children's betrayal had to be unbearable. Rosemaria and Silverstein looked at each other knowing they were experiencing the same feelings. They were sickened by the greed of her children and the devastation it was causing this lady. They sat by helpless, watching her suffer.

Silverstein finally spoke. "Do you understand what has happened, Constance? Are you willing to stand up for yourself?"

Mrs. Berkstadt nodded, the tears still flowing down her face. "I am. Tell me what to do, and I'll do it."

"Can I get you some tea or coffee, Mrs. Berkstadt, Mr. Silverstein?"

"Yes, please. Tea would be nice," Mrs. Berkstadt said.

"Coffee for me," Silverstein added.

Rosemaria walked to the door and opened it.

"Karen, would you mind getting tea for Mrs. Berkstadt and coffee for Mr. Silverstein?"

"Not at all."

Rosemaria turned back into her office and sat back down.

"What kind of a deal can we make here?" Silverstein asked.

"I'm going to offer probation. Nobody wants to see Mrs. Berkstadt go to jail. Not even the manager of the club. But there needs to be restitution. There is no way around that. You need to be brave now, Mrs. Berkstadt. You have an opportunity to start a brand new life. As much as you don't want to, you're going to have to sell your house. Out of those proceeds, you will pay back what you stole from the club. You will have plenty of money to buy yourself a condo, maybe in a senior setting, and pay all your bills.

You'll invest the rest and never have to worry about working again. How does that sound?"

"I can do that," Mrs. Berkstadt said hoarsely. "It might be nice to meet new people."

"I'll help you any way I can," Silverstein said. "And my wife and I will make sure you find the perfect place to live where you'll be happy."

"There's one other thing," Rosemaria said. "You can't allow your children back into your life. It will be tempting, but you mustn't do it. You have to fill up that empty place where your love for them used to be with new people to care about. And I'm sure you'll find that."

Karen brought in the tea and coffee. Mrs. Berkstadt sipped it gratefully.

"There's something else I have to deal with," Rosemaria said, "and that is the crime of elder abuse that your children are guilty of." She saw Mrs. Berkstadt start to object and added, "But I'm not going ahead with that prosecution, as of now. I know a trial would be upsetting for you, and you wouldn't want to testify against your children. But I'm telling you right here and now, I will make it clear to them that if they try to manipulate you, or in any way attempt to persuade you to sell your new home, or try to get their hands on your money, I will be on their tail faster than they can call another crooked lawyer. I'm not budging on this, Mrs. Berkstadt, so I'm counting on you to stay away from them and keep them out of jail."

Mrs. Berkstadt was almost smiling. "You're tough. I wish I were like that."

"Well, you're a smart lady, and that's good enough. I'll send papers over to Mr. Silverstein's office for you to sign, and that will be that."

At this, Mrs. Berkstadt put down her tea and started to cry again. "I can't tell you how—" She couldn't get the words out.

Rosemaria stood up, walked around her desk, and wrapped her arms around Mrs. Berkstadt. "You didn't deserve this, Constance. From now on, your life will be a whole lot better. I promise you. Listen to your lawyer. It sounds like he has a nice wife too."

Silverstein shook Rosemaria's hand in sincere gratitude. She could see in his eyes that he was one of the good guys.

She ushered them out of her office and watched them walk away.

Karen was at her desk observing Rosemaria's pleased expression. "Another success story, boss?"

"Yeah, it is. Who do we have next on our agenda?"

CHAPTER TWENTY-EIGHT

In Austin, Mitch and Tony were in the back of the van, surveilling the area a few miles from the industrial site where Dillon and Gold had their offices. They sat up wide awake as the door opened and Larry and Osborne came inside carrying cups of coffee and a bag of baked goods.

"You ask and we deliver," Larry said as he handed over the food and drinks to his fellow cops and sat in a seat behind them. Osborne made himself comfortable as well and took a sip of his coffee.

Mitch greedily took the bag and fished out a sugared donut. "Food of the gods," he said, and half the donut disappeared into his mouth.

Tony took the bag and found a chocolate-covered éclair that he looked at for a moment. "I just have to enjoy the sight of this beauty before it disappears." And with that, he took a bite and closed his eyes in deep appreciation.

"We spent the morning with your attorney general, laying out what we have on Dillon," Larry said. "He's ordered an arrest warrant."

"We just have to get the judge to agree to extradition," Osborne added.

"I've always found that Mr. Manaheim knows all the right judges," Tony said between bites. "No worries there. "It could take a week or so, but considering the evidence we have, even his superstar lawyers can't keep him here. Meanwhile, we have to catch the SOB."

"Nothing yet, huh?" Larry asked.

"Mitch thinks he's still in the area. That's why we're here," Tony said. "At any rate, this is pretty central, and I figure if anybody spots him, we'll be able to get there to assist."

"I just don't see how he could have gotten far with all of the cameras and patrol cars on the lookout," Mitch said. "He's not a magician. He can't just disappear into thin air." Mitch's cell phone rang, and he clicked it on. "Yeah, Mitchell here." As he listened, his face became suddenly animated. "We'll get on it ASAP." He clicked off the phone and turned to the others. "Somebody named Veranza has ordered a plane from a private airport, San Remos on Highway 21, in an hour. The name is probably phony, but the company footing the bill is Matrix Surveillance, one of the ones on the list of offshore businesses you brought us. It could be anybody from Dillon and Gold, or it could be Dillon. What do you think?"

"We could have missed him somehow. And the road checks didn't start for half an hour. He could have gotten out then. We should have known he'd move fast."

"He must figure there's no way we can know about Matrix and is holed up somewhere near the airport," Larry said. "He underestimated our whiz kids."

"Who are the whiz kids?" Mitch asked.

"Our computer guys at BHPD. I think they're all barely out of middle school."

"Yeah, they're the generation that played with iPads instead of rattles when they were babies," Tony said. "I envy them."

"Anyway, what do we do?" Mitch was all business. "I say, let's head for the airport. I think he's flown the coop."

"Agreed everybody?" Tony asked.

Everybody gave a thumbs-up. Mitch jumped up into the passenger seat. Tony climbed into the driver's seat and started the van.

Mitch picked up the handset. "Delta 29 to dispatch, radio clear?"

"Go ahead Delta 29."

"Delta 29 to dispatch. We're leaving surveillance detail and heading toward San Remos Airport on Highway 21."

"Copy that."

Tony pulled the car out slowly from where it was parked near the industrial park. He picked up speed on city streets and sped along the freeway.

"Delta 29 to dispatch. We're on the freeway two minutes out. We need an unmarked unit to meet us at the exit of Freeway 21 and Clarkson."

They saw the sign for the Clarkson exit coming up.

"Unit arriving Clarkson and Third. Do you need any other assistance?"

"Negative on that. Tell any marked units in the area they need to leave ASAP."

"Copy that."

Five minutes later, the van was parked on Clarkson next to a silver Honda Civic. The undercurrent inside the van was charged with urgency. Tony and Mitch sat in the front. The two new cops who, as it turned out, had just come off an undercover assignment near Clarkson, were in the back with Larry and Osborne. They looked at his photo on Osborne's cell phone and discussed the best way to trap him as he drove up to the security gate. Chances were that airport personnel were in the employ of Dillon and Gold and would immediately report police presence. Or, possibly Dillon had reserved more planes under other names at different airports and would go to one of those places instead. There were over two thousand private airports in Texas, and it would be impossible to cover them all. They had to move fast once they were sure that Dillon was in the car, but if he wasn't visible, either because he was lying down in the back seat or behind tinted glass, how would they know what car to stop? It was a conundrum.

"It's time to call the attorney general," Osborne said. He got out his cell phone and called. He raised his forefinger at the others as they exchanged puzzled looks. "Hello, Mr. Manaheim, this is Sergeant Osborne calling. I have an urgent request to make of you. How soon could one of your rich donors make reservations for four of his or her employees to fly to Dallas on a private plane out of San Remos Airport? None of those people have to show up. We just need their names. We're two minutes from the airport now. And tell them to add the names of—" The two cops held out their driver licenses for Osborne to read. "—'Sal Mancuso' and 'Avery Lucas' to the list. Those are the false identities of two undercover cops with us. Those names will check out with Dillon's people if they run a trace on them.— Thank you sir. We also need the tail number of a plane reserved by someone named Veranza. We'll explain once we have Dillon in custody." He clicked off his phone. "God willing and the creek don't rise. He'll call me back once it's done."

"What are you cooking up, Darryl?" Larry asked.

"Our only chance is to get someone inside the terminal," Osborne answered. "'Sal' and 'Avery' will drive up to the gate, show their licenses, and tell the guard that the other passengers on their flight, whose names would have been called in by Manaheim, are coming in another car. You'll go inside the terminal to wait, keeping your eye on whatever car drives up to the plane with Veranza's tail number. See if you can see Dillon in the car as it drives by. Whether or not you do, call us. Then, casually stroll up to what we presume is Dillion's car. We'll flash our badges at the entrance, drive through the security gate, and hopefully nail him. If the car tries to drive back through the gate, other units will block their exit."

Everyone in the van was nervously optimistic. "It was fortunate for us you were the closest car to the airport," Osborne said to the undercover cops. "If only the rest of this plan falls into place as well."

Osborne called dispatch and asked for four more unmarked cars to stand by a block from the airport. His cell phone rang. "Osborne." He grabbed his pen and notebook out of his jacket pocket. "Got it." He ripped off a page and handed it to "Sal." "This is the tail number and the names of the fake passengers. The guard at the gate will have them on his computer. I'll wait for your call."

"We're on it." Sal opened the door and said, "Good luck." Then, the two stepped out of the van and got into the Honda.

Larry watched them drive away. "Maybe he won't even show up and he's at some other airport."

"We'll know soon," Mitch said. "His plane is due to take off in half an hour."

"Here come reinforcements," Osborne said.

Two cars parked a block behind them. No one got out.

Larry was intently typing into his phone.

"What are you looking for?" Osborne asked.

"I'm wondering if Matrix Surveillance is the company Haynes uses to track down the girls. I found the Matrix website. Their logo is an eye inside a camera lens. Sounds like they're made up of a bunch of ex-military and ex-contractors."

"Maybe they do more than surveil."

"I don't think Dillon and Haynes would be that obvious."

"Remember how well Dillon distanced himself from all his companies? Who'd ever know if Dillon or Haynes got his assassins from Matrix? But most of these companies have their employees fingerprinted. I'll suggest in our report that our tech unit see if they can somehow find out if the fingerprints of the assassins match any Matrix employees."

Osborne's cell phone rang. He listened for a moment, then clicked it off. "It's a go! A car just came through the gate and drove up to the plane with the correct tail number, and somebody who looks like Dillon is in the back seat."

Mitch called dispatch. "Dispatch, it's unit Delta 29. Tell all available units near San Remos Airport to block the entrance to the airport!"

Tony hauled ass up the highway, got off on San Remos, and saw police cars coming from every direction. He just made it to the gate before he was cut off. He flashed his badge at the guard. "Open the gate! Now!" The guard did as he was told. The cop cars waited outside the entrance.

They could see "Sal" and "Avery" standing next to their Honda in the small parking lot. They casually walked toward a gray Toyota next to Dillon's plane. Two men got out of the back seat of the gray Toyota and walked around to the trunk to take out their suitcases. Before they had a chance to do that, "Sal" and "Avery" were on them, guns drawn, ordering, "Hands in the air! Down on the ground!"

At the same time, Mitch pulled the van next to the Toyota, which proceeded to turn to the left around the van and head full speed for the entrance gate. The four cops inside said "Shit!" pretty much at the same time. Mitch yanked the steering wheel around, burning rubber as he followed.

When the driver of the Toyota realized it was hopeless to try to get through the gate, he turned right and headed at breakneck speed down a road that ran parallel to the runway. Mitch followed close behind as everybody in the van held their breath. They all grinned as they saw a squadron of police cars coming from the other direction, with lights flashing and sirens blaring, blocking any escape routes. The Toyota screeched to a stop. Mitch stopped at the Toyota's bumper, and several cops got out of their cars and pointed their guns at who, hopefully, would turn out to be Dillon and his driver.

From one of the police cars, a voice called out from a loudspeaker. "Throw your guns out and get out of the car! On the ground! Do it now, or we will proceed to fire!"

The driver slowly opened the door, threw out a gun, and fell prostrate on the ground.

The cop on the loudspeaker got impatient. "Out of the car now! We will give you three seconds before we fire! One, two—!"

The passenger side opened, and Dillon, dressed in casual clothes and a crumpled cloth fisherman's hat, stepped out of the car.

The cop on the loudspeaker was not kidding around. "On the ground! I said on the ground!"

Dillon slowly sank down to his knees and inched himself down to the ground.

Mitch, Tony, Larry, and Osborne watched as Austin cops handcuffed the two men, jerked them to their feet, then hustled them into a cop car. "Sal" and "Avery" drove up in their Honda with the two prisoners in the back seat. The cops gathered around Mitch and Tony. They may have wanted to do high fives but retained their professional demeanor. All were grinning ear to ear.

"Mirandize them, bring them down to our precinct, and we'll book Dillon on assorted charges and Dillon's men for aiding and abetting a fugitive's escape," Mitch told the uniformed cops. "Then, we'll get Dillon to Beverly Hills to face murder charges. And I guarantee he won't be staying at the Beverly Wilshire!"

This got a laugh out of everybody. Osborne, with Larry right behind him, pushed himself to the center of the circle. He shook the hand of the officer in charge. "I just want to say, that the Austin Police are the greatest bunch of cops I've ever had the pleasure to work with. The way you came roaring up the road like it was the Texas Rangers riding to the rescue was chilling."

The officer laughed. "We are the Texas Rangers. The attorney general thought you might want some help with heading them off at the pass, so to speak."

Larry was shaking his head. "Police, Rangers, anytime any of you want to visit Beverly Hills, you're staying with me. I'll have to okay it with my wife, of course."

Everybody was chuckling as they walked back to their cars. The guard had opened the gate, and everybody drove out in tandem.

In the van with Tony, Mitch, and Osborne, Larry was in his element. "Whoo! What a day! I've got to call Vanessa."

"Checking in with the boss?" Tony teased.

"Yeah, always."

Osborne said, "Show him Vanessa's picture. That'll nip this in the bud."

Larry pulled Vanessa's picture up on his cell phone and handed it to Tony, who was mightily impressed. "Wow! She is gorgeous!" He showed it to Mitch.

"I've seen her before. She's on TV. This woman married *you?*"

"Hard to believe, but yeah," Larry took his cell phone back and dialed. "Sweetheart, how are you?"

Vanessa, Rosemaria, and Karen were seated at Vanessas's kitchen island eating salads and lasagna.

"Larry, it's so good to hear your voice!" She nodded excitedly at the other two. "Is everything okay?!"

"Better than okay. Tell Rosemaria we got Dillon, and he'll be heading to California real soon. We're trying to move him out before his lawyers can start throwing up roadblocks."

"You can do that? Is that legal?"

"This is Texas, honey. We shoot first and ask questions later."

"So, you'll be home tomorrow?"

"Probably in a few hours."

"Okay, see you then. I love you."

"Love you too." He hung up and looked at the other cops. "And don't say anything."

Tony said, shaking his head, "Not me."

Osborne's cell phone rang. He answered, listened for a minute, and gave a thumbs-up. "The judge already signed off on the extradition. Larry, can you hire us a plane and get us out of here in an hour?"

"Why not?"

"You're rich too?" Mitch was in awe. "Prepare your guest room."

"Anytime, pal." And he dialed the Austin airport.

CHAPTER TWENTY-NINE

Rosemaria was too excited to eat. "How on God's good earth did they manage that? I thought he'd be protected by a squadron of killers and an army of lawyers."

"Never underestimate the resourcefulness of the BHPD," Vanessa said proudly, speaking with her mouth full of garlic bread.

Karen sipped her wine and gave voice to what they were all thinking. "This could make Haynes even more determined to find the girls before he gets arrested."

"It's agony not being able to protect them," Rosemaria said.

"You couldn't do any more than what Curtis is doing. But we can get more evidence to convict him," Vanessa said.

"You mean the bear?" Karen asked.

"Yeah. That bear would connect him directly to Maryanne and the murder of the phony talent scout," Rosemaria said.

Vanessa picked up her cell phone. "Let me call Mrs. Haynes. I'll tell her what's going on. She hates her husband. If she's part owner of the pied-a-terre, then she has the right to let anybody in to search the place. Haynes may have put the bear away in a drawer with his underwear and forgotten about it. Or it could still be in a suitcase."

"But what if she doesn't want her son's present to be the thing that gets him put away for life?" Rosemaria said. "What if she doesn't want to do that to her son? What if she doesn't want to be known as the ex-wife of a murderer? Then she might tip him off and have him get rid of it."

"How else would we get the bear?" Vanessa asked

"I wonder if the authorities in DC will arrest Haynes," Karen said. "Then how will we get him back here to face charges?"

"That's a good question," Vanessa agreed.

"I don't know about that either, but I think we'll have to call Mrs. Haynes and ask her to find the bear. I don't see any other way." Rosemaria sipped her wine thoughtfully. "But I need to figure out how to approach her without her going off in the other direction."

They went back to their meal, subdued and thoughtful.

* * * *

Maryanne stood in the doorway of the kitchen and observed the group seated around the breakfast table. The mood was upbeat as everyone chatted and enjoyed their food. Two of the guards who were headquartered down the street had slipped into the house before dawn and joined the others for breakfast, which had been prepared by Maryanne and Tiffany. They both were dressed in sweatshirts and jeans. Erik, a dark-haired young Latino from Texas, and Coby, a female ex-Marine from Alabama, in her thirties, were almost as buff as Curtis. Both looked like they could handle anybody with evil intentions toward the girls. Martin had shopped up a storm the day before, and the table veritably groaned from the weight of all the food. There were muffins, cornflakes, pineapple chunks, cantaloupe, sourdough toast, hash browns, and a perfect vegan omelet made from a recipe that Officer Boa had taught Maryanne, Tiffany, and Rosemaria at the Marina condo.

Maryanne had to laugh remembering how difficult it was for Rosemaria to conquer the omelet-making technique. Maryanne, on the other hand, took to cooking like a duck to water. Maryanne found that she enjoyed it.

Who knew? But then, she'd never been able to shop for whatever groceries she needed before or had a chance to cook for people she loved. Everything had changed last night. Now, she and Tiffany no longer felt like victims. If the worst happened, they were prepared, and they had the best people in the world on their side.

Coby looked up at Maryanne, who was lingering in the doorway. "You look pretty happy, Maryanne. And you should feel proud. This is a spread the likes of which I haven't seen since the last time I was at a family reunion back home."

Maryanne moved to stand behind Tiffany and put her hands on her shoulders. "It was a team effort all the way."

Tiffany stopped eating long enough to say, "She was the boss. I just followed orders."

Curtis was proud. "Sit down and enjoy the fruits of your labor before things get cold."

"Yes, sir." Maryanne sat and plucked a muffin off the serving plate, slathering it with butter and jam. She took a big bite and contemplated her good luck.

Everyone continued eating, relaxed and happy, until there were only a few crumbs of food left. Curtis and Martin began carrying dishes into the kitchen. "Curtis and I are on KP," Martin said. "Everybody else relax."

Erik stood for a second in the center of the living room, then he walked over to the front window, where he moved a chair so he could easily see the street and sidewalk without being seen. Maryanne stood next to Coby as the former Marine looked out the side window. "Thank you for inviting us over," Coby said. "I won't have to eat for the rest of the day."

"I wish we had done it before. I didn't know you were allowed."

"It's not a good thing to do on a regular basis, but we were careful coming over here," Erik said. "No one saw us. And while we're with you, Sandy and Peter are on constant alert, so you have nothing to worry about. I think Curtis didn't want any neighbors to see any foot traffic between our place and yours, wonder what was going on, and call the police."

"Well, we'll have Sandy and Peter over next time so we can meet them too." Tiffany had sprawled on the couch all the better to digest her breakfast. "You're all doing so much for us."

"We served under Sergeant Curtis in Afghanistan, and we'd do anything for him. But I have to be honest—your friend Larry is not shy about giving us a very generous salary."

"But being willing to risk your lives for two people you don't know is above and beyond the call of duty," Maryanne said.

The four of them heard the familiar sound of Curtis's cell phone ringing in the kitchen and cast worried glances in that direction. If this was it, they were ready.

In the kitchen, Curtis was on his cell phone. Martin laid his towel on the counter and stared intently at Curtis.

Curtis's friend Jack was on his single bed, in a dingy room somewhere in southeast Asia. He was sweating profusely in a T-shirt and jeans, even with air conditioning on and leaning back against the ancient iron headboard with a self-satisfied grin on his face. "I tracked down the video."

Curtis nodded and gave a thumbs-up to Martin. "My man! How'd you do it?"

"Am I good, or am I good?"

By this time, Maryanne and Tiffany had moved into the kitchen while Erik and Coby stayed where they were. The girls knew immediately from Curtis's upbeat expression that the call was not something to be worried about.

"Yeah, you're good. You're the best. Now tell me how you did it."

Jack, wiping perspiration off his face with the back of his hand, was feeling the love. "Well, like I said, a friend of a friend knew the wife of the cameraman but didn't know where she was living. He got the address from the manager of the TV station that her husband used to work for. The landlord there told him that she and her daughter had moved to Tuol Kork, a suburb of Phnom Penh, where she had found work as a maid for some rich people."

"As it turns out, the wife had, at some point, tried to sell the video and had made copies, but apparently, like her husband, she was asking too much and there were no takers. But five years ago, she did sell a copy to a man whose name she didn't remember, but he paid a lot of money. She got a different job, left the videos, along with some other stuff, in boxes in the rich people's storage shed and forgot about it. My friend told her he was writing a book about the brief insurgency and would like the video for historical reasons. She bought his story, gave him the video, and now I have it."

"Were you able to look at it?"

"I was afraid it would be old and moldy by now, but I found a DVR player, and yeah, I looked at it."

"And?"

"The guy was such a putrid coward. It'll make your stomach turn."

"Can you convert it to a flash drive and send it to me?"

"Sorry, there's no place near here that does that, and I don't have that kind of equipment. I'm laying low a little off the beaten track right now. I'll send it by army courier. You should get it in three days."

"Okay. Send it to the Beverly Hills Police Department and mark it urgent to Sergeant Osborne."

"I hope this is what you need to nail that dirtbag."

"It'll help. As a matter of fact, I think it will turn out to be invaluable. And whatever I can do for you in return, I'll do."

"Seems to me you already did it in Afghanistan. And who keeps track anyway? So long, Sergeant." And he was gone.

Curtis looked at Martin, Maryanne, and Tiffany staring at him, waiting for an answer. "We got the tape of Haynes running out on his wife and kids."

"So, this was the blackmail they had on him," Martin said. "No wonder he would do anything to keep it quiet."

"I'll call Osborne and Rosemaria and let them know," Curtis said. "I want to tell Erik and Coby."

The three of them walked into the living room, but Erik and Coby had disappeared.

Curtis's cell phone rang. "Curtis," he answered, listening. "Good work, Osborne. Also, someone is sending you the DVR of Haynes leaving his wife and kids to save himself. Blackmail material— Yeah, we'll be ready. You don't have to worry about us."

He turned to the others. "Dillon has been extradited to LA. This could make Haynes even more desperate. He needs to get rid of witnesses before Dillon implicates him. We may have to make our move soon."

CHAPTER THIRTY

L AX was a nightmare of astronomical proportions. Josh hated coming here and dealing with the crowds of people moving in every conceivable direction. He was waiting on the sidewalk, constantly being bumped into by people who seemed unaware of anyone or anything but their own agenda. He was keeping in contact with Joell on his cell phone as she moved through customs. He had been there an hour already, waiting for her plane, then enduring the agonizingly slow wait as Joell deplaned. She was given some VIP treatment but still had to get her baggage and prove who she was. He saw her walking toward him, an attendant trailing behind her, wheeling her suitcases in a baggage cart.

She fell into his arms. "That was horrible! I'm never traveling coach again! How do people do it?"

He took her hand and led her toward his car. He'd borrowed a handicapped placard from somebody a while back and didn't feel too much guilt using it at LAX.

"My car isn't far."

"I must sound like such a snob, but this is not how I usually travel." She ignored the glances of people who seemed to recognize her. She had taken the first plane out of Berlin and had one stopover. She had been cramped by wide passengers on either side and hadn't slept in twenty-four hours.

"I appreciate your coming back so soon."

"I canceled Stockholm and Prague, but I'll make it up to the promoter later. I told him it was a family emergency."

Josh saw his car was still where he had parked it and was grateful it hadn't been towed. He opened the passenger door so Joell could get in and then opened the trunk for the attendant. After the luggage was in the trunk, he slammed it shut and gave the attendant a $20 tip.

In the car, Joell settled back in her seat, exhausted. "I don't know if I'm more sleepy or hungry. But I think hungry. The food on the plane was inedible. Can we stop somewhere and eat?"

"Absolutely. There should be something on Century Boulevard." They had only driven a short distance before a Denny's appeared on their right. Josh loaned Joell a baseball cap he had in the back seat. Then, she put on her huge sunglasses that covered half her face, and they went inside. Joell was famished. She ordered a stack of pancakes and coffee. He ordered a salad. There wasn't much on the menu for vegans. As they waited, Josh began to fill her in on what was happening with Sammy.

"Pastor Diehl has set up a meeting for us with Councilman Moretz tomorrow morning at 11:00 downtown. He told Councilman Moretz a little bit about what we want to do, but since he didn't know the details of—" He stopped as the waitress placed a carafe of coffee and cups on the table. Josh continued as he poured a cup for Joell and one for himself. "Pastor Diehl didn't know how and when you're going to set up a press conference and how many homeless people, celebrities, and activists for Sammy you want to be there. We'll fill Councilman Moretz in on that when we see him. Pastor Diehl will be there too."

"I had a lot of time to think on the plane."

She looked so serious, Josh's heart just about stopped. He was afraid she had changed her mind.

She touched his hand and smiled. "Don't worry. I'm still all in."

Josh breathed a sigh of relief.

"It's important to do this just right. I want my press agent to be there tomorrow morning as well. She's very good at manipulating the press and getting the right message out to the public."

"They need manipulating?"

"Yes, Josh, they do. They must be convinced to be on our side in case any animal-hating homeless activists show up. My friend, a famous singer who shall remain nameless because she couldn't stand the heat, ran into those kinds of people when she went to testify for Sammy in front of the City Council. Some of the activists hated her—asked why she was there to testify for an elephant. Why wasn't she there for the homeless even though there were a lot more people testifying for the homeless than for Sammy. There's always going to be people like that who think that you have to bottle up compassion in one container or you won't have enough to go around. Ridiculous. The more love you give, the more love you have. That's the message we want to give the press—that there's more than enough compassion to go around, and the homeless have as much as anybody."

"That makes sense. I'm sure happy you're in charge of this and not me."

"My PR person will write up a press release that'll get everybody on our side. The City Council will have to vote in favor of this or antagonize Sammy's supporters and look like they hate the homeless."

"Or they can vote for it and become all-around heroes."

"Exactly. Then, all we have to do is organize a concert, which will be the easy part. Don't worry, I have people who will do that as well." She looked at him sideways. "I have one small favor to ask of you in return."

Josh looked wary. "Uh-oh. I thought you were doing this for Sammy and the homeless."

"Yes, of course. But I want one small thing from you. Promise me."

Their food came, and Joell dug in without hesitation. Josh was too nervous to pick up his fork.

"What is it?"

"Promise me first."

Reluctant but grateful, Josh knew he could not get out of this. "I promise."

"You will perform one of your songs at the concert."

Josh was stunned. "In front of all those people with famous musicians on stage? How could you ask me to do that?"

"I've heard you sing your songs on demos, remember? You're better than any of them. But don't bother arguing. You already promised."

He watched her happily devouring her pancakes and knew there was no way out.

* * * *

Karen and Tariq were chatting outside Rosemaria's office when she joined them, looking a bit apprehensive.

"You look like something is weighing on your mind. What's up?" Karen asked.

"I'm going to the gym for a workout and a massage. With everything that's going on, I need to unload some of this nervous energy."

"What gym are you going to?" Tariq asked.

"It's on Wilshire, not far from the 405. It's small, but it has all the machines I like."

Karen nodded approvingly. "Sounds like a good idea. Enjoy yourself for a change."

Rosemaria gave them a wave and headed down the hall. "See you tomorrow."

* * * *

Josh was home sitting at the table, tapping on his laptop. Joell had asked him to check out some of the singers and bands that she had in mind for the concert. According to their social media, some of them were on tour and wouldn't be back in LA for months. Others seemed to be recording albums right here in town. Joell had gone straight for the A-list, and why not? She was one of them.

He looked up and saw Rosemaria come through the door looking exhausted, carrying her gym bag. "You went to the gym? You didn't tell me you were going." He got up and wrapped his arms around her. "Mm, you smell good."

Rosemaria dropped the bag on the floor. "Shampoo." She sank into a chair by the dining table. "Everything always seems to happen all at once with us. You notice that?"

She looked over at Suzi, who was chewing her food on the tray below her usual perch. "Hey, Suzi, not even a hello?"

Suzi took time to say, "Turn on the TV."

"Once we get a TV, do you think she'll stop saying that?"

"You do know she doesn't have a clue what's she saying."

Rosemaria sat up suddenly. "What happened when you met Joell? She's not backing out, is she?"

He sat down opposite her. "You wouldn't believe it. She's taken over. Joell and her PR person, her promoter, her whole team. She canceled two dates in Europe to come back and do this."

"Wow. That's amazing."

"So, tomorrow we meet at Councilman Moretz's office, lay out our plan, and hopefully have his support. I don't know why not. He's been trying to get Sammy to a sanctuary for a long time."

She grabbed his hand. "Oh, Josh. I'm so happy for you and for Sammy. And you're doing a great thing for the homeless as well."

"I wish Martha didn't hate crowds so she could take some credit. She's the one who gave me the idea. There's something else."

She looked at him, wary, not liking his tone. "What's wrong?"

"Joell wants me to sing at the concert."

"That's fabulous! You agreed, right?"

"She made me promise before I knew what she was asking me."

"You'll be wonderful."

"We'll see."

Rosemaria stood up and took his hand. "Do you mind if we just lie on the bed while I tell you about my day?"

He followed her, and they lay down, still holding hands. She hardly knew where to start. "I'm going to first tell you about the investigation and then about what I've done tonight, or rather haven't done. And then I want you to hold me and make me feel like nothing bad is going to happen to my girls. All those goons that want to kill them will regret the day they ever thought of going up against Sergeant Curtis."

"Lay it on me."

She talked, he listened, and afterward she felt a whole lot better.

CHAPTER THIRTY-ONE

At 1:00 a.m., all the lights in the house were off. Curtis had watch duty and moved between sitting in the chair in the front room and peering out the back door, never resting. Martin would take over in two hours. From his post in the front room, Curtis felt rather than heard movement at the back door and then scratching on the door window. He moved through the house and opened the door for Erik. They sat at the kitchen table and whispered.

"I asked Sandy and the guys if they had ever heard of the Matrix outfit your cop friend told you about, and Jones said he had. Said it was supersecret and totally off the grid. They hire mercenaries who'll do anything for money and tech guys who know how to hack into any system on the planet. Gun manufacturers who are rich as all hell provide the best equipment and pay top dollar. They contract out only to countries or dictators who think killing anyone who stands in their way is normal. Jones found out about them by accident through a friend, checked them out and thought he might apply, then realized these guys are psychopaths and, furthermore, scared the living crap out of him. He tried to forget he ever heard of them."

"Does he think the guys coming after us are from Matrix?"

"He says they have massive amounts of satellite surveillance monitors and can track almost anybody anywhere. They can find out more of your history than even you know. They can learn who all your relatives are, where you live, where you have lived, where you served, how much you were paid, and so on. You can't hide from these guys."

"If that's true, we better make our move now. What do you think?"

"The sooner the better. Dillon may have ordered them to come after us before he was arrested."

"Then it's time we let them think we're running and hiding. I'll wake the girls."

Erik went out the back, and Curtis woke Maryanne and Tiffany, who were both asleep in Maryanne's room.

"We're leaving," Curtis told them.

They didn't hesitate or ask questions. Their bags were packed. They followed him to where Martin was waiting by the back door. "I heard," was all he said.

Curtis grabbed his bag. Both men checked their weapons and held them as they went out the door.

The four of them crept down the stairs and around the side of the house, where the SUV was parked on the lawn. They silently loaded their gear and got in—the girls in the back, Martin in the driver's seat, Curtis in the passenger seat. Maryanne and Tiffany seemed calm. No one spoke. They all knew what was coming. They backed out into the street and passed the house with the guards. There was no sign of life there. It felt like they were all alone.

They drove north out of Akron for 25 miles before they came to the trees and rivers of the national park. No one appeared to be following them. In the SUV, Curtis turned on his cell phone and called Osborne. "We're going after those bastards now. Expect a special delivery before morning." He clicked off the phone, smashed it with his boot on the floorboard, and threw it out the window into the river as they crossed over a bridge.

They arrived in the town of Peninsula and stopped briefly for the girls to go to the restroom. Curtis and Martin escorted them both in and out of the ladies' room, draping thick bulletproof vests and jackets over their heads. They continued driving deep into a thick forest, where the road became narrow and rutted with potholes. They crossed a wooden bridge, and soon the road disappeared. They parked the SUV and covered it with brush. Curtis and Martin helped the girls out of the SUV, again covering them with bulletproof vest and jackets. They made their way through the woods as quickly and quietly as they could until they came to a small log cabin surrounded by thick foliage. They entered the dark cabin. All was silent outside.

Fifteen minutes later, two black SUVs drove with no headlights down the same dirt road that led to the cabin. They stopped a mile away, where the road disappeared into thick undergrowth. Four men stepped out of each SUV, all of them dressed in camouflage. Two were carrying sniper rifles, four carried Smith and Wesson 9 mm semiautomatics, and two had 6.8 mm assault rifles.

The men put on their night goggles, then the leader gave a silent signal. They took off in four different directions, dropping to the ground when they come within 50 yards of the cabin. The two snipers headed out alone toward upper ground.

Two of the men in camouflage, both carrying assault rifles, approached the south side of the cabin, constantly peering in every direction through their night goggles. They sensed movement in front of them a split second too late. A bright light came out of nowhere. Exacerbated by the night goggles, the bright light temporarily blinded them, destroying their ability to respond. The light disappeared. Two men in black, in perfect synchronicity, quickly and silently administered a choke hold on the two men until they rendered them unconscious, then pulled them out of sight.

One of the snipers had made his way to the back of the cabin and set up his rifle. He looked through his scope for a sign of life inside the cabin. His finger was on the trigger. He was ready to shoot if he saw the slightest movement. A warning instinct shot through him a split second before a needle was shoved into the side of his neck. He shuddered, his hands fell away from his rifle, and he slumped to the ground.

The camouflaged leader was crouched close to the ground, facing the front of the cabin. He whispered into his shoulder mic. Five of his men responded with their code names, and three did not. He whispered again. Same response. He did not dare retreat. Failure meant severe repercussions for him and his men. Wary now, the remaining five killers began to approach the house with more caution. One of them, on the east side of the cabin, was on his belly, moving toward the porch, looking from side to side and behind him for any signs of life. A man slid an arm out from underneath the porch and dug his fingers deep into pressure points on the killer's neck. The man's head dropped to the ground. He was quickly disarmed and handcuffed.

The leader, unable to reach two more of his men and realizing his mission was in peril, refused to admit defeat. He issued a command into his mic to attack. The two men with assault rifles ran forward, firing into the cabin. Trip wires knocked them to the ground, setting off small explosions and rendering them unconscious. Three men in black flipped them on their backs, checked that they were still alive, and handcuffed them.

The second sniper, who had set up on the opposite hill from his friend, quickly packed up his rifle upon hearing the explosions and ran toward the direction of the black SUVs. The leader had already started running. Their mission had failed, and he would have to face the consequences. He and the sniper arrived at the site where their rides had been parked and realized both SUVs had disappeared. Blinding lights from high up in the trees surrounded them. The two men raised their arms above their heads to protect their eyes against the lights. Four men in black aimed their assault rifles at them. One of them yelled, "Drop your weapons! Down on the ground!"

The two men followed orders and fell on the ground. Immediately they were handcuffed and ordered to stay down. Six men in black dragged the other men out from behind the trees and bushes, grouping them side by side on the ground alongside the leader and the sniper. One of the men in black spoke into his shoulder mic. "Mission accomplished, sir. Would you like to see them before we haul them away?"

From the direction of the cabin, Curtis and Martin made their way through the woods. Two women, one wearing a red wig and one a black wig, were walking with them. Their carriage and attitude made it clear they were military.

Curtis looked down on the would-be assassins. It took all his willpower to keep from kicking their heads in. He spoke in a low, gravelly voice. "Coming after me and mine was your last mistake. I will see you in lockup, and I will see you in court. There will be no bail for any of you this time. Dillon and Haynes will be joining you faster than you can cry for your mamas."

Two trucks pulled into the clearing, and the handcuffed men were dragged into the back of one of them, manacled to steel pipes bolted into the floor of the truck.

Curtis gestured for his troops to gather around him. The two women stood on either side. They were both grinning from ear to ear. "Nice planning, boss," the redhead said.

One of the men in black added, "But we had the hard work of setting everything up."

Curtis smiled. "Very true. You did all the work, and you will get all the glory."

"Nix on the glory part. We work in the shadows, remember?"

"Then Martin and I will share the glory," Curtis said, feeling more relaxed and happier than he had in a long time.

"Shouldn't somebody be playing the *Mission Impossible* theme about now?" one of the men wisecracked.

"Effin A!" someone else said. "That went like clockwork, man!"

"Mount up, everybody!" Curtis yelled. "Before the park rangers show up!"

They cut short their celebration, knowing they better move out quickly in case rangers were nearby and had heard the explosions.

The ex-Marines, including the Maryanne and Tiffany imposters, hopped into the two trucks, four of them into the truck that held the manacled prisoners, and drove away. Martin and Curtis walked back to their own SUV, and Martin drove. As soon as they were near cell towers, Curtis took a cell phone from underneath the seat and called Osborne, then Maryanne and Tiffany to tell them the news.

They drove in silence, decompressing from the adrenaline rush of the past hour. Pulling off the ambush and capture of trained assassins with lightning speed was an incredible accomplishment, but neither one was going to admit it was anything but business as usual. They both knew they had been incredibly lucky. Dillon, being a civilian and not knowing any better, had hired assassins instead of combat veterans. Unlike Curtis's troops, they didn't have the finely honed instincts that would have enabled them to sense the presence of humans surrounding them. They didn't take time to look up in the trees and notice the lights among the high branches. These were thugs who had forgotten any military training they might have had and whose senses had been dulled by too many easy targets, too many mass killings. They might have known how to track their victims and crawl on their bellies toward a kill, but their less-than-average intellect and lack of imagination kept them from anticipating a target who was much better prepared.

Martin pulled their SUV into the parking lot of the motel behind the gas station, where they had left Maryanne and Tiffany a few hours ago.

Before they could knock, the door flew open, and the girls threw their arms around Curtis and Martin and held on for dear life.

"You did it! We're so proud of you!"

Erik and Coby, along with Sandy, a Black man who looked to be in his late forties but still maintained his excellent physique, and Peter, another ex-Marine, lean and ramrod straight in the mold of Curtis, came out of the motel room and waited until they could shake the hands of both men.

"That was one hell of a takedown," Erik said.

The others agreed. "Wish we could have been there."

Curtis shook his head. "Knowing they were safe made it all possible."

Martin pointed to the 24-hour diner across the alley from the motel. "Let's go eat before we all start crying."

Maryanne walked with her arm wrapped around Curtis. "We haven't been able to eat a bite. Now I'm starving."

They arrived at the restaurant and made themselves comfortable in two big booths. The waitress gave them menus while the smells from the kitchen drove them all crazy with hunger. They ordered quickly.

Maryanne still had questions. "Will the DC police let our police take Haynes to California?"

Curtis smiled. "Let's just say this: Very soon, Detectives Harvey and Waite will arrest Haynes in a hotel in Beverly Hills. How Haynes ended up back in LA will remain a mystery. His army of lawyers will descend on BHPD like a swarm of locusts, but I think our prosecutors can handle them."

Curtis asked Erik for his cell phone. "I wanted to call Rosemaria together. Sound like a plan?"

* * * *

Rosemaria was still in bed sound asleep when she got the call. "Hello." Her voice was phlegmy from sleep, and she cleared her throat. "Baker here."

"Baker, this is Curtis."

Rosemaria shook Josh awake, panicked. "What is it? Is something wrong?"

"I'll let you ask somebody else that."

He handed the phone to Maryanne. "Hi, Rosemaria. It's Maryanne."

"Honey, are you all right?!"

"Curtis and his friends got them all!"

"They came for you?!" Rosemaria put her cell phone on speaker so Josh could hear.

"Yes, but we had everything set up. Martin knew about a cabin he went to with a friend when he was a kid, so he and Curtis had their Marine buddies go up there a week ago and planned exactly what they were going to do! It was incredible!"

"What about you? Were you in any danger?"

"No. Curtis left us at a motel with our bodyguards. We weren't in any danger at all."

"Thank God!"

"But there's more. Soon, Haynes will be back in LA under lock and key."

"And all this while, I'm sleeping. How useless am I?"

"Tiffany wants to say hello."

"Hi, Rosemaria."

"Tiffany! I wish I could have been there!"

"Curtis, Martin, Coby, Sandy, Peter, and Erik are here." She pointed at them one by one smiling as she said their names, "They were incredible. Don't worry. We were never in any danger. There wasn't anything more you could have done."

"I guess you're right."

"Our food is coming, so I'll hang up now. We'll call later."

"I love you guys," shot out of her mouth before she had a chance to think.

"Love you too!"

Rosemaria clicked off her phone and threw herself into Josh's arms. "I'm so relieved they're safe. I don't know what to do with myself."

"Well, don't cook breakfast, whatever you do. I'll run down to Starbucks."

He jumped out of bed, pulled on his jeans and T-shirt, slipped into his sandals, and grabbed his wallet.

"The usual?"

She flopped down on the pillow. "No, I want double everything. I'm celebrating. I'll attack my waistline tomorrow."

"Sounds like a plan." And he was gone.

Rosemaria stared at the ceiling for a few minutes, contemplating her next move. "At least I can do something." She looked at the alarm clock and muttered, "They're three hours ahead of us. She should be up." Rosemaria grabbed her cell phone and punched in the name she was looking for. She dialed the number.

Mrs. Haynes was in her bathroom, slathering cream on her face when the landline rang. "Tina? Would you get that?"

After a few moments, the maid brought her the phone and held it out for her. "It's someone who says it's an emergency."

She wiped the cream off her face with a towel and took the phone. "Hello, who is this?"

"This is Rosemaria Baker, Mrs. Haynes. Your husband has been arrested, and I need your help."

Mrs. Haynes was not amused. "Are you some kind of a nut? If you don't leave me alone, I will have this call traced, and you will be arrested. Do you know who you're talking to?!"

"You're Senator Haynes's wife, and I am a former police officer. If you think I'm lying, hang up and check me out with the Beverly Hills Police Department. I used to work for them."

Mrs. Haynes noticed the maid still standing there and waved her away. "How do I know you're telling me the truth about him being arrested?"

"Call his office. He won't be there. Call his cell phone, and he won't answer. It's been confiscated."

"Hold on." Mrs. Haynes picked up her purse sitting on the dresser, dug out her cell phone, and dialed. "Hello, Morgan. This is Mrs. Haynes. Could I speak to my husband, please?" She listened, then put her phone down slowly and went back to her call with Rosemaria.

"He didn't come home, did he, Mrs. Haynes? He wasn't at the office, and he didn't go to his apartment in town."

Mrs. Haynes spoke in a whisper. "Why would he have been arrested?"

"He arranged to have one man murdered and two innocent young girls killed to stop them from testifying against him. He's been completely out of control ever since he was blackmailed in LA, and his blackmailers killed a young prostitute at the Island Hotel."

Mrs. Haynes sank down on her chaise. "Tina! Make me a vodka on the rocks!" She stared blankly at the wall.

"This is going to get really ugly, Mrs. Haynes. Tapes will be used against him that show why he was being blackmailed. They prove that he abandoned his wife and children in Cambodia to save himself. He will be reviled as a coward and then sent to jail."

Mrs. Haynes accepted a glass of vodka from her maid, took a deep swallow, and shooed her out of the room. "I still don't understand why you're calling me."

"I want you to help convict your husband. I want to make sure he gets the punishment he deserves. This is no stand-by-your-man time, Mrs. Haynes. Your husband is a monster who must be put away for good."

Mrs. Haynes took another deep drink. "You think I don't know he's a monster? I knew it before I married him. The money sucked me in. I was an idiot, and I was in trouble. I wanted to be rich. Little did I know."

"That's understandable, Mrs. Haynes. A lot of women do that."

"I'm not surprised he ran out on his family. That's who he is. He's never given a thought to anybody in his life. Anything he does for us is for show, you know what I mean? Gifts, clothes, cars, it's all to make my son and I suitably presentable. The trophy wife and her kid."

"I'm going to ask you to do something very hard, Mrs. Haynes. I want you to go to the apartment in town with a friend and see if you can find a bear that was bought at the Harland Hotel. I want you to take videos with your phone as you search, see if there is a receipt in the bag and send it all to the Beverly Hills Police Department."

"Why in the world would I want to do that at a time like this?!"

"I know it's difficult, Mrs. Haynes. But we need proof that he was at the Harland that weekend. I realize helping convict your son's father is not easy, but it's the right thing to do."

"He's not my son's father."

"Huh?"

"The creep is so self-absorbed he didn't realize I was pregnant when I married him. He didn't even count the months to when my son was born."

"That must have been very difficult for you."

"Why can't the police go get it?"

"It's a matter of jurisdiction. Having them do it could take weeks or more."

"It might not even be there."

"Then, please, Mrs. Haynes. Just go look. You probably hate that place considering the reason your husband bought it, but since it's community property, you're the only person who has the legal right to go in there." Rosemaria figured throwing a zinger in as incentive couldn't hurt.

Mrs. Haynes took another swallow. "I'll do it."

"And take a friend as a witness."

"I have a friend who hates him almost as much as I do."

"And wear gloves, please. The sooner you do this the better. The police could be on their way as we speak."

"Any more instructions?" Mrs. Haynes was getting annoyed.

"Yes. If you find the bear, could you show the bottom of the bear to the camera so we can make out the barcode?"

"The bottom of the bear. Okay. Anything else?"

"No. I'm truly grateful for your help, Mrs. Haynes. Truly grateful."

"So why is this so important to you? You sound desperate for me to find this bear."

"The two girls your husband was trying to kill are friends of mine."

"Oh." That quieted her for a moment. She finished her vodka. "Well, in that case, let's get this show on the road." She yelled, "Tina!" and hung up.

Rosemaria was wrung out. She flopped back on the bed and hoped Mrs. Haynes would follow through. She didn't have long to wait before Josh came through the door carrying a big pastry bag and their coffees. "Starbucks wasn't open yet. I had to go to a twenty-four-hour place." He saw the expression on her face and knew something was up.

"What did you just do?"

"I tried to convince Mrs. Haynes to help us convict her husband."

She walked over to the table and helped him set up their breakfast. "I'm pretty sure she went for it."

"So now you wait. At least the girls are safe with Curtis. Take a day to enjoy it."

"I can't. We still don't know who murdered Maria. It could be one of the assassins from last night or one of the ones who made the attempt before." She sat down and broke off a piece of her blueberry muffin. "Or maybe none of them. Maybe we still don't have a clue who it was."

"I'd look at Dillon's most trusted bodyguards. They arrested a couple of them at the airport, right?"

"Good thought. Who else would he trust with blackmailing a senator? They couldn't be complete goons. They would have to be men with a modicum of intelligence."

"But still would kill without hesitation."

"I wish it were eight o'clock so I could go to the station. They're probably having a big meeting this morning."

"Nothing happening with your real job?" he teased.

She laughed. "Let's eat and think positive about your meeting with Councilman Moretz this morning."

Josh smiled. "I can do that."

CHAPTER THIRTY-TWO

The atmosphere in the conference room at the Beverly Hills police station was one of quiet intensity. Lieutenant Manley sat at the head of the table and was in deep conversation with Celia Mathison, who sat at his right. Larry was on his cell phone, speaking into it in a murmur. Osborne, Sergeant Harvey, and Detective McNamara were perusing pictures spread out on the table. Two people from forensics were speaking with Mal Crews, the medical examiner. Everyone was ignoring the bagels and cream cheese on the table.

The lieutenant stood up and waited for the room to quiet down. "You've all done a great job so far tracking the murders to Dillon and Haynes and getting them locked up in our jail. We have no idea where Gold is. He has completely disappeared. Maybe he's dead, for all we know. But we have legal issues to deal with regarding Dillon, Haynes, and eight assassins our good Samaritans managed to round up for us. Mathison will be the one to guide us through those rocky shoals, so I'll let her explain it all to you."

Rosemaria, out in the hallway, was eager to get inside the room and listen to what Celia had to say, but she desperately wanted to hear from Mrs. Haynes. She had called her on her cell phone but didn't want to leave a message. How long would it have taken to round up her friend, drive to DC, and get into the apartment? It had been a couple hours now. What the heck was taking so long? She gave up expecting a message and quietly entered at the back of the room and sat in a vacant chair against the wall. She hoped the lieutenant wouldn't mind that she was there.

Manley sat down, and Celia pushed her chair back, stood up, and faced the others. "Before I give you my summation of where we are, I want to show you a video. Some of you have already seen this." She pulled down a white screen and nodded at Waite, who used his laptop to project on the screen.

The video is a little grainy, and it is not high def, but Haynes is clearly visible. He is wearing a suit and tie and is seated in a chair in front of an oriental screen and a potted palm. Haynes looks every inch the polished, successful politician that he is.

Someone is interviewing him in English. A male voice says, "Senator Haynes, we have heard rumors that you intend to lobby our government to allow an American army base here in Cambodia. Is this true?"

Haynes looks amused. "Absolutely not. We know how the Cambodian people feel about having foreign troops in their country. That's not what this trip is about."

"What is the trip about?"

"I'm on a purely economic mission here. I would like to explore what the Cambodian people need from us and find out which American companies would be welcomed in this country in order to provide jobs and economic growth for Cambodia."

"As you know, Cambodia allows foreign investments that benefit us. Like everyone all over the world, Cambodians love fast-food restaurants. It seems no one can get enough hamburgers and fries."

Haynes laughs. "I was thinking more along the lines of tech companies and textiles. I want to discuss trade agreements that are beneficial to both countries."

"It is ironic that not too many years ago—"

The interviewer abruptly stops talking. And while the camera is still on Haynes, Cambodian chatter can be heard off camera.

Haynes looks perplexed and worried. "What is happening? Please tell me what that man who just came in is saying?"

The interviewer speaks again. "It seems that some criminal gangs have started looting stores about a mile from here, and there have been shots fired."

"The police will stop them, won't they?"

Haynes is ignored as the chatter continues for several minutes. Haynes stands up and paces, growing more and more anxious.

The interviewer speaks. "It seems that the hooligans are coming closer. They have killed several people in a restaurant near the American Embassy."

Well, what should I do? Will they come to the hotel? I have to get out of here."

"Soldiers have been ordered to bring your wife and children, who I believe you said are having lunch at Romdeng, to the hotel. Your embassy is sending a helicopter, which will land on the roof of the hotel, to get you and your family out. It is too dangerous to go out into the streets. You need to wait here."

By this time, Haynes is sweating profusely. "When will the helicopter be here?"

There was more chatter in Cambodian.

"Soldiers are trying very hard to get to your wife and children, but there is much chaos in the streets. The helicopter will be here soon but will wait for your family."

The roar of a helicopter can be heard above them. Haynes looks up and follows the interviewer with his eyes as the man paces around the room.

"Maybe I should leave now?"

"You must wait for your family. It shouldn't be long."

Gunshots and yelling can be heard outside.

"I can't wait any longer! They may never get here!"

"They are your family! We must wait for them!"

Haynes runs out of the room, followed closely by two white males. The camera is aimed at the floor and then at other spots around the room as it is disconnected from the tripod. The camera follows Haynes out into the hall and focuses on him standing several yards away, punching at the elevator button. When the elevator doesn't show, Haynes runs to the stairwell door, rips it open, and disappears into the stairwell. The camera follows him into the stairwell, but Haynes is gone. Other men, Cambodians, are running after him up the stairwell. The camera keeps filming all the way up two floors to the roof. Haynes is arguing with the pilot.

"They're not coming! We need to leave now!"

Three Cambodians rush toward Haynes speaking in Cambodian and English, all too garbled to understand. Haynes jumps into the helicopter and begins yelling at the pilot. The two white males run into frame and climb in beside him. After another two minutes, the helicopter lifts off the roof. End tape.

The entire room sat in stunned silence. Celia allowed them to sit in contemplation for a few minutes, then spoke. "This is what Dillon's men were blackmailing Haynes with and what they were talking about when Maria overheard them, and it got her killed. They wanted Haynes, a Democrat, to vote against the upcoming assault rifle bill, which would have ended his career. But this tape insured that he would do it. So far, your warrant for Dillon's home or office hasn't turned up the video, but he must have it somewhere. Get warrants for his other homes and see what you can find."

"He has ten other homes all over the world," Waite said.

"Then start with his homes in Texas, where we have a friendly judge. He probably kept it close."

Celia turned back to her report. "The eight assassins who attempted to kill Maryanne and Tiffany were intercepted and detained by Malcomb Curtis and his men. They were flown to a holding site near San Diego. We used every available avenue to identify the eight killers, including Interpol." She nodded to the tech unit guys. "Fortunately, we were able to ID four of them through Matrix Surveillance. We obtained a warrant to hack into the site, and our tech guys found three Americans and one Ukrainian in the Matrix records. We compared fingerprints and have solid IDs. Through Interpol, we determined that one of the others is Chechnyan and three are Russian. All of them have used several aliases and are suspected of countless murders in Europe. The three Americans are being held here and will have access to lawyers. The Chechnyan, the Ukrainian, and the Russians are being held in a nearby facility that detains terrorists indefinitely per the Patriot Act. We have videos of all of them, and Waite and the others are painstakingly going through the footage to try and see if any of them might be Maria's killers. We also arrested Dillon's bodyguards.

"Our evidence against Dillon is solid. We have him on tape ordering the hit on Maryanne and Tiffany. He can't squirm out of that. If we can ID the two men who murdered Maria and connect them to him, which we will do, he is cooked. He has four lawyers from the firm of Masters and Lowe, who are located here in LA, and three lawyers from Austin who are not licensed to practice in California. I guess they are here for moral support. They will use whatever leverage and connections they have to get our extradition warrant thrown out and get Dillon out on bail. That won't happen. We're on solid ground with the judge in Austin and did everything by the book. Furthermore, Dillon showed consciousness of guilt by trying to flee the country. The possibility that he'll be granted bail is a pipe dream. We will continue to find and expose every illegal business he controls. His tentacles reach into many countries, but we will find them. Dillon will never see the light of day once he is convicted. And Gold, wherever he may be, will undoubtedly fade into obscurity while he enjoys his blood-soaked retirement."

Rosemaria kept looking down at her cell phone. What the heck was holding up Mrs. Haynes? Did the cops show up? Did they prevent her from going in? Rosemaria's imagination started running away with her. She should have listened to Vanessa and called her days ago.

She shook her head at Celia, who resumed her report. "We have Haynes's assistant on tape conspiring with Dillon to murder Maryanne and Tiffany. We also have the blackmail video, which shows Haynes leaving his wife and children to the mercy of terrorists. It's possible we can prove Haynes was the person who stayed in room 203 at the Harland Hotel because of the hotel maid telling us she recognized his voice." She looked at Rosemaria, who nodded anxiously and pointed at her cell phone. "We're waiting for additional proof that will be invaluable in backing up her testimony."

Rosemaria's cell phone vibrated, and she looked down at the screen. It was Karen telling her that Lattimer wanted to see her in his office at 11:30 today. She had expected this. At least she would have time to listen to the rest of the meeting. She turned her concentration back on Celia.

"Haynes's lawyers are all from DC and are licensed to practice here. They will claim that spiriting Haynes out of DC was illegal even though a judge in California had issued a warrant for his arrest. We will claim our officers merely responded to a complaint of a man found unconscious in a hotel room in Beverly Hills and discovered he was a wanted fugitive. We have no knowledge of how he got to the hotel. Right now, we still need more proof that he had Dobransky, the talent scout, murdered. We have one witness who may have seen one man walking away from the apartment about the time Dobransky was killed. Maryanne ID'd the man who chased her out of Haynes's hotel room from the gift shop video. Tiffany can ID the men who came for her at the laundromat. So, I'll conclude by saying we need to confirm Haynes was the person in room 203, we need to ID the two men who took Haynes out to the alley and murdered Maria, and we need proof that Haynes and Dillon had Dobransky murdered. We have enough now to convict both of them for several counts of attempted kidnapping and murder, but I would like the evidence against Haynes and Dillon to be so airtight even their lawyers won't be able to breathe."

Celia was ready to close. "I'd love to answer all of your questions if you have any, but please call me later. I have to get back to the office right now. I have meetings with some angry lawyers." She smiled. "My favorite kind. So, call me, and I promise I will get back to you as soon as I can. Lieutenant, do you have anything more to add?"

"Nothing that I can think of right now."

"Thank you for listening, and I'm here for you."

Rosemaria was deeply disappointed that Mrs. Haynes hadn't gotten back to her. She not only wanted it to help her girls nail their would-be killer, but she also wanted to feel like she was a part of the investigation. Like the old days. She hated the feeling of being a helpless outsider. She watched Celia gather up her things and head out the door. The detectives and techs finally dug into the bagels and cream cheese, and Rosemaria was about to pour herself a cup of coffee when her cell phone vibrated. It was a text from Mrs. Haynes. *She had done it!*

Rosemaria ran out the door and yelled down the hall at Celia. "Come back! Mrs. Haynes sent me a video!" She ran back into the conference room and gave her phone to Waite. "Can you project this on the screen?"

"Yeah, it'll take just a few minutes to send it to my laptop." While he worked, Rosemaria sank into a seat beside him and spoke to Larry and Osborne. "You guys sure did a phenomenal job in Texas. Congratulations."

Larry was modest. "The Austin police and Texas Rangers did most of it. I can only imagine the political repercussions of Dillon the gun manufacturer being arrested. They love their guns in Texas."

"They also love their kids, like everybody else," Osborne said. "Things are changing for the better, I hope."

Rosemaria turned to Waite. "Say, Jimmy, could you send me all the photos you have of the perps? I'm pretty good at noticing things. Maybe I'll see something that was missed."

Waite shrugged. "Why not?" He clicked a few times on his laptop, then sat and waited.

Rosemaria looked across the table at Mal Crews. "Mal, could you tell me again how Maria was killed. I mean, in more detail?"

"Okay. From what I can deduce, Maria was smoking a cigarette out by the dumpster around the corner from the exit door when she heard men come outside and start talking. Maybe she didn't even hear what they were saying. She can't tell us that. She finished her cigarette and turned to go back inside. The three men saw her. They must have said or done something threatening, but I believe she turned to run when one of them grabbed her around the neck with his left arm, then used his right arm to pull back on his left to choke her." Mal grabbed Larry and used him as a prop. She moved her left hand around his throat, pulled back with her right and showed how easy it was. "From the bruising on her throat, it was definitely an arm covered with clothing, like a suit arm. I'm strongly suggesting that the man was right-handed since the right hand is stronger and was used to pull back the left. I can't state with certainty that the killer was right-handed, but I put that opinion in the report."

Waite looked up from his computer. "I'm ready." By this time, everybody was back in their seats. The lieutenant and Celia were in quiet conversation at the head of the table.

Waite began the video. *Mrs. Haynes holds the phone up for a waist high selfie. She is dressed in casual pants and blouse, standing in the hallway. Another woman stands behind her, smiling at the phone. Both show they are wearing plastic gloves. "Hello, I'm Tara Haynes, and this is my friend Joanie. We are here to look for a souvenir bear that my husband, Senator Haynes, may have bought at the Harland Hotel and charged to his room on the weekend of the fundraiser at the Island Hotel. This is my first time visiting this apartment. That can be verified by the doorman and by the video camera footage that they save here for three years. This apartment is used mainly by my husband. I, of course, am half owner and am entitled to be here. Joanie and I will now look for the bear." She aims the phone at the lock. "My key card is now being used for the first time, as will be verified by the doorman on his computer." The camera follows Joanie into the darkened apartment. Joanie pulls open the living room drapes to let light in. It is a fairly small unit, minimally decorated like a hotel room. Tara's voice is heard narrating the search.*

"Joanie will look through the drawers to see if he tossed the bear in the dresser and forgot about it. Then, she will go through the laundry bin in the bathroom to see if it ended up in there with his dirty clothes. Last, we will search through his suitcases to see if it ended up in one of them. I will now film Joanie searching." The camera follows Joanie pulling out drawers and carefully searching for the bear. She finds nothing. She moves to the laundry bin and pulls out all the dirty clothes. "I guess he had other things on his mind besides fluff and fold," Tara says. Joanie carefully throws the laundry back into the hamper, one piece of clothing at a time. She finishes searching the dirty clothes, and Tara says, "Not in the hamper." Joanie walks to the bedroom closet and takes down several suitcases. She puts them on the bed and opens the first one. Nothing. She goes through all of them and does not find the bear. The camera aims in different directions. "Hold on. Joanie, look under the bed." Joanie does as she is told and pulls out a carry-on from underneath the bed. "I hope this is it, everybody," Tara says. Joanie rifles through the carry-on and pulls out a small plastic bag

that has a logo on it. She straightens out the bag so the camera can read what it says: Harland Hotel—Hollywood.

Everybody watching the video held their breath.

"Cross your fingers." Joanie reaches into the bag and pulls out a small, fluffy bear. His T-shirt says "Harland Hotel—Hollywood." Joanie inverts the bear, and the camera zooms in on the barcode. Joanie pulls out a receipt. "Looks like we hit the jackpot," Tara says. Joanie is beaming.

Rosemaria felt like the Red Sea had parted in front of her. The room came alive with chatter. Celia shushed the room quiet.

Joanie carefully places the bear back into the bag. Tara aims the camera at herself. "I will pack up this bear, and my lawyer will send him on his way to Sergeant Darryl Osborne at the Beverly Hills Police Department the fastest possible way. The next time I see you people will be at my husband's trial. I'll be the one sitting up front behind the prosecution with a big smile on my face." She turns off the camera.

The lieutenant and Celia shook hands and grabbed shoulders. Everybody was giving Rosemaria attaboys. Celia looked at Rosemaria from across the room and said loud enough for everyone to hear. "We just put another nail in Haynes's coffin. Good job, Ms. Baker. I don't know how you got her to do that and how you convinced her to present that in such a professional manner, but it was brilliant. I am *now* going back to my office." She walked up to Rosemaria, gave her a brief hug, and went out.

Larry, like everybody else, was smiling ear to ear. He hugged her as well. She told him, "Vanessa warmed her up, you know, and weeded out the chaff. I couldn't have done it without her."

The lieutenant came over and shook Rosemaria's hand. "That was perfect. All the legalities were covered. Good work." She watched him walk away and thought how much she missed this place. She loved being a prosecutor, but this was where the action was. She hit a number on speed dial. "Mrs. Haynes, you did great."

"Yeah, well, the reason it took so long to get there was because I wanted to get advice from my lawyer, and he told me what to say and what not to say. Pretty good, huh?"

"Everybody at BHPD said you were amazingly professional. The prosecutor said all the legalities got covered."

"I hope I get to testify against that SOB. And when he's put away, I'll be an independently wealthy woman, unless the lawyers take all his money. That reminds me, I better clean out our bank accounts before that happens."

"I hope I see you again soon, Mrs. Haynes."

"Make that Tara. Tara Fletcher. Looking forward to using that name again. Bye."

"Goodbye." And the connection was broken.

She found a quiet place to make her phone calls. First Karen, then Curtis and the girls, and then Josh, who she would pray for this morning with every fiber of her being.

CHAPTER THIRTY-THREE

ouncilman Moretz didn't keep them waiting. His office was fairly large and traditionally decorated with dark wood furniture, an immense desk, and bookshelves loaded with legal tomes, notebooks, and a few framed family photos. There were introductions all around—Josh, Joell, Miranda Telfer, Joell's pint-size, redheaded public relations representative, Harvey Morgan, Joell's concert promoter, who looked more like a mild-mannered, middle-aged accountant, and Pastor Diehl. Moretz had arranged seats for all of them around his desk. His secretary, Ms. Winters, came in. He introduced her to everyone and sat down.

Moretz wasted no time getting to the point. "Ed Hahn has extended an offer to the Milwaukee Zoo for Sammy. He is asking for a meeting with council members to approve the sale."

Joell jumped in. "They won't do that, will they?"

"I don't think so. Most of us realize that selling Sammy would be a huge public relations blunder. But there are those on the council who are tired of decades of protests, billboards, and editorials demanding Sammy be taken to a sanctuary. If Hahn decides to use his political connections to keep pressuring the council members, you never know what will happen."

"So, loss of campaign contributions could decide Sammy's fate?" Josh asked.

"I have some friends on the council I count on to stand with me on this, but I wanted you to understand what we're up against."

"We need that press conference to happen immediately," Joell said. "Like, within the next few days."

Pastor Diehl spoke up. "My constituents at the mission have generally responded well to the idea. You must understand, these are people in need. They are, for the most part, decent people who have landed on the streets through no fault of their own, and yet they are willing to do their part to help us. I've talked to a couple of organizers downtown, and they will arrange to have some of their people show up as well. I've refrained from talking to belligerent activists who would think of this as extortion for the sake of an animal."

"Yes, they appear in front of the City Council on a regular basis and always berate us for doing anything for shelter animals or pet adoption centers," Moretz said. "If we organize quickly, we can avoid having them show up."

"Miranda, why don't you tell everybody what you have planned?" Joell asked.

Miranda jumped in enthusiastically. "I've spoken to all of the local TV channels, cable network news shows, and newspapers, and I have arranged a press conference in front of Pastor Diehl's mission for Monday morning at 11:00 a.m. I have a press release that I won't email them until early on Monday to keep the text from leaking. I merely told the media that Joell and some of her celebrity friends had a huge announcement to make regarding the homeless. They were all over it, as I thought they would be."

"What will the press release say?" Josh asked.

"I haven't even made copies of it for fear it would get into the wrong hands. Basically, it says that Pastor Diehl, his associates at the downtown mission, Joell, whatever musicians she can convince to take part, and a representative from PAWS are sponsoring a huge concert at the Greek theater on Saturday, two weeks from now, in order to raise over one million dollars for the homeless and for Sammy's freedom. In a generous quid pro quo agreement, the homeless and their representatives are requesting that in exchange for the money raised at the concert, Sammy is to go to a sanctuary. Councilman Moretz will be putting the agreement up for a vote at the City Council on Tuesday, and the passage of the bill will result in the most fabulous win-win arrangement in the history of the city."

She was on a roll. "We will use more of that same kind of hyperbole to garner the support of not only animal and homeless activists but the general public as well. Pastor Diehl, Joell, or someone else, will announce at the end of the news conference that tickets for the concert will go on sale at Ticketmaster as soon as the City Council vote is taken, and we expect a sellout crowd." She finished her presentation and expectantly turned her attention to Moretz.

He nodded appreciatively. "The City Council will have nowhere to turn. If they vote against it, they will be voting against both Sammy and the homeless. They will be aggravating an awful lot of voters. Some of the zoo apologists and homeless activists may speak out against it, but they'll lose." He smiled. "At least that's how I visualize it happening."

Joell looked at Harvey. "So, tell them who we have so far."

Harvey looked a little apprehensive. "Joell will be our headliner, of course. It's a bit difficult to arrange for big name musicians to appear at such short notice, but the ones I've talked to are trying to rearrange their schedules and will get back to me. Other groups are recording in town, and they have said they definitely will do the concert. They include Natasha McBain, Monsta Minds, Farley Soring, Crowd of Glory, Hayden Pierce. All of them have major hits and huge followings. The ones I'm waiting to hear from are even bigger, and hopefully by tomorrow I'll nail down as many of them as I can. It's a big PR coup for them, and they know it."

Joell looked over at Josh. "What do you think, Mr. Mastermind? You started all of this. Think we can pull it off?"

Josh was momentarily startled at being singled out. "Yes, we can do this." He looked at Joell. "Without you, none of this would be happening, and without you, Pastor Diehl, my plan would not have worked. I do want to help the homeless, of that there is no doubt, but fulfilling a promise I made to Sammy the day I first started working at the zoo is a dream come true."

"Wait, wait!" Joell exclaimed. "I forgot to say one thing. Josh Sibley will be performing one of his songs at the concert. It will be his debut. I have known for two years how good he is. Now the world will know." She applauded and cheered, and the others joined in. Josh was mortified, but for Sammy, he would do whatever it took.

* * * *

An hour later, Josh walked up the path to Sammy's prison. A man and woman with two small children had just stared, pointed, and yelled at Sammy, as so many thoughtless zoo visitors did, never noticing his eyes were barely open, and his feet and toenails were torn and bleeding. Josh walked up to the fence and spoke in a whisper as he always did with Sammy. "It's Josh, Sammy. We're getting you out of here. Don't give up, pal. It's really going to happen this time." He wished he could go inside the compound, but he didn't dare. He knew he better leave before someone reported him to Hahn. But somehow Sammy seemed to understand, or maybe it was his imagination. Either way, soon Sammy would be free. He stood for a few more minutes, speaking softly to his friend and wishing Sammy could know how many people cared for him.

* * * *

Frank Lattimer, head deputy D.A. at the Airport Courthouse, was not looking forward to this meeting. Rosemaria Baker so far had a perfect record in the short time she had been working for him. And that despite that moron nephew of the attorney general trying to sabotage her every move. He had worked hard to earn his position, and his friendship with the attorney general could mean even bigger things were on the horizon for him. Despite that friendship, this thing with the nephew and Baker couldn't go on. But maybe now Atkins had finally found something solid to use against her. His phone buzzed, and he picked up.

"Ms. Baker is here."

"Send her in."

He looked up and saw the poised and very pretty Rosemaria Baker walk into his office.

"You can close the door behind you."

She did and walked toward his desk. Her face registered no nervousness. She looked rather free of any kind of emotion. He indicated for her to sit in the chair in front of his desk, which she did.

"Do you know why I've called you into this meeting?"

"I can't say that I do."

"You had many good people recommending you for this job both in New York and LA, and you haven't disappointed me. However, something has come to my attention."

"Yes?"

Damn, she seemed impervious to his most intimidating tone. She'd make a great witness in any trial.

He opened his laptop and stared at the screen. "Something has come to my attention regarding the Kazinsky case."

"What would that be?"

"I'm afraid you were filmed talking to Kazinsky yesterday afternoon at the Wilshire Gym and Spa. You talked to him for at least fifteen minutes without his attorney present and, at some point, disappeared from view."

"That's not true."

He started the video and turned the laptop around so she could view it. The camera had followed Rosemaria's car as it pulled into the driveway of the gym, toward the rear parking lot. Two minutes later, it showed her wearing her green and black workout pants and jacket with a hoodie, walking from the back parking lot to the front entrance of the gym. Then, the camera was stationary as it filmed her going inside.

The time stamp showed that an hour later, a woman looking very much like Rosemaria, and dressed in the same gym clothes, came out the front entrance. Her face was hidden and turned away from the camera. She approached Kazinsky, where he was standing with a group of men, and spoke to him. They both walked away from the group, and the woman appeared to be asking Kazinsky questions. They seemed to be very friendly, with Kazinsky's face clearly visible in the video and the woman in partial profile. They walked around the side of the building together, and a few minutes later, Kazinsky came back around the building, started his car, and drove out the back entrance of the building. The woman never reappeared, and the video ended.

Rosemaria pushed the laptop back around to Lattimer. "The woman who came out and talked to Kazinsky is not me."

"She is wearing an outfit that is identical to the one you were wearing, and her red hair is clearly visible despite the hoodie you have on."

"A lot of people buy that same outfit. They sell them at the gym. If you notice, the second woman's jacket is a different design than mine. The hem of my jacket goes straight down while the other woman's jacket has a band of black elastic at the bottom holding it tighter. She can do that because she's thinner than me. The jacket I bought camouflages my hip and tummy problem." She patted her thighs.

Lattimer studied the video.

"Also, I booked an appointment with a massage therapist right after my workout. That would have been happening at the same time as the time stamp on the second part of that video. You can confirm that with the gym. Furthermore, sir, I would never have a secret meeting with any defendant. It would be illegal and harm my career irrevocably. I would never do it."

Lattimer felt a little shaky. "It was assumed that because you used to be a cop yourself, particularly undercover, you would show favoritism to Kazinsky and go out of your way to help him."

"Who exactly assumed that?"

Lattimer sat for a moment. This time Folson's nephew had gone too far and put him in an untenable position.

"I have a right to know who accused me of this ex parte communication."

"I think we both know the answer to that."

"I want to know who is having me followed and recording my movements. This is an incredible breach of trust, and I daresay could mean this person losing his license to practice law if he is an attorney."

"It was Atkins, as you probably assumed. I guarantee he will be dealt with. This is just the latest example of his indefensible actions that somehow never end." Sensing he had said too much, Lattimer resumed his officious tone. "I assure you that he will never bother you or anyone else in this office ever again. Consider the problem dealt with." He hesitated, then added, "Unless you want to bring charges against him."

Rosemaria was unperturbed. "No, sir, I trust you to deal with the situation in your own way."

Lattimer stood up and offered his hand to Rosemaria. "I'm sorry about this, Ms. Baker."

She shook his hand. "No harm, no foul. It's forgotten already."

Lattimer watched her walk out of his office. He was relieved but had a niggling feeling he'd been had. But if she had actually set this up, then it was fortunate she was on his side, using her machinations to get even more guilty verdicts and improve his record as head deputy D.A. He was already preparing what he would say to the attorney general about his worthless nephew.

Karen had been on pins and needles waiting for Rosemaria to come back. When she saw her walking toward her desk, she practically pounced on her. "What happened?! Are you in trouble?"

Rosemaria acted cool, calm, and collected. "It was a very good meeting. And I expect Atkins will be fired before the end of the day."

Karen watched her walk into her office and followed her. No way was she getting away with that nonexplanation. "What did you do? You did something, I know it," she insisted. Rosemaria sat down behind her desk.

Rosemaria looked up at her kindly. "Have we been swept today?"

"Yesterday. There's been no time for anybody to plant new bugs."

"Karen, there may be times when I do some things that are highly irregular. When those times come, I will not share the details with you in order to protect you. I have always followed that rule and always will. Okay?"

Karen scrunched up her face in disappointment. "Okay. I don't like it, but okay."

"Let's schedule a meeting with Kazinsky and his lawyer. I can't seem to get him off my mind."

* * * *

It was Saturday, and Josh and Rosemaria were taking an early morning walk along the beach toward Venice, staying on the cement walkway.

"I have meetings today with Joell and the promoter at one o'clock at his office in Beverly Hills," Josh told her. "We have to try to nail down some more acts and, at the same time, tell them it's contingent on the City Council vote on Tuesday. It's not easy to get people to commit to a maybe. The promoter is keeping The Greek on the hook until Tuesday. He has a lot of things to juggle—advertising, security, and all the rest for the concert a week from Friday. He's not used to doing it all on such short notice."

"Does Moretz think he'll win the majority vote?"

"He's cautiously optimistic."

"I'd rather hear a resounding yes."

"I believe they will cover their political asses and do exactly what we want."

"I totally accept that. After they vote and everything is a go, can we drive up to the sanctuary on Wednesday? We need to make up for not being there this weekend and a couple of weekends after that. Will you have time?"

"There'll be a lot to do here, but why don't you drive up early, and I'll come up after I finish recording a restaurant commercial and probably a couple of meetings? Can you get away from the office?"

"The head deputy D.A. owes me. I'll give Karen and me a day off."

"He owes you?" He let that sink in for a moment. "Aha, your little scheme worked."

"Ask me no questions, and I'll tell you no lies," she shouted, and took off running toward the water. "Last one to Venice buys breakfast!"

He chased after her. "You didn't bring any money!"

"Oops, guess you pay!"

He caught up to her and easily passed her, racing up the wet sand.

They grabbed salads at the Rose Café and sat outside. Josh nibbled as he spoke.

"It occurred to me the other day that you are the most important thing in my life."

"Well, yeah, I told you that a long time ago."

"You might say I had an epiphany I couldn't ignore."

"So, what did you do after having this epiphany?"

"I went shopping."

"Well, retail therapy is always a good thing. I don't have too much time for it myself."

"I bought you a little something."

He unzipped a pocket in his sweatpants and pulled out a small box."

Rosemaria's eyes widened in disbelief. She could barely speak. "Is that what I think it is?"

He handed her the box. "Open it and see."

Her hand shook as she took it from him. She slowly opened the box and breathed in sharply. Inside was an emerald-shaped diamond engagement ring. With trembling fingers, she took it out and placed it on her ring finger. She couldn't stop staring at it. "It's beautiful."

Josh studied Rosemaria's face, lit up with joy, and wondered why he had waited so long. "So, the answer is yes?"

Her smile was radiant. She leaned forward, and they kissed softly, lingering longer than they usually did in public.

Rosemaria slowly pulled away. "Why did you change your mind?"

"Because I recognized during this epiphany that I was acting like an idiot. Ever since I was a boy, I've known nothing but poverty. I've lived in LA for years, struggling every day and drinking my life away. I never wanted to invite another person into that kind of existence. I still don't know if I'll ever be rich. Not like Larry, that's for sure. But I'll always get by okay, and in a few months, I'll have earned my two-year sobriety chip in AA. You've never expected me to have a big bank account or a fancy apartment. You've always accepted me as I am and that I may never have more than I have now. And I'm assuming you must still feel that way."

She looked at him, her face glowing. "My answer is yes, Mr. Sibley. Yes, yes, yes."

"Well, that's a relief. I'm ready to make it official whenever you say."

"Let's wait until after Vanessa has her baby and after we bring Sammy to PAWS."

"Sounds like a plan."

Rosemaria stared into space. "You know, our lives will always be complicated, and mine a little more than yours—"

"Tell me about it."

She looked at him askance. "Don't interrupt. As I was saying, I do tend to have more adventures than you, but whatever I have to face on a daily basis, I have you to come home to. For years I never had that, and now I do. That kind of happiness overwhelms any bad that may come along." She looked at her ring. "And soon I will completely own you, you gorgeous hunk of a man. That feels even better."

As always, he spoke through mouthfuls. "Admit it, I'm your dream man."

She stabbed a big chunk of avocado out of her salad and stuffed it into her mouth. "All day long, my love, all day long."

CHAPTER THIRTY-FOUR

Rosemaria was engrossed in her laptop, and Josh was outside on the patio speaking into his cell phone as Suzi flew around the apartment yelling, "I have to win the lottery! I have to win the lottery!" She didn't seem to want to settle anywhere until Rosemaria held out her arm for her to land on. Suzi pecked her on the mouth. Rosemaria lectured her, saying, "I keep telling you, you can't win unless you play, and who the heck taught you to say that anyway? Must have been one of Josh's old girlfriends." Suzi gave her another peck. "But we don't have to give any more thought to them ever again, and you need to be quiet."

Suzi seemed to take that hard and hopped onto the other dining chair, looking sad.

"I'm sorry, Suzi, but I'm trying to figure something out here. I'm usually so good at this, but now that it's important that I notice something, I can't see anything." She was studying the photos Waite had sent to her of the four assassins who made bail and the eight that were locked up, comparing them to the backs of the two men who took Haynes out into the alley and murdered Maria. "There has to be something to connect them."

She heard the front door intercom and mentally kicked herself. She ran to buzz Vanessa and Larry inside. Then, to herself, she said, "Shit! I forgot to tell Josh."

She hurried over to the patio door and slid it open. "I'm sorry, hon, I forgot to tell you, Vanessa and Larry are coming over to help us celebrate."

He pulled the phone away from his mouth. "When will they be here?"

She cringed. "Two minutes?"

"I'll wrap this up in one."

God, she loved what a good sport he was. She ran to answer the door when she heard the knock.

Vanessa threw her arms in the air and screamed, "You're getting married!" She was holding two bottles of sparkling grape juice.

Rosemaria threw her arms in the air too and screamed. "Yeah, I'm getting married!"

"Let me see the ring!"

Rosemaria waggled her ring finger in front of her.

"Wow! Beautiful!"

Suzi flew around the room, excited. She loved people. The more the merrier. "Gilbert get down! Gilbert get down!" she yelled.

Rosemaria admonished her. "Calm down, Suzi. You can socialize later." Suzi flew around the room a few times and landed back on her perch.

Vanessa spotted Josh out on the balcony. "Get that man in here, and let's open up the bubbly." She made a beeline for the kitchen.

Larry was calmer but just as happy. He gave Rosemaria a hug and followed his wife into the apartment. "You gotta love her enthusiasm."

Vanessa was rooting around in their kitchen drawers, looking for a corkscrew. "You don't have a lot of stuff in here, girl. I need to open this bottle."

Larry took one of them off her hands. "I think you just unscrew these."

Rosemaria joined them in the kitchen, and she and Vanessa grabbed some glasses out of the cupboard, brought them into the living room, and set them on the table. Josh opened the sliding door and came inside. "I heard yelling in here. Is there a fire or something?"

Vanessa waddled over to give him a hug, her belly bigger than ever. "A fire in your heart, I daresay."

Larry was right behind his wife. "Good move, my man." They hugged. "Speaking as the recently wed, I recommend it."

Rosemaria was filling up their glasses.

As Rosemaria passed them out, she asked Larry, "How is Lupe doing?"

"She's staying in an apartment near the Harland, so it will be convenient for work, and my lawyer is drawing up all the necessary papers for her to get her green card."

Vanessa looked at Larry. "He's such an old softy. That's what I love about him." She planted a kiss on his cheek. "Okay, let's get back to the celebration. Somebody give a speech."

Larry feigned to be in deep thought, then spoke. "We were all wondering when this joker would finally come to his senses. I don't know what finally got him there, but he's the luckiest guy alive that this lady stuck around waiting for him to make his move." He lifted his glass. "Here's to the best cop, the best prosecutor, and the best friend my wife ever had and to the man who better treat her right or he's got the entire BHPD to answer to! Cheers!"

They all yelled, "Cheers!" and drank up.

"The wedding will be at our house," Vanessa said. She looked at Larry. "Okay, honey?"

"Fine, just don't expect me to have anything to do with planning it."

"Don't worry, "Vanessa said contentedly. "I'll handle everything."

Rosemaria protested. "But you'll have a newborn baby to deal with, and we haven't set a date yet."

"I can change diapers and chew gum at the same time. As soon as you two decide on a date, I'll hire a wedding planner, and you can leave everything in our hands."

Rosemaria stood next to Josh and gave him a nudge. "See what you started?"

"Let me give you some advice about women," Larry said. "They're stronger, smarter, and more organized than we are. They love doing things we don't like doing. Let them have their way. We get to relax, don't have to get involved, and then we show up for the festivities."

Vanessa nuzzled him. "You sure know how to sweet talk, babe." She suddenly grimaced in pain and put her hand to her stomach. "Whoa." She reached out for a chair and sat.

Larry panicked. "What's wrong? Is it time?"

Vanessa shook her head. "No, I don't think so." She flinched. "I think our kid may be a football player."

Larry knelt beside her. "Are you sure? Do we need to go to the hospital?"

Rosemaria took her glass from her and knelt on the other side. "Your water didn't break, did it?"

"Dry as a bone." Vanessa managed a smile and looked down at Larry. "I promise you I'll let you know as soon as that happens."

"I have to be there, you know." He looked up at the others. "We've been going to birthing classes together at Cedars. I'm helping her through this."

"Okay, no more fussing over me. Rosemaria, will you help me to the bathroom? You men can go out on the balcony and talk amongst yourselves. The two of us have some things to discuss."

Larry stood up. "All right. Just holler if you need me."

Josh led the way, and they went outside.

Vanessa spoke softly in a conspiratorial voice. "I don't need to go to the bathroom. I just want to know how it went with our little plot concerning you-know-who."

"It went very well. Your friend was perfect. You-know-who is getting fired."

"Bravo!" Vanessa clapped her hands together.

"But it's all strictly between you, me, and your friend. No one else knows, except Josh, of course."

"My lips are sealed." Vanessa indicated the laptop. "How the heck did you come up with such a sneaky plan in the first place?"

"It's a long story, but I got the idea from a man I almost prosecuted and a case of mistaken video identity involving his shoes."

Vanessa gave her a puzzled look. "All right, so don't tell me. Anyway, were you working on something when we so rudely interrupted?"

Rosemaria tapped the laptop, and it lit up. "Let me scoot your chair around so you can sit next to me. Maybe you can help."

"I can scoot." She moved next to Rosemaria and looked at the screen. "What are these pictures and videos?"

"I split the screen so I can compare this guy here." She pointed at one of the two men escorting Haynes out the back door of the Island Hotel. "See this guy on the left? He's right-handed according to his actions with a clumsy bus boy on the video just before this. The other man is left-handed. Mal Crews told me she is ninety-five percent sure the man who choked Maria to death is right-handed. I'm trying to see if either of these men could be one of the men who have been arrested, but they keep their heads down. All you can see are the backs of their heads, the tops, and the sides." Rosemaria is exasperated. "I'm usually so good at spotting little differences, but this time, I've struck out."

Vanessa glanced at the screen for a few seconds. "I can tell you right now that the guy on the left is wearing a piece."

Rosemaria studied the screen. "What? How can you tell?"

"I'm an actress. I've worked with plenty of men who wore hair pieces. Some are really good and can't be spotted right off, but most are painfully obvious. One actor, Simon York, had one that was so good I didn't even realize it during our love scene. But during his close-up, I saw it. This guy has one almost that good. But if you'll notice the hairpiece doesn't quite match his own hair and is not blended in well."

Rosemaria is stunned. "A vain assassin?"

Vanessa shrugged. "A lot of men are that way about their hair."

Rosemaria started bringing up booking pictures of the twelve would-be assassins. "Let's go through them slowly, okay?" She started with the eight men who had attacked Curtis in the woods and were now safely locked up.

Vanessa carefully studied the photos one at a time.

"Anything?" Rosemaria asked hopefully.

"Not yet."

They went through all eight pictures, then Rosemaria pulled up booking photos, front and both sides, of the four who had invaded Curtis's house, had been arrested, and had gotten out on bail.

"That's him." Vanessa was pointing at Mark Dornan.

"Are you sure?"

Vanessa leaned back in her chair. "Yep. Same man. Same piece."

Rosemaria blew out a lungful of air. She was relieved to know who the murderer was but deeply disappointed that he was one of the ones who had escaped and was beyond their reach.

Vanessa saw her disappointment. "Didn't I help you?"

Rosemaria rushed to assure her. "Oh yes, you did, Vanessa. More than you know. But this particular man was arrested and let go, and now we have no idea of where he is."

Josh and Larry came back in. "Why are you two huddled over the computer?" Josh asked.

"I have good news and bad news," Rosemaria told them. "Vanessa identified Maria's killer, but he's one of the men who was let out on bail in Ohio."

Larry stepped close to Vanessa and took her hand. "Good detective work, wife."

"How do you get him back?" Josh asked.

"I don't think we do. Can you think of anything, Larry?"

"Not off the top of my head. Maybe the tech guys can track him down through Matrix somehow."

"How did Vanessa manage to identify him?" Larry asked.

"Your brilliant actress wife recognized his hair piece in both pictures, which is more than I was able to do."

Larry pulled Vanessa to her feet. "I think I'll take her home and spoil her now, if you all don't mind?"

Vanessa pecked him on the cheek. "That's all you ever do. One of these days, you're going to get good and sick of catering to my every whim. Then what will I do?"

Larry walked her to the door. "I'll answer that in greater detail at home."

Josh and Rosemaria joined them at the door. There were hugs and congratulations all around. "Thank you for coming, guys." Rosemaria said. Suzi flew over and landed on Josh's shoulder, sorry the party was over.

"Bye, Suzi. We'll stay longer next time," Vanessa said.

They disappeared down the hallway, and Josh closed the door. He could see how disappointed Rosemaria was. "Darn! So close! We had him and didn't even know it."

"Have faith in the tech guys. They might come up with something."

"Yeah, they might. I remember Celia saying the same law firm that got the four assassins off is one of the two handling Haynes. Those lawyers probably know where he is."

"I don't think your cops are going to hack into a law firm website."

"You're probably right. There's got to be a way." She looked at Suzi on his shoulder. "Let's give her a treat. I think she feels ignored lately."

She watched him walk into the kitchen with Suzi. Despite the setback, she felt content. She picked up her cell phone off the coffee table and hit speed dial. She waited for her father to answer. "Hey, Dad, I've got some awfully good news for you."

* * * *

Senator Haynes looked around his temporary living quarters. For a jail cell, he figured it wasn't that bad—clean, comfortable cot, decent food delivered three times a day on schedule. He had plenty of time to confer with his lawyers in a small conference room. But this wasn't how he had envisioned his next trip to Beverly Hills would unfold. It seemed like a lifetime ago that he had been relaxing in his condo awaiting the arrival of one of his attractive, amenable lady friends who would cater to his every need, no matter how unusual they might seem to his more conservative constituents. His women were always paid handsomely to do as asked and feign pleasure as they administered to his needs. He insisted on that. And who knew? Maybe they did enjoy it. He liked it more if he could convince himself of that.

After coming home to his condo, he had shoved unpleasant thoughts of Dillon, blackmail, and hired killers out of his mind. He was confident that everything would work out. It always had before. He had showered and shaved after doing a hard day's work for the people—meetings, luncheons, interviews, all designed to stop the anti-gun law Dillon had forced him to stand against. He was a schmoozer extraordinaire and believed he could do what Dillon demanded. Knowing he was committing political suicide, he had resisted doing Dillon's dirty work at first, before that video was shoved in his face, but Dillon promised that he'd donate to Haynes's campaign chest when he would be forced to run for reelection to the Senate as a Republican.

He was relaxed and ready for a night of pure delight with Marni, his absolute favorite, when the door to his condo had crashed in. Four men wearing dark suits and ski masks grabbed him and roughly manhandled him out the door. His mouth and nose were covered with a wet, foul-smelling cloth. He woke up much later, finding himself blindfolded, bound, and gagged in the back of a limousine. After what seemed like an hour's drive, the car door opened, and two men grabbed him on either side and forced him up a flight of stairs onto a plane. Someone helped him to the restroom twice during the long flight, otherwise he was completely ignored, no food or water, still bound and gagged. His face was again covered with a damp cloth, and the next thing he knew, he woke up in a hotel room in Beverly Hills and was arrested.

He, Senator Haynes, one of the most important politicians in Washington, DC, was being treated like a piece of trash. His lawyers must have raised hell on his behalf. At first, he was certain it wouldn't be long before he was released and wreaking revenge on this pathetic little Podunk police department. If they thought they could get away with treating him with such complete disregard, they were sadly mistaken. But here he was, days later, his lawyers making excuses, saying they needed more time, don't worry, blah, blah, blah. He had paid them hundreds of thousands of dollars through the years, and now when he really needed the sons of bitches, they were failing him.

It wasn't until his lawyers told him that Dillon was here as well, locked up in another cell, that Haynes felt the first stab of fear in his gut. What did the police know about the bribes and the payoffs? At least there was no way they could have learned about the blackmail, or connect him to the murdered girl at the Island, the hit on the pimp, and the attempted hits on the prostitutes. After all these years of having a free pass for his indiscretions, was he finally being made to pay? He couldn't let that happen.

Haynes shook off his doubts. He was meeting his lawyers again in a few hours, and they would tell him that some judge had agreed that what the cops had done was illegal. They would be filing a flurry of motions to put an end to this monstrous miscarriage of justice. But he had another reason for looking forward to this meeting.

He was consumed with the desire to destroy the person who he was certain had spearheaded this vendetta against him. Again and again, the same name came up—Rosemaria Baker, an ex-cop and a friend of the two sluts his idiot assistant had arranged for him to meet after a successful day of fundraising at the Island. Instead, he had witnessed a murder and fled back to his room at the Harland to arrange a flight out of town as fast as he could. He figured at least one of those girls had seen him there. He'd managed to get rid of the pimp who sent them, but because of that Baker women, he hadn't been able to get to the girls. He couldn't tell his lawyers about the last attempt on their lives that Dillon had arranged. All he knew was that it hadn't worked, and he had no idea where the men Dillon had hired through Matrix were now. Those girls were being protected like they were the crown jewels. Two hookers, for God's sake! Why all the fuss over two useless girls who would never amount to a hill of beans? If this case ever went to trial, which he was certain it would not, they would not be alive to testify.

His lawyers hadn't been given the evidence the cops had against him yet. They were filing motions to get their hands on all of it. What could they have on him? The word of two worthless women? He was a respected statesman, a hero who risked his life to save his family. His wife would testify for him. She'd do anything for money. Whatever money that was his that she was getting her hands on now was chump change to him. She was for sale like everybody else and didn't know diddly-squat about his business with Dillon. He was untouchable, as his enemies would soon find out.

Meanwhile, he would find pleasure in causing pain and death to this interfering bitch, Baker. He would make her disappear, and her disappearance would never be connected to him. But before she died, she would know who killed her. The thought of that gave him immense satisfaction.

Haynes could still destroy witnesses and anyone else who dared to think they could diminish his power. Dillon was just a businessman. Sure, he had connections in Congress and paid plenty to block any bills that would stop the constant flow of guns into the hands of anybody who wanted them. He had manipulated politicians for years. But the public had grown to despise men like Dillon and blamed them for every school shooting and every little kid's death. Ridiculous, to be sure. Guns don't kill people. People kill people. Haynes loved that slogan. But even he had to admit it was wearing thin. However, Dillon had gotten out of scrapes before and he would get out of this one. The power brokers in Washington would come through for them. Haynes would emerge unscathed. Baker would learn the hard way who was boss. And it wasn't her.

CHAPTER THIRTY-FIVE

ollywood Boulevard was a mob scene of news trucks, reporters, curious residents, and tourists. The boulevard had been cordoned off to vehicle traffic between Whitley and Wilcox, but the very sight of camera crews drew pedestrian onlookers like flies to honey. The press conference was not scheduled for another half hour, but to the news media, the lure of Joell and other famous musicians making an announcement of this magnitude was irresistible. News channels and the printed media had received the press release early this morning—a concert would be held to raise over a million dollars for the homeless and for the release of Sammy the elephant from the zoo. Joell herself was the driving force behind the plan. The large group that had gathered inside the mission was visible through the large plate-glass windows. Everyone waited with bated breath to see who would take part in the news conference.

Inside the mission, Miranda Telfer, the PR lady, was trying unsuccessfully to gain the attention of the group. A piercing whistle assaulted the ears of everyone in the room, drawing their eyes to the offender. Josh took his fingers away from his mouth, smiled, and gestured toward Miranda. Gratefully, she proceeded to remind the people in the room, who were now giving her their full attention, the order of the speakers.

Josh was relieved he could fade into the background and didn't need to say a word. Joell was standing beside Miranda and gave thumbs-up and smiles every time Miranda announced a name. Joell would be the first speaker at the press conference. A couple of musicians who had agreed to perform, should the council vote yes, would then say a few words. The representative from PAWS, where Sammy would make his home, would speak next. Pastor Diehl would be the second-to-last speaker, Councilman Moretz would be last, and Joell would wrap it up. Then, they would open the press conference to questions.

* * * *

Rosemaria and Karen walked quickly down the hall and into the court-house kitchen to pick up their midmorning snack. Both were a bit apprehensive. They would be watching Joell's and Sammy's big moment in the conference room. O'Malley, on his first day back at work, was sitting guard at a table in the conference room. Rosemaria, Karen, Tariq, and a three of his fellow interns, David, Eddie, and Zach, would be watching the news conference there. O'Malley's job was to make sure the TV stayed tuned to the local station without interference from any other prosecutors who might come in the conference room to eat their lunch.

Rosemaria took a plate out of the refrigerator that held a slice of pie covered by plastic wrap. "I have to eat something sweet when I get nervous."

"Hey, I'm not here to judge," Karen said as she pulled out a small bowl of mixed fruit in a plastic container.

"I feel your scorn, though."

"It's a special occasion, and there is no scorn in my tone." Karen took a banana from a bowl on the counter.

"Okay. I'll do better tomorrow."

They walked quickly to the conference room, where their friends were waiting, keeping their eye on the TV screen.

"They keep saying five more minutes, then ten minutes go by," Tariq said.

"Every press conference is like that," Karen said. "Drives people crazy."

Everybody seemed filled with positive enthusiasm, even O'Malley. "This is big stuff your fiancé has come up with, boxing in the City Council like that. I think Joell will pull it off today."

"She's wonderful," Rosemaria said. "If I died, I'd let her have him."

"Stop with the dying stuff," Karen said.

"Nothing will happen to me. I have too much to do." She looked at O'Malley, who still looked very thin and pale. "It's good to have you back, Terrence. Try not to do anything like that again."

"I'll do my best."

Suddenly, they all sat up and took notice of the screen. The people inside the mission were coming out to stand in front of the microphones. Rosemaria grimaced. "Oh God, here it comes. I'm so nervous."

* * * *

On Hollywood Boulevard, Pastor Diehl came out first, followed by two homeless activists. They acknowledged the press, and the crowd then stepped aside as Josh, Natasha McBain, Farley Soring, and Miranda Telfer came out. Councilman Moretz was next, and finally Joell stepped up to the microphones. There were noticeable gasps from the onlookers as they recognized the musicians and then the goddess of song, Joell. Loud, enthusiastic cheers broke out and traveled up and down the boulevard from Highland to Gower, overwhelming in its intensity. For Josh, it was music to his ears. The City Council couldn't ignore the people, and the people loved Joell. She acknowledged the cheers, and after a while, she held her arms up, indicating she wished to speak.

"Thank you all for being here," she said. "I have appreciated your love and support for many years, and it's time for me to give back. As someone who has lived in Los Angeles all her life, I have seen the plight of the homeless grow worse with every year. Money is always allocated for them, and then it seems to disappear where no one can find it. We expect to change all that." The entire crowd was listening to her with rapt attention. "We are going to raise, we hope, if people will be kind enough to buy tickets, over one million dollars for the homeless by giving a concert starring the best musicians in the country!" Her voice crescendoed, and the audience cheered. "But this money will be personally overseen by Councilman Moretz and his committee, and any citizen who wants to know where the money is going can find out anytime they want! There will be no political shenanigans where this money is involved! It will go directly to the homeless!"

Pastor Diehl and the homeless activists looked as if they had finally arrived at the Promised Land, and even hard-core reporters were smiling. "Pastor Diehl, who works his heart out for the homeless here at the mission, reminded me that people who are poor and have no place to live are still good citizens who care about others. Many of them have animals whom they love and who are their constant companions. And so, at *their* suggestion, they have demanded a quid pro quo because they, too, want to give back. Tomorrow morning at the Los Angeles City Council meeting, Councilman Moretz will be announcing a vote on a bill to release Sammy the elephant from his prison at the zoo and allow him to live out the rest of his life in a sanctuary. If the City Council votes yes, the concert will be held, the homeless will be given over one million dollars, and Sammy the elephant will be set free! It's a win-win for all of us! Working together, we can make this happen! I now give you Natasha McBain!" Joell stepped back and hugged Natasha, who stepped up to the microphone.

"Hey, LA. I love you!"

People on the sidewalks and street could not believe their good fortune at having been strolling down the boulevard and running into this incredible spectacle of famous people. They had struck celebrity gold without even looking for it. They went wild at Natasha's words.

"I love the homeless, and like they do, I love animals! Hey, City Council! Let's make a deal!"

* * * *

In the conference room, everyone at Rosemaria's table was under Natasha's spell.

"I love her," Tariq said.

Zach agreed. "She's incredible."

"Is Josh going to speak?" Karen asked.

Rosemaria shook her head. "Are you kidding? He handed the show over to Joell. It's her's now."

"Farley's coming up!" Karen said. "I have his new CD. I've listened to it a million times in the car."

* * * *

The crowd on Hollywood Boulevard had grown exponentially. The police had their hands full keeping them from pushing forward and getting in the way of the reporters and TV cameras. Everybody was eager to get close to their favorite stars.

"Thank you, everybody, for showing such great support for the homeless!"

The noise was constant now. Farley had to yell even louder to be heard.

"We're looking forward to a great concert, and we hope all of you will come! A week from Saturday. Will you be there?!"

The crowd screamed yes, and a few enthusiastic fans escaped the first line of police but were caught by the next. Miranda had no idea the press conference would draw this many crazed onlookers. It was more than she could have hoped for. She'd have to tell the other speakers to edit their comments, or they'd all be overrun by fans before Moretz even got to speak. Farley was wrapping it up.

"We love the city of angels, and that's just what every one of you are! See you at the Greek real soon!" As the crowd roared, he joined Natasha, who was standing next to Josh in the back. The lady who represented PAWS, Candace Morelli, stepped forward.

* * * *

"How do you think we're doing?" Rosemaria asked her friends. "Can we pull this off?"

"I'm waiting for hard questions from reporters," O'Malley said. "We'll know then."

"I'm convinced," Tariq said. "If there's a concert, I'm going."

* * * *

Joell joined Candace at the mic. "This wonderful lady works at the sanctuary that will accept Sammy and make him the happiest elephant in the world as soon as the City Council gives their say so. Please welcome, Candace Morelli!"

The animal activists, many of whom had protested for the release of Sammy, were out in full force. They blended in with the rest of the crowd, so it wasn't obvious how many were there. At this point, they cheered wildly. Everything they had worked for since Sammy was imprisoned in the zoo might finally happen. Candace was a young, attractive lady with a commanding voice, but her personality shone with compassion. When she began to speak, the noise dimmed, and the crowd listened.

"I want to thank the homeless people who contributed to this win-win deal for them and for Sammy. Their generosity and selflessness are an inspiration to all activists on both sides who volunteer countless hours to make this a better city for everyone, including animals."

Cheers greeted her words.

"We are ready to welcome Sammy with open arms. His suffering began when he was just a baby, beaten into submission and treated like an object of entertainment his entire life. We want that to end! It's time for Sammy to be free!"

Joell, the musicians, and everyone else behind Candace cheered and waved their arms in the air, inspiring everyone listening to do the same.

"Joell, Natasha, Farley, the other musicians, and the homeless people of LA have given Sammy an incredible gift, and all the City Council has to do is say yes! They've been saying no for twenty-five years. It's time to say yes! Yes! Yes!"

The people behind her took up the chant, and the crowd followed. "Yes! Yes! Yes!" They repeated the word over and over again. All over LA and on cable news, the words echoed throughout the country.

"Thank you, LA!" Candace shouted. "And Sammy thanks you!"

Joell stepped forward and gave her a hug. Pastor Diehl came up to the microphone.

As the cheers died down, he said, "I don't know how to follow that, but everyone I talk to on the street and who comes to the mission are all in on this. I've been working with people in need for twenty years, and their generosity of spirit does not surprise me one bit. The narrow-minded and stingy need to find another place to call home because they won't find it here!" He stretched out his arm toward the mission as he spoke, and the response was deafening. He waved to the crowd as Moretz came up behind him and put an arm around his shoulders. He kept Pastor Diehl by his side as he spoke.

"I'm Councilman Moretz, and I approve this message!"

It seemed that the noise could not get any louder, but it did.

"I'm introducing the motion to free Sammy directly to the Los Angeles City Council tomorrow morning along with my friend and fellow council member Jodi Adams. And we are urging that the vote be a unanimous yes!"

The crowd again started chanting, "Yes! Yes! Yes!"

"We look forward to the day in the very near future when Sammy is driven to his forever home up north! We are in this together!"

Joell walked forward and stood between Councilman Moretz and Pastor Diehl. "Thank you, Councilman Moretz! Let's do it!"

Joell calmed the crowd down and spoke to the reporters. "We stand here before you ready to answer any questions you have."

Miranda wondered how long it would be before some reporter asked the most important question of the day. She had personally coached one of Pastor Diehl's homeless men, Barney Tortoff, to answer the question. He had put up with her for all of about thirty seconds before he put an end to her advice-giving.

He was short and chubby with gray stubble on his face. He had a crew cut and intelligent blue eyes nestled in a mass of flesh and wrinkles, and his clothes were old but clean. "Thank you very much, but I can speak for myself. I know how I feel, and I know what I want to say." And with that, he turned and walked away. Since he was going to answer the all-important question, she was now riddled with anxiety. She saw him standing a little bit apart from the group but seemed alert and ready. Pastor Diehl noticed her nervousness and calmly smiled and nodded.

* * * *

In the conference room, everyone at Rosemaria's table was optimistic. They had been studying the other people in the room who were watching the news conference, trying to assess their reactions, and from what they could tell, they were all positive.

"I think that went incredibly well," Karen said. "Actually fabulous."

Rosemaria had been studying Josh the whole time, and she could tell he was pleased. "I hope the whole City Council is watching this."

O'Malley chuckled. "Oh, they are. You can bet on that."

They turned their attention back to the TV to listen to the reporters' questions.

* * * *

Miranda's stomach was in a knot as her people responded easily to some softball questions, then she saw Clark Romano of Channel 2 square up to ask a question. *Here it comes*, she thought.

"Joell, I have a question for you. If by some chance the City Council should vote no on moving Sammy out of the zoo and into a sanctuary, does that mean you would call off the concert and the homeless would not get their much-needed funds?"

Joell moved as if to go to the mic when Barney pushed his way forward. He elbowed some people aside and stood directly in front of the mic. Joell gestured for him to take the stage. Barney was all business.

"My name is Barney Tortoff, and I am a person who has found myself without a permanent home for some time now. Pastor Diehl has been kind enough to help me in every way he can, and I am working on making my life better. Do you think that because we are in need that we only live for ourselves? Yes, many of us are to blame for where we are today. Some of us are addicts and may be lost forever. I don't know. But most of the people I meet on the street care for each other. We help each other. We share what we have no matter how little it may be.

"People who represent us have gone to the City Council many times to ask for this and that, and much is promised, but nothing changes. We, like Sammy the elephant, live in a prison. Our prison is made of sadness and hopelessness. We are the same, Sammy and us—he is sad and feels hopeless too but lives in a real prison you can see and touch. We are in this together with Sammy. We all want out of our prisons. So, this time, when we come to the City Council, we are not coming to ask them for something. We are coming to give the gift of life to Sammy and to ourselves.

"If the vote is no, we are willing to give up the money from the concert because we will have won our self-respect, which is more helpful than anything else in getting us out of our prisons. We will have taken a stand for something that is right. Something big. But the terrible thing is that Sammy would be doomed to live in sadness without hope until he dies. And where is the self-respect in that for the City Council? They have a chance to do something big too, just like us. And I think they will."

Barney had been stoic throughout his speech, but now was overcome with emotion. He stumbled backward, and Pastor Diehl caught him in his arms. Everyone took turns hugging him as the cheers echoed up and down Hollywood Boulevard.

Joell announced the end of the press conference and encouraged everyone to go to Ticketmaster as soon the City Council voted. She raised her arms and acknowledged the cheers of the crowd.

* * * *

O'Malley stood up and picked up his tray. "No wonder that woman is a star. She can sing, yes, but man can she control an audience."

"Barney put the cherry on top of the whipped cream," Karen said. "He was wonderful. By this afternoon, everybody in the whole country will have seen that press conference, and millions of people will be on the side of Sammy and the homeless."

Everyone stood up and then looked down at Rosemaria, who sat rooted to the spot.

"What's wrong?" Karen asked.

"I'm just so happy," Rosemaria said. "I'm so happy, I forgot to eat my pie."

"You can eat it in your office. Come on, boss, you've got people to incarcerate."

The others patted Rosemaria on the shoulder as they walked by. "I'll call you later," O'Malley said.

Rosemaria finally stood up and shook off her mood. "I feel inspired." She asked Karen, "When is Kazinsky coming in?"

"One o'clock."

"Let's cheer up his day."

* * * *

Joell, Josh, and Miranda were in Joell's office on Wilshire Boulevard. It was large and comfortable, with homey furniture that included a grand piano loaded down with charts and store-bought sheet music. The walls were hung with gold and platinum records, and pictures of Joell with dozens of celebrities. The view was of the boulevard and the art museum a block away. Josh looked out the picture window, lost in thought as Joell and Miranda chatted away over their cappuccinos.

"What are you thinking, Josh?" Miranda asked softly.

Josh wandered over to the piano, sat down, and struck a few soft chords. "I'm just wondering how the hearing will go tomorrow."

"From what I hear, Ed Hahn and his zoo flunkies will be there in force. Our side will be overwhelmingly bigger. Everyone who wants to say something gets a minute or so to talk, and then they vote."

"We'll all be there, Josh," Joell reassured him. "You won't be alone when we get our answer."

"This must be more nerve-racking than being up for a Grammy. Of course, I've yet to experience that firsthand."

"Speaking as someone who has been through that a few times, yes, this is worse. Someone's life is at stake." Joell looked at her awards on the bookshelves. "Sammy's life is worth a lot more than these."

Josh played softly, and the ladies came over and leaned on the piano. "Sing something for us, Josh." Miranda said. "Give us a preview."

"I would, but I can't sing a note until I know what will happen tomorrow. I guess you'll have to wait for the concert. If it happens, it will be because of the two of you."

"You're giving us too much credit, big guy. All we did was follow your lead, and the rest was easy, right, Miranda?"

"Absolutely."

Joell leaned toward Josh and whispered, "What do you think, Josh? Think we can pull it off?"

"We've got one big hump to get over, and then Sammy is free and clear."

CHAPTER THIRTY-SIX

Waite was in the computer room when his phone rang. He saw that it was Rosemaria calling again. He had nothing but respect for the woman. She was his friend. But she was the most persistent, demanding person he had ever known. Every other day, she called to find out if he had found anything new on the investigation and, whether or not it was approved of by the higher-ups, he told her everything. She had called him immediately when she found out Mark Dornan was the probable suspect in the murder of Maria Ramirez and expected results from him overnight. She had no concept of what it took to search the Matrix site and various other sites owned by Dillon's company, let alone sort through hundreds of records of employees of those companies. He'd already been working on that for weeks. She didn't seem to understand that BHPD was investigating Hayes, Dillon, and their hit men practically 24/7. He picked up the landline.

"Yes, Rosemaria."

"Anything yet?"

"Didn't I say I'd call you?"

"Yes, but I thought maybe you could tell me if you're getting close."

"It doesn't always work like that."

"All right. You know how much this means to me."

"It's important to all of us."

"All right then. Call me if there's anything. I'm sorry if I'm bothering you."

"No bother."

"Talk to you later."

"We're all rooting for Josh."

"Oh, Jimmy, thank you! And thank everyone else for their support!"

"Will do."

"Bye."

Waite hung up and went back to his keyboard. He looked at the other guys in the tech unit, heads down, intent on their work. This was the unit that he was supposed to have left behind when he joined Osborne's murder investigation. But here he was again, his punishment for doing his work too well. After he helped convict the two monsters ensconced in their jail and all their cohorts, that would be it. He would insist he wanted to be a real investigator and not stuck behind a computer screen. Until then, he would make it his mission to find Mark Dornan, whatever rock he may be hiding behind.

* * * *

Kazinsky sat with a smirk on his face next to his lawyer, who didn't look all that smug. Kazinsky was sure that he had given this prosecutor chick a successful snow job about the whole stupid case against him. He was good at fooling people. That's why he would have made a great undercover cop if his lack of money hadn't made him do something stupid. This prosecutor used to be a cop, undercover even. She wanted to believe him in the worst way. He saw her smiling at him but let his lawyer talk first.

"Ms. Baker, now that you've had time to think over Mr. Kazinsky's side, I'm sure you can see that it was all a misunderstanding by the Santa Monica Police. Mr. Kazinsky had no intention of joining the burglars in spending their illicit gains."

Still smiling, Rosemaria asked, "Then why did Mr. Kazinsky hide his illicit gains in his garage behind a wall board?"

"I was saving it as evidence," Kazinsky said, positive he was getting through to her.

"You had weeks to bring it in as evidence. You had weeks to contact your superior in the police department and give him the names of the fences and everyone else involved. You completely dropped off the grid and didn't show up again until you were caught in the act of burglarizing a house."

Kazinsky felt everything slipping away. His grin was replaced by an anxious scowl. "I was waiting for the right time." Even he had to admit he sounded pathetic.

"Mr. Kazinsky, the case against you is so obvious, the night janitor could take it to court and win. I'm charging you with first-degree burglary, which is a felony. Your crime is punishable with up to six years in state prison. I'm offering you three, with the possibility of parole in two. I'm being very generous here considering the fact that you committed your crimes while working as a police officer. Whatever punishment the SMPD decides to inflict on you is up to them. Take it or leave it, Mr. Kazinsky."

All the air had gone out of Bernard. He was finished. He'd be lucky if he got a job as a ditch digger when he got out. He hung his head and didn't speak. His lawyer accepted the deal.

Kazinsky didn't look at her as he walked out the door. His lawyer shrugged and followed. Rosemaria knew she had been generous with Kazinsky, but since she had used him to get rid of Atkins, she figured she owed him something. Any way you looked at it, his life was ruined.

Reid Smith stuck his head in the door. "The Grover Vick case is scheduled for a month from now." He saw her confused look. "You know, the guy who tried to kidnap you?"

"I'm sorry. My mind was somewhere else."

"You'll be testifying. But it's a long way off. We have plenty of time to put our heads together."

"He's still safely locked up, right?"

"Secure and comfortable in the county jail."

"Keep him there, okay?"

"We have him dead to rights. Don't worry. He won't get out."

"Thanks, Reid. I won't let you down. Do you know yet who's replacing Atkins?"

"Not yet."

He waved and was gone. She decided to dig into her apple pie that was still sitting on her file cabinet. Waste not, want not.

* * * *

Curtis was surprised that after all the violence that they had experienced in the past few weeks, the girls would still be interested in learning how to shoot—especially since they had been the targets.

Curtis was standing behind Maryanne at an indoor shooting range, tutoring her on how to hold the Ruger .22 and aim at the target while Tiffany watched. He had chosen the .22 because of its small size and the likelihood that the girls would hit the target. No sense in getting them discouraged early on. Both girls, for whatever reason, seemed very focused on their lessons, and he wondered if they were considering law enforcement or the military as careers. He would let them make the decision to talk to him about that. Meanwhile, he would encourage them in any endeavor they chose. Having worked with many women in the Marines, he didn't differentiate or judge according to sex when it came to getting the job done. This was their third lesson, and already the girls were hitting the target more often than not.

After her bullets were spent, Maryanne took off her earmuffs. She waited for Curtis and Tiffany to take off theirs. "Not bad for the third time, sir."

"You've got a long way to go, recruit, so don't get ahead of yourself."

Curtis packed up the .22, and they walked outside to the parking lot.

"I'll bet you're wondering why we want to learn how to shoot," Maryanne said.

"I figured you'd tell me in your own time."

"What are the chances that someone will still come after us once Haynes and Dillon are put in prison?"

"I'd say slim to none. There would be no reason for it. Haynes wanted you dead because he thought you'd be witnesses against him. He thought you both saw and heard him at the Harland and wasn't taking any chances. It's extremely doubtful that he has access to assassins now that he's in jail. If and when you are called to testify, you will be protected by your personal army of bodyguards. After he's locked up in a federal penitentiary, there'd be no point in going after you."

"But he still might continue on with appeals, and his important friends might help him and all that," Maryanne said.

"As I said, not much chance of that."

Maryanne and Tiffany looked at each other.

"Well, we kind of like the thought of being able to protect ourselves no matter what," Tiffany said. "It just makes us feel safer."

Curtis considered that for a moment. "I can go along with that. But that means learning everything about your weapon, including how to take it apart and clean it, put it back together, and store it safely. You also need to know when to use it and when to not use it."

"And you'll teach us all that?" Maryanne asked.

"Of course."

"Sounds good," Maryanne said.

They came to the car. Before opening the doors, Curtis paused and looked off into the distance and then back at them.

"I had a phone call from Rosemaria earlier."

"How is she?" Maryanne asked.

"She's good. She says she has a place for you two to live if you want it. A house in Simi Valley. No rent until you get jobs and save up for a while."

The girls looked down and then at each other.

"That's great," Maryanne finally said.

Curtis unlocked the car doors. Maryanne and Tiffany made no move to get in. "What's wrong?"

"We know that we've interrupted your life in a big way," Maryanne said, "but is there any chance that we could stay with you a little while longer?"

"Yeah," Tiffany added, "like, to learn about guns and self-defense and all that."

They both looked at him, hopeful.

"You can stay as long as you want," Curtis said and coughed as his voice cracked a bit.

"Yeah?" the girls said together.

"Yeah."

They got in the car, Curtis driving, Maryanne in the passenger seat, and Tiffany in the back.

"It's not that we don't appreciate Rosemaria and everything she's done for us," Maryanne said.

"We really do care for her a lot," Tiffany agreed.

"It's just that, well, we never had a real father." Maryanne felt she had gone too far and cut herself off. "Sorry, I didn't mean to say you should want to be that for us."

"No, that would be asking too much," Tiffany hurried to add. "We don't expect that."

Curtis's hands tightened on the steering wheel. "I'd be proud to have daughters like you, and like I said, you are welcome to stay as long as you like. And, Maryanne, this might be a good time to call your aunt and let her know you're okay."

Maryanne stared out the window for several seconds. "I will. I already decided to do that."

No one said another word for a long time, and then Maryanne reminded Curtis they needed to go to the market to shop for things she needed to make dinner that night. The subject quickly turned to catching up with their schooling, finally doing some shopping for new clothes, and possibly scheduling lessons in Krav Maga. Curtis said he'd have to think about that last one.

What he hadn't told them was the devastating news Rosemaria had shared with him, that they knew who Maria's murderer was, but he had now disappeared without a trace. He was one of the men who had invaded Curtis's house, intent on killing his girls. The murderer had been just a few feet away, but Curtis had been oblivious. He had failed Maria again. Curtis couldn't go after the killer himself. He had the girls to think of now. But he would talk to his buddies. Maybe his friend Jones, who came close to working for Matrix, could chase down a lead. Letting the killer walk away from murdering Maria was unthinkable. He would find him. Somehow.

* * * *

The elevator in the courthouse was crowded with people eager to go home and get Monday over with. They clutched their briefcases and looked forward to doing a minimum amount of work at home and having a nice dinner alone or with significant others. Rosemaria smiled at familiar faces but wasn't in the mood for small talk. She was eager to see Josh. He must be as nervous as all heck. She wondered if he would be up for going out to dinner or if he just wanted to stay home so he could pace back and forth and worry about the vote in the morning. They had a couple of decent microwavable meals in the freezer. She could always pop those in for four minutes and eat the tiny portions that vegan companies seemed to think were enough for an adult human being even though they weren't. Maybe they had some rolls in the refrigerator that she could heat up and slather with vegan butter. That would do it. She had thought that by joining Josh in his vegan lifestyle she would lose weight. That had yet to happen.

The lobby doors opened, and outside she found herself alone as she walked to the far end of the parking lot. Oh well. She needed the exercise.

"Guess what, bitch? I got fired!" Out of nowhere, Atkins was walking beside her, an ugly sneer on his face. "I sure as hell know you were behind it!"

Rosemaria moved away and walked faster. "You got yourself fired all by yourself. And may I remind you you're on camera?"

"The camera can't read my lips, bitch! I won't forget what you did to me, and I'll make you pay!"

"Speaking in clichés, Atkins? You can't do better than that? Your epithets are a little redundant."

He kept up with her stride for stride. "You'll never see it coming, Baker. And no one will know it was me!" He heard high heels clicking on the pavement behind them and moved away from her. "Live with that, you douchebag pathetic excuse for a prosecutor!"

The two young ladies with the clicking high heels caught up to Rosemaria. One of them asked her, "Are you okay? That guy looked like he had a screw loose. Was he bothering you?"

Rosemaria stopped behind her car. "Thank you for coming to my rescue, ladies. And yeah, he does have a screw loose. I'm okay now though."

She gave them a friendly wave and got in her car. She sat for a moment before starting the engine. She needed time to pull herself together. Atkins had totally lost it. She knew from the get-go that he was mentally unbalanced, but getting fired had taken his persecution complex to a new level. Would he really attack her one night when she least expected it? From his threatening tone, she had to admit it was a good possibility. Rosemaria had no doubt she could handle anything he dished out, but she didn't want to have to physically hurt him. He needed to be locked up in a mental ward, not beaten up by another prosecutor. She shuddered at the thought. Rosemaria doubted if the mayor would come by and congratulate her for that. She would worry about it later. All she would focus on tonight was Josh on the eve of his dream for Sammy coming true.

CHAPTER THIRTY-SEVEN

"This is great pesto." Josh was enjoying the vegan microwave dinner Rosemaria had prepared.

She sat across from him at the table enjoying her own dish of lasagna. "I don't just put these things in the microwave, you know. I have certain things I do to make them better."

"I know. You are the genius of the microwave."

"That sounded a bit sarcastic."

"Not at all."

"What you're really saying is you'd rather have me heat up frozen dinners than make anything from scratch."

"Isn't that much easier for you?"

"I want you to know I'm not hurt by your continued negative assessment of my culinary skills. As a matter of fact, it does make my life much easier."

"As always, we're in perfect accord."

"I talked to Curtis today and then the girls. It seems they want to stay with him a while longer. I'm thinking he's become somewhat of a father figure to them."

"I agree with that. You shouldn't be hurt that they don't want to come back right away."

"I'm not hurt. Really, I'm not."

"Good."

"All right. Maybe I am, a little."

"You can call them all the time. They'd love to hear from you."

"I hope so."

He picked up a roll and took a bite.

"I heated those rolls in the oven. And put lots of your favorite vegan butter on them."

"They're perfect."

"Can I ask you a question?"

"Uh-oh. Go ahead."

"If the movie is a hit, and your record goes to number one, and women start throwing themselves at you, would you still want to be with me?"

Josh dropped his fork and looked at her in astonishment. "Where the heck is this coming from?"

"Well, I'm thinking of you and Joell, and how close you've become. She's beautiful, and rich, and really nice. Most men would kill to spend as much time with her as you do. And the truth is, hard as it is to say—I'm jealous. I'm admitting it here and now. I'm jealous. I'm this plain, ordinary working woman who can't even begin to help you like she has, and it scares me that you might like her more than me—there, I've said it." She hung her head down.

He grabbed her chair and pulled it close to his. He took her by the shoulders and made her face him. "Look at me. Lift up your head and look at me."

With great effort, she lifted her head and looked him in the eyes. "I don't even recognize the person I used to be anymore. I used to be tough. Nothing got to me. Now the thought of losing you terrifies me."

"There will never, and I mean never, be anyone for me but you, Rosemaria. See that ring on your finger? As far as I'm concerned, that means forever. Joell is a wonderful woman, and yeah, men all over the world would love to be with her. So what? You have my heart. No one can change that. I want to be with you till the day I die. Understand?"

"What if I die? Would you want to be with her then?"

"No. You want to know why? Because that thing that's there between two people who love each other is either there or it isn't. It isn't there between Joell and me and wouldn't be even if you were gone. So, don't get any ideas about leaving me."

She leaned forward and put her head on his chest. "I love you so much."

"I know that. Does that mean you're feeding me dessert?"

"If you'll make the coffee, I'll spoon up the frozen Rice Dream, and we can have our dessert on the balcony."

"You got it." He picked up their plates and carried them into the kitchen.

A few minutes later, they were seated at the rickety patio table, looking out over the lights in the distance, eating their vegan ice cream, and sipping their coffee. The late winter chill had warmed somewhat and reminded them that an early Los Angeles spring was around the corner.

She took his hand and held it. "About fifteen hours from now, you'll finally have your answer. I know it must be hard to have to wait that long."

"You have no idea." To her, he looked as apprehensive as a defendant waiting for a not-guilty verdict in a murder trial—trying his best not to show any emotion.

"I'm sorry I'm such a nudge. Is there anything I can do to make it easier for you?"

"Just be here."

"I wouldn't be anywhere else."

He took a sip of his coffee and clutched her hand tighter. "Whatever happens, I couldn't have asked for better friends through all of this."

"By now, you have millions of people on your side. And they don't even know you exist."

He chuckled. "Yeah, I'm the most famous nonperson in the country."

"Everybody who matters knows you are the driving force behind all this."

"Only one thing really matters. Sammy's freedom." He thought for a moment. "How would you like to take a drive to Santa Monica and walk on the beach?"

"You took the words right out of my mouth."

* * * *

Karen stood in the doorway of Rosemaria's office and looked at her boss, who was sitting behind her desk and facing away from her. She seemed frozen in place, staring out the window at blue sky and the buildings next door. "Hello. Anybody home?"

Rosemaria whirled her chair around. "I'm sorry. Don't mind me. I was just thinking about the council meeting."

"Keep busy, then you won't have to think."

Rosemaria closed her eyes and and breathed heavily. "You're right. We have a meeting soon, don't we? With—"

Karen laid a file on her desk. "You'll find the rest in your computer. Janey Butler and her lawyer will be in here at eleven."

"Janey Butler. She's the one who—"

"Pushed her husband's girlfriend in the pool, poured red paint all over her Mercedes, emptied her garbage on the woman's front lawn, and threatened her with bodily injury if she didn't stay away from her husband."

Rosemaria groaned. "What is wrong with these people? If your husband doesn't want you, then divorce him, don't make an idiot of yourself." Rosemaria suddenly recalled her jealous meltdown the day before and bit her lip.

"What is it?"

Rosemaria pulled herself together. "Nothing. It's just that I think women should try to retain a bit of dignity and pride—" Rosemaria shook her head. "Never mind. I get where she's coming from. Totally."

Karen was surprised. "You do? What she did is not your style at all."

"I know, but I understand it." She looked at the file. "So, this Sunny Feldman reported Janey to the police and is pressing charges for assault and battery and destruction of property. Why doesn't Janey just pay for the Mercedes to be detailed and send her gardener to clean up Sunny's yard instead of clogging up the court calendar with petty squabbles?"

"I thought you said you understood?"

"I do, but that doesn't mean I endorse stupidity—no matter who may wallow in it."

Karen backed out of the room. "Okay, something is going on here that you don't want to talk about, and since I'm not the prying type I'm going to the lunchroom for a mocha. You want anything?"

"Thank you, no. My stomach is in knots."

As soon as Karen left, Rosemaria picked up her cell phone and called Josh. She tapped her fingers on the desk as she waited for him to pick up. "Josh! Are you there yet?"

Josh was sitting alone at a table outside a coffee kiosk in downtown City Hall. "Yeah. I'm here waiting for Miranda and Joell to show up. They're still working on trying to get some celebrities to come to the council meeting. Although, at this point, I don't think it matters. The members must have their minds made up by now."

"Can't hurt to let the fence sitters know the spotlight is on them."

"Apparently Hahn has been leaning hard on Councilman Chang to lean on the fence sitters."

"Hahn is desperate. He sees the writing on the wall."

"I hope you're right."

"I wish I were there with you."

"You have work to do. I'll call you as soon as they vote."

"Okay. Love you."

"Love you too." And they hung up.

Rosemaria found the Butler file on her computer and read the details of the crime and the charges. The assault was obviously a misdemeanor punishable by a fine and less than a year in jail. Janey would have to pay restitution for the damage to the Mercedes, and that could amount to a pretty penny. It was a brand-new car worth $80,000. If the case went to trial, Rosemaria doubted that Janey would face a prison sentence. She hoped Janey and her husband were well off. According to their address, they were. What a mess. And all because of love. Relationships sure could go sideways.

* * * *

Rosemaria noticed as she came into the room that Janey Butler had defiance written all over her. A tall woman with short dark hair and average looks, she carried herself as if everybody owed her a living. Her husband, Troy, was good-looking. He had dark blond hair and was extremely well built. He trailed behind his wife like a naughty child who had been told by his mother he had to be there. Both were thirty-five but behaving like teenagers. Cameron Bowers, their lawyer, entered last. Fifty-ish, well-built, with a ruddy complexion, he made the introductions, and everyone sat down in front of Rosemaria's desk.

Bowers spoke first. "My client realizes that her actions were inappropriate and takes responsibility for the confrontation with Ms. Feldman. But seeing as Ms. Feldman was the provocateur in this situation, we think charges against Mrs. Butler should be dismissed, no harm, no foul, or else we will go to trial. My client rejects any plea deal where she is found solely responsible for the actions of both parties." He waited for Rosemaria to respond. Troy looked like he wished he were anywhere else. Mrs. Butler was working hard to restrain herself from talking. She must have been told by her lawyer to stifle herself or find another lawyer.

Rosemaria addressed Bowers. "What exactly is the other side of the argument? How is Ms. Feldman to blame for the assault on her person and the destruction of property?"

"My client's husband and Ms. Feldman had been carrying on an affair for three months. Four weeks ago, Mr. Butler informed Ms. Feldman that he no longer had any interest in pursuing the affair. Ms. Feldman was not happy at having the affair end. She had what you might call a tantrum and threatened to call Mrs. Butler and reveal everything. Mr. Butler placated her and promised to call her the next day. When he didn't, Ms. Feldman started showing up at his office, driving by his house, and calling the landline and hanging up."

"How long did this behavior continue?"

"She kept this up for two weeks."

"And how long before the assault did Ms. Feldman stop harassing Mr. Butler?"

"About a week and a half."

"When did your client find out about the harassment?"

"She didn't know until a week after it stopped."

"Then what was the inciting incident that you say provoked Mrs. Butler to act as she did?"

"Mr. Butler had agreed to meet Ms. Feldman for coffee to talk her out of harassing him. That's why she stopped. My client found her husband's behavior suspicious. At this point, she still didn't know about the affair. She followed her husband to the restaurant where he was meeting with Ms. Feldman and confronted them. At that point, everyone was yelling, and they were escorted out of the restaurant, where the argument continued on the sidewalk. All details of the affair came out, and Mr. Butler had to forcefully separate the two women. He then escorted his wife to their car and drove away."

"Did the harassment continue after that?"

"There were no more incidents, but Mrs. Butler lived in constant fear that Ms. Feldman might try to attack her."

"Why was that?"

"Mrs. Butler ran into Ms. Feldman in a coffee shop, and words were exchanged that made Mrs. Butler think that Ms. Feldman was not through with her vendetta."

"Vendetta? That's what Mrs. Butler felt was in play?"

"Definitely."

"Did Ms. Feldman track down Mrs. Butler to this coffee shop?"

Bowers and his client shifted in their seats. "Not exactly. Mrs. Butler had found out from her husband where Ms. Feldman liked to buy her coffee in the morning."

"I see. Thank you for clearing up a few things for me, Mr. Bowers. Mrs. Butler, do you have anything to add?"

Mrs. Butler looked at her lawyer. "No, I have nothing to say."

Rosemaria pursed her lips and looked down at her computer. "You certainly have every right to go to trial with this case, Mrs. Butler, but you may not be happy with the verdict. When it comes to a defense for committing assault, you would have to prove you were in imminent danger. Apparently, you brooded over the betrayal of your marriage for several days, during which time you had no contact with Ms. Feldman until you confronted her in a coffee shop. You then went to Ms. Feldman's house, shoved her in the pool, and wreaked your revenge. The timeline is as clear as day. If you go to trial, you could end up spending time in jail as well as paying the fines and restitution, which there is no way out of. I would recommend—"

Rosemaria's phone rang. She picked it up and gasped. "Excuse me. I have to take this. It's an emergency."

Rosemaria all but leaped out of her chair and left the room, closing the door. She saw that Karen was not at her desk. "Josh! What happened?!"

Josh was standing in the hallway outside of the Council Chambers. The hall was filled with smiling, celebrating, high-fiving people. They swirled all around him, congratulating him, punching him in the arm as they went by.

"They voted yes!"

Rosemaria sank down in Karen's chair. "Yes? They voted yes? Oh my God, Josh! You did it!"

"We won! Can you believe it?! It's a miracle is what it is. After all these years. I have to go tell Sammy. I don't care if he can understand or not. I have to tell him."

"I'm so happy for you. I can't tell you how happy."

"Now we have to plan the concert and hope a lot of people come."

"They will, honey, they will."

"I better go. I have to meet up with the others."

"All right. I'll see you at home later."

She clicked off her phone and slumped down in Karen's chair in exhausted relief. She looked up to see Karen staring at her.

"Was it yes?"

Rosemaria flew out of her chair and wrapped her arms around Karen. "It was yes!"

* * * *

The three people in Rosemaria's office were grumbling among themselves as Rosemaria came back in. They undoubtedly had heard her celebratory phone call and wondered what was going on. She behaved calmly, as if nothing out of the ordinary had happened.

"What I can offer you is this. A sentence of 180 days in jail suspended, and $2,000 in fines for a Class B misdemeanor. A fine of $15,000 for vandalism, ten days in jail suspended, and restitution to be paid to the victim of $25,000 or more depending on how much is required to get the car back to its original condition." She looked at Mrs. Butler, who was boiling.

"I have to pay money to the woman who ruined my marriage, who harassed my husband, who should burn in hell for what she did?! No way! I'm going to trial! Bowers, tell her!"

The lawyer hesitated while the husband slumped down in his chair, seeming as if he wished he were invisible.

"That's your choice, Mrs. Butler," Rosemaria responded. "In that case, I will charge you with a Class A misdemeanor for the assault and battery, ask for one year in jail, plus a fine of $4,000. Since you caused damage to property worth more than $80,000, I will charge you with felony vandalism and ask for another year in jail. And you will be required by the court to pay restitution." She smiled at Mrs. Butler and waited.

Mrs. Butler was simmering. "You have got to be kidding! I am the victim here. I am the wronged party. She should have to pay me!"

Rosemaria addressed Bowers. "I leave it to you to explain the law to your client. She stood up. "See you in court." She held out her hand, and Bowers shook it. Troy Butler stood and reached out as well, happy at the thought of getting out of there.

"Sit down, Troy," Mrs. Butler snapped. We'll take the deal."

CHAPTER THIRTY-EIGHT

Osborne and Waite were in the conference room studying their laptop screens as the rest of the team straggled in. Bud Elliott was short, baby-faced, and had short dark hair. Desmond Hawk was thin, with a crew cut and rimless glasses. Benny Doyle was just as thin, with long blond hair. All three men were from the tech unit. Larry, Sergeant Harvey, and finally Lieutenant Manley came in and sat at the head of the table. He cleared his throat, and everyone stopped what they were doing and gave him their attention.

"Thanks to all of your hard work, we have solid cases against both Haynes and Dillon. We have the tape of Dillon setting up another hit on the girls, and we have proof that Mark Dornan was one of two men working for Dillon when he presumably threatened Haynes with blackmail and murdered Maria Rodriguez. Matrix, a murder-for-hire company, has been traced back to Dillon, and Elliott, Hawk, and Doyle are connecting more dots every day. We have positive proof, thanks to Mrs. Haynes, that Senator Haynes was the person staying in room 203 at the Harland, and that he had his people chase Maryanne and try to kidnap her. The pimp who was hired by Haynes's men and subsequently murdered had been told by Haynes's men to send the girls to room 203, which connects Haynes to that killing."

He took a deep breath, looked around the room, and continued. "The extradition of Dillon was by the book, and as for Haynes, he was found passed out in a room at the Island Hotel. The maid told the manager, the manager called police, and we arrested him and brought him here. We have no idea how he got there, had nothing to do with it, and apparently the cameras in the condominium hallways were temporarily on the blink, so the DC cops don't have a clue what happened. Mathison says we are totally in the clear. We will continue to gather evidence and charge them both on Friday, at which point we will have to turn over the state's evidence to the defense lawyers. They will then find out that it wasn't Maryanne or Tiffany who positively identified Haynes as the man in 203 but a Hispanic maid, Lupe Saldana. She will receive our full protection."

As he was speaking, everyone in the room looked away from the lieutenant, turning their attention to the massive figure of Captain Hubbard standing in the doorway. He was African American, 6' 4", 250 pounds, and wearing his dress blues. The captain was an imposing presence. He didn't usually get involved with individual cases, but this one was an exception. The investigation had been massive, with all hands on deck and every resource employed. Their efforts had paid off in mass arrests, certain prosecutions, and guilty verdicts.

The lieutenant turned around, saw Captain Hubbard, and indicated for him to take over.

The captain's voice was deep and sonorous. He spoke softly. "I wish I could say that is the scenario that will play out, but I can't."

Everyone in the room had expected this but had hoped it could be avoided. Osborne voiced the obvious question. "The feds?"

"Yes, the feds. Someone from the FBI called the police commissioner, and he called me. US Attorney General Soderberg is sending agents to this station with a federal court order authorizing them to take all the prisoners back to DC. That includes the assassins now residing in the Van Nuys jail. Our witnesses and our evidence will never be heard in a court of law. The attorney general of the United States will bury this case deeper than a fracking well in Oklahoma. The political-powers-that-be have spoken, and we, I'm afraid, are at their mercy. Mathison is on her way here and has a call in to the AG."

"There's nothing we can do?" Larry asked. "With all due respect, Captain, we worked our butts off on this case. These guys are psychopaths, for God's sake. They need to be locked up."

"Agreed, but there's not a whole lot I can do. I'm going to make a few calls, see if this can be delayed for a few days. It's the best I can do right now." He nodded gravely and left.

The lieutenant looked at his men, and it was all he could do to control his anger and not verbally lash out at a system that could allow such a travesty of justice to occur. But that wasn't his style. They all sat at the table downcast, staring at the wall and wondering how and why all their efforts could come to naught. It was inconceivable.

Celia breezed through the door. "Now, now, I don't like seeing all those long faces. We don't give up this easily, do we?" She set her briefcase down on the table. Her cell phone was in her hand.

"So, what can we do?" Larry groused. "They hold all the cards."

"Not necessarily. At least we have to—" Her cell phone rang, and she clicked it on and listened. "Yes, this is Celia Mathison. I'll hold." She held up crossed fingers as she waited. "The Feebs were just pulling up out front when I drove in." She spoke into her cell phone. "Yes, I'm still here."

She waited for another minute, then nodded to the others in the room. When she spoke, she sounded as sweet as a Sunday school teacher speaking to a room full of six-year-olds.

"Hello, Mr. Soderberg."

Every cop in the room exchanged surprised glances.

"This is Celia Mathison. — Yes, I wasn't happy to hear that you intend to kidnap our defendants and whisk them back east, where they will disappear forever into the DC swamp." A smile remained fixed on her face. "I'm afraid I have little faith in the word of politicians, Mr. Soderberg. We prefer to put the defendants on trial right here in Los Angeles."

She listened, looking as if it were taking every bit of control she had to reign in her temper. "I do know who you are, Mr. Attorney General, and I do not respond well to threats. But you need to understand who I am and the people I represent and protect." Her tone became more strident. "Sir, I think it will be in your best interest not to hang up and listen to what I have to say. I assure you; you will regret it if you do not hear me out."

Celia was on a tear, a force to be reckoned with.

"This is Beverly Hills, Mr. Soderberg. You may think of us as an insignificant little town of pretty people and movie stars. But we have something else. We have the greatest screenwriters in the world. We have writers who can wring tears from a stone, who can make people laugh, who can frighten audiences and make them shiver in their seats with terror, and who can raise the ire of a nation."

She listened to the attorney general for a moment, tapping her fingers impatiently on the table. "I will be more than happy to explain Mr. Soderberg. Please listen carefully." She paused for effect.

"If you go forward with your plan, we intend to hold the biggest news conference this country has ever seen. In preparation for this news conference, during which we will announce to the public your intention to protect hired assassins and murderous politicians from justice, our writers will become our most valued asset. They will work with mothers who have lost children to gun violence, with Me Too leaders who will speak up for the two girls whom the defendants tried to kill, with beloved celebrities who will inspire their loyal fans to action, and with your political opponents who will *annihilate* you." She emphasized the word.

"Using extraordinary powers of persuasion, our writers and directors will work together to evoke outrage in every man, woman, and child in this country. Everyone except gun nuts and women haters will rise up against you and excoriate your boss in the Oval Office. I can practically guarantee every last one of you will go down in flames in the next election, if not before."

She doubled down in her intensity.

"Our writers are that good, Mr. Soderberg, and they have the Emmys and Oscars to prove it. If your men are not gone from the front of our building in three minutes, I will call the Writers Guild and begin to put our plan in motion. Being professional screenwriters, they work fast, and the first news conference will begin in, I'd say, about four hours. Is it worth it, Mr. Soderberg? Is protecting mass murderers worth your career and unanimous scorn? I'm sure you'll make the right decision. Thank you very much for your time."

She clicked off her phone and looked around the room. "I told Kowalski to call me."

The room was silent as they waited. About two minutes went by. Then, her cell phone rang, and she answered. "Thanks, Kowalski." She hung up and smiled. "The Feebs are pulling away."

There was a mass exhale of breath as Celia immediately picked up her briefcase and readied to leave. "Let's file Thursday, okay? I want to get this show on the road."

The lieutenant shook her hand. "I should have had more faith."

"I can't take all the credit," Celia said. "I was inspired by a news conference I watched yesterday. Some animal activists cornered the LA City Council in a way that blew my mind. I was very impressed and decided to do a little bit of that myself. Soderberg's choice was to do the right thing or try to escape mass retribution after doing the bidding of the gun lobby. He knows which way the political wind is blowing and decided discretion was the better part of valor."

"It took you to make him see the writing on the wall," the lieutenant said.

"Good work, Mathison," Osborne added. "We won't let you down."

"We're still digging up more dirt," Waite assured her. "We'll have it by Thursday."

Larry stood and picked up his laptop. He thought of Rosemaria, how deeply disappointed she would have been if the criminals responsible for terrorizing her girls had been set free. They may not have arrested Maria's murderer yet, but they would. Meanwhile, Rosemaria would have the satisfaction of knowing Dillon and Haynes would stay behind bars for the rest of their lives.

Celia walked down the hall to the sound of murmurs from a roomful of happy cops. She had to admit, this felt good.

* * * *

Josh and Rosemaria were in bed, both sitting up, working on their laptops.

Rosemaria thoughtfully scratched Suzi, who was sitting on her pillow. "Joell yesterday, Celia today, both kicking butt like crazy. I think women are taking over the world."

Josh was engrossed in his work. "Uh-huh."

"What a fabulous planet this would be if women were in charge."

Josh stopped typing and looked at her. "What?"

"Suzi would like to have a TV, and I think we should buy her one. I know you think it sucks creativity right out of a person's brain, but it would be nice to enjoy movies every once in a while, and Suzi would like watching it when we're not at home."

He went back to his work. "That's fine."

Rosemaria perked up. "Wow, you're easy. We'll go out and buy one right after the concert and we take Sammy up to the sanctuary."

Josh seemed engrossed in his laptop. "Suzi wants to win the lottery too, but I'm not buying lottery tickets."

"I thought you weren't paying attention."

"I was."

She put her laptop on the little table by her bed and snuggled closer. He put one arm around her as Suzi flew off to her perch.

"What time are you driving up to the cabin tomorrow?" he asked.

"Actually, I took all day off, but I'll stop in and see if anything has come up and leave straight from there."

"I have a meeting at two, and after that I'll head on up."

"I'm going to take a little hike after I get there. You know how we always stop in the same place and come back? I've always wanted to keep walking and go down into the valley and up to the top of the second hill. The view of the ocean from up there must be awesome."

Josh frowned. "I'd rather we did that hike together."

"Don't worry. I won't get lost. I have a compass, and I'll have lots of food and water in my backpack in case I wander around a bit."

"I don't want to have to call out the rangers to find you once I get there."

"Don't you dare humiliate me like that! Besides, I'll probably be back before you arrive. But if I'm not, don't panic. I am woman. Hear me roar."

He closed his laptop and placed it on the floor. She turned out the light.

They turned toward each other, and Josh began touching and stroking her softly in all the right places. He put his hand behind her head, pulled her face close to his, and nibbled on her lips. "Don't roar too loud, woman. The neighbors might call the police."

"Don't worry. I know how to deal with their type," she whispered, then lost herself in his warmth and expert explorations of her most sensitive places.

* * * *

Rosemaria traveled up the 110 and the 101, finding little traffic on both. Midmorning seemed a good time to drive the freeways of LA while Karen had everything under control at the office, Sammy was going to a sanctuary, and Dillon and Haynes were in jail. She was allowing herself this day to just enjoy being alive. Work would have to trouble her brain on another day. She had never been much of a nature lover until she and Josh rented the cabin to be near Noor and Gilbert. Now, she needed her regular dose of clean air and ocean breezes like she needed oxygen. They would spend the night with their kids sleeping under the stars. It seemed impossible to believe that after all the Sturm and Drang of the past few weeks, she could finally relax and just be.

* * * *

The killer followed her loosely. She was an ex-cop and would easily spot a tail. Besides, he knew where she was going—to their cabin in a canyon past the Santa Ynez Valley. His orders were to kill her up close and personal. He had been told to strangle her and let her know who had sent him, so that's what he would do. He didn't mind watching someone struggle trying to get loose from his grasp. The whore at the hotel had been small and weak, not as much fun as his stronger victims. He enjoyed seeing the light in their eyes slowly dying as their body shut down and they were on their way to meet their maker. It made him feel like God.

Matrix had been good to him. When he was with Dark Water as a military contractor, he mostly killed people in the Middle East. Since he had joined Matrix, he had been paid to travel all over the world and take care of loose ends, as that idiot Dillon liked to call the people he murdered. He'd never met the man, but he sure sounded like a class A phony who pretended to be a badass living a dangerous life through the people his company hired. Dillon never got his own hands dirty and always acted in public like he was as pure as the driven snow.

Now Matrix was dead and gone and Dillon was locked up. Life sure was funny. Senator Haynes, with all his political connections, was sure to get out of the jam he was in. Haynes had plenty of cash lying around in various places and was happy to give some of it to a man who would kill a hated enemy. He was grateful that Haynes had picked him for the job, especially after what he had done to that worthless piece of crap politician in the alley at the Island. Somehow Haynes had tracked him down through some flunky in his lawyer's office who had access to Senator Haynes's accounts. Haynes's burning hatred of this broad must be killing him to take that kind of a chance. But Haynes had gotten away with all kinds of shit for decades, so he probably figured he'd get away with this too. The Baker broad had helped protect the two girls so well, even he couldn't get to them. He had to admit the retired Marine and his buddies were good. He knew a lot of those types who worked for Matrix. He had no beef with them. He got paid no matter what.

He would park his car up the highway a bit and then make his way through the trees to the cabin. He would kill her in the cabin if he had too, but if he was lucky, she would decide to go on a hike, he would follow, then jump her, strangle her, drag her body under the trees, and bury her under a pile of rocks. Haynes wanted her to disappear for good. He could manage that. If she saw him following her, he could shoot her in the leg or shoulder to make it easier to strangle her. But the shot might be heard by other hikers.

He didn't really want to do that. He had to get back to his car unseen. Hunting wasn't allowed in those hills, so he couldn't walk around with a rifle and risk somebody calling the rangers on him. He had his Magnum, and that would do the job if she gave him any trouble. Haynes would be happy as long as the broad was dead.

CHAPTER THIRTY-NINE

osemaria felt a sense of well-being come over her as she puttered around the cabin and put away the groceries she had bought on the way up. She figured it was good for her to spend a few hours alone up here. Sometimes she needed to remind herself who she was—independent, self-reliant, and strong. That's who Josh had fallen in love with, and she never wanted to lose that part of herself. Joell and Celia were both independent women. They had no significant others in their lives and managed very well on their own, thank you very much. As long as she remembered who she was, Rosemaria felt she had the best of both worlds.

Still, it wouldn't hurt to do a little cleaning up and dusting before she went on her hike. She worked for half an hour and decided she'd better get going if she was going to take the long hike she'd told Josh she wanted to take. She made a couple of sandwiches, put some potato chips in a small plastic bag, picked out a Snickers bar from the variety pack in the refrigerator, and stuffed them all in her backpack. She grabbed a bottle of water, and put that in its little holder on the side of her backpack. It was warm outside, but she dressed in sweatpants and a T-shirt, and she tied a sweatshirt around her waist in case it took her longer to get back. She took her little .22 out of her purse and stuck that in the backpack. There were coyotes in the hills, but they never bothered humans. She didn't think there were any mountain lions in the area, but she hoped that if there were, they wouldn't come after her. She could never shoot a cousin of Gilbert's. She wouldn't be able to look him in the face ever again. *Death or shooting Gilbert's cousin?* She banished the thought from her mind. She decided to bring her cell phone even though there weren't any towers close by. Every once in a while, the phones worked. Maybe they'd put in those new towers they'd been promising to put in for the safety of hikers. She kept it on, just in case. Josh would worry if she didn't.

She stepped outside, locked the door, and took a deep breath of pure mountain air. The sky was blue, with a few white clouds floating high above. They had found a bit of heaven here, all because Josh had promised Noor and Gilbert he'd always be close. She headed out in the usual direction and easily found the trail. This was easy. She didn't know what Josh was so worried about.

The killer waited patiently as his target fussed around in the cabin. Maybe she wasn't going to go out at all. Perhaps he'd have to attack her inside the cabin, then drag her up the hill to hide her. That would be a hassle but doable.

He was relieved when she finally came outside and started walking up the trail. He followed far behind. He had no fear that she would know he was there. Stealth was his middle name. He would stay far enough away so that if he did have to shoot her, the shot wouldn't be heard by passersby on the highway. Besides, he loved stalking prey. They were always so helpless and so surprised when he finally made his move. He enjoyed the look on their faces when they realized their life was over. Some begged, others tried to escape, and a few were hostile to the end. It didn't matter to him; it always ended the same way.

After Rosemaria had climbed up the first hill, she drank a big gulp of water and wiped the sweat off her forehead with the sleeve of her sweatshirt. A run on the beach wasn't nearly enough exercise to keep her in shape. She vowed to go to that gym she had just joined for the sake of trapping Atkins. She had a month's membership. Might as well use it. She turned, doing a 360-degree survey of her surroundings, and saw a flock of doves suddenly take flight out of the trees a half a mile away. An involuntary shudder ran through her. She knew something or someone had to be there for the doves to fly off like that. If it was another hiker, he or she would keep walking in her direction. Or maybe the other hiker had merely stopped for some reason. She stood stock-still and stared at the spot for a good three minutes. Nothing moved. She didn't hear a sound. She had read once that women were the first to feel imminent danger. It took men a little longer. But women were also the first to dismiss the possibility of danger. She didn't think that was so smart.

Rosemaria walked slowly forward, listening carefully to every sound. She set down her backpack, took out her .22, and put it in her pocket. A small animal had probably frightened the doves, but she'd stayed alive this long by taking nothing for granted. Now what? Keep going forward, dismiss her well-honed instincts, or go back? Either way, if someone was following her, she would still be a target. She decided to go forward, find a place to shelter, and wait where she could defend herself against an attack. Who would be after her? It couldn't be Atkins. He would be completely helpless out here. Had Haynes or Dillon hired someone? What would be the point?

This whole thing could be just her overwrought imagination. Thoughts of killers and kidnappers had permeated her mind the last few weeks of her life to the point where she was probably primed to see them everywhere. She didn't want this beautiful day ruined by bogeymen who didn't exist. She took another gulp of water and kept walking.

The killer cursed his stupidity. He hadn't noticed the flock of birds in the tree above him. He had inadvertently disturbed them and betrayed his presence. Now he had to remain still until the target relaxed and moved forward. He would wait until she reached the bottom of the valley before circling around and waiting for her to pass. She was staying on the path, so that would be easy. He would have his arm around her neck before she even knew he was there. He waited patiently. He was good at that.

Gradually, when she heard nothing behind her but small animals in the underbrush, Rosemaria relaxed. There was an abundance of trees in the area, so she had a lot of shade from the sun. She stood on top of the hill and looked down into the valley. She would hike down and then climb up the opposite hill, which looked more like a mountain to her. But she needed the challenge. Rosemaria was determined to make it to the top and be rewarded by a glorious view of the ocean. The path down the hill was rocky, and she stumbled a few times, causing small rockslides, but she managed to maintain her footing. Slowly, she made her way down and decided to rest once she got to the bottom. What a wuss. No wonder Josh had never brought her this far. She'd whip herself into shape and run circles around him next time.

She found herself a smooth rock to sit on and took out her cheese and tomato sandwich. It was halfway to her mouth when she heard rocks sliding that was definitely not caused by a small animal. She dropped the sandwich and ran. Heavy footsteps pounded into the ground several yards behind her. As she ran, she kept looking for a place to hide and shoot. Her backpack was light and didn't slow her down much. She heard the footsteps getting closer. She veered off the path and ran through the underbrush, looking for a rotting log, a large rock formation, or anything to hide behind. It was better to hide than to keep running like a scared rabbit, making a target of herself. She found a tree with its branches partly wrapped around a high rock. It would have to do. She set down her backpack, retrieved her .22 from her pocket, and crouched down behind the rock and the thick branches. He wasn't coming through the woods the same way she had come. Was he circling around? Rosemaria's heart was pounding. She was being stalked like prey. She was completely hidden from view where she was. The killer was patient. She would be even more patient. The sun was sliding down past the mountain. She had told Josh not to call the rangers if she wasn't there when he arrived. Big mistake. Now she didn't dare make a phone call. She had to turn off her cell phone.

The killer hadn't been able to avoid the rocks. The entire hill was surrounded by them. They caused him to make his second mistake. She had left the path at some point, so he would have to wait her out. Prey never had the patience to wait. Sooner or later, they chose to move and try to make their escape. That was always their fatal mistake.

* * * *

The meeting at two o'clock had been postponed until tomorrow, so Josh was happy he could surprise Rosemaria by showing up early. If she was still out hiking, he would stop by and visit with Noor and Gilbert for a while. He had watched Joell, Miranda, and Harvey work the telephones for a couple of hours and thought they were the most persuasive people he had ever met. Acts were fighting to be on the bill. They were willing to take time off their tours or to take a break from recording in New York, England, or wherever they might be to come be part of the concert. It was amazing. He had stopped by the zoo to see Sammy the day before and told him his prison sentence was coming to an end. Maybe on some level he understood, but soon he would find out his suffering was over. Sammy would be free because of the incredible people who had become a part of his life. Considering the many famous acts that would be appearing, Josh wondered what he could sing to be worthy of being on the same stage. He would have to choose a song he already had. It was too late to write anything new.

* * * *

Rosemaria's back was aching from staying frozen in place for so long. It had to have been at least forty-five minutes since she'd hidden behind the rock. She'd heard nothing from her stalker. There was no way she would be able to find her way back to the cabin in the dark, let alone with someone following her who wanted to kill her. She was certain of that now. It had become a game of cat and mouse, and she was the mouse. She wasn't used to that set of circumstances but didn't know how to change things around to her advantage. She racked her brain to try and figure out a strategy, but nothing came to her. Her brain was numb and so was her body. Being the stalker was easier than being the prey.

The killer waited. The dark would be his friend. She would never stay out here all night. He knew she would move.

It was late afternoon when Josh arrived at the cabin and went inside. It was way past time for Rosemaria to come back from her hike. He took out his cell phone and called her. It went straight to voicemail, which meant her phone was turned off. Why the hell would she do that? She never turned off her phone. And she would never worry him on purpose like this. A bad feeling came over him. He had promised her that he wouldn't call the rangers, but in a couple of hours it would be pitch-dark outside, and she would never find her way back to the cabin. He pondered what to do. He opened the door and looked up the hill to where she had probably gone. Doing nothing was not an option. Somehow, he knew she was in trouble. A light went on in his head, and he raced for his car and jumped in.

Rosemaria knew she would have to make a move before it became dark. Even if she risked exposing her position, she needed to find out where he was in order to take him out before he killed her. She moved one leg and arm at a time, stopping herself from crying out in pain as she dug herself out of her hiding place. She left her backpack behind and slipped through the brush as quietly as she could. She moved in the direction of the hill that she had come down. Somewhere, he was waiting for her. Her head and eyes were in constant movement as she crept forward, the .22 in her hand.

Josh pulled up to the private gate of the sanctuary and jumped out of the car. He hurriedly unlocked the main gate with his new key card and saw Noor already pacing inside the second one. Gilbert stood beside Noor, who was coiled and ready to spring. With apologies to Gilbert, Josh let Noor come out through the inner gate and unlocked the outer one. She ran past him and ignored his orders to get in the car. Sensing danger, every instinct in Noor made it impossible for her to obey.

Something evil was nearby, and she raced as fast as she could toward that evil—down the cement road, across the highway, and into the hills. She could smell the fear of her human. She knew she was in mortal danger.

The killer saw his target through the trees and waited for her. He observed her hesitate when she came to a narrow clearing, and he made his move.

Rosemaria saw him an instant before he could grab her, and she shot out a fist that caught him in the throat with full force. Choking and tearing up, he threw her down. Then, she kneed him in the groin, causing him to bend over in pain. It gave her a chance to scramble to her feet and run.

A shot rang out, and she screamed, then fell. Her leg was hit, and the .22 dropped to the ground.

Noor heard the shot and the scream and ran faster. She raced up the hill effortlessly and leaped through the trees and over the rocks, lifting her nose to the wind to find the scent and follow the direction of the sound.

The pain in Rosemaria's leg was excruciating. She had lost her gun somewhere in the leaves that covered the ground. The stalker walked toward her, and she finally saw his face. It was the man she had been looking for—Maria's murderer. He had a weather-beaten, lined complexion, with eyes as dead as his stone-cold heart. She stared at him defiantly. He said nothing as he came closer. She crawled backward, reaching behind her to try to find her gun. He saw her desperation and smiled.

A massive roar echoed through the hills, and for a split second, Rosemaria's entire body was frozen in shock. Then, she opened her mouth and screamed, "Noor!" The killer looked confused, wondering if his eyes were deceiving him as he saw a black panther racing down the side of the hill. In a panic, he aimed at the panther but missed his shot. While he was distracted, Rosemaria was on her knees searching through the leaves for her gun. She fumbled for a few terrifying seconds until she found it and turned. Before the killer could get off a second shot at Noor, Rosemaria emptied her .22 into his chest. He looked down at the blood spurting from multiple bullet holes and seemed surprised. Noor came sailing through the air, knocking him down and pinning him to the ground. The killer looked up at Noor's open jaws and yellow eyes. Noor stared at him like the devil himself was about to devour him. The killer opened his mouth in terror, then died before he could make a sound.

"Noor! It's okay!" Rosemaria was in a panic, afraid that Noor would maul the body and she or another cat would get blamed and be hunted down. "Come here, Noor!"

Slowly, Noor moved away from the body and stood guard next to Rosemaria. She remained vigilant as her female human wrapped her arms around her, trembling and making choking sounds as her tears soaked into Noor's fur. Noor was not distracted. Her eyes searched the hillsides for other predators. All her senses were on alert. She saw Josh running down the hill, rocks sliding down in small avalanches. He ran toward them, then bent down and pulled Rosemaria into his chest.

Rosemaria's body was shaking uncontrollably, and as Josh held her in his arms, the full impact of what had happened unleashed a tidal wave of emotions. The possibility of Noor getting killed had terrified her. She looked up at him, wide-eyed and anguished. "He was going to shoot Noor, Josh! He was going to shoot Noor!" Rosemaria cried repeatedly as Josh held her tight. "He was going to shoot Noor!"

Rosemaria sobbed as if her heart would break. It took a few minutes, and Josh's gentle whispers, for her body to stop trembling. She wiped her face with her shirt and willed herself to calm down. She flinched in pain as Josh wrapped his shirt around her leg to stop the bleeding.

Noor paced relentlessly. She must keep her humans safe, and dark was coming. She heard them talking quietly. The female urged Josh to go. He finally came to Noor and said, "I have to get you back before the rangers come, Noor. They can't know you were here." Josh stopped to say something to the female, then headed up the hill. With one last look at the female and the evil thing, Noor followed Josh.

Rosemaria watched Noor and Josh disappear over the hill. She felt strangely alone and still frightened, even though the killer was lying dead on the ground beside her. Josh was going to call the rangers after he had safely delivered Noor back to the sanctuary.

With great effort, she managed to stand, grabbed a fallen branch, and slowly began to scuff up the crime scene, making sure that any evidence of Noor's presence was obliterated. Paw marks nearby and on the hill would look like they could have been from any mountain lion who had happened to wander by in the last few days. If they found anything suspicious, the cops would trust the word of a fellow law enforcement officer regarding what had happened. The man had been hired to kill her, and she had shot him dead to defend herself. Case closed.

She looked down at the man who had murdered Maria, had tried to murder Maryanne and Tiffany, and today had done his best to murder her.

He was as ugly on the outside as he was on the inside. What point could there possibly have been for this hideous man to be vain? She snickered at him in contempt and reached down and yanked off his hairpiece. He had a receding hairline with a few stubbles of hair in front. She saw more of Noor's paw marks in the dirt around him and used the hairpiece to scrub them away. After she was finished, she threw the hairpiece on his face. To hell with preserving the crime scene.

* * * *

The four of them lay on the grass in the private sanctuary enclosure. Rosemaria was sandwiched between Noor and Gilbert, and Josh was on the other side of Noor. The events of the past few hours kept running through her mind. Josh had called 911 and reported the shooting. Then, he told Jason, who was still in his office, what had happened, trusting him to ignore Noor's involvement and the surveillance video. In no time, using the fire roads, the park rangers, sheriffs, and EMTs had shown up to pronounce Dornan dead, preserve the crime scene, and ask her questions. The EMTs patched up her leg. Lastly, the medical examiner arrived to do a cursory examination of the body and transport it to the morgue. The rangers had arrived at the scene even before Josh had safely put Noor back behind the gates and made his way back to Rosemaria. She had handed over her .22 to the sheriff, explained to him who Mark Dornan was, why he wanted to kill her, and who had probably hired him. She described how he had stalked her and where she had hidden, leaving behind her backpack that was now in evidence. She recounted how they had fought, how he had shot and wounded her, and how she had found her gun and managed to shoot him with her .22 before he could fire his Magnum at her again. She explained that he had probably been told to kill her up close and personal, which is why he shot to wound, not kill. The sheriff checked out her story with the BHPD and congratulated her on managing to survive a hit by a hired assassin. Not exactly protocol, but he treated her like the fellow law enforcement officer she used to be. He told her they could have a short interview via Skype on Friday. No need to drive back up. She told him she appreciated that.

The best part of the day was calling Curtis and the girls to tell them that Dornan was dead. He thanked her profusely and made sure she was okay. The girls asked if she wanted them to come back right away, and she told them that she was happy they had found someone who loved them and to stay as long as they wanted. It was all she could do to say goodbye.

Her leg where the bullet had grazed her flesh was throbbing, keeping her from falling asleep. "Josh?"

"Yes."

"Do you think Gilbert feels left out because he wasn't a part of everything?"

"No. I think he's fine."

"Okay. I don't want him to feel left out because Noor is so—well, you know, dominant."

"I'm sure he accepts that."

Noor shifted slightly and made a noise that sounded like a grunt.

"Noor doesn't like when we talk when she's trying to sleep."

"All right then. Good night, sweetheart."

"Good night. I'll just lay here and think for a while."

The throbbing in her leg seemed to die down a bit. The night air was cold, but even through her sleeping bag, she could feel the warmth from the two bodies tucked in close beside her. She looked up at the sky and felt lucky to be alive.

* * * *

Josh walked slowly up the stairs to the detective division at BHPD. His rage had invaded a primordial place in his brain that had remained dormant since his father murdered his brother, Scott, all those years ago. Yesterday, when he had held a sobbing Rosemaria in his arms, the anger he felt toward Haynes and Dillon rekindled that same hatred and thirst for revenge that had consumed him then. He felt removed from any kind of normalcy, but his focus was razor sharp.

Shelly, who was seated at the reception desk behind the glass, looked concerned when she saw him. "Hi, Josh. I heard what happened yesterday. I'm so sorry."

"If Larry is here, would you ask him to come out?"

Shelly quickly assessed his dark mood, got up without another word, and went to find Larry.

The two of them immediately came out to reception. Larry opened the door and joined Josh in the lobby. "What can I do for you?"

Josh turned away and walked a few steps away from the reception area. Larry came over and stood next to Josh, who was staring at the pictures on the wall, seeing nothing. "What's going on, Josh?"

"Dillon and Haynes."

"They're both locked up safe and sound right here."

"Did either one of them have visitors recently besides their lawyers?"

Larry stared intently at Josh, who gave him back the same.

"Haynes had a visit from a paralegal, Julian Saber, who came in fifteen minutes ahead of the appointment time with his lawyers," Larry said. "We brought him in for questioning."

"He passed the message to Dornan from Haynes?"

Larry averted his gaze as if he were studying something down the hall. He waited a few seconds, then looked back at Josh. "It looks like that's what happened."

"At the Harland, Haynes's man was saying Julian, not Julia."

"I think so."

"I want to see Haynes," Josh said quietly.

Larry hesitated. "You won't—"

"I won't hurt him, if that's what you're asking."

"Okay then. Let's go."

They took the elevator down to the jail and walked to where Haynes was locked in his cell. He nodded at the officer in charge to unlock the cell door. A look was exchanged between Larry and the officer. "No one will bother you. You were never here," Larry said to Josh. Larry opened the cell door, Josh walked in, and Larry slammed the door behind him.

Haynes was laying on his bunk. He sat up when he saw Josh. "Who the hell are you?"

Josh took two steps into the cell and grabbed Haynes by the throat. Haynes struggled, but his neck was caught in a vise. Josh pulled him to his feet and shoved him against the wall, one hand still around his neck. Haynes could barely get his words out. "You can't do this," he whispered hoarsely.

Josh put his face close to Haynes. "I'm a friend of the woman you tried to murder yesterday. You will never attempt to do that again."

Haynes whimpered in protest.

"Shut up, or I'll kill you right here!" Josh spoke in a menacing whisper. Haynes was shaking, his eyes wide with terror.

"If my friend so much as trips on the sidewalk, if a gust of wind so much as moves a hair on her head, I will blame you, and I will come after you."

Haynes shook uncontrollably. His face was bathed in perspiration.

"I will have my friends kidnap you when you are being moved to or from the courthouse, and you know they can. I will have them drop you in some dark place where only wild animals live." Josh took out his cell phone. He brought up a picture of himself with Noor and Gilbert and shoved it in Haynes's face. "I have friends who are predators and follow my orders. You could say I'm like Dr. Doolittle, but my animals like to kill." He brought up a picture of Noor with her fangs bared. "This one especially loves the taste of human blood."

Josh's eyes narrowed into catlike slits. "I will come with her and others to where you have been dropped off by your kidnappers. I will track you down, and when I find you, I will order my cats to tear your body to shreds. I will have them rip out your heart with their teeth, chew it up, and spit blood on your mutilated body." He shoved Noor's picture in Haynes's face and pressed it against his forehead. "I promise you, this face will be the last thing you ever see!"

Josh threw Haynes back on the bed. Josh glared at him with pure venom. "Be sure of this—if anything ever comes close to even irritating or annoying that woman or the two girls, you will wish you were in hell instead of what I will put you through!"

Josh backed away. "Do you understand me?"

Haynes stared at Josh like he was the devil himself. He was barely able to nod his head.

Josh held up his forefinger. "Not a hair on her head!"

He knocked on the cell door, still glaring at Haynes.

The door opened, and Josh walked out. Haynes lay on his pillow and wept.

* * * *

Karen was at her desk, giving orders to her boss. "I'm telling you, stay away from here today. If you show up, I have friends who will pick you up and bodily carry you to your car and drive you home, if necessary. You got that?"

Rosemaria was seated on her balcony. A steaming cup of coffee was on the table. "Geez, I didn't know you could be so bossy."

"You've been to hell and back, not to mention shot, barely over twenty-four hours ago, and Josh needs you healthy and supportive in the next couple of days. O'Malley is taking the meeting with the woman who attacked her psychiatrist, and the assault and battery doesn't come before the judge until Tuesday. If anything comes up in the next couple of days, we will handle it."

"You know how to make a girl feel needed."

"Self-pity doesn't become you. And, oh, I blew off the mayor, who wanted to come by again."

Rosemaria sat up straight and winced in pain. "What?!"

"Just kidding. I'm sure he knows you're busy."

Rosemaria sat back gingerly. "A pox on you and all your minions."

"I'm sure we'll survive. See you at the show, boss."

"See you," she all but grumbled.

She walked back into the apartment and Suzi landed on her shoulder. "Turn on the TV! Turn on the TV!"

"I wish we had one now, Suzi. I don't know what else there is for me to do. I've become redundant."

She grabbed her cell phone from the table. "My father offered to take me out to lunch. I think I'll take him up on his offer. What do you think?"

"Let's win the lottery! Let's win the lottery!"

"We already have, silly girl." And she dialed.

* * * *

Josh stood backstage, off to the side, and looked out at the audience. The Greek had sold out within twenty-four hours once tickets were available on Ticketmaster. Up front and to the side sat the people involved in this incredible moment in time—Pastor Diehl and his large group of homeless people were in the very front. Animal activists who had been pushing for the release of Sammy for decades had organized a carpool to get them to the theater. Councilman Moretz sat in the same section with his wife.

Farther back, in the middle, were Rosemaria, Karen, Larry, Vanessa, and Rosemaria's father. He could see them chatting and laughing, but he knew Rosemaria was nervous. She had hardly been able to eat breakfast this morning and hugged him especially hard before he had to leave for the theater. "I'm so nervous. I feel like it's me going out there instead of you—sorry, I'm not helping." He reassured her he was feeling just fine. He'd performed in front of audiences in nightclubs back in the day. How different could it be to perform in front of thousands? As he looked out over the sea of people, he realized it would be much different. He saw Ken and his wife sitting next to Kevin and Jerry. Jennie, who had believed in him and pushed him so hard to succeed, was sitting with a friend. He looked like a nice guy. Josh wanted her to be happy.

The sound and video checks, rehearsals, and last-minute lighting place-ments had all gone off without a hitch. Egos were kept down to a minimum, and everybody was sharing mobile homes. Nobody wanted to be a prima donna and take money away from the reason they were there. Joell herself was too busy to spend time in her trailer. He marveled at how she could organize and perform in the same show. His heart skipped a beat as the house lights went down. The show was about to begin.

Out in the audience, Rosemaria's heart was in her throat. Her friends tried to calm her down and told her to just enjoy the music.

"You're going to be seeing some of the most incredible singers and musicians in the world tonight," Vanessa said. "Personally, I am looking forward to seeing Farley Soring in person. I absolutely adore him. I hope this kid in here doesn't get any ideas about making an appearance before Farley comes on."

Larry patted her knee. "He or she wouldn't do that. We're going to have a very considerate kid who won't cry at night, throw up his food, or interrupt Josh's concert."

She smiled at him hopefully.

Karen leaned over and whispered in Rosemaria's ear. "Don't worry. Josh knows what he's doing. I think he'll surprise even you."

"You think so?"

"I've heard you play his demos in your office. His voice is special. He has an incredible gift. The audience will feel it. You'll see."

Suddenly, there was a crash of drums joined by a screaming guitar and a throbbing bass. The spotlight came on Haydon Pierce, standing center stage at the microphone. The audience went wild, and the concert began.

Song after song, singer after singer, rock, blues, country, and rap, the enthusiastic audience cheered and clapped. They knew this was a rare treat—all these acts together for one night in one place. Pretty special.

Karen, Vanessa, and Larry were as enthralled as everybody else in the audience, and Rosemaria did her best to join in the celebration. She wasn't about to spoil the evening for her friends. She sang along with familiar songs and laughed when she flubbed the lyrics. She had to admit, Joell had produced a fabulous show. There weren't any programs, and she couldn't remember who performed before Josh. She just knew that Joell had scheduled him just before her set, which was the very last. It seemed like the show had gone on for hours before Joell came out, stood before the microphone, and began speaking. *This was it!*

"Before I have the privilege of performing for you—" The audience cut her off with wild cheers. She raised her arms and waved in appreciation. "Thank you. I love you all too." She waited until their cheers had died down. "Before I sing for you, there is someone I would like to introduce who is responsible for this concert and everything that led up to it. He got the idea of freeing Sammy from one of his best friends, who used to be homeless. Because of her, he realized how we could all help each other. He has chosen to remain in the background throughout this entire endeavor, but I persuaded him to let me introduce him to you. He is a singer and songwriter and my very good friend. Please make him feel welcome—Josh Sibley."

Rosemaria watched Josh walk out to center stage toward Joell, holding his guitar. They embraced warmly, and she left the stage. As the audience gave Josh a cordial welcome, she thought she would pass out. Josh, however, looked perfectly at ease and waved his thanks at the audience. She was observing him as the strangers around her saw him—tall, blond, good-looking, with a quiet charisma any performer would be grateful to have. Her nervousness disappeared. She saw that he was in control and relaxed.

A stagehand brought a high stool for Josh to sit on. Josh sat, adjusted the mic, and strummed a note. "This is a song that I wrote for my brother, Scott, who was killed when he was very young. He was an incredibly special little boy, and I miss him still. I hope you enjoy it."

Rosemaria had no idea that Joell had arranged for her own orchestra to back up Josh and was surprised to hear soft strings in the introduction as Josh played chords on his guitar. She had first heard him sing this song almost three years ago and thought he had the most beautiful voice she had ever heard. Finally, because of Joell, he was going to share the song with an audience.

He began to sing the haunting melody.

I'm walkin' down a road to nowhere.
I lost you long ago.
And dreams of tangled memories
whisper soft and low.

I wander down the path where only
fading secrets sing.
Wondering how I'll face the night
and what the dark will bring.
The road to nowhere,
The road to nowhere,
why can't it bring . . .
why can't it bring . . .
me back to you?

The times we had together were precious
but too few.
I still remember every moment
when our world was new.
You chased away the darkness
and taught me a new song.
We'd find a place, the two of us,
where we'd both belong.
The road to nowhere,
The road to nowhere,
why can't it bring . . .
why can't it bring . . .
me back to you?

As he sang the bridge his voice increased in emotion and volume.

I'll find you somewhere. I'll do my best
to let the sadness go and keep the rest.
You're everything that's good, and I can see
you never really left your special place with me.

The times we had together were precious
but too few.

I still remember every moment
when our world was new.
You chased away the darkness
and taught me a new song.
We'd find a place, the two of us,
where we'd both belong.
The road to nowhere,
The road to nowhere,
why can't it bring me back to you?
why can't it bring me back to you?

After the music faded to silence, there was a moment when the audience sat still as a mouse. Rosemaria held her breath. Then, a thunderous ovation began in front, spread out over the entire audience, and lasted for five minutes. Karen, Vanessa, and Larry took turns hugging her as Josh took his bows with genuine humility. He began to walk off the stage, acknowledging the audience every step of the way. Joell came out and grabbed him before he disappeared backstage, brought him back to the mic, held his arm high, and said, "I think I just discovered a star, and now I have to follow him." The audience clapped, and her orchestra began to play her first number. "But I'll do my best!" She began to sing, and Josh slipped backstage.

Rosemaria barely remembered Joell's performance and seeing all the performers gather on stage together for the finale. Somehow, she found her way backstage after the show. She fought her way, limping painfully, through the crowd that had gathered around Josh congratulating him. He saw her and ran toward her. Then, she was in the car with him on her way home. It was unreal. Like a dream. They barely spoke a word, each lost in their own thoughts.

At home, he walked her outside to the patio table, sat her down, and went back inside to make coffee. He brought the coffee outside, set down the cups, and took her hand.

"I feel like I never really knew you," she said.

"I'm still me. Nothing's changed."

"I never appreciated you like I should have."

"You saw me at my worst and loved me anyway."

"Now you'll be famous. The video will be all over the internet tomorrow. You'll record and go on tour and never have to do commercials again."

"I thought you loved my commercials."

"I'll take care of the kids when you're gone. But they'll miss you."

"I'm not going anywhere. I'm happy where I am."

"That's what you say now. Wait till the offers come pouring in."

"You wanted me to be rich."

"Yeah, I like that part."

"Let's get Sammy moved to his new home, and then we'll figure out the rest."

He tightened his hold on her hand, and she finally exhaled. It was all going to work out fine.

* * * *

Josh and Jerry were there when Sammy was moved into the PAWS truck. The four men from PAWS, who were experts in moving elephants, coaxed Sammy inside while Josh and Jerry stood on either side speaking softly to him. Their voices were familiar, and they wanted him to know he was safe and would not be hurt. At last, he was inside. Everyone breathed a sigh of relief.

Riding in Jerry's SUV behind the PAWS truck and out of the zoo was a moment of exultation for Josh. What had seemed impossible for so long was now reality. Sammy was really on his way to freedom. Rosemaria was in the back seat. Next to her was a picnic basket with sandwiches in case they got hungry during the six-hour drive to the sanctuary in San Andreas.

"Will Sammy be okay for such a long trip?" she asked.

"His caregivers are in the back with him behind a partition," Jerry assured her. "They'll watch him every second."

"He must be scared."

"In a few hours, he'll know he's in good hands," Josh said.

Another SUV followed behind them. A cameraman inside was filming the trip and Sammy's safe arrival so it could be shared on social media with the thousands of people who had come to love him. Joell gave orders that no one else could join the caravan. She wanted Sammy's trip to be peaceful and free of gawkers. The day and time of his release had been kept a secret.

The drive seemed interminable. Sammy's fear and confusion was foremost on their minds every minute. They wanted it to be over.

When they reached the sanctuary, they followed the truck through the gate and into the area where Sammy would spend his first few days in quarantine being treated by the veterinarians. As the cameraman filmed, the men from PAWS opened the back of the truck, and Sammy was urged to back up and come down the ramp. It took some time for him to make up his mind that it was safe to do so. Josh and Jerry were by his side as he backed down into the enclosure. Sammy was hungry after the long trip and headed for the water basin and a trough filled with hay. The ground was soft under his feet. Josh hoped he knew his new home would be nothing like his old one.

The PAWS workers sensed how difficult it was for Josh, Jerry, and Rosemaria to leave Sammy. They encouraged them to stay as long as they wanted to and say their goodbyes. There would be no regular trips to the sanctuary to visit him. This would be goodbye for a long time. Sammy needed to heal and then hopefully bond with other elephants without the presence of unnecessary humans, even those who loved him.

Jerry and Rosemaria waited in the SUV as Josh stood beside Sammy and talked softly to him. Josh was sure he saw that some of the sadness in Sammy's eyes had faded. He sensed a glimmer of hope within Sammy's body and spirit. Soon, that hope would be realized as Sammy explored his new life, free from pain, with many miles to roam. With a final gentle touch on his cheek, Josh left Sammy to his new keepers.

As they drove away, it was a bittersweet moment. They had worked so hard to get Sammy here. Now, they had to let him go. They were happy that everything had been caught on film. Sammy's story needed to be told so more elephants could be freed.

EPILOGUE

Josh and Rosemaria sat on a hill in the cat sanctuary overlooking the lake. The full moon was reflected on the water. Noor and Gilbert lay at their feet. The past week had been busy for both of them. Josh had recorded a commercial, managers had vied for Josh's attention, and the premiere of Ken's movie had finally been scheduled. Rosemaria had been cleared in the shooting, and her job at the courthouse was still waiting for her when she came back.

The proceeds from the concert, including a generous donation from Larry and his family, added up to $2.4 million. A check had been handed over to Councilman Moretz and Pastor Diehl at a celebratory press conference. There was no doubt that they would spend the money wisely.

Josh and Rosemaria fulfilled their promise to Suzi to buy a TV and had the Geek Squad connect everything. They could watch movies on Netflix when they felt like vegging on the couch and eating popcorn. Now Suzi wouldn't feel so lonely between visits from the pet sitter when they weren't home.

One day, Larry called to catch Rosemaria up on what was happening with the Haynes and Dillon cases. Everybody was trying to get plea deals, but Celia was playing hardball. She wanted maximum sentences for every one of them. Vanessa interrupted the conversation to say her water broke. They all raced to the hospital, where Vanessa wasted no time in delivering a perfect baby girl named Melissa. Grandma and Grandpa were exceedingly proud. The other set of grandparents were on their way.

Rosemaria laid her head on Josh's shoulder.

"When life is this perfect, it's scary, don't you think?"

"It will get complicated again, don't worry."

"Yes, lots of things can go wrong. It's comforting to know that."

"You deal with a lot of crazy people every day. Who knows what they're capable of?"

"It boggles the mind."

"And then there's the premiere. We'll probably argue about you having to walk the red carpet."

"Yeah, that could get ugly."

"We might disagree on our wedding date."

"I want it as soon as possible."

"Me too."

"Well, that's out. But we might argue about how many people to invite."

"There's that."

"Nothing we can't handle."

I have an important question for you."

"And that is?"

"So, what have you decided you're going to be, a cop or a prosecutor?"

"Rosemaria scrunched up her face for a moment. "I think I'll be both."

"You're going to be law *and* order?"

"Why not?"

"That kind of hubris has brought down many a powerful personage."

"But they didn't have you in their corner."

"Nevertheless, I foresee trouble ahead."

"See, we have a lot to look forward to."

"So very true."

She yawned. "I'm about ready to go back to our exceedingly lush accommodations in our private enclosure. How about you?"

He stood and pulled her to her feet. Noor and Gilbert immediately sprang up and began to run ahead of them as they walked.

"Speaking of children," Rosemaria said.

"We were?"

"I think we have the best-looking kids of anybody."

"And the smartest too."

"But they do snore and keep me awake."

"We'll ask them to let us sleep in tomorrow."

"Done."

They followed Noor and Gilbert to their enclosure as the moon slipped behind a cloud. The world was shrouded in darkness as Noor and Gilbert settled into their favorite spots. Josh and Rosemaria tucked into their sleeping bags and, as always, they were filled with a sense of wonder and contentment as they looked up at the starry sky.

THE END

Britt Lind is an actress, singer, and writer who has performed in television shows, movies, and on stage in Los Angeles, New York, and Vancouver, British Columbia. She has written several screenplays and wrote and directed a short film titled *Obsession*. She came in as runner-up in the Washington State Screenwriting Competition for her screenplay *A Light in the Forest* and recently won the Beverly Hills Book Award for her memoir *Learning How to Fly*. *A Fate Worse Than Death* is a prequel to her second book, *Deception—A Hollywood Mystery*. All are available on Amazon. Britt lives in Thousand Oaks, California, with her husband, Nick Alexander, a screenwriter, and their three feral cats—Teeny, Toughie, and Baby Hughie—who used to live a hardscrabble life in the cold and rain in the frozen north and now enjoy a life of luxury in the sun, as is their due. Britt is also president of a nonprofit, People for Reason in Science and Medicine (PRISM), a pro-health, pro-environment, anti-vivisection organization. Her website is www.brittlind.com

To find out more about PRISM, please go to
www.peopleforreason.org and www.facebook.com/gotoprism
Follow PRISM on Twitter @gotoprism
and Gab @gotoprism